STARFARERS

TOR BOOKS BY POUL ANDERSON

Alight in the Void
All One Universe
The Armies of Elfland
The Boat of a Million Years
The Dancer from Atlantis
The Day of Their Return
Explorations
The Fleet of Stars
Harvest of Stars
Harvest the Fire
Hoka! *(with Gordon R. Dickson)*
Kinship with the Stars
A Knight of Ghosts and Shadows
The Long Night
The Longest Voyage
Maurai and Kith
A Midsummer Tempest
No Truce with Kings
Past Times
The Saturn Game
The Shield of Time
Starfarers
The Stars Are Also Fire
Tales of the Flying Mountains
The Time Patrol
There Will Be Time

POUL ANDERSON

STARFARERS

A TOM DOHERTY ASSOCIATES BOOK · NEW YORK

STARFARERS

A Tor Book
Published by Tom Doherty Associates, Inc.
175 Fifth Avenue
New York, NY 10010

Tor Books on the World Wide Web:
http://www.tor.com

Tor® is a registered trademark of Tom Doherty Associates, Inc.

Library of Congress Cataloging-in-Publication Data

Anderson, Poul, date
    Starfarers / Poul Anderson. —1st ed.
        p.   cm.
    "A Tor book."
    ISBN 0–312–86037–4 (alk. paper)
    I. Title.
PS3551.N378S727   1998
813'.54—dc21   98–21766

First Edition: November 1998

Printed in the United States of America

0 9 8 7 6 5 4 3 2 1

TO
JIM FUNARO
WHO HAS LED MANY A CONTACT MISSION

ACKNOWLEDGMENTS

For information, advice, and much else, I owe thanks to Karen Anderson
(as always), Víctor Fernández-Dávila, editor Robert Gleason, the late Ken-
neth Gray, G. David Nordley, and Aharon Sheer. Special thanks are due
Robert L. Forward and Sidney Coleman. The idea of a nuclear "time machine" is the former's. An idea of the latter's suggested the concept behind the zero-zero drive to me; he kindly sent me a copy of his paper, but
it turns out that my speculation is quite unlike his real-science thought
and may even contradict it.

The lines of verse quoted in Chapter III are from *The Book of Songs*,
translated by Arthur Waley, copyright © 1937, renewed 1965 by Arthur
Waley, by permission of the publisher, Grove/Atlantic, Inc.

The lines of verse by Jorge Luis Borges and their English translation by
Richard Howett and César Rennart quoted in Chapter IX are from *Selected Poems 1923–1967* by Jorge Luis Borges, edited by Norman Thomas
di Giovanni, copyright © 1968, 1969, 1970, 1971, 1972 by Emecé Edi-
tores, S.A., and Norman Thomas di Giovanni, by permission of the publisher, Bantam Doubleday Dell.

The lines of verse by Rudyard Kipling quoted in Chapter XVII are in
the public domain.

Chapter XXI first appeared in a different form as "Ghetto" in *The
Magazine of Fantasy and Science Fiction*, May 1954, copyright © by Fantasy House, Inc., renewed 1982 by Poul Anderson. The lines from the bal-
lad "Jerry Clawson" quoted in it are copyright by the author, Gordon R.
Dickson, and used by his permission.

Chapter XVII first appeared in a slightly different form as "The Tale of

the Cat" in *Analog Science Fiction and Fact*, February 1998, copyright ©
1998 by Poul Anderson.

No person here named is in any way responsible for any mistakes or
other flaws in this book.

ABOARD THE STARSHIP ENVOY

Captain: Ricardo Iriarte Nansen Aguilar
Mate and first pilot: Lajos Ruszek
Second pilot: Jean Kilbirnie
Engineer: Yu Wenji
Second engineer: Alvin Brent
Physicist: Hanny Dayan
Planetologist: Timothy Cleland
Biologist and physician: Mamphela Mokoena
Biochemist: Selim ibn Ali Zeyd
Linguist and semantician: Ajit Nathu Sundaram

STARFARERS

PROLOGUE

"**Look yonder.**" The man pointed northeast and aloft. "That very bright star in the Milky Way. Do you know it?"

"Yes," answered his son. "Alpha Centauri. The nearest to us. It's two, really, and a third that is dim."

Don Lucas Nansen Ochoa nodded, pleased. Juan was barely past his seventh birthday. "Now look up from it, a little to your right. That other brilliant one is Beta Centauri."

"Is it close, too?"

"No, it's far off. Almost seventy times as far, I have read. But it shines thousands of times as bright as our sun. Most of those we see are giants. Else our eyes could not find them across their distances."

Man and boy sat their horses for a while in silence. They had drawn rein after leaving well behind them the house and its outbuildings, walled off by a cedar grove. The autumn air rested cool, still, and altogether clear. They had light enough without a moon, stars crowding heaven, galactic belt gleaming frosty. The Paraguayan plain rolled away through this dusk toward darkness, grassland broken by stands of trees and big, stump-shaped anthills. No cattle were in view, but now and then a lowing went mournfully through the early night.

"Where are *they*?" whispered the boy at last. Awe shivered in his words.

Don Lucas's hand traced an arc along the constellation. "Look on upward from Beta, to your left. Epsilon—do you see it?—and, past it, Zeta. The name Zeta means it's the sixth brightest in the Centaur. That's where the signs are."

"At Zeta?"

"No, as nearly as I can find out from the news, that star just happens to be in our line of sight to the things. They are actually far beyond it."

"Are they . . . are they coming here?"

"Nobody knows. But none of them are headed straight toward us. And we don't know what they are, natural or artificial or what. All the astronomers can say is that there are those fiery points of X rays moving very fast, very far away. The news programs yammer about an alien civilization, but really, it's too soon for anybody to tell." Don Lucas laughed a bit. "Least of all an old *estanciero* like me. I'm sorry, you asked me to explain what's been on the television, and I cannot say much more than that you must be patient."

Juan pounced. "Are you?"

"*Um-m,* I hope they'll corral the truth while I'm still above ground. But you should surely live to hear it."

"What do *you* think?"

Don Lucas straightened in the saddle. Juan saw his face shadowed by the wide-brimmed hat like a pair of wings against the sky. "I may be wrong, of course," he said. "Yet I dare hope someone is faring from star to star, and someday men will."

Suddenly overwhelmed, cold lightnings aflicker in him, the boy stared past his father, outward and outward. It was as if he felt the planet whirling beneath him, about to cast him off into endlessness; and his spirit rejoiced.

He became the grandfather of Ricardo Nansen Aguilar.

✳

With never a sight of beautiful, changeable Earth, Farside gained a night which stars made into no more than a setting for their brilliance. And the Lunar bulk shielded it from the radio noise of the mother world; and the stable mass underfoot and the near-vacuum overhead were likewise ideal for many kinds of science. It was no wonder that some of the most gifted people alive were gathered here, in spite of monastic quarters and minimal amenities. Besides, Muramoto thought, those should improve. Already the desolation of stone and dust was redeemed by an austere elegance of domes, detectors, dishes, taut and silvery power lines.

As his car neared observatory headquarters, he glanced through its bubbletop and found the red beacon light that was Mars. *People there too, nowadays.* An old thrill tingled. *Yes, man does not live by bread alone, nor by economics and politics. It was the vision of ships flying through heaven that got us back into space in earnest. Damn it, this time we'll stay, and keep going!*

He reached the topside turret, linked airlocks, crossed over, and descended. The corridor below felt doubly drab by contrast. However, he could move fast along it, enjoying the long, low-gravity lope. Ordinarily an officer of the United States Aerospace Force was expected to be more formal.

He had called ahead. The director awaited him in her office. She greeted him a little warily, offered him a chair, told the outer door to close, and sat down again behind her desk. For a few minutes they exchanged ritual courtesies—how were things going here, how were things back home, how had his flight from Earth been and his drive from Port Apollo?

Then Helen Lewis leaned forward and said, "Well, I'm sure your time is as valuable as mine, Colonel. Shall we get directly to business? Why have you requested this meeting, and why did you want it to be confidential?"

He knew she shared the distaste for the military that had been common among intellectuals at least since the Siberian Action. His best approach was straightforwardness. "You seemed to prefer it that way, Dr. Lewis. May I be frank? You've entered a request for a large expansion of your facilities. The wide-orbit interferometric system, especially, would count as high priced even in free and easy times, and you know how tight budgets are at present. I'm afraid a wish list of research projects won't open any purses soon. After all, you're still discovering marvelous things with the equipment on hand. What do you really want to search for?"

Her gaze challenged his. "Why do you, why does your service, want to know?"

"Because we've gotten hints that this may be something we'd go for, too." Muramoto lifted his palm. "No, please, not with any idea of warlike application. If our guess is right, it is an area that concerns us strongly, but 'we' are not just a few men and women in uniform. We include civilians, scientists, and certain members of the President's Advisory Council."

She flushed beneath the gray hair. A fist clenched. "My God, does that clique decide everything these days?"

Muramoto had his own wistfulness about the republic that Jefferson helped found, but it wasn't relevant today. "Myself, I hope your request will be approved. Yes, and I'd like it to be an international undertaking, as you've proposed. So would my superiors, partly to save American money, partly on principle. We aren't blind chauvinists."

Taken aback, she sat quiet for a while before she murmured, "I . . . presume . . . not."

"But you haven't given us reasons to fight for what you want," he said. "If you'll tell me what you have in mind and why it shouldn't be publicized"— he smiled —"you'll find we military are pretty good at keeping our mouths shut."

Lewis reached a decision. She actually returned his smile. "The truth is nothing desperate. It's bound to come out in due course, and certainly should. But the potential for sensationalism—" She drew breath. "You see, our latest observations lie at the limits of sensitivity available to us at present. They could be in error. An announcement, followed by a retraction, would do worse than wreck several careers. It would harm this whole institution."

"I see. I thought so," he replied. Intently: "You think you have found more starship trails, don't you?"

She nodded. Although he was not surprised, his mind whirled back through time, twenty-seven years, and again he was a boy, watching the news, listening to the discussions, feeling the dream explode into reality.

Pointlike sources of hard X rays with radio tails, crisscrossing a region in the Centaur. Some have come suddenly into being as we watched, others have blanked out. Parallax measurements taken across interplanetary spans show they are five thousand light-years distant. Therefore maximum transverse motion joins with Doppler effect to show they are traveling at virtually the speed of light.

What can they be but the trails of material objects blasting through the interstellar medium?

Slowly, grudgingly, more and more physicists admit that the least fantastic hypothesis is that they indicate spacecraft.

They aren't many, less than a hundred, and they seemed confined to a volume of perhaps two hundred parsecs' diameter. Why that is, why they don't range everywhere, why they haven't come to us—those are among the mysteries. But all at once, humans around the whole Earth want us also to be in space.

Through a quickening pulsebeat, he heard Lewis's carefully dry voice: "Lately, here, using the Maxwell superconducting telescope, we've found what appear to be similar phenomena elsewhere. The traces are faint, scattered, from sources far more distant than those behind Zeta Centauri. They are few, and none is as rich in objects as that region is. But there they are. Or so we think.

"To confirm, we need better instruments. That will also let us pinpoint them in the galaxy. More important, new theoretical work suggests that improved data will give clues to what the power source is. There's the great stumbling block, you know. Where does the energy come from? I honestly believe we're on the verge of a revolution in our understanding of the universe.

"I can show you around, introduce you to the people doing the research, let you judge for yourself before you report to your group. Would you like that?"

"I—I would," he answered inadequately. "And—no promises, you realize, but—I expect you'll get what you want."

✳

It happened that Avery Houghton launched his coup on the day that Edward Olivares recorded a television interview. Nothing had overtly begun when the physicist reached his office, but the crisis had been building up

for weeks—demands, threats, demonstrations, riots—and was now unmistakably close to the breaking point. Most Americans who could stayed
home, huddled over the newscasts. The amber-hued Hispanic façades of
Caltech stood on a nearly deserted campus, impossibly sunlit and peaceful, while fighter jets drew contrails across the blue above them.

Olivares was stubborn about keeping promises. He arrived at the appointed hour. The camera crew was already on hand, trying hard not to
act nervous. Joanne Fleury succeeded in it. She had her own professional
pride.

"I fear we won't draw much of an audience," Olivares remarked while
the crew was setting up.

"Maybe not for the first showing," Fleury said, "though I imagine a fair
number will tune in around the world regardless of our troubles here.
But the rebroadcasts will pull their billions."

"We could postpone—"

"No, if you please, sir. This is going to be a classic in science journal-
ism. Let's do it while we've got the chance."

Planning and a sketchy run-through had gone before, and the business
went more smoothly than might have been awaited. But then, it offered a
brief escape from what was outside.

After the cameras had scanned the book-lined room, the battered desk,
the portrait of Einstein, while Fleury gave her introduction, "—scientist,
mathematical physicist, as famous as he is modest— We'll discuss his latest and greatest achievement . . ." they moved in on her and him, seated
in swivel chairs. A projector spread a representation of the galaxy behind
them, ruddy nucleus and outcurving blue-tinged spiral arms, awesome
athwart blackness. Somehow his slight frame belonged in front of it.

She gestured at the grandeur. "Alien spacecraft traveling there, almost
at the speed of light," she said. "Incredible. Perhaps you, Dr. Olivares, can
explain to us why it took so long to convince so many experts that this
must be the true explanation."

"Well," he replied, "if the X-ray sources are material objects, the radiation is due to their passage through the gas in interstellar space. That's
an extremely thin gas, a hard vacuum by our standards here on Earth, but
when you move close to c—we call the velocity of unimpeded light c—
then you slam into a lot of atoms every second. This energizes them, and
they give back the energy in the form of hard X rays."

For a minute, an animated diagram replaced the galaxy. Electrons tore
free of atoms, fell back, spat quanta. The star images returned as Olivares
finished: "To produce the level of radiation that our instruments measure, those masses must be enormous."

"Mostly due to the speed itself, am I right?" Fleury prompted.

Olivares nodded. "Yes. Energy and mass are equivalent. As a body approaches c, its kinetic energy, therefore its mass, increases without limit.
Only such particles as photons, which have no rest mass, can actually

travel at that velocity. For any material object, the energy required to reach c would be infinite. This is one reason why nothing can move faster than light.

"The objects, the ships, that we're talking about are moving so close to c that their masses must have increased by a factor of hundreds. Calculating backward, we work out that their rest masses—the masses they have at ordinary speeds—must amount to tens of thousands of tonnes. In traditional physics, *this* means that to boost every such vessel, you would have to annihilate millions of tonnes of matter, and an equal amount to slow down at journey's end. That's conversion on an astrophysical scale. Scarcely sounds practical, eh? Besides, it should produce a torrent of neutrinos; but we have no signs of any."

Fleury picked up her cue. "Also, wouldn't the radiation kill everybody aboard? And if you hit a speck of dust, wouldn't that be like a nuclear warhead exploding?"

A jet snarled low above the roof. Thunder boomed through the building. Cameras shivered in men's hands. Fleury tensed. The noise passed, and she found herself wondering whether or not to edit this moment out of the tapes.

"Go on, please," she urged.

Olivares had glanced at the galaxy, and thence at Einstein. They seemed to calm him.

"Yes," he told the world. "There would have to be some kind of—I'm tempted to say streamlining. The new spaceborne instruments have shown that this is indeed the case. Gas and dust are diverted, so that they do not encounter the object itself, but flow smoothly past it at a considerable distance." An animation represented the currents. The ship was a bare sketch. Nobody knew what something made by nonhumans might be like. "This can, in principle, be done by means of what we call magnetohydrodynamics."

Fleury had regained her smile. "A word nearly as knotty as the problem."

"It takes very powerful force fields," Olivares said. "Again we meet the question of energy. Of course, the requirement is minuscule compared to what's necessary for the speed."

"And nobody could build a nuclear power plant to supply that."

"No. If you did, you'd find you had built a star."

"Then where does the energy come from?"

"The original suggestion was that it comes from the vacuum."

"Could you explain that? It sounds like, well, Alice's Cheshire cat."

Olivares shrugged. "A good deal of quantum mechanics does. Let me try. Space is not a passive framework for events to happen in. It is a sea of virtual particles. They constantly go in and out of existence according to the uncertainty principle. The energy density implied is tremendous."

"But we don't know how to put the vacuum to work, do we?"

"Only very slightly, as in the Casimir effect. You see, the more energy you 'borrow' from the vacuum, the shorter the time before it must be 'returned.' Both these quantities, energy and time, are far too small to power a spacecraft."

"But now you, Dr. Olivares, have shown how it can be done," Fleury said softly.

He shook his head. "Not by myself. I simply pursued some speculations that go back to the last century. And then the new information started to come in from the new instruments."

Fleury gestured. The galaxy gave way to the observatory on Lunar Farside. After a few seconds the scene swept across millions of kilometers to the devices in their huge orbits. Representations of laser beams quivered between them and back toward the Moon, bearing data. An antenna pointed at a constellation. Briefly, the outlines of a centaur stood limned amidst those stars. It vanished, and a telescopic view expanded. It zoomed past a globular cluster of suns, on toward the one called Zeta, and on and on beyond. Tiny fireballs twinkled into existence, crawled across the deep, and died back down into the darkness while fresh ones appeared. "The bow waves of the argosies," Fleury intoned.

The animations ended. The galaxy came back.

"Details we could not detect before, such as certain faint spectral lines, are now lending confirmation to my cosmodynamic model," Olivares said. "And that model, in turn, suggests the energy source for such spacecraft. That's all," he ended diffidently.

"I'd say that's plenty, sir," the journalist responded. "Could you tell us something about your ideas?"

"It's rather technical, I fear."

"Let's be brave. Please say whatever you can without equations."

Olivares leaned back and drew breath. "Well, cosmologists have agreed for a long time that the universe originated as a quantum fluctuation in the seething sea of the vacuum, a random concentration of energy so great that it expanded explosively. Out of this condensed the first particles, and from them evolved atoms, stars, planets, and living creatures."

Excitement throbbed beneath the academic phrases. "At first the cosmologists took for granted that the beginning involved a fall to the ground state, somewhat like the transition of an electron in a high orbit to the lowest orbit it can occupy. But what if this is not the case? What if the fall is only partway? Then a reservoir of potential energy remains. For an electron, it's a photon's worth. For a universe, it is vast beyond comprehension.

"I've shown that, if the cosmos is in fact in such a metastable condition, we can account for what the astronomers have observed, as well as several other things that were puzzling us. It's possible to tap energy from the unexpended substrate—energy more than sufficient, for lengths of time counted not in Planck units but in minutes, even hours."

Fleury whistled. "How can we do this?"

Olivares chuckled. "I'll leave that to the laboratory physicists, and afterward the engineers. In principle, though, it must be by means of what I'll call a quantum field gate. We can use a Bose-Einstein condensate to generate a certain laserlike effect and bring all the atoms in two parallel, superconducting plates into the same quantum state. The consequences are nonlinear and result in the creation of a singularity. Through this the energy of the substrate flows. Presumably it will distribute itself evenly through any connected matter, so that the acceleration is not felt."

"Hoo, you're right, this is kind of technical." A touch of practicality should liven it. "How does the, um, pilot get the ship headed the way he/she/it wants to go?"

"A good question," Olivares approved. "I'm glad you know the difference between a scalar and a vector. I think the velocity vector must increase or decrease linearly. In other words, when the ship acquires the new energy, she continues in the same straight-line direction as she was moving in. I'm still working on the problem of angular momentum."

"More technicalities," Fleury said ruefully. "You mentioned having this energy for a period of maybe hours. Must it then go back?"

Olivares nodded. "Yes, just as with the familiar vacuum, a loan from the substrate must be repaid. The product of energy borrowed and time for the loan is a constant. However, with the substrate the constant is immensely larger—a multiple of the Planck energy, which is itself enormous. The quantum field collapses, reclaiming the borrowed energy for the substrate."

"But the ship can take out another loan right away?"

"Evidently. The instruments have, in fact, detected flickerings in the X-ray outputs that correspond quite nicely to this. From the inverse proportionality of energy and time, it follows that every jump is of the same length. My preliminary calculations suggest that this length is on the order of a hundred astronomical units. The exact value depends on the local metric—" Olivares laughed. "Never mind!"

"Maybe we can talk a little about what a voyage would feel like, aboard a ship like that," Fleury proposed.

"Why not? It'll take us back to less exotic territory."

"Could you review the basic facts? For some of us, our physics has gotten kind of rusty."

"It's simple enough," Olivares said, quite sincerely. "When you travel at relativistic speeds, you experience relativistic effects. I've mentioned the increase of mass. The shortening of length in the direction of motion is another. Of course, you yourself wouldn't notice this. To you, the outside universe has shrunken and grown more massive. And your observations are as valid as anybody else's."

"What about the effect on time? I should think that'd matter most to the crew."

"Ah, yes. Time dilation. Loosely speaking, if you're traveling at close to c, for you time passes more slowly than it does for the friends you left behind you. One of those spacecraft may take several hundred years to cross the several hundred light-years between her home port and her destination. To those aboard, whoever or whatever they are, a few weeks will have passed."

Before she could head him off—but it could be edited out later if need be—Olivares continued: "The new theory modifies this a bit. If you travel by way of the quantum field gate, you never get the full time dilation you would if you accelerated to the same velocity by ordinary, impossible rocket means. However, at high energies the difference becomes too small to be worth thinking about. Contrastingly, the less energy you borrow from the substrate, the worse the ratio is. You could take an extremely long time by your clocks—theoretically forever—to transit the fixed distance of a jump at an ordinary speed. You'd do better to use a regular jet motor.

"So the quantum field gate is not for travel between the planets. Nor do I expect it will serve any other mundane purpose."

"But it will take us to the stars," Fleury breathed.

She guided the conversation from that point, retracing much ground, expanding explanations, weaving in a few personal, human matters. It would be raw material for a program that should awaken eagerness in every thinking person who saw it, around Earth, on the Moon and Mars, faring to the ends of the Solar System.

At last the two stood up. She shook his frail hand and said, "Thank you, thank you, Dr. Olivares, for this hour," which had actually been almost three, "and thank you infinitely more for everything you have given the human race." *That* would remain in the tapes.

Immediacy closed in. Blasphemous though it felt, she could not help herself; she went to the television set in his office and tuned in a newscast.

Terror leaped from the screen. Houghton's junta had seized the Capitol and White House. He had declared a state of emergency and martial law. A number of military units, here and there across the country, had mobilized to resist, and battle had erupted at several locations. She saw combat in the air above Seattle, street fighting in Houston, a city block burning in Minneapolis.

She turned and seized Olivares's hand again. Through her own tears she saw his. "No, God damn it!" she cried. "We've got work to do, you and I!"

—Conflict sputtered out in the next few days, as Houghton prevailed. After all, he and his cause were widely popular. He was now the permanent Chief Advisor to any and every President of the United States. The trial and execution of his predecessor assured the docility of Congress and the courts. His reign lasted until his death, nineteen years later.

Olivares lived much longer in history.

✳

Once an aspect of nature is known, quantum computers and nanotechnic construction make for rapid progress. Barely ten years passed between the publication of his theory and the departure of the first spacecraft for Alpha Centauri.

Surely billions of eyes watched on screens as it left Earth orbit. A few persons on Himalia were luckier. That little moon of Jupiter chanced to be near when the vessel passed by. For many hours before and after the moment, work ceased. Almost everyone crammed into the habitation domes from which it would be directly visible.

Dmitri Sumarokov and Karl Vogel did not leave their station. They and their robots were prospecting the Stephanos Crater area. It might have been more exciting to watch with a group, but would certainly have been more uncomfortable. The partners simply donned spacesuits, took what optical gear they had, and went out of their roundhut.

Low above a topplingly near horizon, the giant planet loomed close to fullness. Larger in this sky than Luna in Earth's, lion-tawny, banded with clouds and swirled with storms in subtle hues, a glimmer of rings offside, it flooded most stars out of vision. The radiance fell soft over ice, rocky upthrusts, scars, and pockmarks. Breath and pulsebeat sounded loud in the silence.

Trouble with the air recycler had caused a delay. Repairs couldn't wait; dead men can't watch anything. With scant time to set up, they wasted none in speech, except for an occasional muttered curse. But when they had their telescope aimed and an image appeared in the display, Sumarokov whooped, "There! See, Karl, see!"

A point of light swelled rapidly within the frame. It turned into a jumble of glints and shadows. It became a bright spheroid from which reached structures that seemed as fragile as spiderwebs. The telescope swung, tracking. Vogel peered along it. Pointing, he said, his tone not quite steady, *"Selbst das Schiff."* In the English they shared: "Someday our children will envy us, Dmitri."

The naked eye saw a spark flit above a crag and across the night. It could have been any satellite, catching the rays of the sunken sun. Two Galilean moons outshone it. But Sumarokov and Vogel stood enthralled.

It faded, dwindling away into distance. Their gaze went back to the display. Abruptly the magnified image vanished in a flare. They glimpsed the reality as a wink near the Jovian disc. "What was that?" Sumarokov exclaimed.

"The jet fired," Vogel answered. He had studied the subject more closely than the other man. "Approach maneuver."

"So soon?"

"You would not want to operate a plasma jet in Jupiter's radiation belt."

"No. . . . No, certainly not." Again the shape was in telescopic view, coasting along on gravity and momentum, shrinking, shrinking. "The day will come," Sumarokov said raptly, "when none of this will be necessary."

"Um, I don't know," Vogel replied. "They, those robots, they do have to be well away from the sun before they turn on the zero-zero drive. Something about space not being too warped."

Sumarokov blinked at him. "Zero-zero?"

"That is what they are lately calling the quantum field gate drive. Have you not heard? A ship springs from the energy state normal in this universe, what they call the zero level, to the superhigh energy level it gets from below the universe, and then falls back down again to normal, over and over."

"I see."

"First they may as well save fuel by letting Jupiter pull them out of the ecliptic plane and aim them at the goal." Vogel spoke absently, his attention on the image. Soon it would be invisibly small.

"Yes, yes, I know that," Sumarokov said. "Everybody does." Enthusiasm thrust irritation aside. "I mean the technology will improve. Jets will be screened. Fuel will be less important. And it will be humans, not machines, who go to the stars."

"If machines do not become as intelligent as humans, or more so."

"That will never happen. I know some neuropsychology. Consciousness, creative thought, that is not merely a business of electrons in circuits. It is something the entire living human organism does."

"Well, maybe. But all of us here would be in a bad way without our robots."

Talk broke off. Both men were watching the starcraft too hungrily.

When it was gone from them they went back inside, and presently back to work, as if awakened from a dream.

Yet the work had its fascination, establishing a settlement in the Jovian System, coordinated with the outposts on the asteroids—steps in the industrialization of space, until the wealth of the planets flowed to Mother Earth and humans need no longer maim and defile her.

Such was the hope of the far-seeing. The hope of most people concerned in the endeavor was to make a profit. And this was right and necessary. No civilization, whatever its social and economic arrangements, can continue forever throwing resources into a void. It must eventually start to reap some kind of material return.

—Eight and a half years after the spacecraft left Sol, its first laserborne messages arrived from Alpha Centauri. What they revealed was wonderful. Three years later, transmissions ended. The unforeseeabilities of navigating among rock swarms between two suns had overwhelmed the computers. The vessel perished in a collision. Its wreckage became another small heavenly body.

By then, however, the first ships designed to carry human crews were taking their first flights.

1.

"Man down."

Ricardo Nansen was floating weightless, looking out a viewscreen, when the alarm shrilled and the words followed. He never tired of this sight. As the ship orbited into morning and the sun rose red from a peacock band along the edge of the planet, blue-and-white marbled beauty drove night backward across the great globe. He could almost have been at Earth. But the sun was Epsilon Eridani, there was no moon, and here Sol shone only after dark, a second-magnitude star in Serpens Caput. That fact turned splendor into a miracle.

The call snatched him from it. He took off, arrowing along a corridor. Captain Gascoyne's voice rang from every intercom: "Pilot Nansen, prepare to scramble."

"On my way, sir," he replied. "Who's in trouble?"

"Airman Shaughnessy. Wrecked. And that was the only flyer currently operating."

Mike Shaughnessy! shocked through Nansen. The man was his best friend in the crew.

This shouldn't have happened. Aircraft, like spaceboats, had been tested for reliability, over and over, under the harshest available stresses, before the expedition set forth. Thus far they had come handily through everything they met. And Shaughnessy had simply been on his way back to Main Base after delivering supplies to a team of biologists on an offshore island.

At least he lived. Nearly eleven light-years from home, any human life became boundlessly precious.

Second Engineer Dufour waited at the launch bay of Nansen's craft to help him make ready. Ordinarily that wasn't needful, but urgency ruled today. While she got him dressed and otherwise outfitted, he kept his attention on the intercom screen at the site. His briefing snapped out at him, verbal, pictorial, mathematical.

Information was scant. Shaughnessy had radioed a report of sudden, total engine failure. He didn't think he could glide to a landing and was going to bail out. Minisatellite relays carried his message to the ship. When she swung above his horizon, her optics found him at the wreckage. Evidently he'd guided his motorchute to chase the crashing flyer. His communications were dead, though, even the transceiver built into his backpack. He seemed unhurt, but who could tell? Certain it was that his tanked air would shortly give out.

To make matters worse, a hurricane raged along the seacoast west of him. To wait in orbit till the window for an approach from the east opened would squander time. Besides, weather along that flight path had its own nasty spots. This atmosphere was not Earth's. Steep axial tilt and rapid rotation increased the treacherousness. Meteorologist Hrodny was still struggling to develop adequate computer programs. Crewfolk argued about whether to recommend naming the planet Satan or Loki.

"We have a course for you that should skirt the big storm," Gascoyne said. "Do you accept it?"

"Yes, of course," Nansen answered.

"Good luck," Dufour whispered. *"Bonne chance, mon bel ami."* She kissed him, quickly. He cycled through the airlocks.

As he harnessed himself before the control panel, the boat told him, "All systems checked and operative. Launch at will."

Nansen grinned. *"¡Ay, la sensación del poderío absoluto!"* Beneath tautness and concern, exhilaration thrilled. The mission wasn't crazily reckless, but it challenged him. He touched the go pad.

Acceleration pushed him back in his seat, gently at first, then hard. Aft, the ship receded from sight. Forward, the globe swelled until it was not ahead, it was below, the circle of it bisecting his universe.

The drive cut off. Slanting steeply downward, the boat pierced atmosphere. A thin wail grew into thunder, the view turned into fire, he lost contact with the ship. The force on him became brutal. He could have taken an easier route, but he was in a hurry.

Slowing, the boat won free of radio blackout. Vision cleared, weight grew normal. Wings captured lift. His hands ordered the airjet to start. He flew.

An ocean gleamed below. Broad patches of weed and scum mottled its azure. A darker wall rose over the rim, higher and higher, crowned with alabaster cloud.

"Damn!" he muttered. "The hurricane. It's not supposed to be dead ahead."

The ship had passed under his horizon and couldn't help. His own instruments probed. Unpredictably, incredibly fast, the tempest had veered.

"Advise returning to orbit," said the boat.

Nansen studied the map unrolling in a screen. *We can't simply fly around,* he agreed. The boat was too awkward in the air for such a maneuver. Normally it dipped into the stratosphere and released a proper aircraft when an exploration party wanted one. The two made rendezvous at that height when the time came to return. *Someday we'll have boats that can perform as well in atmosphere as in space. But today—*

"No," he decided. "We'll push straight through."

"Is that wise?" The synthetic voice remained as calm as always. Once in a while you had to remind yourself that there was no awareness behind the panel, no true mind, only a lot of sophisticated hardware and software.

"Aborting and trying again would take too long," Nansen said—needlessly, since command lay with him. "We have enough momentum to transect the fringe at this altitude, if we move with the wind." *Unless we hit something unknown to pilots on Earth. Into Your hands, God—*

"Go!" His fingers pounced on the controls. The boat surged.

Far downward, he glimpsed monstrous waves on a sea gone white. A skirling deepened to a cannonade. The hull shuddered. Darkness and fury engulfed him. Rain hammered like bullets. The boat dropped, battled upward again, pitched and yawed. He did not now pilot it. With manifold sensors, multiple flexibilities, computer nodes throughout, and a nuclear power plant, it flew itself. His was the will that drove it onward.

They burst forth into clear day. The violence diminished. Nansen gusted a breath and sank back. His ears rang. Sweat dripped off his skin and reeked in his nostrils. Flesh ached where the forces had slammed him against his harness. But what a ride it had been!

The storm fell behind, the air quieted. He flew over a continent. Sandy wasteland, stony hills, gullies carved by rain, and talus slopes spalled by frost stretched dun toward distant mountains. Here and there, sun-flash off a lake or a river gave bleak relief. Soon the map showed he was where he wanted to be. "Land according to plan," he said. The order was scarcely necessary, except as a sound of triumph.

Don't stop to celebrate, he thought. *Not yet.*

The site had been chosen from space, the nearest spot that looked safe without being close enough to endanger Shaughnessy should something go wrong. The boat slewed into vertical alignment, landing jacks extended, dust whirled up, impact thudded. The hull began to tilt. The jack on that side lengthened itself to compensate, and the boat stood stable.

Nansen unharnessed and squirmed his way downward, aft, to the vehicle bay. He could have walked the rest of the distance, but Shaughnessy might need carrying. For a few minutes he was busy donning his equipment. He already wore the gloves, boots, and hooded coverall that protected him from ultraviolet. He slipped on his backpack, with its air tank and other gear, snugged goggles and breathmask over his face, opened the inner lock valve, and pushed the little groundrover through. The chamber expanded to accommodate them, barely. The valve closed, Nansen's fingers directed the outer valve to move aside. A certain amount of interior air was lost in the local atmosphere. He gave the rover a shove to send it trundling down the ramp that had deployed. On the ground, he climbed to the control seat and drove.

Strange, he thought, as often before, how half-familiar the scene was. The Solar System, where he had trained, held more foreignness than this, from red-brown Martian deserts under pale-red skies to the grandeur of Saturn's rings. Here he weighed about the same as on Earth, the horizon was about as far off, a sun that looked much like Sol stood in a blue heaven, the breeze was just comfortably warm, sand gritted under wheels and dust eddied lazily over their tracks. But the oxygen-poor air would choke him, and everywhere around stretched barrenness.

The thought was equally old in him: *Well, why should we ever have expected more? Life on Earth took three billion years to venture from the seas to the land. Our giant Moon, a cosmic freak, may well have hastened that by the tides it raised. Give this life here a few more geological ages. Yes, of course it was disappointing not to find woods and flowers and big, fine animals. But we knew the odds were against it. Meanwhile, what a dragon's hoard of scientific treasure we're winning.*

Steering by inertial compass, he topped a ridge and saw the fallen aircraft. Although it had dug itself half a meter into gravel, the composite body showed small damage. Impact had doubtless smashed most things inside. Nansen's gaze strained. Shaughnessy—

Yes, there, tiny across a kilometer but on his feet! Nansen's heart sprang. The rover rumbled downhill.

Shaughnessy staggered to meet him. Nansen stopped and dismounted. They fell into one another's arms.

"Are you all right?" Nansen gasped.

"Barely, barely. It's foul my air has gotten. Let me hook up." Shaughnessy plugged into the large tank on the vehicle.

Weight penalty or no, Nansen thought, backpack units ought to include recyclers, the same as on spacesuits. Yet who could have foreseen? Every interstellar expedition was a leap into mystery. Oh, yes, you could send robots ahead, as had been done at first, but then you'd wait too long for less news than humans would bring.

"Ah-h-h!" Shaughnessy sighed. "Like the breeze off a clover meadow. Or so it feels by our modest standards hereabouts. My father thanks you, my mother thanks you, my sister thanks you, my brother thanks you, and I thank you."

The crew seldom spoke of kinfolk. When they returned home, the crossing would take a few days of their time—and a quarter century would have passed on Earth. You didn't want to dwell on what time might have done meanwhile. Nansen forgave the tactlessness. He was too glad that his friend lived.

Anxiety: "Are you well otherwise, Mike?"

"I am. I did take a tumble on landing, which split my transceiver apart. We need a design more robust. Otherwise just bruises, not like my poor flyer. I'm afraid my fellow airmen will have fewer missions in future, Rico, for I'll be claiming my share of them."

"They'll get enough other work to keep them out of mischief. So will you." The groundside teams were turning up more surprises than they could handle. All extra help would be jubilantly welcomed. "Have you any idea what caused this?"

"I have a guess, after prowling and poking. I recorded it, in case I didn't survive, but indeed I'd rather speak it in person over a mug of beer."

"I can supply the person. The beer will have to wait." A tingle went along Nansen's spine. "What was it?"

"To my eye, the airscoop has corroded. You may recall, earlier I deposited chemosamplers at the Devil's Playground hot springs. Sure, the material of the flyer is supposed to be inert, but that's a hellish environment. My guess is that microscopic life is invading the land, and some kind of germ somehow catalyzed a reaction, maybe with the fullerene component. Let the scientists find out. The biochemistry here is so crazily different from ours."

"*¿Qué es?*" Nansen exclaimed. Alarm stabbed him. "Do you mean . . . our ship—"

Shaughnessy laughed, rather shakily, and clapped him on the back. "Not to worry, I do believe. Otherwise the whole gang of us would be dead. Those bugs must be confined to that area. Anyhow, exposure to space would doubtless kill them. We've lost an aircraft, but we may be about to make a great discovery."

Discovery is what we came here for.

"If you're fit to travel, let's get back to the ship," Nansen proposed.

"I am, if you go easy on the boost," Shaughnessy said. "Especially with that beer waiting!"

"Oh, you'll take the high road and I'll take the low road,
And I'll be in Scotland before you;
But me and my true love will never meet again
On the bonnie, bonnie banks of Loch Lomond."

Jean Kilbirnie sang only the chorus, almost under her breath. It faded away into the silence that had fallen since she and Tim Cleland reached the height. For a while, again, all they heard was the soughing in leaves overhead.

They sat on a bluff above a river. The westering sun, Tau Ceti, cast rays down the length of the vale, and the water shone like molten gold. Trees shaded turf, which nonetheless gave off fragrances to the mild air. After three terrestrial years, the first humans ever to see this world were calling it, in their different languages, Puerto, Limani, Kiang, Harbor.

Yet little here truly recalled Earth as Earth once was. The sward grew low, dense, a mat of minutely convoluted soft nuggets. Some of the trees curved their twin trunks upward, lyre-shaped, until they broke into shoots lined with feathery foliage. Others lifted columnar in a pelt of leaves. Others suggested huge, fringed spiderwebs. Nothing stood green; everything was in tones of yellow or orange, save where a patch flared red. Nothing could properly nourish the visitors, and much would have sickened them.

It didn't matter. That two evolutions, sundered by half a score of light-years, had been this alike—that you could walk freely, breathe the air, drink the water, rejoice in the beauty—was enough.

"You surprise me," Cleland blurted.

Kilbirnie turned her head toward him. "How so?" she asked.

"Oh, I, well, if you're feeling sentimental I . . . I wouldn't expect you to show it. You'd be extra cocky. Maybe you'd sing one of your bawdy old ballads."

Kilbirnie smiled. Her husky voice took on more than its usual slight burr. "We Scots can wax unco sentimental. Read your Burns—or ha' you no heard o' him?" She dropped back to everyday English. "This *is* our free day, our last day of peace." On the morrow their group would break camp and ferry up to the spaceship. She had said she wanted to go off afoot, into the countryside. He promptly proposed coming along. She didn't refuse him, but had not spoken much as they walked. "Our last look at this fair land."

"You could have taken more time groundside," he reminded her. "I suggested it—"

"Often." She paused. "Don't mistake me, Tim. I'm not complaining. There were simply too many wonders, in three short years." Her gaze went upward, beyond white clouds and blue sky. "I had to choose. And, of course, I had my duty." She piloted one of the boats that not only bore aircraft to and fro but had carried explorers throughout the system.

"I mean, well, you could have negotiated more Harborside time for yourself. I wish you had. We could have . . ." His words trailed to a halt.

She gave him no chance to continue them. "You were aspace too on occasion."

"Very little." He was one of the three planetologists who studied this globe rather than its sisters. His excursions off it had been for the purpose of observing it from outside. "I could wish I'd gone where you did. It was fascinating."

She laughed. "Sometimes too fascinating."

A ring of rocks whirling around the mighty fourth planet; a sudden, chaotic storm of fragments headed for the moon where Lundquist and his robots were at work; she, skillfully, heedlessly, defiant of doctrine, blasting from orbit elsewhere, down to the surface to snatch him off, even as the first gravel sleet and stone hail smote. Cleland reached toward Kilbirnie. "Oh, God—"

She didn't respond to the gesture, merely shrugged. He flushed and said defensively, "Harbor hasn't been a hundred percent safe, either, you know." He'd had a close call or two.

She nodded. "Untamed. Part of its charm. I envy the future colonists."

"You've talked about . . . becoming one of them. I've thought about it."

Kilbirnie sighed. "No, not for me." She glanced at him, caught his stricken look, and explained: "I've been thinking further. It'll be a long while before the first emigrant ships leave Sol for anywhere. They'll need better information than a preliminary expedition like ours could collect; and each voyage to here means a twenty-two-year round trip, plus time spent on site. And then the transports must be built, except first they must be financed, and— No, we'd grow old on Earth, waiting. Likeliest we'd die. Better to starfare."

"Do you really want that? For the rest of your life? Returning each time to . . . to an Earth grown still more foreign?"

The somberness that had touched her deepened. Her voice lowered and shivered. The blue eyes sought his. "It was foreign already when we left, Tim. What will we find when we come back? After a generation. . . . At best, I'm afraid, worse crowding, more ugliness, less freedom. I doubt I'll care to stay. And the rest of the Solar System—well, we know too much about it. Nothing really new there."

"You'd rather explore like this?" He groped for understanding. "Back here?"

She smiled afresh. "That'd be grand." The smile faded. "But probably no such berth will be available in any reasonable time. Too few starships, too many stars." Resolutely: "I'll take whatever I can get, as soon as I can get it."

The wind whispered through the leaves.

"You—you've been brooding," he faltered. "That's not like you. I hate seeing you . . . bitter."

She had been hugging her knees, staring outward. Now she straightened, flung her head back, and cried, "Why, I'm not!" Quieter: "I'm sorry for other folk, but myself, no." Her voice clanged: "A whole universe to adventure in!"

"Maybe never another world like this," he argued desperately. "Nothing but d-d-desolation, poison air, like those other places we've heard of—nothing but a ship for your home, till you die somewhere terrible—" He spread his hands in their helplessness. "Jean, no, please."

She patted his shoulder. "Och, I'll be fine. And so will you, Tim. You're bound to get a high position at some research institute or university or whatever they'll have when we come back. The data we'll bring, and all from the other expeditions, they can keep a scientist like you happily busy forever."

He slumped. "Busy, yes. Happy, no."

She withdrew her hand and sat wary.

He clenched his fists. "Jean, I love you," rushed from him. "I don't want to lose you. I can't."

She bit her lip. A flight of small creatures buzzed past, their wings glinting.

"I'm sorry, Tim," she said at last, low. "You're a sweet man. But— Well, but."

"Somebody else?" he mumbled.

"No." Her utterance sharpened. "Hasn't that been plain to see? I just want to wander."

Shaken, he let loose what had been locked in his mind. "Was your life so miserable before?" Immediately: "I'm sorry. That was uncalled for. I'm sorry."

"No need," she answered. "I do wish, though, you'd take me at my word. I've told everybody what a good childhood I had, and then splendid times in Solar space before I got this berth, everything I could ask for. If I am a bit cross today, it's because I recall how the things I loved, moors, woods, old towns full of kindness, old lifeways, I've seen them crumbling and by now they may be gone." She shook her head. Gladness flowed back. "But the stars!"

She got to her feet. He stood up likewise, awkward and abashed. She caught his hands in hers. "Why this blethers about me? Oh, Tim, poor dear, I know how you feel, I've known for this past year or longer, and I *am* sorry."

She kissed him. His response was shy. She laid her arms around his neck. His arms went around her waist. The kiss gathered strength.

She disengaged lithely. "Come," she said, "we'd better get back to camp before sunset."

3.

While they waited, Yu Wenji fell to remembering and hoping. She could not but say it aloud. ". . . and this time I'll show you much more than my home village. We'll go around the valley. Where the Hwang Ho winds among springtime blossoms—the loveliest land on Earth."

"You may be prejudiced, my dear." Wang Xi spoke absently, most of his attention on instruments and controls.

Yu, seated beside him, smiled. "City boy."

"Well, I'm willing to be convinced."

The screen they faced did not show the heavens as the naked eye would have seen them. At the center of the view, an image stood steady athwart darkness. Its blinding brilliance stopped down, Sirius A shone a hard blue-white; prominences like red tongues licked from the disk. The corona, its own light enhanced, was an opal mane. That amplification also brought background stars into vision. Sol happened to be in their direction, one spark amidst a throng.

The screen was not for scenery. It monitored an optical system that Yu had lately had to overhaul. Perhaps a lingering uneasiness about it—he was such a worrier, she often thought, such an overconscientious darling—struck through when Wang added, "Of course, you assume those things we knew will be there still."

Yu stiffened. "They will be. They must. We won't have been gone too long." A year here, observing, probing, establishing robotic instruments which would remain to transmit further revelations. Seventeen years to and fro—aboard ship, less than a month.

"We'll see." They had been over this ground too often.

Happily, at that moment a bell tone sounded. "Hold!" Wang said. "It's begun!"

Readings and displays came alive. He lost himself, concentrating on them. Yu's attention ranged more widely, watchful for any possible malfunction. He was a researcher, she an engineer. But her work required a deeper knowledge of physics than many physicists possessed. Husband and wife had become a scientific team.

The data pouring in were more than an hour old. No living creature dared come near that huge sun, nor to its companion. They radiated too fiercely. This newly activated station was the first to take orbit around Sirius B.

A visual showed the latter star white-hot. It flickered at the edges. Ghostly whirls raced across it, flung in and out of view by a frantic rotation: storms in an atmosphere compressed to a thickness of a few kilometers. The image drifted over the screen and out of sight, out of detection range, borne by the thirty-odd million kilometers per hour at which the white dwarf whipped around A.

But a probe had sprung from the station and hurtled inward. Heavily shielded, its instruments had beamed their findings with lasers that plasma clouds could not block. Rage ramped—

The screen went blank. The probe's defenses had been quickly overwhelmed. Yet its kamikaze dive had given far more than a brief spectacle. Knowledge of mass distributions, vectors, fields, fluxes, a thousand different aspects of reality had been gained. More was still arriving from the station, a tumble of terabytes.

"All seems well," Yu said, not quite steadily.

Wang leaped from his seat and danced across the deck. This near the spin axis of the ship, weight was only about a fourth of Earthside; he bounced around like a ball. "Wonderful, wonderful!" he caroled. "Now we'll learn something!"

Yu left her own chair and joined him. They were both young.

"And we can soon go home," she said when they stopped for breath.

His forebodings came upon him again. At this victorious moment he defied them. "And we will cope with whatever we find there."

Her gladness wavered. "Do you truly expect trouble?"

"We'll come back with a fame we can turn into power. We'll cope." His fingers stroked her cheek. "Do not be afraid, blossom."

"Never," she told him, "while we have one another." And she murmured a few ancient lines that she treasured, from the *Book of Songs*:

"Wind and rain, dark as night,
The cock crowed and would not stop.
Now that I have seen my lord,
How can I any more be sad?"

4.

The mad old man lay dying. To him came Selim ibn Ali Zeyd.

The suite was high in a hospital. Windows, open to an autumnal afternoon, let in the barest rustle of traffic. A breeze fluttered gauzy white drapes. The windows looked out over the crowded roofs of Istanbul, a Byzantine wall, and the Golden Horn, on which danced boats and little waves. Beyond, hills lifted in tawniness darkened by trees and lightened by homes.

Zeyd trod softly to the bedside and bowed.

Osman Tahir squinted up from his pillow. Bald head, mummy face, shriveled hands, brought forth the massiveness of the bones underneath. His voice was almost a whisper, hoarse and slow, but the words marched without stumbling. "You are very welcome."

He spoke in Arabic, for Zeyd had no Turkish. Either one could have used English or French. The courtesy was regal.

"I am honored that you wanted me here, sir," Zeyd answered. "So many wish to pay you their last respects, and the physicians will let so few in."

"Officious bastards. But, true, I've only driblets of strength left." Tahir grinned. "Time was, you may recall, when I could rough-and-tumble in the Assembly all day, run ten kilometers before the evening prayer, carouse till midnight, make love till dawn, and be back ahead of the opposition, ready to browbeat them further."

You old scoundrel, Zeyd could not help thinking. *Nevertheless it's more or less true.* This man, soldier and politician, had shaken history and gone on to reach for the stars. *We're all of us mortal, though. Bio-*

medicine may have given us a hundred years or better of healthy life, but in the end the organism has used itself up. "It is as God wills," he said.

Tahir nodded. "We'll not waste time on politeness. I had my reasons for insisting you come. Not that I'm not glad to see you—however much I envy you, envy you—"

Zeyd had been to Epsilon Indi.

Tahir must draw several harsh breaths before he could go on: "The damned nurse will throw you out bloody soon. I need to rest ha! As if an extra three or four days till I'm done make any difference."

He was always like this, Zeyd thought. *A trademark. And he made shrewd use of it.* "What can I do for you, sir?"

"You can tell me . . . the prospects . . . of the *Envoy* mission."

Startled, Zeyd protested, "I'm not in the organization, sir. I admire what you have done for us, but I know nothing except what the news releases say."

An English word snapped forth. "Bullshit! With your record, the connections you are bound to have in the space community—" The voice had risen. Overtaxed, it broke in violent wheezing.

Alarmed, Zeyd stooped close. Tahir waved him back. "Be honest with me," he commanded.

Zeyd straightened, as if coming to attention. "Well, sir, yes, I—I do hear things. I can't confirm or disconfirm them. The status of the project is certainly unsure."

A fist doubled on the coverlet. "Because of the war, this damned, stupid, useless war in space," Tahir rasped. The hand unfolded, trembled outward, groped for Zeyd's, and clung like a child's. "But they're not going to cancel the undertaking, are they?" Tahir pleaded. "They won't?"

The most straightforward answer possible would be the best, Zeyd decided. "As nearly as I can discover, no. It's on standby now, as you know, and all the bureaucrats of all the countries involved are being noncommittal. But it does seem as if people within the Foundation, working together regardless of nationality—I do get the impression they're holding their own. We can hope work will resume not too long after hostilities end." *Whenever that may be.*

Tahir's thought must have been similar, for he said as he let his arm drop, "That lies with God. But thank you, young man, thank you. Now I, too, dare hope—" A fleeting wistfulness: "I did hope I'd live to see the ship set forth."

His achievement, his obsession for the past half century, for which he used all the power he had been gathering: wherefore they called him mad. But he got the mission started, he got it started!

"You will watch from Paradise, sir," Zeyd said.

"Maybe. God is compassionate. Otherwise, what do we know?" Tahir's eyes, sunken and dim, sought the visitor's. "You, however, you can *go.*"

Tahir stood mute.

"You want to go, don't you?" Tahir asked anxiously. "Already you've sacrificed so much."

Strange, the lure that caught me. A spectrogram taken by an orbiting network of instruments—oxygen at a planet of Epsilon Indi, a sign of life—and I divorced Narriman, that she be free to find another man, a stepfather for our children—and here I am back, my reputation made but in a world grown more alien than I had imagined. . . .

It would be wrong, a sin, to make a promise to this man that might never be kept. And yet— "Any who go must needs be . . . somewhat peculiar," Zeyd said.

"Everybody realized that from the beginning. I'd like to believe I've met one of them."

"What happens lies with God, sir."

Tahir tried to sit up. He fell back. His voice, though, took on force. "This is to His glory. And, ten thousand years from now, when everything around us today is gone with Nineveh, you will remember, Zeyd, you will tell— But it's not for that, it's for mankind. Mankind, and the glory of God."

"Yes—"

A nurse entered. "I'm sorry, Dr. Zeyd, but you will have to leave," she said in English.

Tahir did not roar her down as once he would have done. He lay quietly, drained.

Zeyd bowed again, deeply. "In God's name, farewell, sir, and peace be upon you." His eyes stung.

He could barely hear the answer. "Fare *you* well. Well and far."

He is not mad, Zeyd thought as he departed. *He never was. It is only that his sanity went beyond most men's understanding.*

5.

Early sunlight slanted over old buildings. The mansion stood as it had stood for centuries, red-tiled and amber-walled. The same family dwelt there as always. Modernizations throughout its history had not changed its appearance much or stolen away its soul. Barn, shed, and workshop were likewise little changed, although now they held only artifacts of the past, exhibits. Trees—chestnut, cedar, quebracho—shaded a broad stretch of lawn. Flowers trooped their colors. Several members of the staff were outside, some doing minor tasks, one showing a party of tourists around. Their talk lifted cheerfully but was soon lost in the wind.

It blew slow from the south, cool, scattering insect hordes. The odors awakening in it were as green as the grassland that billowed onward to the horizon. Anthills dotted the plain like dull-red stumps; groves stood scattered, murky except where tossing leaves caught the light. A few emus walked sedately, not far off, and the sky was full of wings, partridge, thrush, dove, parrot, vulture, and more: wildlife that came back after the cattle were gone.

Ricardo Iriarte Nansen Aguilar and Hanny Dayan rode off. He could have shown her more if they had taken a hovercar, and later they would; but when he suggested an excursion on horseback for her first morning here, she accepted eagerly. To her it was an exciting novelty, to him a return to memories.

Hoofs thudded gently, leather creaked, otherwise they went in silence until they were well out in the open. The whisper of wind through grass became an undertone to the whistles, trills, and calls from above. Dayan looked right, left, ahead, over immensity. She had arrived yesterday evening, when the welcome she got took all her time before she withdrew to her guest room.

"A beautiful country, Paraguay," she said in the English they shared. "I've trouble seeing how you can leave it . . . forever."

Nansen shrugged. "It isn't my country," he replied without tone.

"No? It's your family's, and I can see they're close-knit, and your own roots are here, aren't they? Your grandnephew told me—"

She hesitated. That man was gray and furrowed. The man at her side was still young, under fifty. He sat tall in the saddle, lean, shoulders and hands big for such a build. Under straight black hair, his face bore blue-gray eyes, Roman nose, chin clean-depilated and strong. His garb was nothing uncommon— iridescent white shirt, close-fitting black trousers, soft boots—but he wore it with an air that she thought might, long ago, have been a gaucho's.

Well, he had been to the stars and back.

"—your grandnephew, Don Fernando, told me your ancestor who founded this place came from Europe in the nineteenth century," Dayan finished. "A history like that must mean a great deal."

Nansen nodded. "Yes. Though we weren't all *estancieros*, you know. One son would inherit. Most others went into trade, professions, the Church, the army, sometimes politics in the democratic era—eventually, when the time came, into space."

"Then don't you belong here?" Dayan persisted. "The land, the portraits on the walls, books, goblets, jewels, mementos, traditions—the family." She smiled. "I studied you up beforehand, Captain Nansen, and now I'm seeing for myself."

"You see the surface," he replied gravely. "They are cordial to me, yes, because I am of the blood, and they're proud of what I've done and will do. But they're strangers, Dr. Dayan." He fell quiet, gazing before him. A hawk swooped low. She recollected from news accounts of him that in his boyhood he had been a falconer. "Or . . . no, it is I who am the stranger," he said. "I came home from Epsilon Eridani, and many of the same people were still alive. Things had not changed beyond recognition. Already, however— It seemed well to join the 61 Cygni expedition."

"Surely not in despair?"

"Oh, no. An exploration. My calling, after all. I don't regret it. Those planets, lifeless but full of astonishments and challenges."

His look went aloft. Beyond the blue shone the Centaur. Five thousand light-years hence, other ships fared, and their crews were not human.

"You're familiar with our reports, I suppose," he said flatly, as if realizing he had shown more of himself than he wanted to.

Dayan would not release him. "You returned again and everything was different."

"Yes." Once more his tone carried a trace of emotion. "When I was growing up, something of the old way of life remained," the seigneurial way, hard-riding, hard-drinking, athletic, but also cultivated and gracious. "No doubt it had already outlived its time, but it was alive, oh, very alive. For instance, we still learned Guaraní as a courtesy to the Indios who worked for us, although they themselves spoke mostly Spanish. Today the language is extinct. The Indios have vanished into the general population. Cattle breeding is as obsolete as the building of pyramids, and our few horses are for sport. The Nansens have kept some of their property by turning it into a nature reserve and themselves into its caretakers."

"Is that bad?"

"No. It is simply change."

"But you feel rootless enough to make the great voyage."

He scowled. For a moment she was afraid she had given umbrage. He was not one to tolerate prying. His laugh barked, but relieved her. "Enough of me. More than enough. I invited you for a visit—Fernando agreed—for me to get acquainted with you." His glance sought hers. "The captain needs to know his crew, doesn't he?"

She had expected that. "Ask whatever you like, sir. I do hope you will accept me."

"Frankly, it is not clear to me why you volunteered."

She could not resist teasing a bit. "Maybe I'm crazy. Maybe everyone aboard the *Envoy* will be."

"We can't afford any like that," he said sharply. Not when sailing into the ultimate loneliness.

She sobered. "True." In an effort to show she had given the matter hard thought: "Osman Tahir could become obsessed with the idea of contacting the Yonderfolk. He could spend the last half of his life and the whole of his political capital to get a ship built that can go there. But he was just obsessed, not insane. Why should anybody actually leave? Ten thousand years' round trip! Each of us must be an odd creature. I've wondered about you, Captain Nansen. That's why I tried to sound you out."

He shaped a smile. "Fair is fair. Now explain yourself to me."

"You have seen my résumé, and surely a fat dossier as well. We have talked."

"In some offices. Over some dinner tables. It's time for me to get to know *you*."

"And decide if you want me aboard."

"Yes. No offense. You seem too good to be true. As you say, the volunteers have been few, and nearly everyone wrong in the head or unfit for anything at home or otherwise useless. You are young, healthy, apparently well-balanced. You have proven your competence. You are personally attractive."

Despite the reserve he wore like a cloak, he knew how to say that, and how to regard her while he did. He saw a woman small but firm and rounded of figure, with high forehead and cheekbones, eyes large and hazel between long lashes, curved nose, mouth full and accustomed to laughter. Red hair fell wavy to her shoulders. A pendant in ancient Egyptian style gave a touch of flamboyancy to her coverall.

"Then why," he demanded, "do you want to go on a voyage that will be like traveling beyond death?"

She straightened in the saddle. "You know why. I'm in danger of my life."

He drew rein. She followed suit. They sat confronted. The horses lowered their heads to graze. Butterflies and a hummingbird flashed above rippling green. Wings beat on high, cries drifted through the wind.

"Is that really true?" he asked.

She met his eyes. "You want to be sure I am not a hysteric."

"I've read the biographical material you submitted. More than once. But would you care to tell me the parts you think are important, face-to-face?"

"For you to judge my personal style?" She had done some of her graduate studies in North America; occasionally it showed in her speech. "How far back shall I go?" She threw him a grin. "Your family claims a distant kinship with Fridtjof Nansen. I'm a direct descendant of Moshe Dayan. What else is so special about my life?"

"Almost everything," he said.

She was born in Latakia, where her father was stationed, an officer of the Israeli Hegemony. Her mother was a reclamation engineer. Thus, as a child, she was exposed to considerable foreignness, until they returned to Jerusalem. Having taken her doctorate in physics, rather precociously, she went to work for the Central Technical Supply Company, mostly among the asteroids but also in the Jovian and Saturnian Systems, helping develop instruments for operations in a variety of surroundings.

"You should have a brilliant future," he added.

She grimaced. "Yes. I should have had. Then I ran afoul of the Cosmosophists."

"That was a foolish thing you did."

"Probably. An impulse." Blood rose under the clear skin. Her words throbbed. "But I hated them so. I always will."

His gaze measured her. "I agree in principle. Philo Pryor was an outrageous charlatan, and his successors have done questionable things. However, I am not violent about it."

"They are."

"What you did was provocative."

She tossed her head. "It needed doing."

Every northern summer solstice on Mars, the Order of the Received Cosmosophy brought forth from Pryor's tomb the device he related finding in a cave on Ascraeus Mons, left by the Galactics to await a genius who could endure to use it. Since his translation to a higher existence, it again lay inert; but a procession carried it to the Temple of Truth for solemn ceremonies before returning it to its resting place. Perhaps another genius would appear, in whose brain the quantum mechanical resonances would pulse anew, bringing further manifestations from the Ones. Meanwhile its appearances reminded the faithful of the doctrines their prophet had received, which the Synod of Interpreters rendered into day-by-day commandments. Such a communion will not take kindly to an outsider who loads with instruments an apartment that the procession must pass, afterward publishing her data and explaining how they show that the circuits in the box do nothing and never could do anything.

"Why did you?" Nansen pursued.

"I've told people over and over," she spat. "To expose the fraud."

"You haven't, you know," he said. "Devout believers go on believing, and call you the liar. You are not stupid. Nor do I think you are completely naive. It was a good deal of trouble to go to, for what you should have foreseen was a pointless prank. Why? What drove you to it?"

She swallowed hard, red and white surging across her face. The sun made flame of her hair. He waited.

"All right," she got out. "I didn't put this in my file because I didn't think it was anybody else's business. But I suppose it is yours, and you'll keep it to yourself. I had a dear friend. He owned property on Mars. The Order wanted it, and did him out of it, blackening his name in the process. He . . . got drunk, got careless about his air supply in the desert, died. The body wasn't found till too late for revival. I was angry."

Nansen nodded. "I see." He refrained from inquiring about the friend. Instead, after a pause, he said, "Your account describes several attempts on your life since then. Police records corroborate three of them. How do you know the Order is responsible?"

"Who else would be?" Dayan looked past him, toward the horizon. "Oh, I have my connections in Israel. I could arrange a well-guarded cocoon for myself. But what sort of life is that? Or I could sign onto an interstellar expedition, if one will take me, and come back after my enemies are dead. But I doubt fifty years will be enough, and nothing longer is planned, except yours." She was still for another moment. The wind in the grass, the sound of the horses cropping, seemed to louden. "How very much longer!"

"An extreme way to go for safety."

"I'd rather shoot those swine, of course. But the law doesn't allow, and anyhow, I can't identify the individuals who've tried for me."

"You would hardly be going into a safe refuge."

"I know!" As she went on, allurement overtook rage and her mood brightened. "That's one thing making it . . . not a loss to me. Yes, I'll mourn for the people I love, everybody, everything I'll never see again, but—what'll we find out there? What'll we *do*? And when we return, this will be a whole new world, too."

"We must explore the question further," he said quietly. "I like your spirit."

"And I—I—well, I don't expect your company will be dull," she told him.

For two or three seconds they considered one another.

Nansen touched heels to horse and took up the reins. His briskness declared that the captain should not allow any sudden, real intimacy to flower. "Come, that's plenty for the time being. Let's enjoy the day. You're not an experienced *caballista*, are you?"

She chuckled. "Isn't that obvious?"

"Let me show you a bit of technique, and then we'll ride!"

6

From the *stoep* of Mamphela Mokoena's little house, Lajos Ruszek saw widely. Westward the Transkei heights rose green with plantations, shrubs and trees producing their various organics under a hard blue sky. Northward and southward the city reached beyond sight, towns swollen until they ran together, brightly colored modules clustered along traffic-swarming streets, towers rearing among them, hovercars weaving above, and everywhere people on foot or on motorskates, their voices a daytime overtone to a machine throb that never ceased. Eastward the Indian Ocean glared with sunlight. The city sprawled out into it: platforms for residence, thermal energy, and mineral extraction; maricultural mats; boats and attendant robots plying between. No matter how pure the industry, a faint reek lay in the air—chemicals, particulates, humanity.

Mokoena came from inside bearing a tray with a pitcher and two tumblers of iced tea. She set it down on a table and herself in a woven chair across from Ruszek's. Her guest snatched his drink and gulped.

"Ah-h-h!" he exhaled. "Goes good. Thank you, mademoiselle."

Mokoena smiled. "That title doesn't fit me well, I fear," she replied in English less accented than his.

"Eh? I meant— I understood you have not married."

"True. However—" She waved a hand at herself, a gesture half humorous, half rueful. Her dashiki covered a frame fairly tall and formerly slender but putting on weight now that she was in her late thirties. Her face, brown-skinned, broad-nosed, under bushy black hair, remained smooth, and the eyes still shone like a girl's.

"No matter," she said. Her voice sounded twice melodious after his gravelly basso. "I appreciate the thought. And it is most kind of you to have come all this way just to pay a visit."

"I want to meet everybody in the crew," Ruszek admitted in his blunt fashion. "Get some beforehand knowledge of them. We'll be a long time together."

Mokoena's smile faded. "Long—" It was as if the shade in which they sheltered had gone chill. *Ten thousand years and more.*

Ruszek's prosaic question brought her back. "What should I call you?"

She studied him. Neither his manner nor his appearance suggested courtliness. Of medium height but powerful build, he had made the mistake of wearing a naval-style tunic and trousers, and was sweating copiously and pungently. The bullet head was totally bald except for bushy brows and sweeping black mustache. Brown almond eyes looked out of a broad, rather flat countenance. His age was fifty-five.

She relaxed. "Oh, I suppose 'Dr. Mokoena' will do till we feel free to be less formal. What do you prefer for yourself?"

Ruszek poured more tea. Ice cubes clinked. "Whatever you want. I've been many things."

"So I've gathered. Although the information's remarkably scanty, considering how the journalists are after us. Did you make them hostile to you on purpose?"

"I give the pests what they deserve."

"Forgive me, but is that quite wise? Especially when you will be second in command."

"And a boat pilot," he reminded her, veering from a subject he disliked. "That interests me much more."

She went along with him. "I'm sure it does, from what I've heard about you."

"Besides, Captain Nansen won't really need any second."

His tone had altered. "You sound as though you admire him," she said.

"There's no better man, in space or on the ground."

"Is that why you enlisted? To serve under him? I didn't know you'd met before."

"We hadn't, till I applied. Then I found out."

"May I ask why you did join?"

Ruszek forced a laugh. "I came here to ask you that, Dr. Mokoena."

"It works both ways, Mr. Ruszek."

"Well, adventure, challenge, if you must have big words."

"There are closer stars, shorter voyages, no dearth of discoveries and great deeds."

"Could I get a berth on any such expedition? Not fucking likely—uh, pardon me. Too few starships so far. Too much competition."

"Yes, I suppose so. As you say, adventure and challenge, and the time away from home isn't usually too many years."

He grinned. "Don't forget the profits. Crew members get their lecture fees, endorsements, book contracts, fat Earthside jobs. The Foundation, or whoever has built and backed the ship, gets the specimens and samples to sell—and the entertainment rights, the documentaries and dramas. Oh, it pays."

"It pays us all, in knowledge, in hope—hope of meeting other intelligences, settling new worlds," she said earnestly.

"Why are we trading these duck-billed platitudes?" he retorted. "To get to your point, Dr. Mokoena, *Envoy*'s the one starship with no serious competition for berths."

"Nevertheless—"

He cut her off. "All right, God damn it, all right, I'll tell you about myself. Don't blame me if you already know everything.

"Born in Budapest, lower middle class, rough-and-tumble boy, left home at sixteen and odd-jobbed around the world a few years—yes, sometimes had to dodge the busybody law—till I joined the Peace Command of the Western Alliance. Surprise, I liked that and buckled down to getting an education. Got posted to military construction on Luna and in free space, got piloting skills, but kept being broken in rank for this or that trouble. At the end of my hitch I found me a civilian post, with the Solmetals Consortium, and piloted around, everywhere from Mars to Saturn. Saw some action in the Space War."

Her eyes widened. "Really? But you were a civilian then, you said. And a European."

He shrugged. "It wasn't a decent old-time kind of war, remember. A nasty, drawn-out, sniping thing between the cat's-paws of the big powers, for who should control this or that out there. Even after Europe withdrew, the Chinks— Argh, it's years past. I came through with experience, a record, that made Captain Nansen push hard for the Foundation to accept me. Are you satisfied?"

"An active life," she murmured, her gaze contemplative upon him. "Often harder than you admit, I'm sure."

His irritation subsided. "You have an eye for people, Dr. Mokoena."

She smiled. "Perhaps. My business."

"Your turn. I know hardly anything about you."

"There isn't much to know. Quiet years, unlike yours."

"Then why are you going?"

"I can be of service."

He sat back, ran a palm over the sweat that sheened across his pate, and said, "Well, we certainly do need a biologist and a physician, and if they come in the same package, God is very obliging. But you do well enough on Earth, no? Why should you want to leave it?"

She sipped her tea, buying time, before she answered slowly, "The reasons are personal. Captain Nansen and the Foundation directors know, of course. You shall eventually. I would rather it not come out before the public, to avoid embarrassing . . . certain persons." Decision: "Well, you won't spill it to the media."

He grinned again. "Guaranteed."

"What do you know about me?"

"Um . . . you studied medicine, and worked for years among the poor, first in this kingdom, later with relief missions elsewhere in Africa. At last you stopped, went back to school, became a biologist, and did good science, especially on the specimens brought back from Tau Ceti. Is this why you want to go with us, research?"

"It will be fascinating."

"You may never publish it, you know. When we come back, we may not find any world here."

"I realize that. I dare hope—meeting the Yonderfolk, learning from them—will matter to humankind." Mokoena fanned the air dismissingly. "But I don't want to sound stuffy, either. By going, I can set something right here and now."

"What?"

She sighed. "It hurt, forsaking medicine. The need is so great. I felt so selfish. But I—I did not think I could stand seeing much more utter misery, unless I hardened my heart to it, and I didn't want to do that. My parents are ministers of the Samaritan Church. My work was through it, on its behalf. When I quit, they felt betrayed." Her fingers tightened around her tumbler. "*Envoy* badly needed one like me. I joined on condition that the Exploratory Foundation make a substantial grant to their church, a sum that'll make a real difference. We are reconciled, my parents and I. They say they'll wait for me in the afterlife and welcome me gladly. I don't, myself, know about that. But they are happy."

He regarded her somewhat wonderingly. "You're a saint."

She put down her drink, threw her head back, and let laughter ring. "Ha! Absolutely not, Mr. Ruszek, nor ambitious to be one. I expect I'll enjoy most of what happens. I usually have."

After a moment: "In fact, since we'd like to get acquainted, why don't you stay for dinner? When I cook for myself, I cook well, but it's more fun to do for company."

"That's the best offer I've had all week," he said, delighted.

"One thing—"

"Oh, I have a room at the Hotel de Klerk."

"No, no, what I meant was— It had slipped my mind, but we have a chance to learn something about our second engineer."

"Alvin Brent? I've already met him."

She grew grave. "What was your impression?"

"Why, . . . not bad. He knows his business. Not too much the physics of the quantum gate, but the nuts and bolts. If anything happens to Yu Wenji, Brent can get us home."

"But as a person? You see, I've never met him. I've only seen the reports and some news stories."

"His background is no worse than mine."

American, born in Detroit, parents service providers struggling to keep afloat amidst depression, taxes, and controls. Alvin was their single child, apparently wanted more by the father than the mother; she was dutiful, as the New Christian Church commanded women to be and the Advisor commanded citizens in general to be. A misfit in school, he showed a talent for computers and machinery, which his social isolation reinforced. On recommendation of his local gang boss—the Radiums were in favor with the regional commissioner—he won appointment to the Space Academy. There he flourished. Though still not given to camaraderie, he got along, and his grades were excellent. Having trained on Luna and between planets, he became involved in the Space War, aboard "observer" ships that saw occasional combat. During those four years he did several courageous things.

They availed him little. Having been stripped of most of its interplanetary possessions, the United States must needs scale down. Discharged into a hand-to-mouth existence, Brent finally got a minor position with Consolidated Energetics. He was well aware that a robotic system would replace him as soon as the capital to install it became available. *Envoy* offered more. Whether for weal or woe, nobody knew.

"I am thinking of his ideas," Mokoena said.

"What difference will they make, where we're going?" Ruszek countered.

"Bad for our unity, our morale, if they are offensive. He's been in the news quite a bit, you know, because of those things he keeps saying. But what they mean isn't clear to me."

"Don't worry. If he should get obnoxious, I'll sit on him. But he struck me as fairly sensible. About as sensible as anybody can be who'd go on an expedition like this."

"I saw on the news that he'll give a live talk in Australia about that North Star Society he belongs to. At 2100 hours. In a few minutes, our time."

"And we can watch it happen, hm? All right, if you want to."

"I'd rather. When so much of all our input is recorded or synthesized or virtual— Call it a superstition of mine, but I think we belong in the real world."

"I do, too. When we can get at it."

Mokoena rose and led the way inside. Ruszek glanced around. The living room was clean but cluttered: cassettes, folio books, printouts, pictures, childhood toys, seashells, souvenirs ranging from garish to gorgeous, woven hangings, old handicrafted pieces—tools, bowls, musical instruments, fetishes, masks, two assegais crossed behind a shield. She sat down on a worn and sagging couch, beckoned him to join her, and spoke to the television.

It came alight with a view of an auditorium. The building must date back at least a century, for it overwhelmed the hundred-odd people who had come in person to hear. However, on request the net reported that some twenty million sets were tuned in around the globe. Doubtless several times that number would carry replays, or at least excerpts. "Aren't we the sensation, we *Envoy* crew?" Ruszek gibed. "Every sneeze and fart of ours is newsworthy. How long till they forget, once we're gone? Six months?"

The scan moved in on Brent as he advanced to the forefront of the stage. He was a forty-year-old of average height and soldierly bearing, dressed in plain military-style gray tunic and trousers, a Polaris emblem on the collar. His black hair was cut short, his beard suppressed. His features were regular and sallow, distinguished mainly by intense dark eyes.

"He is attractive," Mokoena remarked.

Ruszek raised his brows. "Heh? I wouldn't know. He doesn't seem to chase women."

Mokoena smiled. "Part of the attraction." Seriously: "And his . . . his burningness."

The invitation to speak had come from a group sympathetic to his views. Australia, too, had suffered losses in space. The chairman introduced the guest speaker rather fulsomely. By sheer contrast, Brent's level tone caught immediate hold of the attention.

"Thank you. Good evening. To all on Earth who share our concern, to all like us through the Solar System, greeting.

"I am honored to be here, I who will soon leave you for a span longer than recorded history. Why have I come? To offer you a vision. To tell you that hope lives, and will always live while men and women are undaunted. My own hope is that you will follow this vision, that you will redress our wrongs and start the world on a new course, that what I find when I return will be glorious."

The voice began to pulse, and presently to crash. ". . . yes, the North Star Society says we were betrayed. In the Federated Nations they bleated about 'peace' and brought every pressure to bear on us they could; but no more than a token on our enemies. The intellectuals, the news media, the politicians squealed about nuclear weapons let loose on Earth if the fighting got 'serious'—as if it wasn't! The bankers, the church bosses, the corporation executives, they had their hidden agendas. Believe you me, they did. And so we withheld our full strength. We pretended we were not in a war at all. And brave Americans, brave Australians, died for lack of our aid. Do you want them to have died for nothing?"

"*NO!*" the audience shouted.

"It's no wonder his government is discouraging that club of his," Mokoena muttered. "This is explosive stuff."

"Oh, I don't know," Ruszek answered. "They're not stirring up any mobs." His mustache bent upward with his sneer. "The mobs are at home, wrapped up in their virtual-reality shows. Maybe that's why he signed on with us—frustration. He can't do any harm where we're bound."

Mokoena shook her head. "I don't think he is an evil man. I think he's terribly embittered and— Yes, let's see if we can help him heal."

"Let him do his job and I'll be satisfied. Not that he'll have much to do, while Yu is in charge."

"A mere backup. It must be a hard knowledge."

Brent continued. His tone grew shrill when he denounced the conspirators and called for a rebirth of Western will. Toward the end, though, he quieted again; and tears were on his cheeks as he finished:

". . . I leave the work in your hands. I must go, with my comrades, across the galaxy, to meet the nearest of the great starfaring civilizations. You, your children, your children's children, they must found our own, and take possession of the stars for humankind. What we in our ship will find, nobody knows. But we, too, will carry destiny with us, human destiny. And when we return, when we bring back what we have won, to join with what you and your blood have built, humankind will go onward to possess the universe!"

The audience cheered, a sound nearly lost in the hollowness around them. Mokoena told the set to turn off. For a minute she and Ruszek sat silent.

"Do you know," he said, "I think he really believes this."

"Destiny? Yes, I daresay he does. And you don't?"

"No. I believe in—slogging, is that your word? Slogging ahead, the best way we can; and if we fail, then we fail. Bad luck, nothing else."

"I feel there must be some purpose to existence. But the purpose can't be that we take over everything at the expense of . . . everybody else."

"Words, just words. I tell you, don't worry about Al Brent. I've known men with wilder notions who operated perfectly well. Captain Nansen wouldn't have accepted him—no matter how scarce qualified volunteers have been—if he was any kind of danger."

She eased. "You two should be shrewd judges." Slyly: "And I confessed he's attractive."

"That is something our crew members will decide about each other," he answered.

She smiled. "We could begin now."

The evening and the next few days passed very pleasantly.

7.

Seen from afar, against blackness cloven by the Milky Way and crowded with stars, Earth a blue spark lost in the glare of the dwindling sun, spaceship *Envoy* was jewelwork, exquisite in her simplicity. Two four-spoked wheels spun with glittering speed, an axle motionless between them. From the after hub projected a lacy cylinder, the plasma drive accelerator. From the forward hub reached, far and far, thin and bright as a laser ray, a lance, the wave-guide mast for the shielding force field. Both were now inactive. The ship had reached the desired velocity and was outbound on a cometary orbit. There was no immediate radiation hazard.

Hurtling closer, Jean Kilbirnie saw the true enormousness swell before her. Those wheels were four hundred meters across, their toroidal rims ten meters thick, each spoke a six-meter tube. They counterrotated almost one hundred meters apart. The accelerator extended 40 meters, the mast a full kilometer. Other starcraft had similar lines, but none were like unto this. *Envoy* bore a quantum gate with capacity to give a gamma, a relativistic mass-length-time factor, of a full five thousand. She must carry everything that ten humans and their machines might imaginably need on a journey into the totally unknown.

Not yet had she embarked on it. This was a one-month shakedown cruise within the Solar System. The zero-zero drive would not awaken. Nothing about the ship required testing. Robots had done that, over and over, and all flaws were mended. The crew were testing themselves.

Kilbirnie peered at viewscreens and instruments. Subtler clues flowed into her through the bioelectronic circuits. Almost, she *was* the spaceboat. The ship waxed as if toppling upon her. The axial cylinder filled her vision, a curving cliff of sheening metal plated on composite whose strength approached the ultimate. Turrets, bays, dishes, tracks, ports, hatches, the whole complexity leaped forth athwart shadows. It was the outer hull, fifty meters in diameter. The inner hull projected slightly at either end, twenty meters wide, encased there in sleeves that held the magnetic bearings of the wheels. Kilbirnie was overtaking from aft, as doctrine required. No person was in that wheel, only machinery, supplies, and equipment awaiting whatever hour they would be wanted.

Time! Her fingers commanded full thrust. Deceleration crammed her back into the recoil chair. Blood thundered in her ears, red rags flew across her sight. The brief savagery ended and she floated weightless in her harness. She had not set those vectors. Living nerves, muscles, brains were too slow, too limited. Yet hers was the mind that directed the robotics that animated them. "Ki-ai!" she shouted, and spun *Herald* around.

The next maneuver was actually trickier, but did not rouse the same exuberance. Having matched velocities just as she came even with her dock, half a kilometer off, she boosted delicately inward. The dock extended arms, caught hold, swung the boat parallel to the ship, drew her in, and made her fast.

Kilbirnie sat still, letting her heartbeat quiet down. The comscreen lighted. Captain Nansen's image looked grimly out. "Pilot Kilbirnie," he said, "that approach was total recklessness. You left no margin of safety."

She pressed for transmission. "Och, *Herald* and I knew what we were doing," she replied.

He glared at her. Blood still atingle flushed a narrow face with strong bones, straight nose, broad mouth, and blue eyes under thick black brows, framed in light brown hair bobbed below the ears. Coverall-clad, her body was rangy to the point of leanness. It was thirty-three years old, but Tau Ceti had added twenty-five to its calendar.

"You endangered your boat, the ship, the whole mission," he snapped.

Lajos Ruszek broke in, though he didn't bother with splicing to video. His vessel, *Courier*, sister to *Herald*, had barely come into naked-eye view, a blunt bullet tiny among stars. "Captain, I gave her leave to do it," he said. "I knew she could. We've maneuvered enough together, we two."

"Why did you?" Nansen demanded of Kilbirnie.

"Not to show off or experiment, sir," she explained, slightly chastened. "That would have been foul, taking unnecessary chances. It was to practice. We've unco short time left for reinforcing our skills. Then we're off on the big jump and can't again for a year. Who kens what we'll meet at the far end? Lajos and I had better be well drilled."

"Pilot's judgment, Captain," Ruszek reminded.

Nansen relaxed a little. "Very well," he said. "I withdraw the reprimand. But do not repeat this or anything like it, either of you." He gave her a wry smile. "We aboard want to keep our sanity in condition!"

Kilbirnie lowered her head. "I'm sorry, sir. I didn't think of that."

"We learn by mistakes." Nansen switched off.

"Including you by yours?" she muttered. "Dinna think I havena heard what a hotshot you were in your own piloting days."

Her cheerfulness revived. She disengaged the sensory interfaces attached to her skin, unharnessed, and floated to the bow airlock. The dock had mated a transit module to it. She passed through. Inside the great hull, a passage stretched bare and bleakly lighted. Maybe someone would brighten it up in the course of the journey. Hands grasping, feet thrusting at inset rungs, Kilbirnie sped forward. At the end, a perpendicular corridor brought her to a lock near the inner hull. Beyond it she entered a padded compartment with several seats, into one of which she secured herself.

The compartment was the cabin of a shuttle. It did not jet, it jumped across the ten meters to the wheel. Magnetohydrodynamic forces captured it along the way and eased it into contact with a port in that spoke which happened to be whirling past at the right instant. The radius here being short, the impact was slight, as was the weight Kilbirnie suddenly felt. She unbuckled, cycled through this pair of locks, and emerged on a platform projecting into the cylinder. From there she could have taken a railcar to the rim. She preferred to climb the fixed ladder.

The climb could as well have been called a descent. Weight increased as she proceeded, until at the end it was a full Earth gravity. She came out into a corridor, lined with doors, which curved upward to right and left, although the deck was always level beneath her feet. The overhead cast gentle light. At the moment, a breeze bore an odor of pine. She inhaled gratefully. While a boat trip might be exciting, undeniably the ship had a better air system.

Tim Cleland stood jittering to and fro. He was a tall young man, carelessly clad, sparely built, his countenance round and snub-nosed, with brown eyes and curly brown hair. "Jean," he croaked.

She halted. "Losh, what a face on you," she said.

"I was . . . terrified." In haste: "Not for me. For you. If you'd crashed—" He reached toward her.

She ignored the gesture. "No danger of that," she assured him. "I like being alive."

His arms dropped. He stared at her. The ventilation whispered.

"Do you?" he asked slowly.

Her smile died. Her look defied him.

"Do you?" he insisted. "Then why are you throwing it away, ev—everything that is your life? . . . Ten thousand years sealed inside this *shell*."

Kilbirnie strengthened her burr. "Nobbut two years altogether, ship time. In between them, five years of Elvenland."

"You don't like what Earth's become," he pleaded. "In ten thousand years, it'll be—what?"

Her teeth flashed in the wide white smile that was especially hers. "A high part of the whole faring, to see what." The husky voice went low. "But if you feel like this about it, why are you bound along?"

His shoulders slumped. "You know why. I've told you, how often?"

She nodded. "It's because I am. Tim, Tim, that's not a sane reason."

He attempted playfulness. "I'll wear you down."

"I think not, Tim. You're a dear, but I think not. Best you resign, before 'tis too late. We do have some standby volunteers, you remember."

Cleland shook his head. "No. They're second choices. By now, I'd feel like a traitor." He caught a breath. "Besides, well, the scientific prospects are dazzling, that's true. What kinds of planets, what kinds of beings? And—and, uh, I've explained how I never was very adept socially. Not a leader, not a follower, not a joiner. I'm giving up less than most men would." He gulped. "But I'm not giving up on you."

"Forgive me," she said softly. "I must go now. I have a date."

He stared as if she had slapped him. She laughed. "With Mamphela in the gym. We'll trade teachings of old dances, Highland and Zulu."

He gaped. "Right after . . . getting back from space . . . the way you did?"

"When would a girl more want to kick up her heels?" she answered joyfully, and left him.

The engines of the plasma and zero-zero drives were aft in the inner hull. Most of their servicing facilities were nearby. However, the forward wheel held lesser workshops of various kinds, as well as laboratories. Its circumference gave ample room.

Passing by one of these, Chief Engineer Yu Wenji heard sounds through the door, opened it, and went in to see. Alvin Brent, her second, sat hunched over a table, at work on a circuit board. Tools and materials lay scattered before him. A faint ozone pungency in the air spoke of an ion torch lately used. Computer screens displayed diagrams.

"What are you doing?" Yu asked.

Brent twisted around on his stool. For an instant he glowered. She stood her ground, a short, sturdy woman with blunt features between high cheekbones, bronzy complexion, black hair swept up and held by a comb. Her embroidered jacket and blue trousers seemed to rebuke his soiled work clothes.

He smoothed the irritation off his face and said carefully, "I've worked out an idea for an improvement in our missile launch control. Minor, but it could make a difference someday. Now I'm putting together the hardware. There'll be time on this cruise to install and test it."

She stiffened. "You told me nothing about this."

"I saw no reason to, ma'am. It's not connected to your engines. Not your responsibility."

"Every apparatus aboard and every program to run it is my responsibility. Bad enough that we carry weapons—"

"How do you know we won't need them?" he interrupted.

She sighed. "I don't, of course. But I cannot believe that civilizations thousands or millions of years old continue such obscene follies." Coldly: "You will consult me in advance about any further ideas you may have, Mr. Brent. Meanwhile you will stop this project until I have evaluated it."

"What harm?" he protested. "You'd have known before I tried anything. Everybody would have."

"I would not have had an opportunity to analyze it for any effects on the entire, integrated system. Have you thought of every possibility? Furthermore, this is a matter of principle. You cannot decide unilaterally what use of your time is best for the ship."

He slammed the board down on the table. "Use?" he exploded. "What do you expect me to do? Stand idle like another of your machines till you feel like switching me on?"

She lifted a palm and replied with quick mildness, "I have wondered if you would care to teach our shipmates something of what you know and can do, in case you suffer misfortune. I need not explain to you the value of redundancy. We do not have nearly enough."

"Who in this gang of freaks has that kind of talent?"

"Why, surely Mate Ruszek, Pilot Kilbirnie, and Dr. Dayan, at least. Probably more. They will be wanting worthwhile occupation on our journey. We all will."

"You the most," broke from him.

"I beg your pardon?"

"You probably have more need to forget than anyone else does. Or do you imagine your precious Chinese culture will still be here when we get back?"

"That will do, Mr. Brent," she clipped.

He swallowed, stood up as if at attention, and conceded stiffly, "I apologize, ma'am. I shouldn't have said that."

Again she softened. "Well, but you are under stress. We must not make it worse. If you will prepare a report on this device of yours, I will be glad to review it and, if it has merit, discuss it with the captain. Good daywatch."

Before he could reply, she turned and left. Her strides down the corridor were quick but not entirely even. Tears glimmered in her eyes. She blinked them away.

Presently she reached the common room. As yet it was plain, monotone, like most of the interior. Decoration would help occupy the time of voyage. Already it reached spacious, comfortably furnished, equipped for games, recorded entertainment, or live performances. Interference projectors could block sound from those who might want to sit undisturbed. It offered a change from their private cabins.

At this hour it was generally deserted. People were more actively engaged. As Yu entered she saw Ajit Nathu Sundaram in an armchair.

He rose and bowed. She returned the courtesy. He was a small man on the verge of middle age, fine-featured, chocolate-colored, the black hair beginning to frost. As usual, he wore merely pajamas and sandals. "Good afternoon, Engineer Yu," he greeted. His voice was rather high, its English devoid of any regional flavor.

"Yes, it is afternoon by the clock, is it not?" she responded more or less automatically. "Likewise to you, sir. You look happy."

"I have no reason not to be." He regarded her. She had not hidden every sign of distress. "A few of our friends are less fortunate."

She grabbed after conversation. "What were you doing, if I may ask?"

"Thinking. Not very productively, I fear."

She in her turn gazed long at him. "Can anything shake you?" she murmured.

"Too many things. They should not, true." He smiled. "Since you are here, apparently at loose ends, would you care for a game of chess?"

"I—I suspect you notice more than you pretend."

"Not really. I am a theorist. Whatever expertise I may have is abstract, in the underlying structure and logic of language," said humankind's most famous linguist and semantician. "But perhaps I can put some blood and fire into my chessmen."

"Thank you," she said low. "A game is exactly what I would like."

At 1930 hours the crew came to the wardroom from wherever they had been in the wheel. Selim ibn Ali Zeyd encountered Hanny Dayan near the entrance.

He halted to look her up and down. *"Quelle surprise délicieuse,"* he greeted, politely but with unmistakable appreciation.

She stopped, too. Her lips quirked upward. A deep blue gown, full-length and low-cut, hugged her figure. The Egyptian pendant was colorful above her breasts and a silver fillet held the red hair. "Thank you," she said.

"When the captain requested that henceforward we dress for dinner, I did not expect anything so splendid."

"We knew he would."

This was to be after acceleration ended, weight became purely centrifugal, and the travelers had moved from the cramped gimballed decks. This gathering would celebrate the completion of settlement in their proper quarters.

"So I brought a few extra clothes along," Dayan finished.

"Greatly to the gain of the gentlemen among us," Zeyd told her.

She gave him a glance as frank as his own. "You are quite elegant yourself."

The biochemist stood slim and dark, hawk-faced, with sleek black hair and closely trimmed mustache, in well-tailored whites. "How kind of you," he answered. "Also to wear that ornament. I am an Egyptian, you may recall."

"Not yet mummified."

"You seem in a merry mood."

She grew briefly thoughtful. "I've . . . put regrets behind me, as best I could. Let's move onward."

"An attitude more than sensible. It confers radiance."

Wariness edged her tone. "Thank you, Dr. Zeyd."

"Since we are to play at formality," he said, his geniality undiminished, "may I?" He offered her his arm. She smiled back at him and took it. They went into the wardroom and sat down together.

Savory smells mingled. The nanotechnics of the adjacent galley could provide everybody with his or her choice from the menus of the world. Tonight it was to be a surprise, but individual preferences, religious injunctions, and the like were in the database. Napery rested snowy beneath a gleam of tableware. A servitor rolled about, its arms deftly placing the hors d'oeuvres and the first bottles.

When the whole company was seated, Nansen tapped his goblet with a knife. The chime brought talk buzzing to a halt. Attention swung toward him, at the head of the table in a gray tunic with gold trim. "Silence, please," he said. "A moment for those who wish to bless our meal."

He crossed himself. He was nominally a Reform Catholic, as observant as he felt good manners required. Ruszek did likewise. Zeyd bowed his head. Mokoena looked down at her folded hands and whispered. Yu and Sundaram grew meditative. The rest waited respectfully.

"Well, ladies and gentlemen," Nansen resumed, "now that we are properly on our cruise, let's do more than practice being a crew. Let's take pleasure in each other and in the voyage we'll share." His cordiality gave way to seriousness. "I promise not to make speeches at you as a regular thing, but on this first occasion a few remarks do seem in order. You are all aware of these matters and have given them much thought. I would simply like to set them forth in a few words, to make sure we share the same understanding. Anyone who feels I am wrong about anything, please say so, if not here then at our regular discussion sessions.

"We are going on what may be the greatest adventure in human history. I believe it will be even more an adventure of the spirit than of the body and mind. We've had our different reasons for joining it, and not all those reasons are happy. But let us leave sorrow, guilt, and doubt behind us. Let us expect wonders.

"Nevertheless, we will be more alone than ten souls ever were alone before. Only ten—"

Lesser expeditions had borne more, as many as fifty, not individual scientists and technicians but teams of them. Advances in computer systems and robotics had not brought the desirable number quite this low. But willingness and competence rarely came together for a voyage like *Envoy*'s; and, yes, a skeleton crew required less mass of supplies and life support, which meant that the ship's drive, unprecedentedly powerful though it was, could bring them still closer to c, slicing centuries off the journey time; and, psychologists thought, an uncrowded interior should make for less human friction, which might well prove important. When the very objective of the mission was unknown, you proceeded according to your best guess to do the best you were able with what you had.

"We can never return home. When we come back to Earth, we will necessarily come as foreigners, immigrants. I think that what we bring will make us welcome, and we will find new friends and found new homes. But none can ever be close to us in the way that we are—that we must be—to each other. We have to become more than a crew. We have to become a family.

"I wish we could start with established, stable relationships between us, especially between men and women. But we are who we are, the handful of people best suited for this voyage, and we cannot wait for a full set of arrangements to develop, or the voyage will never begin. So we must not only be brave, we must be tolerant, sympathetic, and generous. Let us remember always, above and beyond everything else in us, we are the crewfolk of humankind's *Envoy*.

"All this is perfectly obvious. But—word magic, if you like—I felt it needed saying forth. Now, if you please, I will propose one toast before we dine." He lifted his dry sherry. "To the stars."

Coming from anyone else the speech might have been pretentious. Don Ricardo knew how to carry such things off.

8.

After the ship returned to high Earth orbit, her people had six weeks' liberty before she departed for the Centaur.

Steel rang. Nansen parried and riposted. Light flashed at the tip of his saber as it made contact. *"Touché!"* acknowledged Pierre Desmoulins. *"Très belle!"* In a series of lunges, glides, and thrusts, Nansen had driven him back halfway across the floor.

For a minute they stood breathing hard, faces agleam with sweat and smiles. Other pairs contended around the *salle d'armes*, a dance of bodies and blades, but several had stopped to watch these two. *"Encore une fois?"* Desmoulins invited.

Nansen shook his head. *"Merci, non. J'ai—"* His French broke down. He spread his palms. *"Une femme."*

Desmoulins laughed. *"Ah, mais naturellement. Bon jour. Bonne nuit."* Jauntiness dropped from him, forced off by awe. *"Et . . . bon voyage, M. le capitaine."*

Nansen shook the proferred hand. His own smile died. He could not altogether keep a catch out of his voice. *"Adieu, mon ami."*

This had probably been the last fencing he would ever do. He didn't think anyone aboard ship would care to learn, and virtuals were a pathetic surrogate. Ten thousand years from this evening, who would know there had been such a sport?

He could come back here if he chose, of course, but he wouldn't. Too little time remained for too much else.

He walked quickly off, turned in his outfit, put his street clothes on, and went forth to the rue de Grenelle. Though the air was warm, he wore a cloak with the hood up—not uncommon hereabouts, and it might keep him unrecognized. A gaily striped awning over a sidewalk café tempted. He could use a cold beer. But no, he had to bathe and change garments at his hotel before he met Odile Morillier. She'd wait if need be—few women would not have waited for a man of the *Envoy*—but someone so beautiful wasn't used to it, nor did he want to seem arrogant.

A live symphony concert in the Parc Monceau, then dinner in a private room at the Vert Galant, then perhaps a walk along the river or under trees fragrant with spring, and then, yes, the night, and the days and nights to follow. He had cut enough swathes in the past and had begun to think wistfully about marriage, children. . . . No, the stars had made him an alien. Let him know one woman well and learn to hold her dear—as well and as dear as time allowed—and take the riches away in his memory. That would be worth the pain of farewell. He hoped she would not share it, but remember him kindly and with pleasure.

A constabulary guard in the foyer verified Yu's identity and saluted as he admitted her to the ascensor. She rode in blessed solitude to the fiftieth floor. After the crowded streets, people yelling and shoving toward her even as she crossed from her cab to the entrance, this cool quiet was like another world. She found the number she wanted and touched the door. It must have been instructed from below, for it immediately contracted and let her through.

The room beyond was spacious, furnishings sleekly up-to-date, but the vases from which lilies and jasmine perfumed the air were antique. Set for transparency, the south wall showed bustling modern Rehavia. Eastward she saw the Old City, the Temple of the Reconcilement, and the Mount of Olives under a Mediterranean sky where aircraft darted like glittering mites.

Dayan had sprung from a chair. She ran to meet the visitor. "Wenji, welcome—*shalom*!" she cried, and hugged her. "Come, make yourself comfortable." She led her to a recliner. "What would you like: tea, coffee, something stronger?"

"Thank you, whatever you take," Yu replied. She sat down but remained tense.

"Speak up, do. I can barely hear you. It's kind of early in the day, but, I decree, not too early for a beer. One minute." Dayan went through an arch to the inner suite. She returned almost as soon as promised, bearing a tray with two frosty steins and a bowl of salted nuts. Setting it down on a minitable, she dropped into the seat opposite and beamed. "Oh, I am glad to see you."

"Thank you," the engineer whispered.

The physicist raised her drink. "*Mazel tov.* I don't know what they say in Chinese."

Yu smiled a bit. "*Kan bei,* in my part of the country." She barely sipped.

"What a grand surprise when you called."

"I . . . hesitated. Are we not generally keeping away from each other on this last furlough?"

"No doubt. But you're a breath of pure oxygen, Wenji." Dayan scowled, drank, and made a chopping gesture. "This damned guarded existence."

Compassion deepened Yu's voice. "Do you feel imprisoned?"

Dayan sighed. "Not exactly. I do want to be with my . . . parents, brother, sister, their children, our kin, our friends—be with them as much as possible. But the government's carrying its concern for my safety too far. I'm not supposed to leave Jerusalem, or go anywhere outside without an armed escort, or— All those eyes, always watching. I don't want to disappoint or grieve anybody, but—" She snapped a laugh. "That's plenty about me! Tell me why I'm having this break in the routine."

Yu was still for a moment before she said, with difficulty, "I, too, feel watched."

"How? I took for granted you'd spend your leave in China. You've spoken of your home so lovingly."

The old tile-roofed village in the old green countryside, the Hwang Ho mightily flowing, a bell at twilight, lifeways and a reverence for them that had changed their outward guise only a little as the millennia swept past; science and machines could ensorcel a girl, she could snatch at a scholarship and lose herself in the marvels of city and university and a certain young man, but always, always she would yearn back.

"I cannot," Yu said. "No, I mean I will not."

Dayan stared. "What?" When the other did not respond at once, she murmured, "I've heard something about your having political difficulties, but you didn't seem to want to discuss it and I didn't want to pry. We've ample time ahead of us." Her tone sharpened. "Surely, though, you, your fame and . . . and standing—they can't deny you admission. I should think they would make you a national hero."

Yu had gathered resolution. "They would," she said starkly. "I will not . . . appear in public with them, accept their medals and praises, let them lick glory like dogs."

"This must be hard for you to talk about."

"It . . . is. I divorced my husband. You will all on the ship hear the real reason . . . eventually. I can trust you now, Hanny, if you care to listen. But first promise me to say no word to anyone until we have left. If the truth came out, they—my beloved government—would be embarrassed. They have a hostage who would suffer."

Dayan caught Yu's hand. "I swear. May God and my mother forsake me if I don't keep silence till you set me free."

She let go and sat gripping her mug tight, while Yu's words trudged. "When Xi and I came back from Sirius, we were horrified. The Space War had occurred, and in China the Protector was overthrown but the Council of Nine was worse, and— Nevertheless he took the professorship promised him at Nanjing University. I did interplanetary work, developing some of the asteroids China had annexed. We were too much apart. We planned on emigrating to Australia. But without my knowing, he became involved with the Free Sword Society. Yes, he believed democracy could be raised from the dead, in our country and around the Earth. They caught him. They told me they would pardon him if I volunteered for *Envoy* and was accepted—pardon him and let him go wherever he wished after I was gone, but I must take this on faith and the truth about the bargain must never come out. They want the credit, they want to say they sent a Chinese to meet the Yonderfolk, but they had nobody else quite suitable. I went through the pretenses and the motions. I did tell the Foundation directors I am still fond of Xi and asked them to press for his release. They promised to. I can hope it will happen, and he will guess what is behind it, but I will never know."

She fell silent, staring before her, her tears long since exhausted. Dayan shed a few, rose, leaned over, and embraced her. "Oh, my dear, my dear."

The steely calm in Yu entered her, too, and she sat back down.

"Do not pity me," Yu said. "We will experience wonders. And it does honor me far beyond my worth, that I will keep alive something of what my country and my people were."

"You . . . haven't yet told me . . . why you came here."

"I thought I would spend these weeks seeing the best things on Earth. But there is no peace for it. Everywhere the journalists, the cameras, the crowds. And always I must watch my tongue."

Dayan nodded. "You need a refuge, where you can take a meal without twenty hands sticking autograph pads under your nose and a reporter firing questions about your love life. Well, you've come to the right place."

"I do not wish to intrude," Yu said, diffident again. "A day or two, if you will be so kind—"

"Nonsense." Dayan's tone grew animated. "You'll stay with me till we go. I have tough men with firearms to keep me unmolested, and we'll share them. My family, my friends will be delighted to meet my shipsister." She rubbed her hands together. "We'll show you some fun, too. And maybe we'll learn to eat gefilte fish with chopsticks."

"You are too generous."

"Not at all. Self-interested. I told you this existence was getting dismal. You'll liven it up, in your quiet way." Dayan paused. "And—hm—I would like to slip out by myself once in a while, alone, nobody knowing. A gentleman or two, do you understand?"

"That is not for me," Yu said gravely.

"I suppose not. But I think we could work out a scheme where you cover for me. If *you* will be so generous."

For the second time, Yu smiled. "An interesting technical problem."

"Hoy, you've hardly touched your beer. Don't you like it, and too polite to speak?"

"No, no—"

"What will you have instead?" Dayan jumped up. "Don't hang back. We have a lot of living to get done in the rest of this furlough."

Mokoena's living also included gentlemen—more than one or two—and festivities that sometimes became uproarious. After she complained about pestiferous strangers, her king issued an edict, which was enforced with discouraging sternness. However, her guards were mostly a jolly lot, who contributed their share to the fun, as well as to traditional pageantry in her honor.

Yet this was, actually, a rather small part of what she engaged in. She was much with her parents and their immediate circle, calmly and piously. As time passed, she spent increasingly more of it in hospitals. The patients, the children among them above all, were heartwarmingly happy to meet and talk with a person who was going to the stars.

Isla Floreana loomed steep and dark from a brilliant heaven. Light burned on the sea. Jean Kilbirnie waded out from the beach and went under. Salt kissed her lips. The water slid around her like a caress, cool and silken. Its colors deepened from tawny green toward blue as she swam downward. The bubbles from her breathmask glinted, streamed, danced. Fish darted past. Two seals drew playfully nigh. Farther off, ghost-dim, a dolphin went by. She exulted.

Poor Tim, she thought for a second or two. It had not been easy to deny him leave to come along. She didn't want to hurt him. But he would have been sure to spoil the tricks by which she traveled about incognito. Besides, in any case, she couldn't be bothered. For the same reason, she had declined an offer of company from a quite charming young man she met. She enjoyed male society and had had a few affairs, but acknowledged cheerfully to herself that her sex drive was low. The energy radiated outward, into the world and the universe.

Last week Alaska and Mount Denali. This week the Galápagos. Next week the Andes, followed by a trek through Amazon Park— Virtuals were adequate for historical and cultural monuments. Here was the reality of living Earth, what remained of it; she had not many days left, and nobody knew what lay at the far end of her voyage or what she might find if ever she returned.

* * *

For a generation after he was gone, memory of Ruszek's passage through taverns and women lingered in the rowdier corners of cities around the globe. Several men felt the weight of his fist, and twice only his status kept him from jail; the authorities strongly suggested he go elsewhere. But when not provoked to anger he was a leviathan of openhanded, noisy good humor.

He had other interests that would have surprised his drinking companions and partners in bed, but he reckoned they could wait.

His shipmates were unwittingly indebted to him. The colorful copy he provided took some of the publicity pressure off them.

Evening light slanted long above the roofs of Cairo. The call to prayer rang from minarets that it touched with gold. Zeyd heard directly, not electronically, for he had opened the windows of his apartment now that the day's heat was waning. He prostrated himself on the carpet. Its biofabric responded with a sensuousness lost on him in this moment.

After the words had been said and the thoughts had been thought, he stayed for a while, his mind still speaking to God. He knew that was not quite orthodox, but he had been influenced by a largely European education.

Peace to the soul of Osman Tahir, greatest man of the Ahmaddiyah Movement since Abdus Salam. *He inspired me to this, for Your glory.*

Peace to you, darling Narriman, and to the children. You, God, Who see my inmost heart, You know I was not being wholly selfish when I forsook them to go to Epsilon Indi. Was I? Yes, the science lured, but it would surely benefit mankind. It did. Primitive though the life on that planet is, we learned much there, and already the physicians have use of our findings. And always, as Your prophet Ahmad taught, through the knowledge of Your works we exalt and come nearer to You.

A visiphone sang. Zeyd rose to answer. The caller, an old acquaintance, gave him specific information about arrangements to bring him discreetly to a certain establishment. A Cordon Bleu meal was in preparation—yes, vintage wines—and the entertainment afterward would be rather special.

"Indeed I will come," Zeyd said. "Many thanks." He had his ideals, but no pretensions to being a holy man.

A nearly full Moon rose over the mountains and threw a trembling glade across Lake Louise. A breeze lulled, cold and pure. Cleland wished he could linger. He had an appointment, though, and the chance might not come again. With a sigh, he made his way to the lodge.

Banners still flapped around the paved lot, but the torches and their bearers were gone. The speaker had spoken, his listeners had cheered, now the rally was over. Police were the last solid evidence of it, a squad that had not yet left, hostility and suspicion on their faces.

Cleland passed unchallenged, unrecognized, and went inside. An ascensor took him from the fake ruggedness of the lobby to the top floor. The speaker's door admitted him to the suite.

Brent got up from a table on which stood whiskey, ice, and splash. "Hi," he greeted, advancing to shake hands. "Sorry I couldn't meet with you sooner, but you saw how it was."

"Ye-es," Cleland said hesitantly. He hadn't attended. Instead he had enjoyed the beauties nearby: manicured, overused, nonetheless beauties such as he might well never see again in anything but virtuals.

"Not that it was a big deal," Brent admitted. He took the other man's elbow and urged him to a chair. "The government, you know, did everything possible to damp us down. I wish they had more reason to. How do you like your drink?"

"Mild, please. . . . Thanks."

Brent took a stiffer one and seated himself also, leaning back, legs crossed, attitude and quasi-uniform suggesting a soldier at ease after a battle. "Well," he said, "I can hope we'll grow. That our cause will, everywhere."

Because his aim was to explore this man, Cleland made bold to reply, "We'll never know, you and I, will we?"

Though Brent's voice stayed level, something kindled in it. "Maybe we will. Even after ten thousand years, what we do in this day and age may matter." He shrugged, smiled, and sipped. "At least it'll be nice having a sympathizer aboard ship."

Cleland mustered bluntness. "I—I came . . . to find out. I don't necessarily agree with you."

"Besides," Brent said shrewdly, "you hadn't anything much better to do, did you?"

Taken aback, Cleland floundered. "Uh, well—why, I could have—"

"Sure, all sorts of stuff. Most of our crew are taking advantage, I gather. But you're not the type."

"Since we—we'll be living side by side—"

Brent took him off the hook. "Okay. Why don't I give you just a few words tonight, then we'll relax? We can argue on the trip if you want."

"I—when I got in touch, I told you I was interested to hear your side of things. The news—"

"Yeh, the news," Brent scoffed. "It makes the North Star out to be a pack of ravening chauvinists who want to start a second Space War and wouldn't mind nuking targets on Earth. How many people *listen* to us?" His lip curled. "Governments find us inconvenient. We might stir up a real popular feeling. Naturally, they and their toadies make us out to be dangerous lunatics."

Cleland swallowed before he managed: "I must say, I don't think Americans should die to get General Technology's asteroids back for it."

Brent slammed a fist on the arm of his chair. "Slogans!" he exclaimed. More calmly: "Okay, the North Star has a slogan, too, but is it really unreasonable? 'Renegotiate from a position of strength.' Do we have to be forever victims? Look, the Jews decided two, three centuries ago they'd had a bellyful of that; and today, the Israeli Hegemony. Are we any different?"

"What do you mean by 'we'?" Cleland challenged.

"Ordinary folks like you and me. North Americans, Australians. I'd say Westerners, if the Europeans hadn't crawfished and the South Americans hadn't stood aside. You were born and raised hereabouts, weren't you? Well, think back. Look around. What's wrong with our people having their fair share of the Solar System? What's wrong with the whole human race, if we can get it together under the right leadership, taking its fair share of the universe?"

A vision, Cleland thought. *A certain grandeur.*

He wasn't convinced, but Brent was worth hearing, and proved surprisingly likeable.

Sundaram sat on the ground, on a bank of sacred Ganges, and gazed across the water. It rippled and sheened beneath the Moon, through the night, broad, powerful, with now and then a glimpse of darkling wings or a crocodile gliding past. One could forget that works of man controlled and purified it, and imagine it as eternal. Leaves rustled overhead, a stand of bamboo rattled ever so faintly, in a breeze warm and full of silty odors.

He was alone in this mite of a park. The multitudes who revered him and clamored for a touch of his hands gave their mahatma his solitude when he needed it, and fended outsiders off.

They might have been bewildered to know that, sitting there, he did not contemplate the Ultimate. His thoughts were of the Yonderfolk. What language was theirs? The principles of mathematics and physics hold true across the cosmos, from fiery beginning to cold extinction. Is there, then, a basic law for communication? How shall we talk with that which is utterly strange to us?

He had won his fame by proving relevant theorems. More stirred within his mind.

9.

Falling free, each second laying more than a hundred new kilometers between her and a shrunken Sol, *Envoy* was about to enter the deep.

Her crew had not been aboard during the weeks of outward acceleration. There was no need of adding that to the unforeseeable stresses ahead of them. Two high-boost spacecraft overtook while the living cargo rested dreamless under brainpulse in weight-supportive tanks. Roused at rendezvous, they said their farewells and shuttled across to the starship.

It was the last valediction. Word from Earth would have taken an hour to reach them. After all the pomp and speeches, they agreed this was a mercy. Nevertheless it was lonely watching the other craft vanish into remoteness.

Here, at their distance from the sun's mass, space had flattened enough that the quantum gate could function. As nearly as instruments could tell, they were aimed close to Zeta Centauri, a marker on their way to the goal. It set the direction in which the energy from beyond spacetime would take them: speed, a scalar, becoming velocity, a vector.

They went quickly to their individual stations, a business rehearsed so often that now it was automatic and felt not quite real. In a sense, the feeling was right. Computers, circuits, machines would do everything. Humans only commanded, and at this hour the only commander was the captain.

His voice rang over the intercom: "Stand by for shield generation"—purely ceremonial, but ceremony had grown very needful.

A whirring followed as the main fusion plant came to full power, and ebbed away in steadiness. Eyes watching electronic viewscreens saw no

change. The stars crowded brilliant against blackness, images reconstructed to hold fast though the wheel turned and turned. But gauges
registered current through great superconducting coils, and magnetohydrodynamic fields sprang into being as a shell surrounding the ship at
twenty kilometers' remove.

"All well," said the quasi-mind governing them.

"Stand by for zero-zero drive," called the master.

Muscles tightened, fists clenched, throats worked. No one feared.
Crews had traveled like this, unharmed, for generations. Though *Envoy*'s
gate was the most capacious ever built, to bring her gamma factor to an
unprecedented five thousand, robots had tested and retested it, had
even taken animals along, proving utter reliability.

However, the gate was mighty because the journey would be.

"Go," said Nansen quietly.

Aft in the inner hull, switches flipped. Most of them were not material,
but the quantum states of atoms. An eerie oneness awoke to existence.
Between the two plates appeared a naked singularity, wherein the familiar laws of physics no longer held. Through it flowed a little of that
underlying energy which the universe had not lost at the instant of its
birth.

A little—enough to multiply the mass of ship and payload five thousand times and send her hurtling forward at a minuscule percentage less
than the haste of light.

No sensation struck, except that viewscreens went chaotic, with swirls
and flashes of formless hues. The energy entered everything equally, almost instantaneously, a quantum leap.

Notwithstanding, the power plant within labored close to its limit,
while the governor of the shielding fields calculated and issued orders at
a rate possible to nothing but a quantum computer. Space is not empty.
Apart from stars and planets, it may be a hard vacuum by our standards;
but matter pervades it, dust and gas—hydrogen, some helium, traces of
higher elements—averaging about one atom per cubic centimeter in
Sol's neighborhood, and cosmic rays sleet through it well-nigh unhindered. Had the ship rammed directly into this at her speed, radiation
would soon have been eroding her; the crew would have been dead
within the first few seconds. No material defense would have availed.
Multimegawatts must go to work.

Guided and shaped by the boom forward, the fields were an envelope
of armor. Laser beams, aimed forward, ionized neutral atoms, which the
forces thereupon seized and sent as a wind that bore other stuff with it,
flung aside and aft. In effect, a giant, streamlined shape flew through the
medium, cocooning the vessel inside.

X rays did pierce it from dead ahead, made fiercer by Doppler effect,
but no more than wheel and hull could ward off. Otherwise aberration
caused them to pass through an aftward cone, attenuated both by
distance and by lengthening of their waves. Well did *Envoy* guard her

people. Yet the battle was incessant and the power requirement high. Meanwhile she must fill her capacitors with still more energy.

Thus did she run, for some two hundred astronomical units, far out into the Oort cloud of comets. Observers orbiting Sol registered the time as a bit more than an Earth day. To her and those aboard her, it was slightly under twenty seconds. And both were correct. Her relativistic time dilation was the inverse of her gamma factor, and just as real.

Then the loan fell due. The quantum field collapsed, the high-energy state ended, she moved on trajectory no faster than she had done before, about 150 kilometers per second; for her, lengths and passages of time were the same as they had been at home. Like the acceleration, the deceleration happened too swiftly and pervasively to be felt.

She must repay her loan in *full*. She had done work, moving interstellar matter aside, moving herself farther from Sol. The collapsing field would have reclaimed the deficit from her atoms, disastrously, were she not prepared. As it was, the energy in her capacitors flowed into the field and satisfied. The net expenditure had been precisely zero.

"Jump one!" cried the captain, as was traditional.

It was a gesture, not repeated. Already, in a fractional second, the gate had reopened and *Envoy* was again running on the heels of light.

The optical system soon compensated, and viewscreens once more displayed the stars. Three showed the heavens weirdly distorted by speed, for purposes of monitoring the flight. The rest took photons captured in the brief intervals between jumps and let computers generate an image shifting evenly from point to point. Thus far the scene had scarcely changed. A few light-days, a few light-years, are of little consequence in the vastness of the galaxy. But Sol dwindled fast from a small disk to the brightest of the stars, and second by second it diminished further, as if it were falling down a bottomless black well.

Nansen and Dayan stood in the command center, looking. They belonged together in this first hour, captain and physicist. Theirs were the intuitions, instincts, judgments that no artificial intelligence could ever quite supply. Did it seem best to abort the voyage, they would decide.

They found no reason to. Around them instruments gleamed and gave readings, the ship murmured impersonally, a breeze pretended to blow off a field of new-mown grass. They watched their sun waning, and silence was upon them.

Nansen broke it with a whisper. ". . . *el infinito*
Mapa de Aquél que es todas Sus estrellas."

"What?" asked Dayan, almost as softly.

"*Ay*—" He came out of his reverie and shook himself, like a swimmer climbing ashore. "Oh. A poem that crossed my mind. '*The infinite map of the One who is all His stars.*' By Borges, a twentieth-century writer."

She regarded the lean, grave face before she said, "It's lovely. I didn't know you were such a reader."

He shrugged. "There is much time to fill, crossing space."

"And it makes a person think, doesn't it?" She stared out at the cold galactic river. "How insignificant we are to everything except ourselves."

"Does that trouble you?"

"No." The red head lifted defiantly. "Ourselves are what we have to measure everything by."

"I am not so sure of that. The fact that there are countless things we will never know, and many that we could not possibly know, does not mean they do not exist—only that we cannot prove it. I am a philosophical realist."

"Oh, me too. No physicist today takes seriously any of that metaphysics that sprang up like fungus around quantum mechanics in its early stages. I meant just that we're tiny, an accident, a blip in space-time, and if and when we go extinct it won't make, we won't have made, a raindrop's worth of difference to the cosmos."

"I am not so sure of that, either."

"Well, your religion—" She broke off, half embarrassed. "I'm not observant of what's supposed to be mine."

Nansen shook his head. "If anything, what faith I have comes from this material universe. It doesn't seem reasonable to me that something so superbly organized, its law reaching down beneath the atom, out beyond the quasars, through all of time, that it would throw up something as rich as life and intelligence by chance. I think reality must be better integrated than that, and we are somehow as much a part of it and its course as the galaxies are." His smile quirked. "At least, it's a comforting thought."

"I guess I'd like to share it," Dayan said, "but where's the actual evidence? And we don't need comforting, or ought not to. Whatever we are, we can be it in style!"

He considered her. "Yes, you would feel like that."

She met the look. "You would, too, regardless," she answered.

For several pulsebeats they stood mute, unmoving.

"I should get back to my laboratory," she said quickly. "Everything seems in order here, and you remember I have some experiments going. At our gamma factor, who knows what we might detect?"

Journey commenced, the rest of the expedition had, in an unspoken mutuality, sought the common room. Together they sat watching Sol recede. In a few more hours of their time, it would no longer be the dominant star. In a day and a night of their time, thirteen and a half years would pass on Earth.

Sundaram rose from his chair. "I believe that suffices me," he said. "If you will pardon me, I shall retire."

"For a nap?" Kilbirnie asked, as lightly as she was able.

"Possibly," he replied in the same spirit. "Or possibly I can pursue an idea a trifle further." He went out.

Brent squinted after him. "Good Christ," the second engineer muttered, "is he anything but a thinking machine?"

"Much more," Zeyd told him sharply. "I have taken the trouble to become acquainted."

Brent lifted a palm. "No offense meant. If he doesn't care for women, it makes things easier for me, if he doesn't make a pass at me." He saw frowns and tightened lips. "Hey, sorry, just a joke."

Yu stood up. "I think we would be wise to inspect the recycler systems," she said.

"Why, is there anything to fear?" Zeyd wondered.

"No. I am confident they have themselves well in hand. However, the final responsibility lies with my department,"—responsibility for the nanotechnics and processings that turned waste back into fresh air, pure water, food, and the luxuries that were almost as vital. "One more go-through, now that we are under zero-zero, will secure us more firmly in our teamwork."

"Oh, all right," Brent said.

"Actually, a welcome diversion." Zeyd made a gesture at the awesomeness in the screen. As the biochemist, he was involved.

"Should I come, too?" asked Mokoena, biologist and physician.

"No need, unless you wish to," said Yu. She led Brent and Zeyd out.

Mokoena stayed. "That was neatly done," she told those who also remained. "She defused what could have become an awkward situation."

Cleland stirred, cleared his throat, and spoke tentatively. "Do you mean Al might have, ah, lost his temper? I don't think so. He's not a bad man."

"I didn't say he was," Mokoena answered.

"Besides," Ruszek put in, "I think what Wenji wants is to give her group something to do. The sooner everybody's busy, the better. Sitting and gaping at . . . this . . . is no good."

Mokoena chuckled. "As for that, we can trust our captain to have some ritual planned for our first supper."

Ruszek shrugged. "Probably. He didn't approach me about it."

Kilbirnie jumped to her feet. "Meanwhile, we do jolly well need a break," she exclaimed. "Who'd like a hard game of handball?"

Ruszek brightened. "Here's one," he said. Side by side, they left for the gymnasium.

Cleland started to follow but sank back down. "Wouldn't you care to join them?" Mokoena asked.

His glance dropped. "I'd be too slow and clumsy."

"Really? You've handled yourself well in some difficult places."

He flushed. "That was . . . competing against nature . . . not people."

"You mustn't let jealousy eat you, Tim," she said gently.

His head jerked up to stare at her. "What do you mean?"

"It sticks out of you like quills." She leaned forward and took his right hand in hers. "Remember what the captain told us on our shakedown. We cannot afford hostility or bitterness or anything that will divide us."

"I suppose we . . . should have made . . . our personal arrangements before we embarked."

"You know that wasn't practical. Especially when relationships are sure to change as we go."

"You and Lajos—"

"It is friendly between us," she said. "But it's not binding on either one." Her smile offered no more than kindliness, a kindliness without urgency or need to be anything other than itself.

10.

The town began as a district in a small city. Humans tend to cluster together, the more so when their way of life makes them ever more foreign to everybody else. As time passed, the district became a community in its own right. And it abided, while change swept to and fro around it like seas around a rock.

On this day, descending, Michael Shaughnessy saw it as roofs and sundomes nestled among trees. A powermast reared from their midst as if pointing at the clouds that drifted by, billowy white against blue. Otherwise grass rippled boundless. Sunflowers lifted huge yellow eyes out of its silvery green. A herd of neobison grazed some distance to the south, unafraid; only wild dogs and master-class men hunted them, not very much. Crows flocked about, black, noisy, and hopeful. Northward a long, high mound and a few broken walls were the last remembrances of Santa Verdad. Grass hid scattered slabs and shards, as it had hidden the remnants of earlier farmsteads. This region of central North America was now a vicarial preserve.

Shaughnessy set his rented vehicle down in a lot on the edge of settlement and got out. Air blew mild, full of odors the sun had baked from the soil. There was no guard, but neither was there any call for it. He walked on into town.

The street he took was immobile, with antique sidewalks. Its indurite was beginning to show the wear of feet and wheels through centuries. The trees that shaded it were younger, replaced as they grew old and died. Behind their susurrant leafage, homes stood in rows, each on its patch of lawn and garden. The houses were ancient, too, but not the same age. Most were half underground, topside curving in soft hues up to a dome: a style archaic enough. Some, though, harked further back, even to times when forms still more outmoded were enjoying revivals—a rambling ivy-grown bungalow or a peaked roof on two stories of brick, with windows and a chimney. Most displayed a token of the family who held it—a nameplate, a *mon*, an ancestral portrait, a line of calligraphy, a stone from a far planet—and the crests of ships on which members had served. Nevertheless, perhaps because they were all of modest size, perhaps because they were all in one way or another marked by time, they engendered no disharmony; they belonged together.

Not many people were about at midafternoon in this residential section. A few children sped past, a whirl of color, shouts, and laughter. A few adults walked or rode purring motorboards. Here among their own kind, they were generally in traditional groundside garb, which ran to flamboyancy. The headbands of men glittered, their tunics were of shimmering metalloid mesh, colorful trousers banded with gold went into soft half-boots. Women's coronets were gemmed or plumed, filmy cloaks fluttered from shoulders, lustrous biofabric shaped and reshaped itself to them as they moved. None of them knew Shaughnessy, but they greeted him with an upraised palm, a gesture he returned.

A young woman who came striding toward him stood out amidst them. She was in uniform, an opalescent sheathsuit with a comet emblem on the left breast, beret slanted across the black curls. Doubtless she was bound for a rendezvous with other officers of her ship, a business meeting or a party. Although her outfit was new to him, he realized what the ship must be.

Seeing him, she broke step. Her hand snapped to her brow, a formal salute that had not changed. He stopped and reciprocated, enjoying the sight. She was short and dark—as more and more starfarers seemed to be—and comely. He smiled. "That was kind of you, Ensign," he said.

Her eyes searched him. He stood gaunt, tall, and gray; his own uniform, which he had donned on impulse, was blue with red trim. "You are . . . a captain, aren't you?" she asked.

Her accent was not too strong for him to follow. Spacefolk's English was apparently stabilizing—especially after English ceased to be the main language spoken on this continent.

"I am that by rank, though not a shipmaster," he replied. "How did you know?" The bars on her shoulders were the same as they had been when he wore them, but his present sunburst was quite unlike the spiral nebula that identified a captain nowadays. *No doubt emblems will also eventually stabilize,* he thought.

"We learn the history in school, sir."

"You do? I am happy to hear that. We did in my youth, but a lot has happened since then." *Yet what are we without our history?*

"You must be newly back from a long voyage, sir," she said. "That would be the *Our Lady*."

"Indeed she is, home again from Aerie and Aurora."

"I'm leaving soon," she said eagerly.

"And that would be the *Estrella Linda*, for a longer circuit than ours was. May the passage be easy, the worlds welcoming, and your return gladsome."

Her eyelashes vibrated. "Thank you, sir."

She'd like to talk more, he thought, *and I would, too, but we're bound on our separate ways. Later? Yes.* "A good day and evening to you, Ensign."

Both of them proceeded.

Shaughnessy's route took him past a number of shops and service enterprises. Some were family-owned, operated by hirelings or retirees. Others belonged to outsiders: who might, though, have lived here for generations. All were antiquated. *Well, when you are gone for twenty, thirty, fifty, a hundred years, you had better have something familiar waiting for you.*

He came to a house on another street of homes. A veranda fronted its stucco walls. He had called ahead from his aircar and the occupant stood in front. "Greeting, Captain," Ramil Shauny hailed. He waved the visitor ahead, onto the porch. "Please have a seat. What may I offer you?"

Stooped and white-haired in a plain brown robe, he somehow kept the bearing of an officer. His aspect was not a shock; Michael Shaughnessy recalled the young Ramil Shauny, but you had to expect that decades would do their work, and anyhow, they had met again, not long before. What felt odd was that Ramil, a hundred and ten biological years of age and the mayor of the town, should defer to another who was just seventy. But then, Ramil was Michael's great-grandson.

They settled into formchairs, side by side. A neochimp servant—a type of creature new to Michael, and the idea a bit repugnant—took their orders for drinks. For a while they sat unspeaking in the shade and breeze, looking out at the street. One girl who walked by carried a batcat on her wrist. Michael wondered what provision she'd make for it when she grew up and shipped out. If she did, of course. Maybe she would rather forsake the kith of the starfarers. Theirs wasn't an easy life. Maybe she, being smart as kithfolk usually were, could get a well-paid position in a guild or in the vicarial bureaucracy. Or maybe she, being pretty, could become a mistress of a local magnate and ride forth in twilight to fly her batcat at homing crows. Or maybe she would choose the stars.

She passed on out of sight.

"And how did your travels around Earth go?" Ramil asked.

Michael grimaced. "Not well. I thought something of Ireland would be left. I was away less than a century."

A swing around by two suns with a planet apiece where humans can live. I should be grateful for the few such we've found. Without them, would any starships besides Envoy *be running yet? It is the colonies and their need, their need less for material goods than for human contact, novelty, more word than a laser beam can bring—and, rarely, a passenger or two—it is they and what trade they carry on among each other that keeps us going.*

Oh, yes, we make our occasional exploratory ventures, and

sometimes one of them reaps a great profit, but most do not. I think the only reason for them, or for any starfaring, is that some people still wonder about what there may be beyond their skies.

May they keep on wondering. The voyages, the discoveries, the adventures! But meanwhile, at the heart of it all, is Earth growing old?

"I have no more wish to settle there," Michael said.

"Well, it's been a hard century," Ramil conceded.

"So I gather."

The servant brought the drinks, whiskey and soda for Michael, wine of Maian skyberries for Ramil, together with kelp crackers and garlic nuggets. Ramil gazed into the air. "In many ways I envy you," he said. "I wish I could have gone back to where you've been. But Juana would never have been happy aboard a ship. And now it's too late for me."

"She was worth giving up space for, though, wasn't she?" Michael replied softly.

Ramil nodded. "Oh, yes. You remember her."

Michael did—her, and the wedding, for it chanced to be when he was last on Earth. From time to time starfarers were bound to marry outside their kith. And Ramil's earlier voyages had been rather short. He was not too alien for her.

Yes, Juana was a darling. But my Eileen—your great-grandmother, Ramil—who died in my arms while the light of Delta Pavonis streamed through the ports—I had the better luck.

"Don't mistake me," Ramil added. "I am not sorry for myself. There's still fight and fun to be had."

"Keeping our autonomy here?" Michael asked, partly for the sake of tact, partly because he didn't know. He hadn't yet caught up with events. When he left, the Greatman of Mongku had been Earth's ruler, not a figurehead for whatever cabal had most recently seized power.

"No, that isn't in any danger," Ramil said, obviously relieved to get away from matters too close to him. "Not so far. Our ships, our cargoes give us leverage. Nothing critical, you know, but the pure chemical elements, the special feedstocks, the new data—yes, above all, the new information, for science or industry or sparking fresh, saleable ideas—those pay off."

"As always." Does always mean forever?

Ramil's tone harshened. "The Vicar of Isen, though, the overlord hereabouts—he's a greedy sod. Unless we can keep playing him and his fellows off against each other, the taxes will eat us."

Michael frowned. "Why can't you be getting help, pressure on your behalf, from the Lunarites, the Martians, or the Outerfolk?"

"None of them have any strong incentive to give it. They do help indirectly, just by being. I've lately been hinting that if we're pushed too hard and drained too dry, we can take our business elsewhere in the Solar System."

"Why not? From what I've heard about the current situation, mightn't we be more comfortable?"

"It would not be Earth," Ramil said.

No, Michael thought, *Luna, the asteroids, the moons of the giant planets, even Mars can never be, no matter what humans have done for them. Earth is our mother, no matter what humans do to her. . . . Oh, the colony worlds at other suns may beckon, but they're changing their people still more than happens here. We starfarers—our starfaring keeps us changeless.*

"I understand," he said low. "Without this much of a tie between us, a home port, we'd drift away from what we are. Earth is where we meet."

And marry. Those who love space will marry into us, those who can't stand the hardships will leave us, and so as genetics and usage work onward, we evolve from a handful of crews to a people, a kith.

Ramil smiled wistfully. "Besides," he said, "they'd be sad aboard *Envoy* if they came back and found nobody like ourselves to greet them."

Michael sighed. "I am not sure they will, whatever we do. Ten thousand years is an unholy stretch of time." *And they are only—what?—750 years into their journey. To them, less than two months, hasn't it been? . . . Nonsense, sheer malarky. Under these conditions, "simultaneity" is an empty noise.*

Ramil glanced at him. "You knew Ricardo Nansen, didn't you?"

Michael nodded. "I did. We were on the first Epsilon Eridani expedition. He saved my life on that grim world."

Ramil took a goodly swallow from his tumbler. "Well," he said, "this has wandered from the subject."

Michael chuckled. "Do you mean we had one?"

"I'm sorry your visit has disappointed you."

Michael's humor faded. "You did not tell me the Ireland I knew is gone."

"But it isn't," Ramil protested. "They've kept part of it, at least, green and beautiful."

"For the pleasure of its vicar," Michael spat. "Oh, common folk may nest in their villages if they choose, like us given leave to stay in this burg of ours, but they are not my folk anymore."

"I'm sorry. I would have told you, if I'd understood what you had in mind." Their histories had flowed too far apart. "Well, if not there, why not here? We would be honored to have you in Kith Town, and a man like you would never lack for work. In fact, brokerage—"

Michael shook his head. "I thank you," he interrupted, "but for now I have given up the idea of settling on Earth."

Ramil gave him a startled look. "What? But—"

"I've queried. *Estrella Linda* could use another experienced officer."

"But . . . but she's leaving soon and—you've only been here a few weeks. Surely, if you must go, you can take your ease for a year or two first, till *Our Lady* heads out again."

"Ordinarily I would," Michael said. "But *Estrella Linda* is off on a wide sweep. As far as I can find out, nothing else like that is planned for the next several decades, just twenty- or thirty-year shuttlings. I'll snatch the chance and—" His gray head lifted. He laughed. "Greatmen, vicars, I'll outlive the bastards."

As the days aboard *Envoy* mounted to weeks, her crew settled into their various ways of filling their abundant free time. You could share sports, games, recorded shows of every kind; you could pursue hobbies, studies, even research; you could teach two or three interested shipmates something you were knowledgeable about, such as a skill or a language; you could help arrange live entertainment, a play or a concert or whatever; you could think about questions that were not trivial but for which there had always somehow been too many distractions; you could simply talk with someone, long conversations, perhaps over a drink or two, and get to know that person better.

It did not work perfectly for anyone, and did not work as well as it should for certain ones. Then the temptation was to seek the pseudolife of an interactive virtual-reality program. Every cabin was equipped. But you rationed yourself pretty strictly; prudence and unspoken social pressure remained powerful.

A popular, productive activity was the improvement and decoration of the interior. Individuals or teams contributed according to talent and inclination, after general agreement had been reached on what to do in a given area. One daywatch about three ship months after departure, Mokoena and Brent met in the common room for this purpose.

With the two of them alone there, it felt cavernous. Kilbirnie, Dayan, and Zeyd had painted the bulkheads and overhead in cheerful colors, with flourishes. A wall screen showed a mural composed by Yu: black-and-white scene of mountains and river, house and bamboo grove, a poem of Li Bo inscribed in the upper right. She was programming a second picture. Mokoena thought the place also needed something dynamic, but something that was solid, touchable, not an engineered mirage. Nobody objected.

Brent hunkered at the base of an aluminum framework. It suggested a miniature fir tree stripped bare, with intricately curved boughs and subbranchings. Motor-driven, they could undulate, twirl, and interweave, swiftly, randomly. He had built it in the machine shop according to her design and today, with strength and skill she lacked, secured it to the deck and made sure it operated properly. As it whirled back to quietude, he rose. "There," he said. "Seems okay. Will it do?"

She beamed, a flash of whiteness in the dark face. "Splendid. I can't wait to put on the ornaments." Mirrors, jewels, shining fractals—her creations; they should move and gleam and glitter endlessly variable, almost alive. "Would you like to help with that, too?"

"No, I'm not the artistic type."

"Well, then, thank you twice as much."

"No trouble. I had nothing else to do. With my hands, anyway."

Mokoena's smile dissolved. "Yes, I have thought that must be difficult for you, Al."

Resentment broke abruptly loose. "Yu Wenji's just-in-case backup."

"Why, you stand your watches, you have your jobs—"

"Busywork. Nothing a robot couldn't do as well or better. Keep the clod occupied, because if you don't he might stir up trouble for lack of any other interests."

She frowned, straight into his eyes. "Now, that's nonsense. In the first place, you knew full well what the situation would be en route—"

"Oh, yes. In theory. Practice turns out to be harder. Don't worry, I'll last out the monotony, hoping we'll find what'll make it worth going through."

"In the second place, Al, we all know you are not an oaf or a monomaniac, and you know we know it. We've heard you mention pieces of history we never learned, and snatches of the music you play for yourself, and on Christmas Eve," celebrating a date that existed only in the ship's calendar, "over the cognac, when you fell to talking about—" She stopped. Abashed, she had to ask: "What was his name? The composer."

"Beethoven."

"Yes. I'd like to know more about him and his music."

His countenance brightened, his voice lightened. "You would?" Bitterness returned. "You'd be damn near unique. How many give a politician's promise any longer about the heritage?" The last word he used quite without self-consciousness.

"Times change," she answered. "Ideas, tastes, ways of doing and saying things, even thinking and feeling."

"Not necessarily for the better." He grew earnest. "That's one reason I came along. So that somebody would remember what Western civilization was, and bring it back again to Earth."

Surprised, she said, "You never made that clear to us, Al."

"I didn't expect anybody would understand. Well, Tim Cleland, a little. And Nansen, maybe, except he's given up on it. He hugs his traditions to himself and just tries to be the perfect captain, the perfect robot."

"You're being unfair. Speaking for myself, I admit I don't know much about this. We had other things to think about in Africa, including our own traditions. But I'd be happy to learn."

"Really?" Brent stood motionless. When he spoke again, it was warmly. "Why, that's wonderful, Mam."

"I'm not sure how—"

"We'll find our way forward. Look, let me put these tools away and then we'll go off by ourselves and begin."

He edged closer. She retreated a step. "That may not be wise, Al."

He halted. "Huh? You—"

"I think I see what you have in mind. No, I'm not angry. It's very natural." She trilled a laugh. "A compliment, actually. Thank you."

He stiffened anew. "But you won't."

"Not so suddenly."

"You and Lajos Ruszek are open enough about what's between you."

"Our business."

"And Tim, lately—"

"Hold on!" she snapped. "For your information—" She paused. "Do you mean you didn't know? I thought, as often as you two have been talking— Well, he is a private person. He's having a thorny time. I'm trying to help him through it. I do not want to make matters worse."

He reddened. "Instead, you're serious about that Ruszek hooligan? Because if you're just screwing for fun—"

"I told you, mind your own business!" she shouted. "And keep a civil tongue in your head, fellow."

He gulped and glowered.

She relaxed, bit by bit. "Oh, I understand," she said after a while. "You're overstressed." *Less stable than we believed,* she did not add. "Please come see me at my medical office. There are plenty of helpful pharmaceuticals. And I don't gossip about my patients, Al."

"I don't need that kind of help."

"Well, I can't compel you," she sighed. "Only remember, do, it's always available and you're always welcome. Meanwhile, shall we forget this incident?"

"All right." He sounded half strangled. Collecting the tools, he stalked off.

In his cabin he selected a program, made the bioelectronic connections, lay back, and went questing through the wilderness with Daniel Boone. The native women were very hospitable.

12.

On a hilltop above the valley of the Kshatriya, old Michael Shaughnessy sat alone. Delta Pavonis warmed him, akin to the sun of his childhood, but two daylight moons hung wan among clouds whose whiteness was streaked orange and amber by tiny life. The air he breathed blew pure and sweet, but through its odors of grass and wild thyme drifted a sulfury hint of surviving firebrush. The land swept down to the shining river and rolled back upward on the farther side in familiar curves sculptured by wind and rain, but from one slope jutted a many-towered bulk of clay and small stones that had been the nest of animals now extinct. Beside the river stood a town, but its rounded pyramids and spiraling spires were like nothing he had ever beheld elsewhere. The people who dwelt there were peaceful and kindly, but time and their world had made them altogether foreign to him.

The old man sat on a log and plucked a harp. He had fashioned it himself, and he half spoke, half sang to its notes, in a tradition that died before he was born and would die anew, forever, when he who had resurrected it was gone.

"I have come to you, Feng Huang, who have never been another Earth and never can be nor should, I have come to lay my bones in your soil. First, however, I will tell you of Earth, I will say to your winds what Earth was when last I walked upon her.

"She lay bleeding, Feng Huang, and the shadow of many deaths over her, and the fear of many more to come. New dreams were astir, as ruthless as the new ever are, and the ancient overlords with their ancient ways stood against it, hoping to kill the newborn dreams and those who bore them. A mighty war was in the making, and none could foresee what ruin it would wreak or what the whims of chance might spare.

"I, who neared the end of my days, wept for the young. I, who was about to depart, went about bidding good-bye to those things that remained on Earth, wonderful, beautiful, and defenseless, from all the ages she had known. I would not be content with images and illusions; I wanted memories of having myself met what had been shaped by hands, seen by eyes, trodden by feet, kissed by lips long down in dust.

"In a green country wet with springtime I found the great stones of Newgrange, where a folk forgotten once buried their kings; and along its western cliffs, where the sea roared gray, I went into a little parish church from when the people found their hope in Christ, and I knelt before his altar.

"Light streamed on me in many colors through the windows of faerie York Minster and soaring Chartres Cathedral. At the University of Salamanca, which remembers the wise Moors, I lost myself in books.

"I looked into the big eyes of the Empress Theodora at Ravenna and knew why men had loved her. I saw Michelangelo's Judgment Day in Rome and wished that the doom in our cosmology had such a meaning.

"The columns of the Parthenon rose before me, broken, eroded, but softly golden from centuries of weather, and they made my spirit stand as true as they.

"In the tombs of Egypt, where the paintings still cried forth love of life, I wondered at the steadfastness that hewed them from the rock beneath that furnace sky.

"Shwe Dagon recalled another faith, which yearned beyond life for oneness but which wrought splendor.

"I stood on the Great Wall, where brave men had kept watch against the barbarians, and I searched through the Forbidden City for the loveliness that dynasty after dynasty had gathered together.

"Under blossoming cherry trees in a Kyoto twilight, it was as if I heard temple bells ringing again.

"The halls where Washington and Jefferson spoke of freedom are no more; but I have walked over the Virginia hills that they knew.

"On an Andean mountain I did homage to the stones of Machu Picchu, whose builders followed dreams of their own.

"I tell this to your winds, Feng Huang, that they may strew it wherever they will. There is no other remembrance known to me.

"Now soon I shall lay my bones in your soil, where my Eileen laid hers these many centuries ago."

13.

Sixteen hundred light-years from home, her clocks reading four months into the journey, *Envoy* paused. Shielding force fields down, she moved on intrinsic momentum, at mere tens of kilometers per second, through space that was not shrunken and time that went not as in Elf Hill, among stars that the eye saw in their own colors and at their own stations around the heavens. Need was to take fresh, more accurate navigational sightings and realign the velocity vector accordingly. Here was an ideal place for that, where those aboard who were able to could meanwhile do science.

Spacesuited, Dayan worked outside. Induction boots held her fast to the outer hull; similar footings secured her instruments. Cleland stood by, her assistant.

The great cylinder reached fifty meters right and left. At either end spun the wheels, cliff-sheer, but stars agleam beyond them and aflicker when spokes hurried across. Metal glimmered in the light of star throngs, icily tumbling Milky Way, querning nebulae, galaxies dimmed only by distance. But instruments and minds were aimed straight outward. It had been planned that *Envoy* would pass within a few light-years of the open cluster NGC 5460.

Some forty suns were gathered close together, a fire-swarm of ruby, gold, and diamond. The brightest burned with the radiancy of more than a hundred Sols. Like Venus at its most brilliant in the sky of Earth, they cast shadows, but they did not glow, they were frozen flame.

Dayan adjusted a spectrometer, switched off the control panel illumination, and waited in weightlessness for night vision to return to her. The noises of her body were the barest flutter beneath silence. When she again saw fully, she breathed, like a prayer, "*Yafeh*— The glory of it."

"And—and the questions," Cleland stammered louder.

"Yes. I'll be analyzing these data for I don't know how long. I think we'll discover things they never could, peering from the Solar System."

"There may well be some remarkable planets. Formed under those conditions," in the roiling gravitational fields of huge masses swinging near each other. "And life?"

"I doubt we'll find signs of that," in the spectra of planetary atmospheres. "Supernovae going off at such quarters, within ten parsecs or thereabouts, wouldn't they kill it off?"

"Be that as it may, what could exist— Do we *have* to go on right away?"

Dayan's rapture yielded to sympathy. "We're committed, Tim." Her gloved hand patted his. "Don't worry. You'll find plenty of interesting stuff where we're bound, I'm sure."

His mood plunged. "No doubt. I can keep busy."

Dayan looked at him. His face in the helmet was a chiaroscuro of darkness and faint highlights. "You miss Earth badly, don't you?" she asked.

"No point in that, is there? The Earth we knew is—is in its grave, with . . . all we cared about . . . forgotten."

"And you are maybe feeling you have given it up for nothing?"

He had avoided mention of the situation between him and Kilbirnie, obvious though it was to everyone. He straightened so fast that the motion was plain in his spacesuit. "No, of course not. I said I'll have my work. Everybody will. Work like, uh, like no work ever done before."

Again Dayan's hand sought his, and now squeezed. "That's the spirit, Tim. Don't give up personal hope, either."

He stared through the enormous night. "What? Do you really think—" Dayan and Kilbirnie were friends, often talking privately.

"We'll have to see," the physicist replied. He could not tell whether she was unwilling to disclose confidences, or had none to share, or had been too sharply reminded of her own losses. She turned back to the instruments. "Let's get on with our observations."

Like the voice of a providence, Nansen's sounded in their helmet receivers. "*Hola*, out there. I think you two should suspend your project and come inboard as soon as possible."

The physicist tautened. Unknownness reached everywhere around. And lately the captain and chief engineer had seemed troubled about something they did not speak of. "What's the matter?"

"Nothing wrong." Nansen's tone had regained a lilt. "But Yu has tuned the neutrino detectors as you requested. They seem to be registering a nonstellar source—from the cluster."

Dayan and Cleland poised rigid. The blood thundered in their ears.

"My God," the planetologist said, "that could mean nuclear power plants. A high-tech civilization."

"Life after all," Dayan whispered. "In spite of everything."

"Now we do have to go see!"

"First we learn whether this is real. Come on, let's bundle up our gear and get inside. We have more urgent business!"

In a dozen zero-zero jumps, the ship took as many vantage points and harvested data for the computers to interpret: interferometry, spectroscopy, analysis, done on every aspect of matter and energy available to her. Among those crew members not engaged, talk rattled and swirled, except for those who drew back from the excitement to think.

They all met in the common room, as they did whenever Nansen called a session. He stood before his crew, who had taken chairs in a semicircle. For a short while, nobody spoke. Ventilation rustled, stronger and cooler than usual. Views of space filled two large screens, the cluster splendid in one of them, the Milky Way chill in the other.

His glance went over the gathering from left to right. Sundaram sat calm, a trace of a smile on the full lips. Cleland's gaze kept wandering to Kilbirnie, then springing back to the captain. Now and then Yu shivered just a bit. Brent held himself upright, hands flat on thighs. Ruszek had folded powerful arms across broad chest. Mokoena's eyes glistened— tears catching the light? Kilbirnie well-nigh crouched. Zeyd looked deceptively at ease. Dayan's fists lay clenched on her lap.

Our good biochemist seldom fails to position himself with a woman on either side, Nansen thought. The amusement flickered out. "Order, please," he said without preliminary. The dryness was a mask for the turmoil within him, where a fledgling eagerness danced above the concern that had more and more gnawed. "We know why we're here. May we first have a report from Dr. Dayan?" He believed formality as well as reserve was necessary when he presided over a gathering.

She cast a look across the group but addressed herself to him, though he was aware of what she would say. "It's definite. Unless nature is playing some trick we never suspected she could, we've found a source of neutrinos near the heart of the cluster. It appears to be at a star, but is not a star itself. The distributions of energy and type don't fit. However, they do fit a thermonuclear reactor more or less like ours."

A sigh and a stirring went among them. Rumor and conjecture had become fact.

Sundaram raised his hand. "Excuse me," he said, "I am no physical scientist, but how can anything artificial be strong enough to detect at this distance, especially above the background emission of that many crowded suns?"

"Our equipment has the sensitivity, given sufficient data, bearing in mind that the emission *is* different from any that a star would give off," Dayan explained. "Actually, we haven't identified a point source. It may be a number of reactors within a limited region. I expect it is."

"If beings there have such power plants," Kilbirnie wondered, "why haven't they spread through space?"

"No zero-zero drive, apparently," Dayan said.

"But yon stars are clustered! They could reach others using plasma jets, or could at least send robots to explore, and you could detect the ships boosting, could ye no?"

"We can't project our psychology on them," Mokoena said. "They may be nothing like us."

"We'll go find out," Ruszek boomed.

Mokoena winced. Nansen had overheard part of an exchange between them. The mate had not taken well her reluctance to approach the suns. He hungered for a break in a sameness that seemed to wear on him more heavily than he had awaited.

Kilbirnie waved clasped hands above her head. "Whoops, aye, and hear, hear!" she cried.

"Wait a minute—" Brent began.

"Is it wise?" Yu asked simultaneously.

"Would you really pass by a chance like this?" Zeyd demanded of them both.

"Unique," Cleland put in.

Yu lifted her hand. They listened. "I thought likewise at first," she said. "But then I thought further. We have not reached our goal. Here is no starfaring." She cast a glance at Nansen. He stayed impassive. "The environment is unlike anything of which humans have had experience."

Mokoena's face showed complete agreement.

Kilbirnie could not refrain from interrupting. "At the time we left Sol, anyhow. The more reason for us to discover what we can."

"We don't know what the hazards are," Yu continued. "Or the gains, compared to"—her words stumbled—"to what we hope for from the Yonderfolk."

"And the time we'd spend," Brent said.

Zeyd shrugged. "A few extra cosmic years. For us, perhaps a few months."

"How could we learn anything worth knowing about utterly strange planets, whole worlds, in a few months?" Mokoena retorted.

"People worked hard and made sacrifices to send us on our mission," Yu finished. "We should keep faith."

Even if the mission turns out to be empty, Nansen thought. The same foreboding must be in her. *Maybe especially if it does.*

But here we have a fresh prize close by. It may even somehow bear on the mystery of the Yonderfolk, which is beginning to seem darker than we knew.

Yu's reminder had given Zeyd pause. He stared into the air. "True," he mumbled. "Osman Tahir."

"Damn it to hell, this is a scientific expedition!" Cleland exclaimed. They had not seen him so vehement before. "We've come on a scientific treasure hoard. I say our duty is to at least go take a *look*."

"Hurrah for you, Tim!" Kilbirnie cheered. "I second that."

"We'd proceed with due caution, of course," Dayan said.

"What do you think, Captain?" Ruszek called. "You've been as silent as an unpaid spy, these past days."

Yu Wenji knows why.

Nansen had chosen his words beforehand: "I personally favor a reconnaissance, taking no avoidable risks. If we make it, we should make it now. Who knows what will have changed in several thousand years? Besides, on our way back we will likely be tired, we will certainly be older, our ship or equipment may have suffered damage, and in general, the venture will be more dangerous. Here we may possibly learn something that will help us later, in our primary mission."

Kilbirnie bounced on her chair. Ruszek's mustache jutted upward from his grin. Dayan smiled. Cleland nodded jerkily. Zeyd retreated into thoughtfulness. Mokoena appeared to resign herself and then start lightening up; if all she got here was a tantalizing glimpse of some biology, it might still give a new insight. Sundaram sat quiet, with his customary expression of mild friendliness. Yu could not entirely conceal her distress.

Brent stirred. "One thing," he barked. "One thing. If we go on into the cluster and spend time, how does that time count?"

Nansen raised his brows. "What do you mean, please?"

"The contract. The articles we signed. Five Earth years max, after we get where we're going, before we start home. Will a side trip count toward that? I say it should."

"Pardon me," Sundaram said, "but may I ask what difference this makes across ten thousand years?"

"A difference to us. Our lives."

"The question is ridiculous," Dayan snapped. "The articles also provided we can vote to stay longer than five years."

"Yeah, if seven out of ten want to."

"Don't you want to come home with the knowledge that's our whole purpose?"

"Sure, sure. I'm not saying I wouldn't vote to stay, even, if we need to. I just want this point clarified."

"It's valid," Nansen ruled, "but not relevant yet. We'll take it up if we find we should remain in the cluster any substantial length of time. That is if we do choose to investigate here. At present, don't waste thought or energy on incidentals."

Brent glared, swallowed, but kept his mouth shut.

"Captain," Yu said, "we really ought to continue as we were. The traces—"

Nansen's chopping gesture cut her off. "Please, Engineer Yu, we agreed to keep that matter aside till we have better information." She sank back.

"What the devil is this?" Ruszek rasped.

"You will hear in due course," Nansen assured him. "Now I'll only say it would be a distraction, when we need our heads clear." To them all: "I shall not dictate the decision. If there are no further questions or comments, we will adjourn for twenty-four hours. Think, inquire, discuss it among yourselves, and tomorrow we will vote."

It wouldn't be that simple, he knew. For instance, most of them would be calling up everything about open clusters that was in the database and doing their best to understand and evaluate it. He had done so himself.

Nevertheless, he knew what the decision would be.

14.

In carefully planned leaps, *Envoy* neared and entered the cluster.

Within, she all but lost the galaxy. Nebulosity lingered here, dust and gas, still a hard vacuum but enough to dim most of the distant stars out of naked-eye vision. The members of the group shone practically unhindered, to overwhelm the rest; you could see those faint glimmers, but you gave them no heed. Almost half a hundred radiances gemmed the sphere of heaven. Even dwarfs shone as bright as Rigel or Aldebaran above Earth; giants blazed, the red of fire or the blue of steel, like scores of Siriuses come together, and when you turned your gaze aside an afterimage burned in it for a while. The crew fared onward in awe.

Yet the everyday needs of life stayed with them. To these were added the needs of science, which might prove necessary to survival.

"I definitely know the sun we want," Dayan told Nansen at their third stop for observations. The computers had integrated the new data with previous findings and she had read the meaning in the numbers and graphics. "It's a late G type, about four-fifths Solar mass, and, yes, it has planets. The second one shows oxygen absorption lines in its spectrum.

"It is not the source of the neutrinos," Yu added. "Their generators move about through interplanetary space, favoring what's probably an asteroid belt, although we can't pick out something so small at this distance. They are intermittent. It suggests engines, powerful engines, boosting spacecraft to hyperbolic velocities and decelerating again."

"How many?" Nansen asked. The question sent an electric thrill along his spine and through his skin.

"Impossible to say. I have found ninety-five so far, but can't tell which are from the same ship, especially when we jump about across light-years and confuse the proper dates of events. And no doubt most of the time they are all on trajectory, with their reactors running at too low a level for us to detect before we get much closer."

"A big fleet, *de calquier modo*. Has all the industry of those beings moved into space?"

"That doesn't quite make sense to me." Dayan clicked her tongue. "One more anomaly to put on the list."

Nansen seldom barked a question. Now he did. "What else?"

"Well, the sun is hotter than would be standard for its mass. That indicates it's old, still on the main sequence but well on the way to moving off. The metallicity of others in the cluster support that. So does the frequency of white dwarfs. In fact, there's a recurrent nova just a few light-years from the star we're interested in."

"Won't it have harmed life on its planets?"

"I said 'nova,' not 'supernova.' "

Nansen nodded. "I heard that, also that you said 'recurrent.' The outbursts aren't violent enough, then, across such a gap, to raise the background count very much?"

"Right, to judge by what I've observed. The companion is only middle type M. The spectral data show there was a recent eruption, several thousand years ago—I can work out exactly when, if you like—so it'll be quiet for a goodly while to come. But it must have been a spectacular sight in the skies that we are bound for."

Nansen stared into the viewscreen. He didn't know where to find that faded resplendency. Imagination evoked it: two stars whirling close about each other, one a dim and long-lived red dwarf, one a spendthrift giant that had flared up before collapsing into the tiny, superdense, incandescent globe of a neutron star. It kept most of its great mass and gravity. Thus it stole material from its companion. A fiery bridge of gas joined them—no, a river, a cataract, tumbling from the red to the white— hydrogen piling up on the neutron surface, jammed together by weight, heated by the energy of its Lucifer-like fall, until it reached the thermonuclear flash point and exploded, a cosmic bomb, briefly outshining fifty or a hundred Sols. . . . The cycle went on and on, through millions of years, but slowly the one sun would dwindle to a fragment while the other would grow and grow. . . . Finally, perhaps, in a remote future, the last catastrophe, a supernova of Type I, and afterward the mystery that humans called a black hole. . . .

"Of course, the radiation in its vicinity is fierce," Dayan was saying.

Some places in the universe we will never visit ourselves. Only our machines, our robots, dare go, and even they may find they are in danger.

"But I suppose it's irrelevant to us, except as an extra indication that things hereabouts are old," Dayan continued. "We may be bound toward a civilization that was ancient when the dinosaurs ruled Earth."

"Why are they not starfaring, too?" Nansen wondered, half under his breath. "Why have they never come to us?"

"That's what we want to learn, isn't it?" Dayan answered.

Learn. Yes! Nansen straightened where he stood.

The quantum gate could function as near to a sun like this as seven astronomical units. By adroit zero-zero maneuvers, *Envoy* arrived in the ecliptic plane at approximately that distance, with less than it between her and the living planet. However, her relative velocity was of little help. She must go the rest of the way by means of her reaction drive. Nansen chose a continuous half-*g* with turnover at midpoint. That would take about ten days. A higher acceleration was possible but would have squandered more delta *v* than the time it saved was worth, while building up a velocity not easily changed. As it was, she would reach speeds at which she was less nimble than he preferred.

Under such thrust, when linear and angular vectors combined to skew the direction of "down," people must move from their private cabins, from all their comfortable and convenient facilities, to cramped quarters on the gimballed decks, which swung to give horizontality underfoot. The crowding couldn't be avoided. The flexibly coupled sections of deck must be short, to fit in the curvature of the wheel; also, they must not interfere with whatever else was around them, everything from laboratories to the park. There and on the upper level, objects that were not permanently fastened in place had been well secured.

Between the gimbals, the captain occupied his own cubicle, but, crammed with instruments and controls, it doubled as the temporary command center. Two dormitory rooms, for men and for women, shared a bath. Small wonder that the crew spent most of their waking hours in the saloon-galley, where they found screens, games, and a limited selection of hobby materials. An exercise chamber adjoined, where couples or trios could take turns doing workouts that didn't require much space.

On the whole, they took it well. They had rehearsed it in the past; it would not go on too long; and at the end they would find surprises, revelations, adventures. Even those who had spoken against the diversion were, mostly, excited.

Besides, they could leave the area for limited times, if they were careful. Some had to, in the course of their duties. Others chose to.

Hilbirnie skipped along a corridor, leaning over, flexing to and fro with every leap, as if it were a steep hillside. The biomat gave some grip to her shoe soles, but it was slight and she risked taking a tumble. Around the curve into sight came Nansen, bound the opposite way. Though he moved agilely, too, it was not so fast and his left foot used the bulkhead that angled from the deck. They saw one another, paused for a startled instant, and continued more slowly. When they met, they stopped.

Zeyd had decorated this stretch in Pharaonic style—the overhead royal blue studded with stylized golden stars, sides with a marshscape of papyrus, lotus, and wildlife, transcribed from the database. The air happened to be right for it at this hour, warm and moist, simulating a scent of growth. Kilbirnie and Nansen were a little sweaty; flesh odors mingled. They both wore skinsuits, bringing forth his wide shoulders and narrow hips, her spare curves and small, firm bosom.

"Hola," he greeted. "What are you doing here?"

She grinned. "I might ask you the same."

"I've been on inspection rounds. What else?"

Kilbirnie shook her head. The light brown locks stirred across her brow and beside her cheekbones. "I have my doubts," she said merrily. "For what, then, are you doing here?" The burr thickened in her voice. " 'Tis no on any direct route frae bridge or transfer bay or where'er, nor e'en your ain cabin."

"Bien—" He cleared his throat. "Well—"

She laughed and lifted a hand. "At ease, skipper! You have my leave to be honest."

He stared, got back his composure, and said, "I beg your pardon?"

"I'll believe you were making your rounds, dutiful as always. But on the way back, you couldn't resist taking a while to scramble about on these crazily slanted decks, could you? Like me. Except I need no excuse."

Nansen smiled. "Well, yes. We do come to feel rather hemmed in, don't we?"

"Now, I was making for the gym, the real gym, to swing on its rings and wrestle with its machines at twenty-six and a half degrees from the vertical. Do you care to join me?"

He frowned. "That would be hazardous."

"Not really. I know we can't well afford broken bones, but we're in good condition and space-trained. Why don't you join me?"

He stood silent, between an ibis and a crocodile.

She touched his arm. "Oh, skipper, I know you think you must always be reserved and correct and impartial and everything else that goes with a proper aristocrat." Again she went Scots. "But dinna be pompous."

"I did not think I was," he replied stiffly.

She stepped back, stricken. "I—I'm sorry. I didna mean— No, it was, was altogether the wrong word. I *am* sorry."

His pique had dissolved. He smiled more warmly than was his habit. "That's all right. If we couldn't let out a frank word now and then, we would soon have real trouble."

Through the skinsuit, he could see how she tensed herself. "But you won't let yourself speak free."

He could only reply, "How do you know I have anything I need to speak?"

"You're human, aren't you? Maybe you try not to be, but—" She veered off to a kindred matter that had been on her mind. "You and Wenji are certainly keeping a secret."

His face turned expressionless. "No," he said. "It is a matter that we are not yet sure of. Temporary administrative confidentiality—"

She regarded him. He sensed the wicked flicker behind her eyes, threw up his hands, and laughed. "Ha! You're right, Pilot Kilbirnie. I do get pompous."

Gladness flooded. "That's better." Softly, half reaching toward him: "Dinna fash yersel' aboot whate'er 'tis, not till the bogle comes at ye for sairtain. Belike he ne'er will."

He let out a breath. "I dare hope so."

"And meanwhile, here's this grand discovering ahead of us."

"Yes."

His brightening waned. He stood pensive, a crease between his brows. She had recalled to him the unforeseeables and the decisions he must make, which could prove lethally mistaken.

She took his arm. "And meanwhile," she said, "we have our canted gym. What say you to a bout of handball? It ought to be wild."

He hung back. "Well, really—"

"Come along, now." She tugged. He stood for a second more, then yielded.

That was two days before the onslaught.

15.

The sun cast bleak light and knife-edged shadows across *Envoy*. Brightness reduced in a viewscreen, the disk showed tiny; but it was no longer another star. The ship had passed turnover and was decelerating, backing down toward her goal.

Nansen retrieved an image and frowned at it. The optical system had obtained it an hour ago, across a distance of some two million kilometers. A large asteroid lay athwart the sky, slowly rotating. The shape was too perfect a sphere to be natural, and just half a dozen small meteor craters pocked the gray surface. Therefore they must be recent, probably under one hundred thousand years old. It was other gouges and pits that disfigured the surface, black in their depths, jumbled with debris around outlines that were not round but angular. A squared-off bluff came over the horizon as the body turned. Its top was flat, except where holes showed that something had been dug out and taken away.

"A foundation," he muttered. "This was some kind of space center. A port, I would guess, perhaps supporting communication relay towers as well, and who knows what else?"

"And everything was demolished and abandoned," said Yu as low at his side. "Why? Did it become obsolete? A technology capable of building it would scarcely have needed to salvage parts. And why do we find no signs of what replaced it?"

"Spacecraft moving about— Something seems to be going on at a few sites—" other asteroids, two moons of giant planets, but they were off *Envoy*'s path. Nansen glanced at a viewscreen. The living world stood as a blue spark near the sun. "Well, we are on our way to inquire."

A voice broke in, melodious, calm, sexless, the central computer speaking. "Attention. Attention. The detector program reports a thermonuclear power plant brought to full output, driving a plasma jet. It may be a spacecraft moving to intercept."

Yu caught her breath. Shouts, whistles, and a Magyar oath flew over the intercom. Nansen sprang from his seat. "Quiet!" he ordered. "Stand by, ready for action. We need more information."

Kilbirnie could not resist calling back, "You might show a bit of enthusiasm, skipper."

Nansen's grin was brief and tight. "I'm rather busy. We'll have time to cheer later."

Tears shone in Yu's eyes. "Oh, wonderful, wonderful," she whispered.

"No surprise," Nansen said needlessly. "They were bound to notice us." After a moment: "What is surprising is— No, first I have to study the parameters. Engineer Yu, please take your emergency station."

"Not an emergency, Captain. Surely we have nothing to fear. But, yes, we should be alert . . . for surprises." She left the cabin. Nansen sat back down and threw questions at the computer.

Presently he reported to the crew: "Yes, it is an interception boost. She's going at nearly eleven gravities. We just picked up another acceleration farther off, which will bring a meeting, too. The first will be in about three hours.

"That's if we continue decelerating as we are. Instead, we will shut down. We'd want to anyway when we come together, and this will give us time to settle in. It won't affect the rendezvous time much, if those ships change vectors when they see what we have done, which they doubtless will."

"Eleven gravities?" Zeyd cried. "But that planet has only—what?— seven percent more than Earth's on the surface."

"Drugs or fluid immersion for the crews," suggested Mokoena.

"Or they are machines, or God knows what," Nansen answered. "You may all take one hour after shutdown for personal preparations, food, drink, change of clothes, whatever you need." His tone gentled. "A prayer, perhaps. Then go to your stations and make ready for duty."

He entered a command. The drive cut off. Still facing rearward, *Envoy* flew on at high speed, almost in a straight line. Weight inside returned to normal, decks level, bulkheads upright, walking easy.

Time sped, time crept. The crew waited at their posts—Yu and Brent in central engine control, Dayan in the nerve center of instruments, Ruszek and Kilbirnie at their boats, Mokoena in the sick bay–surgery, Zeyd and Cleland at opposite ends of a wheel diameter, poised to go wherever summoned. Sundaram had joined Nansen in the main command center. There might be a sudden need for one who could guess what was meant in an alien language, and immediate physical presence was somehow better than intercom. Words did pass through now and then, fugitive speculations, small talk, attempts at humor. They died away after a spell, and silence brimmed the ship.

She signaled on every available band, and silence replied.

"It is not to be expected that their equipment will be compatible with ours, is it?" Sundaram wondered at last.

Dayan's voice: "They jolly well know the electromagnetic spectrum. If they can't pick up any of our transmissions, and can't at least send a burst of the same kind, they're more stupid than I think is possible."

Cleland: "Maybe they're, uh, sizing us up first. We could be the f-f-first visitors they've ever had."

"We'll see," Nansen said.

Mokoena: "Will we necessarily?"

The stranger hove in optical range, maddeningly minute and blurred to begin with, then the magnified image strengthening second by second. Nansen and Sundaram strained forward, peering.

They did not need to describe what they saw. Every station had a readout screen. A long cylinder terminated aft in an accelerator lattice not unlike *Envoy*'s, the same plasma fire blue-white to drive it onward. At the bow another meshwork formed a great, shallow bowl, pierced by a mast. The hull was dull metallic, well-nigh featureless—except for the second fourth of its length, counting from the bow. That section was bare ribs and stringers, open to space. It enclosed an intricate web, in which solid shapes bulked. No details came through the screening effect of the metal and the tricky light-and-shadow of vacuum.

"About one hundred meters long, apart from the drive assembly, and thirty maximum diameter, apart from that dish in front," Nansen reported. "I can't be sure, of course, but I suspect the dish is intended more for transmission than reception, if it uses radio frequencies. It must be made from a composite as strong as any of ours, to stay unwarped at the acceleration it's been through."

"The entirety seems more and more as though it is purely robotic," Sundaram ventured. "That would fit with an industrialized planetary system, and perhaps the mother world a residential park. When the dwellers became aware of us, they dispatched patrol machines to investigate."

"Too much that we have seen does not fit with that," Nansen said. "Wait. Soon we may know." The tension hurt. He willed his body to ease off, muscle by muscle.

The stranger matched velocities and terminated boost. Half a kilometer away, it hung as if motionless against the huge stars.

"Still no response," Nansen told his crew. "We—*Hold!*"

Magnification showed him and Sundaram the forms that climbed out of the skeleton. Instruments gave dimensions and movements. To unaided vision they would have been mere glints, but they swept swiftly nearer in a V formation.

No screen at a station gave so clear a view. "Robots, yes," Nansen said like a machine himself. "Fifteen of them. Each a cylinder, about three meters long. Four assemblies with nozzles around the circumference at the waist—jet motors, I think, probably chemical. Four landing jacks aft, or so they appear to be. . . . Claws at the ends, perhaps they double as grapnels. Four arms forward, branching and rebranching . . . yes, at the ends, what must be manipulators and assorted tools. An array projecting at the nose—a lens in it? A laser? Gleams and housings elsewhere—sensors?—*¡Esperad!* They are turning about . . . interior wheels, minijets?" Flame flickered. Vapor roiled, thinned, disappeared. "Yes, they are on approach, they are coming in."

The shapes drew close. The optical program tracked them and displayed the images.

"*¿Qué es?* They . . . they approach aft—they touch down—induction grip like our boots? But it is—*¡Madre de Dios, no!*"

The machines were on the plasma drive lattice. They clung as wasps cling to a prey. Radiance sprang from their lenses. Metal glowed suddenly white, sparks fountained, a cable writhed loose, a thin girder parted and a second robot seized the pieces to bend them before they could fuse.

"They're attacking us," Mokoena said, stunned.

"Start the drive!" Ruszek roared. "Burn the bastards off!"

"No," Yu told them. "We have already lost too much feedback for the guide fields. We would melt the entire assembly."

"Stop, please stop," Sundaram begged. His little brown hands bounded over the keyboard before him, seeking to hit on a message that might be understood.

"Shoot their ship!" Kilbirnie yelled.

Sweat stung Nansen's eyes. "Not yet. We know nothing, *nada.*"

Brent's voice rang: "Well, we can defend our own. Lajos, you and me go out and kill those things before they take our whole hull apart."

"By God, yes!" the mate shouted. "Tim, you're nearest the small arms locker. Bring us weapons. Selim, come help us suit up."

"I will go, too," Zeyd said.

"And I," Kilbirnie put in.

"No," Nansen decreed. "Not you two. Ruszek and Brent have the military experience. We cannot risk more." A groan escaped him. He also must stay behind.

Dayan sent him a benediction. "We know how you feel, you, our captain."

"This must be s-s-some tragic mistake," Yu gasped. "They would not—rational beings—"

"They are doing it," Zeyd said.

Sundaram had won back his inner balance. "I am working out a program to transmit," he said fast. "Basic mathematics, flashes for numbers up to one hundred, digital symbols for operators, operations conducted to identify them. And we will vary an amplitude, sinusoidally, parabolically, exponentially, and present a succession of prime numbers. All to show we are not automatons but conscious minds. You can begin now, at every wavelength you have. I will continue adding more."

Nansen set it up for him, without hope. What harm? Doing so took a fraction of his awareness from the destruction outside. Parts were floating free in space, bobbing off into the distance. Several robots left the work to move forward. They flitted around the after wheel and parallel to the hull, slowly, on feathery gusts of jet. Ahead of them lay turrets, bays, locks, vulnerable sensors; beyond the forward wheel stretched the mast that generated and controlled the radiation shield. If he could just bring those forces to bear— But they heterodyned to form a hollow shell, and the requirements of feedback made their very creation dependent on a high background count.

The mother ship waited, mute. Instruments registered its mate, speeding closer.

A shuttle jumped from forward wheel to main hull. Sweeping about on his order, the optics gave Nansen an image of it. The shuttle reached a port and secured itself. The men aboard were cycling through, into the passage beyond. They were bound for the nearest exit to space.

He knew which that would be, and focused on it. After endlessness, while the wrecking went on aft and the scout robots advanced forward, the valve drew aside. Two spacesuited figures clambered out and took stance to peer around them. Their boots clung fast, their hands gripped firearms. More were slung at their shoulders. In the harsh sunlight, they shone like armored knights. The jetpacks on their backs were like the wings of the warrior angel Michael.

They were not symbols, though. Individually fitted suits gave recognition; burly Ruszek, slender Brent. An antenna picked up their radio speech.

"On to the drive," the second engineer said. Ardor pulsed. "Shoot on sight. Bullets. A rocket would blow one into scrap. We want them in condition to study."

"Give them a chance first," the mate growled. "Maybe when they see us they will— Hold! Cover me."

A robot rounded the hull, flying low alongside its great curve. Light sheened off smooth alloy, dendritic arms, watchful pseudoeyes. Still clutching his rifle, Ruszek spread his arms high and wide, a token of welcome.

The laser lens came aglare. His helmet darkened barely in time to save his sight. He leaped, tore free of the hull, floated. Metal glowed where he had been and bubbled along the slash the energy beam left.

Brent was already firing. The robot spun back from impact. The slugs tore through its plating. It gyred off, jets dead. The arms flopped.

Two more appeared. Ruszek knew better than to shoot from free fall. He twisted around, activated his motor, struck the hull, went step by gripping step to join his partner. Brent's rifle hammered.

From aft rose the other machines, a swarm across the monstrous stars. Ruszek slung his rifle and freed his rocket launcher.

Lasers flashed, seeking range. Metal seared.

"The orders for that came from the ship," said Nansen. To it: "No, you shall not kill my men."

A rocket streaked on a white trail of smoke. Its radar found a target, its warhead exploded. A rose bloomed soundlessly, spread thin, vanished. Fragments tumbled where two robots had been, winking in the sunlight.

In vacuum, the concussion had merely tossed the others a little. However, their pack dispersed. For a minute or two they drifted in several directions, as if uncertain.

Nansen had entered his command.

The robots regrouped. They moved again toward the men. Ruszek and Brent stood back to back.

A torpedo slipped from a launch bay in *Envoy*. Nansen sent instructions. The lean shape slewed about and jetted.

Low-yield, the nuclear blast nonetheless filled heaven with incandescence. The fireball became a luminous cloud. When that had dissipated, shards whirled red-hot and molten drops hurtled like comets gone insane.

Nansen's attention was back on his men. They had had the hull between them and the explosion, sufficient shelter; else he would first have used a counterrotator to swing his vessel around. They had not moved from their position. As he watched, Brent shot an approaching robot. Again the bullets ripped thin skin and tore circuits asunder. The machine wobbled backward. Pieces dribbled from it.

The sight was almost pathetic, because the entire band had lost purpose. Momentum bore its members past. Two of them encountered the ship, took hold with their jacks, and stood. Tools on the arm-branches plucked empty space. The rest of the robots drifted by and dwindled in view.

"Hold your fire, Al," came Ruszek's hoarse mutter. "I think we've won."

A few fragments of the slain vessel struck *Envoy*, not too hard, sending faint drumbeats through her air.

Nansen let out a breath. His skin prickled. He smelled his sweat, felt it on brow and in armpits, heard himself as if from afar: "Return inboard, you two. Well done."

"We'd better stay here awhile, on guard." Brent's words were a little shrill, but they throbbed.

"*No hay necesidad*—no need." Nansen hesitated. His thoughts hastened, he believed; it was language that had gone heavy. "At least the probability of more trouble in the near future seems slight. We destroyed the mother ship, do you know? It must have been in charge. The robots doubtless have some autonomy, but without orders, they don't . . . don't know . . . what to do. At any rate, they don't when they meet something as unheard-of as we must be."

Horror spoke from Mokoena: "You destroyed—whoever was on board?"

"They were after us," Kilbirnie snarled.

"No, the ship must have been robotic, too," Dayan said. "The wreckers were—agents, organs, corpuscles serving it. I can't believe intelligent beings would mount a senseless attack. It was most likely due to a program not written for anything like us."

Nansen's tongue began to moisten. It moved more readily. "We'll discuss this at leisure, and lay new plans," he said. "Meanwhile, Mate Ruszek, Engineer Brent, we'll not hazard you further. Come back."

"To a heroes' welcome," Kilbirnie cried.

"First I'd better blow these two here apart," Ruszek said.

"No!" Brent exclaimed. "We want them to study, dissect. The military value—lasers that powerful, that small—"

"Well, I'm God damn not going to leave them squatting on our hull unless I've put their lights out. Right, Captain?"

"Can you do that with a rifle?" Nansen asked.

"We did already."

"Don't shoot them in the same places," Brent urged. "Leave different sections intact. We need the knowledge, I tell you."

"For war?" Yu protested. "Why? I thought we are agreed this was essentially an accident."

"We are not certain of that," Nansen replied. "We'll try to find out. First, of course, we'll assess the damage and commence repair."

Sundaram stirred. "No," he said. "First we should attempt contact with the second ship. It will be here in another hour, won't it?"

"It will not," Nansen declared. "I am about to launch a second missile."

"Oh, no!" Yu screamed. "You cannot tell—"

"I can gauge probabilities," Nansen answered, "and that robot brain yonder may have learned something from what has happened. It shall not get a chance to apply the information. I hope the rest of the fleet will take that as a lesson to leave us alone."

"But, Captain—"

"I am the captain. Let any guilt fall on me. I am responsible for all of *us*."

Sundaram parted his lips and closed them again.

Nansen's fingers wrote a command. Another torpedo eased into space. It turned, searched, found its target, plotted its course, and spurted off. After a while, very briefly, a new star winked.

There was no further sound from the engine center. Perhaps Yu had turned her intercom off. Perhaps she wept.

16.

Robots and humans working together restored *Envoy*'s plasma thruster. It had not been too badly damaged, as short a time as the wreckers were granted. She came about onto a new path and at length took orbit around the planet that bore life.

No more raptors troubled her. "They must have passed word back and forth," Kilbirnie said. "They've learned we're bad medicine."

"Yes, they aren't conscious, but they can learn—within rather broad limits, I'd say—if my guess about them is right," Nansen replied.

"Oh, what is your guess?"

"I'll wait until we have more data."

"Aweel, meanwhile the rest of us can have the fun of making our own." After the brush with ruin, mirth ran high, if a trifle forced.

Moonless, a fourth again as massive as Earth, turning once in forty-two hours on an axis barely tilted, atmosphere more dense, the planet still looked familiar enough to rouse an ache in a human breast. Although ice caps were lacking, oceans shone sapphire and lands sprawled dun beneath white swirls of cloud. The air was nitrogen, oxygen, water vapor, carbon dioxide; it knew rain, snow, sunshine. Life flourished. The reflection spectrum off plants was not that of chlorophyl, but the chemistry was of protein, and animals were abundant.

They included sentient beings. High resolution found large brown creatures with stumpy legs and six-digited hands in villages (?) that consisted mostly of dome-shaped dwellings. They cultivated fields, mined and milled and manufactured, shipped and traveled, with the help of domesticated beasts and modest machines. They crossed the seas under sail; sometimes they flew in lighter-than-air craft. Dams, windmills, and solar collectors supplemented fueled power plants to furnish a certain amount of electricity. Designs were exotic and often suggested sophisticated engineering, but the main energy source seemed to be the combustion of biomass, and apparently much land was given over to growing this. Local variations in everything were noticeable, but nothing like what Earth had known through most of its history. Here might well be a world united under one dominant culture.

It was the ruins that leaped out at eye and mind. Remnants of cyclopean walls and sky-storming towers reared above forest crowns, brush-grown plains, deserted islands. Lesser relics lay everywhere; some had been incorporated into later works. Other traces—old riverbeds, peculiarly shaped mountains, anomalous patterns of vegetation—likewise told of past grandeur.

"Did a war destroy what was here?" wondered Zeyd one evening in the common room. "Could the shipkillers be left over from it?"

"I doubt that," said Dayan. "Nothing looks as if it was broken by anything but neglect and weather."

"Besides," Ruszek added, "those aren't really shipkillers. They tried to dismantle us, is all. When we fought back, they went straightaway kaput."

Mokoena shuddered. "Not straightaway." She caught his hand. "If the captain had been one minute slower, you would be dead now."

"But Lajos is right," Yu said. "They had no real defenses, they were not military machines. Let us not project our psychology onto the souls here. Perhaps they have never made war."

"That would be lovely," Sundaram mused. "If we could get to know them—an enlightenment—"

Nansen dismissed that idea at the formal meeting several days later. "We are pledged to go to the Yonderfolk," he said starkly.

"But the science to do," Mokoena demurred. "A whole new biology."

"The beings," Sundaram added in his quiet fashion. "Their thoughts, feelings, arts, their mysterious history."

"I know," Nansen replied. "But you know, all of us know, we could spend our lives here and not begin to understand it. We're in search of a starfaring race. I only agreed to this diversion because it might somehow bear on"—he faltered—"on certain questions about the stability of high technology."

"Well, doesn't it?" Cleland made bold to ask.

"Yes and no," Nansen said to the half-circle he faced. "Clearly, they never achieved the zero-zero drive. It does appear their time of glory was long ago. Perhaps the civilization we are bound for did not yet exist. Perhaps the haze in this cluster prevented their finding traces of any farther off. It was discoveries like that which led us to the principles of the quantum gate."

"Somebody had to do it first, independently," Kilbirnie argued. "I suspect we would have regardless."

Nansen shrugged. "Who can say? In any event, I have had a few thoughts about the situation here and how it came to be. I've discussed them with Engineer Yu and Physicist Dayan, who carried them further. We have what we believe is a reasonable hypothesis."

Brent glanced at Yu, Kilbirnie at Dayan, with a flash of jealousy. Kilbirnie lost hers in fascination as talk continued.

"A high technology, including nucleonics and doubtless genetic engineering, arose on this planet, and evidently there was world peace, too," Nansen said. "Perhaps there always was. They explored the planetary system. They began to use its resources: energy, minerals, industrial sites that did not harm the biosphere at home. In all this they were like us.

"Then why should they not do what our ancestors thought of doing, and would have done if zero-zero had not made it irrelevant? Send probes to the nearer stars—and in a cluster, every star is near. Robots to survey and study and beam their findings back."

"Our ancestors did, a few times," Cleland pointed out.

Nansen nodded. "True. But they never took the next step, which was to send von Neumann machines."

"What?"

Nansen looked at Dayan. "Would you like to explain?"

"It's simple enough," she said. "We use the same principle every day in our nanotech, and in fact it's the basis of life and evolution. Send machines that not only explore and report to you, but make more like themselves and dispatch those onward, programmed to do likewise."

Brent whistled. "Whew! How long would they take to eat the galaxy?"

"It wouldn't be that bad," Yu told him. "It would be enough to make a few score in any given planetary system. An asteroid or two would suffice for materials."

"A probe wouldn't be a single unit," Dayan added. "We've seen. A carrier, housing the central computer and its program; a number of robots to do the actual work, including to build the next generation of machines."

"But none ever reached us," Ruszek argued, puzzled. "Why not? If it began here, oh, a million years ago—well, we've seen what kind of boost the carriers have. Sixteen hundred light-years, they should have spread through that before now."

"High boost," Brent said, "but limited delta v." He had been pondering the recorded data, as well as starting to dissect the slain robots. "Maybe a fiftieth or a hundredth c."

"Even so—"

Zeyd narrowed his eyes. "The shipkillers," he hissed. "Can they be the reason?"

"Not that simple," Dayan answered. "Our conjecture— But, Captain, you can probably explain it with the least technicalese."

A smile tugged at Nansen's mouth. "Thank you. I'll try.

"Essentially, we think a von Neumann probe went to the double star soon after it had gone nova. We don't know if that was the most recent eruption or an earlier one, but our guess is that it was the latest. The mission was a very natural one, to a remarkable thing, fairly nearby. And doubtless the system has kept a few planets, or at least solid debris in orbit, to use for construction material.

"Now, the von Neumann principle does not mean that immediately on arrival, a machine makes more machines to launch toward farther stars. First it will make more like itself to investigate the system that it has reached. They must cope with many unforeseeables. Their hardware must be complex. But even more, they need sophisticated software, programs capable not just of learning but of developing solutions to problems that arise—and programs that can take advantage of any opportunity they see to do things better, more efficiently.

"Well, our hypothesis is that in the dreadful radiation environment shortly after the nova outburst, a program mutated. Probably several did, in different ways, and perished. It would make sense to take the useable parts of those machines for making new ones. But this mutant went beyond that. It found it could reproduce still more efficiently by actively assaulting others, or any machinery it found, and processing what it took."

"My God, a predator!" Kilbirnie blurted. She stared before her. "No awareness to tell it this was wrong, a bad idea. Evolution, blind as wi' life."

"I imagine the . . . cannibals . . . aren't too specialized," Yu murmured. "They must retain the ability to use raw materials. It is simply a loss of . . . inhibition. But in the end, they devoured all others in the nova system."

"And then they went after new prey," Dayan said, flat-voiced.

"Is that why no such machines ever reached Sol?" Mokoena asked. In her expression, shock struggled with professional interest.

"No," Zeyd said. "How could they overtake the wave of exploration?"

"Wolves didn't wipe out buffalo," Brent added.

"Predator and prey developed an integral relationship," Sundaram said. "We learned on Earth how unwise it is to interfere with the web of life."

"Please," Nansen said. "These are side issues. Argue them later."

"The analogies to organic evolution are not exact," Yu admitted.

"Our guess is that machines capable enough to be useful interstellar explorers are necessarily so complex as to be vulnerable to mutation in their programs," Dayan said. "They need not visit a nova. Sooner or later, if nothing else, cosmic radiation will do it. Generally, they lose their 'wits' and just drift on aimlessly forever. Probably no line of von Neumanns gets beyond a few hundred light-years before it goes effectively extinct."

"More speculation," Nansen said. "We, our crew, will never know with certainty. But the suggestion is that this one mutation was successful in a way. And some of the predators came back to this star. It may have been random, or they may have . . . remembered.

"By then, the civilization here was completely dependent on its industries in space. Suddenly they were wiped out. If the beings realized what was going on and tried to launch weapons against the invaders, those weapons were inadequate, perhaps gobbled up as they left atmosphere. Or perhaps the beings were too peaceful to think of weapons. Whatever happened, their technology collapsed. It must have been horrible."

Mokoena winced. "Famines. Epidemics. Billions dying."

"They seem to have rebuilt as best they could," Nansen reminded her gently. "It looks like a stable population and ecology, a world that can last till the sun grows too hot."

Kilbirnie grimaced. "But then? And meanwhile, ne'er to adventure again?"

"Not while the predators prowl," Brent grated.

"I daresay they've reached an equilibrium, too," Dayan said. "They probably reproduce from raw materials and from the parts of ones that, um, die. Maybe they have combats once in a while, but that can't be the basis of their existence. Their programs remember, though. They remember. And when we arrived—Manna from heaven."

Zeyd jumped to his feet. "Let's hunt them down!" he shouted. "If we do nothing else, we can set these poor beings free!"

Ruszek sat bolt upright, his mustache quivering. Brent stifled a cheer.

"No," Nansen said. "It would take years, if we can do it at all. And we can't tell what the consequences could be. We are not God. We have our promise to keep.

"No, we have not really solved the mystery we found. We have what seems to be a good guess, no more. It is the best we can hope for. If no one finds an unanswerable reason to stay, we will continue on our proper mission within this week."

Zeyd snapped air into his lungs, looked around at his crewmates, and sat down. Silence closed in.

Kilbirnie waved a hand aloft. "Bravo for you, skipper!" she called. "We've plenty ahead of us. Bring us there!"

She, at least, is wholeheartedly with me, Nansen thought. *I'd like to confide in her—tell her why this irrational sense of urgency is riding me—if the thing I'm afraid of turns out to be true.*

And then, looking at her: *Afraid? Why? Our mission is to discover the truth, whatever it may be.*

His mind flew back across light-years, to what was less knowable than that which lay ahead. *May they at home still have a spirit like hers.*

17.

Earth was the mother and her Kith Town the small motherland of every starfarer; but there were other worlds where humans dwelt. At those the ships were almost always welcome, bearers of tidings and wares that bridged, however thinly, the abysses between. It was not perennially so on Earth.

Thus, over the centuries, Tau Ceti became the sun which voyagers from afar often sought first. Its Harbor was as homelike as any known extrasolar planet, and usually at peace. News beamed from Sol arrived only eleven and a half years old; if you had felt unsure, you could now lay plans. Whether or not you went on to that terminus, here was a good place to stop for a while, do business, make fresh acquaintances and breathe fresh winds. A Kith village grew up, stabilized, and settled into its own timelessness.

Spanning the distances they did, vessels could hardly ever prearrange a rendezvous. It was occasion for rejoicing and intermingling when two happened to be in the same port. When three or more did, it meant a Fair.

Fleetwing came to Harbor and found *Argosy* and *Eagle* in orbit. *Argosy* was about to depart, but immediately postponed it. Profits could wait; they were no longer large anyway. Fellowship, courtship, exchange of experiences, renewal of ties, the rites that affirmed and strengthened Kithhood, mattered more.

Ormer Shaun, second mate aboard *Fleetwing*, and Haki Tensaro, who dealt in textiles wherever *Eagle* might be, walked together through the village, bound for the story circle. Tensaro wanted to hear what Shaun would tell; they had become friendly in the past few days, and besides, a real yarn-spinning with a bardic accompaniment was an art practiced in just four ships, which did not include *Eagle*. The two men had met for a beer in the

Orion and Bull before starting out, and continued their conversation as they proceeded. It had gradually, unintendedly, gone from merry to earnest.

"A disappointment, I admit," Shaun said. Sounds of revelry beat beneath his words. "Not so much for me, or most of our crew. But the boy, he was really looking forward to all the ancient marvels."

"We're quite safe on Earth nowadays, I tell you," Tensaro argued. "No more persecution."

"They still don't like us, though, do they? To go by what everybody's been saying."

Tensaro shrugged. "I've seen things better there, but I've seen them worse, too. I think the next generation will be pretty tolerant."

"Up to a point. I doubt we'll ever again be exactly popular anywhere on Earth outside of Kith Town."

"Why not?"

Shaun paused to marshal words. He contrasted with Tensaro, who was slim and intense, clad in formfitting lusterblack with white sash and cloak, and a headband on which a miniature light fountain made a dancing cockade. Shaun stood bigger than most Kithfolk, stocky, his features rugged and his hair a dark mahogany. For his garb today he had chosen a blouse that slowly shifted color across the visible spectrum, a vest of silver links, a broad leather belt studded with Aerian eyestones, a shaggy green kilt, and knee-length boots. A beret slanted across his brow. Both outfits were traditional festival garb, but the traditions belonged to two different ships.

"Earth doesn't have enough to do with space anymore," Shaun said. "People get in the habit of taking their ways to be the only right and decent ways. Governments feed on that. Meanwhile we insist on being peculiar, and bringing in unheard-of notions from elsewhere, and asking troublesome questions."

The street down which they passed seemed to belie him. Turf covered it, springy and pebble-grained underfoot, breathing a slight odor not unlike rosemary into cooling air. On one side a lyre tree curved its double trunk and feathery foliage aloft, on the other side an arachnea spread its web across a cloud tinted gold by the westering sun. The houses that lined the street stood each on its piece of lawn, among its flower beds. They were of archaic styles, tending to pastel walls and red-tiled roofs; time had softened their edges. All were currently vacant. Most of the families that owned them were afar among the stars, leaving machines to tend the property. Everyone staying here, whether as transients or permanently, had flocked off to the Fair.

Between the houses glimmered a glimpse of water. Beyond it the cliffs of Belderland rose white. Opposite, native forest spread red-splashed ochers and golds above the roofs. Long since deeded to the Kith, the Isle of Weyan retained much wilderness.

"Yes," Shaun said, "I think *Fleetwing*'ll elect to make another swing from here—not as long as last time, of course, but we can give Earth forty or fifty years more to mellow further before we show our noses there again. The boy'll be disappointed, like I said. But, what the gyre, learning how to wait things out is part of becoming a Kithman."

"Well, if that's what your crew favors, so be it," Tensaro replied. "I expect you can sell what you're carrying on Aurora or Maia as well as here. It'll probably be exotic enough to fetch a price. But really, you're too pessimistic. I can understand how your last visit to Earth was embittering and made you decide on a long cruise. Nowadays, though—"

A trumpet cut him off. The noise from ahead had been waxing as they walked, voices, foot-thuds, song, boom and bang, the racket of merriment. Shaun and Tensaro came abruptly out onto open ground, where the Fair was. It surrounded the village. They had crossed from the tavern on one edge to this side.

Shaun threw up his hands. His laugh rang. "Haki, us old fools, we've gotten serious! What ails us? Did the beer wear off that fast? Come on, let's get back to our proper business today."

He quickened his pace. His comrade grinned wryly and trotted along.

People swarmed about. Folk costumes from the separate ships mingled with gaudy individual choices, often inspired on other worlds in other eras. A middle-aged couple strolled by, he in the blue-and-gold tunic and flowing white trousers, she in the red frock, saffron cloak, and massive jewelry of *Eagle*. Shaun smiled at a young woman he knew aboard *Fleetwing*. Her brief and gauzy gown twinkling with star points, she walked hand in hand with a young man whose fringed yellow shirt and black knee breeches said *Argosy*. Memory stirred—courtships flowered like fire when crews met, and if the marriages that followed took place quickly, they endured, for the elders of both families had first considered what was wise. Shaun's wife was a *Flying Cloud* girl; but his brother had joined his own bride on *High Barbaree*, because that seemed best. . . . Children dashed about, shouting, marveling bits of rainbow.

Pavilions had been erected throughout the area, big and gaudy. Banners above them caught the sea breeze and the evening light. From one drifted savory smells and the sounds of clinking cups and cheery chatter. In another, a benched audience watched a classic drama, performed live; in another they heard a concert, which included music brought back from artists who were not all human; in another, visual artworks were on display, created aboard ship as well as on remote planets, and in this quiet atmosphere a few officers took the opportunity to discuss business or exchange information. In a clear space, a band played lustily for scores of dancers. Mirth whooped as some tried to learn, from others, measures new to them, the sarali, the Henriville, the double prance.

Nearby stood the Monument Stone. The bronze plate on it shone bright, having lately replaced a worn-out predecessor. The inscription was the same, *Here camped Jean Kilbirnie and Timothy Cleland of the first expedition to Harbor, afterward of* Envoy *and our future in the cosmos,* with a date in a calendar long superseded. Likewise, only scholars could read the language, ancestral to Kithic, but everybody knew what it said. A few meters off, wood was heaped to be burned after dark—fire, evoking prehistoric memories and instincts older still, which were doubly strong in a people who rarely saw it.

The narrators' pavilion lay a little distance onward. About a hundred persons sat inside waiting, mostly adults, mostly from *Eagle* and *Argosy*, though several youngsters and *Fleetwing* crew also felt they would enjoy the performance. They gave Shaun the salute of greeting as he entered, came down an aisle, and mounted the stage. Rusa Erody was already there. She made a striking sight, clad in a long dress of scales that glittered in the subdued light, herself a genetic throwback, tall and blonde. Her fingers drew vigorous chords from the polymusicon on her lap. The song she sang was as ancient as her looks, translated and retranslated over the centuries, because it spoke to the Kith.

> *"The Lord knows what we may find, dear lass,*
> *And the Deuce knows what we may do—*
> *But we're back once more on the old trail, our own trail, the out*
>   *trail,*
> *We're down, hull-down, on the Long Trail—the trail*
>   *that is always new!"*

Words and notes clanged away. Shaun took the chair beside hers. The tumult outside washed like surf around sudden silence.

He lifted a hand. "Good landing, friends," he drawled. A comfortable informality was his style at these events. "Thanks for coming, when you've got so much else you could be having fun with. Well, you men have had my partner to admire, Rusa Erody, biosafety technician and bard. I'm Ormer Shaun, second mate and occasional storyteller. Those of you who docked here earlier have heard others tell of things that *Fleetwing* did or encountered or got wind of, sometimes generations ago. Rusa and I will relate a happening on our latest voyage, just finished."

"But it was well-nigh a hundred years agone, for Aerie is the farthest of all worlds where humans dwell, our last lonely home in the heavens," the woman half sang. Music wove low beneath her voice. Her role was to call forth a mood and bring a scene to life. If she deemed that meant repeating common knowledge, it worked as a refrain or a familiar line of melody does. "Not even our explorers have quested much beyond, where time must sunder them from us more than the hollow spaces themselves."

Shaun frowned slightly. A storytelling was not rehearsed, but improvised. The hint that outwardness was faltering fitted ill with the lightness he intended. *But Rusa generally knows what she's doing,* he thought. *A touch of sad or anxious, like a pinch of sharp spice—* He decided to follow suit for a moment, in prosaic wise, before he went on to his tale.

"Well, being that distant, Aerie gets visitors few and seldom. Previous one, as near as we could learn, was about a century before. We figured to do a brisk trade in the goods and information we offered.

"But also, after what we'd just been through on Earth, we didn't care to see it again soon. Insults, restrictions, place after place that didn't want us for customers, throatgrip taxes—yes, once a mob threw rocks at some of us, and I saw a woman of ours bleed and heard little children of ours crying—but many of you know this, maybe better than we do. To the Coal Sack with 'em. We'd come back after they were dead, if they hadn't meanwhile spawned too many like themselves."

A smile crinkled his face. His tone eased. "Moreover, frankly, a lot of us were curious. What'd been going on, way out at Aerie? What new and odd might we find? We'd been in the Quadrangle Trade from some while and were getting a tad bored with it. Time for a change of scene, a real change."

"The Quadrangle Trade," Erody chimed in. "Biochemicals from the seas of Maia's uninhabitable sister planet Morgana, worth harvesting and transporting because it costs more to synthesize them. Rare, useful isotopes from the system where Aurora orbits. Arts and crafts from Feng Huang. Biostock from Earth, to nourish the Earth life on yonder worlds."

This was not entirely another chorus for Shaun. Neither *Eagle* nor *Argosy* had plied that circuit, and crewfolk of theirs might know of it only vaguely. She did not add that it, too, was declining, losing profitability as the demand for such cargoes diminished. "We fared from the Quadrangle toward the Lion," she finished.

"A long haul, aye," Shaun said. "Considering how scarce traders had been on Aerie, and how small the population and industry probably still were, we loaded a lot of stuff more massive than usual, machinery and so on."

"Besides our several hundred men, women, and children as always, their life support, their household treasures, their tools and weapons that they may have need to wield when we arrive, their need to be together, to be families, and thus keep the life of the ship alive." Not information, for those who sat listening—affirmation, for every Kith member, living, dead, and unborn.

"So our gamma factor was well down, seeing as how our quantum gate's no bigger than anybody else's."

"Not like *Envoy*'s, for none of our ships is *Envoy*, outbound beyond the borderlands of history and bearing no more than her fabled ten. Well could we wish for an engine like hers, but the gain and loss of trade say no, it cannot pay, and though we travel not for trafficking alone, it is by the traffic that we abide as the Kith." More rituality, as a priest at a service may recite an article of the creed to strengthen feeling in a congregation that may know it word by word.

"Ninety-seven light-years took us eight zero-zero months. Oh, we were good and tired when we got there—tired, anyway, and cramped and grubby and ready to settle in for a while."

"Where ground and grass were under our feet, a breeze and unfeigned odors of growth in our nostrils, heaven blue overhead, and strangers around us, new souls for us to know."

"Who hadn't heard every joke and anecdote we could tell, folks who'd think we were glamorous and our wares were marvelous. And they ought to be interesting to us, of course, and have things to trade that'd fetch decent prices back at the heart stars."

"Yet theirs is a harsh holding."

"You know Aerie's not just far off from anywhere else human, it's a lump that never would've been settled if planets where people can settle at all weren't scarce."

"Vanishingly scarce. The sun of Aerie dim, its light across the lands of summer like the light of hazy autumn over Earth. The glaciers north and south, mountain-high. The cold seas that clash around the one tropical continent that our race could make its own. But the rings, the remnants of a shattered moon, the rings on a clear night are very beautiful."

"Well, the land's not that bad everywhere. The region where we set up our pitch, after *Fleetwing* took orbit, was shirtsleeve in its fashion. Naturally, that was the spot we negotiated to stay at, and, naturally, it belonged to the grand high rambuck."

Shaun continued with incidents from first contact, the establishment of groundside camp, trade, personal encounters, mostly as amusing as he could make them. Erody filled in descriptions.

"Our cabins were on pastureland, for they keep herds and sow crops on Aerie," she explained. "They dare not trust entirely to robotics and synthesis, when quake or storm or the mites that gnaw metal may strike terribly in any year. Terrestrial grass stretched away southward from us, deeply green in the pale day, on one side the neatly arrayed houses and shops of the Magistrate's retainers and their kindred. Northward persisted native forest, a murky realm into which few ventured and none deeply. The castle loomed between us and the wildwood, its towers stark athwart the clouds. No need for curtain walls, when aircraft, missiles, and armed men stood watch. The castle was a community in itself, homes, worksteads, chapels, stadium, even laboratories and a museum."

"Aerie's not under a tyranny," Shaun said. "The way things had worked out—at least, as of when we were there—government was mostly by town meetings scattered around the continent. The Magistrate provided peace and order; police, through his militia, and higher justice—court of appeal, court of legal review—through his telepresence. Otherwise he generally left people alone, which most times is the best thing government can do. But after several generations had passed the office down from one to the next, he held a huge lot of assorted properties, and people didn't give him much backchat. He was a reasonable sort, though, in his rough-hewn style. We had no trouble ranging about in our own flitters, seeing things and making deals. And we were on a live, uncluttered world. Yes, that was a good three, four months."

"For us," Erody laid to this. Her music throbbed and keened. "We were not wholly benign. In some whom we met, we from the stars awakened dreams forgotten, wishes ungrantable, and belike we will never know what has afterward brewed from that discontent."

"One boy in particular," Shaun said. "Valdi Ronen, his name was. A bastard son of the Magistrate, raised at the castle in a hit-or-miss way, but with fairish prospects ahead of him. He might become an officer in the militia, for instance, or a rancher or an engineer, he being bright and lively. By Earth reckoning, he was about fourteen."

"A thin lad, shooting upward, his hands and feet too big for him, though he was not overly awkward," Erody remembered. "Pale-skinned, like most on Aerie, hair a flaxen shock, large blue eyes, sharp features. He often went hunting in the wilderness—sometimes alone, despite his mother's command that he have ever a companion or two; and we gathered that at those times he ventured farther in than men thought wise."

"He didn't after we arrived," Shaun said. "No, he hung around us like a moon around a planet. Most of us had studied and practiced the local language en route, of course. It hadn't changed a lot from what was in the database. I got pretty fluent, myself. We could talk, we two.

"I was willing to put up with him when I wasn't too busy, his countless questions, his bursts of brashness, everything that goes with being that age. My son had been, too, not terribly long ago, and had metamorphosed into a presentable human being. Besides, Valdi told me and showed me quite a bit, better than grown-ups probably could, about native wildlife and youngsters' games and lower-class superstitions and whatnot. Some of that might well go into the documentary our production team was planning, might help it sell when we got back. In fact, Valdi couldn't do enough for us. If we asked anything of him, he'd try his best, no matter how tough or dirty a chore it was."

"We meet not wondersmitten youth like this on worlds elsewhere as often as erstwhile, do we?" Erody asked low. "That may be as well. It was painful to see the grief in them when we bade good-bye."

"Yes, I saw what was coming, and tried to head it off," Shaun continued. " 'Valdi,' I told him, 'starfaring is our life and we wouldn't change if we could, but we were raised to it.' "

" 'We were born to it,' I told him," the woman recalled. " 'Our forebears for many generations were those who wanted it. They who could not endure it left, taking their genes with them. Kithfolk today are as chosen for space as birds are chosen to wing aloft.' His ancestors had brought some birds here and several species had flourished."

" 'But people don't grow wings!' he argued," Shaun added. "His voice broke in a squeak. He went red. Just the same, he pushed on. 'People build ships and—and l-l-learn to sail them.'

"I hadn't the heart to answer that nobody but a groundhugger would speak of sailing a spaceship. Instead, I set out the grim side for him. I talked about weeks, months, maybe years crowded into a metal shell or into still more cramped sealdomes, never able to step outside for a breath of clean air, only in a suit—because, I reminded him, planets where humans can walk freely are bloody few, and to make the profit that keeps us going we often have to call at other kinds. I talked about danger, death, and the worse than death that environments may bring down on us, bodies crippled, minds gone to ruin, and little our meditechs can do to remedy things. And coming back from even a fairly short voyage, after ten, twenty, fifty, a hundred, or more years have gone by, the people you knew old or dead, and every voyage leaves you more and more an alien. And how they react to this on the planets—Earth— Oh, I laid it on kind of thick, maybe, but I was trying to convince him he'd better be content with what he had.

"No use. 'You have each other,' he said. 'And you go to all those worlds, you go to the stars. Everything here is always the *same*.'" Shaun sighed. "When did a fourteen-year-old boy ever listen to reason?"

Erody nodded. "Yes, he dreamed of joining us." Her hand struck a chord that was like a cry. "Or else it was the vision that dreamed him, for he came to be consumed by it; nothing else was quite real to him any longer."

"M-m, I don't know about that," Shaun countered. "He stayed smart and cocky. In fact, once in a while he'd revert to his age and be downright obnoxious, like when he slipped what they call a squishbug into Nando Fanion's shoe or, guiding me around in the woods, got me to fall into a lurkfang's muckpit, and in either case stood there cackling with laughter. I'd have decked him if he hadn't been the Magistrate's son." He shrugged. "Or maybe not. A boy, after all, hopelessly in love with what he could never have."

"Our scoldings eventually stopped the pranks," Erody said. "He came to me and asked my help in learning our language. I warned him that would be pointless, but he begged, oh, so winningly clumsily, until I set up a program for him. He applied himself as if he were attacking a foe. I was amazed at how quickly he began to speak some Kithic and how fast he improved. And when he heard how widely used Xyrese is around the heart stars, naught would do but that he study this also, and again he was on his way to mastery."

Shaun nodded. "It got me wondering if he might not actually be recruitable. Planetsiders had joined the Kith now and then in the past. And . . . some fresh DNA in our bloodlines wouldn't hurt.

"I hinted to his father, and gathered that *he* wouldn't mind. He'd never see his son again, but on the other hand, wouldn't have to worry about providing for him or sibling rivalry or whatnot. So I put it to Captain Du one day, privately, just for consideration. He wanted no part of it, though. We were too close-knit, he said, our ways too special, a newcomer would have too much to learn. And supposing he could—which I did believe Valdi was able to—would whatever he contributed during the rest of his life be enough to make up for the time and trouble his education, his integration with us, had cost?"

"Our margin is thin at best," Erody whispered through a rippling of cold string-sounds, "in material profits and still more in the spirit."

"I tossed the notion aside. Naturally, I didn't mention any of this to Valdi. But I felt kind of glad that we'd be leaving soon."

"We know not to this day how he discovered whatever he did discover.

He may have had other, more secret friends among us. Ormer was not the sole Kithperson for whom he did favors. Somebody may have heard something in our camp and given it onward to him. Or he may simply have guessed. Bodies—stance, gait, glance, tone—often say what tongues do not. We know only that of a sudden Valdi Ronen grew most kind to little Alisa Du, she of the brown bangs, freckled nose, prim dresses, and great black cat."

"The captain's daughter, and the midpoint of his universe," Shaun explained. "Nothing untoward took place, nothing erotic at all. She was half his age. But she'd been fascinated by him ever since he made himself a fixture amongst us. To her he was as strange and romantic a figure as any of us was to him. She'd follow him around whenever and wherever she possibly could, maybe lugging Rowl in her arms."

The bard smiled. "Rowl was a ship's cat, a tom, but pleasant enough when chemoneutered as he usually was, quite intelligent, with a mortgage on Alisa's love second only to Daddy's and Mommy's. He shared her bed and each night purred her to sleep. Yes, she became Valdi's adoring admirer, her violet eyes never let slip of him while he was nigh, but Rowl was whom she went back to."

Shaun resumed. "Till now, Valdi hadn't been more than polite to her. That couldn't have come easy to him, but he knew what she meant to the captain—well, to quite a few of us. So he spoke kindly, and sometimes told her a story or sketched her a picture. He had a talent for drawing, among other things. If he expected that'd stop her tagging after him, he was wrong. Talk about counterproductive! However, he bore with the nuisance, because he had to if he wanted to stay welcome in our camp.

"Suddenly this changed. He didn't seek her out or anything, no need of that, but he let her come to him and received her gladly. He'd hunker down and listen to her chatter, carry on a straightfaced conversation like with an equal. He spun longer yarns and drew fancier pictures than before. He showed her flowers and wildlife, took her for a ride in an open hovercar, led her through local skipdances and games like bounceball, till her laughter trilled. And, yes, he took special pains to make friends with Rowl. He brought treats stolen from the castle kitchen, he stroked the cat under the chin and down the belly, he'd sit for an hour or two after Rowl got on his lap and fell asleep, till Rowl deigned to jump off— Ah, every ship has cats. You know what I mean.

"I couldn't quite figure this out. Surely he didn't imagine it would butter Captain Du into approving his adoption—which'd call for a vote anyway, of course. At best, he got the Old Man and the Vanguard Lady to regard him as less of a lout. What use that? Vacuum, poison air, hard radiation, celestial mechanics—they've got no respect for niceness."

The music went briefly sinister. "I wondered also," Erody related. "Could it be a subtle vengeance, striking out at the thwarting of his hopes? Soon we would depart. None now alive on Aerie would see us again, nor would we ever see them. Did he mean to send Alisa off with her heart ripped asunder?" The notes gentled. "No, I could not believe that. Valdi had no cruelty in him—"

"No more than most boys," Shaun muttered.

"—and besides, he must have realized it would not happen. Alisa would miss him for a while, but she was healthy and a child; new adventures awaited her; and she had her Rowl."

"Then things exploded," Shaun said. "The sun was going down, it was getting bedtime for kids—Aerie's got a twenty-six-hour rotation period, you may recall, so we'd easily adapted—and all at once Rowl wasn't to be found. Consternation!"

"The news spread among us like waves over a pond where someone has thrown in a stone," Erody adjoined. "No enormous matter, no crisis of life and death. But throughout our camp, we began to peer and grope about. The bleak eventide light streamed over us, casting shadows that went on and on across the grass, while the castle hulked ever more darkling to north and beyond it night welled up in the forest. 'Here, kitty, kitty!' we cried, ridiculously to and fro, around the shelters, probing under cots and into crannies, while the sun left us, dusk deepened from silver-blue to black, and the rings stood forth in their ghostly magnificence. It mattered not that Captain and Lady Du had offered a reward. Our Alisa wept."

"No luck," Shaun said. "The cats had roamed freely. They seldom wandered far outside our perimeter, and never toward the woods. Things there probably didn't smell right. Rowl, though, even when his tomhood was suppressed, had always been an active and inquisitive sort. Had he, maybe, come on something like a scuttermouse and chased it till he couldn't find his way home? I don't think Alisa's parents suggested that to her. Nor do I think she slept well through the night."

"In the morning, we did not entirely go on preparing for departure," Erody told. "Some who found time to spare went more widely than before, into the very forest. None entered it beyond sight of sunlight aslant between those hunched boles and clutching boughs, down through that dense, ragged leafage. If nothing else, the brush caught at a man, slashed, concealed sucking mudholes, while the bloodmites swarmed, stung, crawled up nostrils until breath was well-nigh stopped. Noises croaked, gabbled, mumbled from the shadows. Hunters in these parts had means and tricks for coping, yet they themselves never ranged deeply. When Captain Du asked whether any of them would help search, they answered nay. If Rowl had strayed into the wildwood, whatever got him could too easily take a human. Those creatures can eat our kind of flesh."

"Just a cat gone," Shaun said. "The girl would get over it. We had work to do.

"About midday, Valdi arrived. I asked where he'd been. He told me his school had gotten flappy about him skipping too many lessons, and he'd had to take a remedial section at the instruction terminal. Once free, he'd come straight to us. I gave him the news, not as any big thing."

"I was there," Erody said. "I saw him flush red." A note twanged. " 'I will go look!' he cried. 'I know the forest, I'll find him!' " Her instrument sounded a bugle call.

"The boy's voice cracked again," Shaun observed anticlimactically. "Sure, I thought, sure; adolescent heroics. He dashed off. After a while he returned, outfitted like a huntsman, green airbreath skinsuit, canteen and ration pouch and knife at hip, locator on right wrist and satphone on left, rifle slung at shoulder, and a plume in the hat on that unkempt head of his. Ho, how dramatic! 'I will find Rowl,' he promised Alisa, who'd heard he was there and come out in fairy-tale hopes. And off he loped."

"Stars kindled in her eyes behind the tears," Erody said. "I thought how callous he was to raise her heart thus, when it must be dashed back down onto the stones. Heedless, rather—a boy, a boy."

"I sort of thought the same," Shaun went on. "However, like the rest of us, I was busy readymaking. Besides, Alisa's no crybaby."

"A gallant little soul. As the day wore on, she swallowed her sorrow and took up her own duties. But she did not smile. Often and often I saw her gaze stray northward to the forest."

"I glanced that way myself, now and then," Shaun admitted. "More and more, I fretted. How long did the pup mean to try? What sense did it make? Had he quit, slunk into the castle, not wanted to tell us he'd failed? Really, he couldn't have expected to succeed. He wasn't that stupid-cocky. Or might he also have come to grief?"

"It was an evil wood." Music hissed.

"Hostile, anyway. You and I weren't the only Kithfolk who worried. Most of us liked Valdi Ronen. We called an inquiry to the castle. Had he checked in? No, he had not."

"Once more, darkness crept over us. The evening star glowed in western heaven. The rings were a banded bridge of pallid hues, around them the true stars and beyond those the galactic belt, as chill as the airs that sent mists aswirl about our ankles. Afar, some animal howled. Did it crouch above its prey? Windows and windows glowed yellow on the black bulk of the castle. Lights flickered like glowflies in the hands of servants and soldiers, out searching for Valdi. Their shouts drifted to us faint and forlorn."

"We Kithfolk huddled in. Our blundering efforts couldn't help. The boy hadn't phoned. No satellite had spotted anything. Well, Aerie didn't have many in orbit. Besides, the leaf canopy hindered their spying. Come morning, when a wider spectrum was available, we'd see what they could see."

"I have heard that now Alisa wept for her friend. Her mother rocked her in her arms for hours before she won to sleep. They do not trust psychodrugs on Aerie."

"Me, I lay awake, too, thinking some harsh thoughts. I recollected tales of what could find a human lost in those woods. And night whistlers, clingthorn—I didn't care to go through the list. Finally I took a soporific. My wife was smarter; she'd already done that.

"Our clock roused us when dawn was sneaking up into the eastern sky. We threw our clothes on and stumbled out, aimed more or less at the nearest mess cabin, desperate for coffee. People grunted and stirred in the shadows around us. Not that I was eager to be fully conscious. When the sun rose, its rays felt as cold as the lingering night mists.

"And then . . . there across the wet, trampled ground came Valdi Ronen."

"His hair hung drenched with dew, his clothes dripped, he snuffled and sneezed," Erody said. "But pressed to his breast he carried a cage, rough-made of withes, and in it stirred and yowled a black furriness."

"We crowded around, jolted wide awake. Huh? He'd found Rowl? How ever? By what crazy chance? And why hadn't he called home? We babbled. He looked straight at me in particular—"

"The level young sunlight blazed from his eyes."

"He answered us quietly, the way a man should. Yes, he'd assumed the cat had strayed into the forest. Being a better woodsman than average, he knew what traces to look for, bent twigs, pug marks in the duff— Well, I'm no tracker myself. I can't detail it. He didn't actually go any big straight-line distance, he said. But the hunt was slow, with many false leads. By the time he'd found the beast, night was falling.

"Then he discovered his satphone was dead. Sometimes on Aerie, in spite of every safeguard, metalmites get into equipment. He should have checked before he started out, but didn't. A boy in a hurry.

"To stumble back through the dark would be too risky. He wove a cage for Rowl out of shoots, so the idiot animal wouldn't wander off, and settled down as best he could. Once, he said, something huge passed by— he didn't see, he heard the brush break, felt the footfalls through the ground—and he unslung his rifle; but nothing happened. At daybreak he started home."

"Alisa jubilated. Will I ever again see such utter happiness, and afterward such adoration?" wondered Erody. "Alisa's mother hugged Valdi to her breast and kissed him in sight of every soul. Her father wrung his hand, while swallowing hard."

"Oh, yes," Shaun said. "Only a cat rescued, a pet. The Dus, the ship, owed Valdi the reward, our thanks, and nothing else. Still, the lad had proven himself. Maybe he'd been reckless, but that goes with being a boy. Besides, he had in fact carried out a difficult operation. Taking a chance when you have to goes with being Kith.

"And, then, we were in turmoil, also in our feelings—close to departure, we'd nevermore see the friends we'd made, this or that love affair was ending— You understand.

"The upshot was, we adopted Valdi Ronen. He's apprentice crew. And, I may say, in spite of his handicaps, quite promising."

"Which pleases Alisa and Rowl," Erody laughed.

For a short span there was silence, beneath the rollicking of the Fair.

Shaun grinned at his audience. "No doubt you're puzzled what the point of this story is," he said. "And no doubt, we being a race of traders, you suspect.

"If so, you're right. I'd had my own suspicions—not unique to me, but I was the officer who took Valdi aside and braced him after the ship was outbound."

"The sun of Aerie lost to sight," Erody murmured, "and around us, anew, the stars."

" 'This was too convenient,' I told him. 'I am now your superior and you will obey orders. I want to know what really happened to that poor cat.'

"He laughed. Not a cackle; a man's laugh, from down in the chest and straight out the throat. 'What poor cat?' he answered. 'A victim? Why, sir, I lured Rowl with delicacies my father enjoys only on feast days. Yes, then I caged him and kept him hidden away till I could carry him off to the woods. But I kept him fed with the same treats.'

"And in fact," Shaun remarked, "it took Rowl a while before he stopped turning up his nose at his regular rations.

" 'Didn't anybody notice that when I let him out he didn't race for food or water?' Valdi asked me. 'I was three-quarters expecting somebody would. But with you about to leave forever, what had I to lose? Uh, sir.' I saw him struggle to keep a sober face.

" 'Well, it was an emotional scene, as you'd counted on,' I said. 'We Kithfolk are slobbery sentimental about things like that.' I gave him my sternest look. 'They include the welfare of an innocent little girl.'

"He had the grace to look down at the deck. 'I'm sorry about that, sir,' he mumbled. 'I didn't really think of her, how hurt she'd be, till too late.' Maybe this was true. A boy, raised in hard company, often neglected, and possessed by a dream. 'I will try to make it up to her, sir,' he finished.

" 'Well,' I said, 'those of us who guessed have kept quiet, which may count as conniving. Punishment would make Alisa cry more. No society could run for long without a certain amount of hypocrisy to grease the wheels. But you had better justify our estimate of you, Apprentice Ronen.' "

Shaun paused. His glance roved through the pavilion entrance, past the dancing and hallooing, to the sky.

"I didn't spell out that estimate for him," he said. "He needed chastening. But our ship needs more bold, clever rascals than she's got.

"Valdi's rambling about the Fair today, in the middle of all the glamour he ever wished for. I imagine he's observing, too, learning, thinking. I hope so."

Erody's instrument clanged.

Shaun brought his attention back to the people who had come to hear him and began another story.

18.

Fickle as Earth's, because in the narrowness of a ship every inconstancy was a tonic to organisms that evolved on Earth, at present the air through the command center blew slightly chill, wet, tangy with ozone, as if a thunderstorm were approaching. The two persons who stood among instruments and screens gave it no heed, unless subliminally. To one side, enhanced against interior illumination, the cluster burned in splendor. They were also unaware of it. Their eyes were on the view ahead, the stars of their destination.

Nansen spoke slowly, trying for dryness and failing: "There is no more doubt. Here, where the detectors get continuous input— The traces are dying out."

"What?" Kilbirnie whispered.

"It wasn't certain earlier. Therefore Yu and I announced nothing. Perhaps that was a mistake. But . . . throughout the region we're bound for—and the region has shrunk—we're receiving signs of less than a fourth as many ships as we observed at home."

She was mute for a span. The ghost storm gusted around her. A strand of hair fluttered below her headband.

"And that's as of more than three thousand years ago," she said at last. "By now, how many are running?"

" 'Now' means nothing across these distances."

"Oh, but it does, in a way, when we're like this, not hell-driving zero-zero but moving no faster than the stars. . . . Have the instruments looked back at Sol?"

Sol, long since lost in the horde, unrecoverable. "No. Why? We would pick up a few traces at best, voyages that were going on when we left."

Kilbirnie's gaze remained fixed on the screen, as if she refused to yield and look away. "It would be a comfort, though."

"I didn't expect you to need comfort," he said.

She fashioned a rueful smile and turned her head about to regard him. "No, not really. I am taken aback. I hoped we'd find the Yonderfolk in an even bigger and finer bailiwick."

His mouth tried to imitate hers. "We all hoped that." Somberness claimed him. "Perhaps we should not be surprised. They never came to us, did they?"

She strengthened her accent. "Aweel, we still want to ken why."

He nodded. "That's why I invited you here, to tell you first. The news would not daunt you."

"Thank you. Though you're unfair to my shipmates."

"None is a coward, I know. But they had their—their different reasons to come aboard, or their demons. Only you wanted to go purely for the sake of going, the adventure. This will be an unnerving shock to them. We may have to make a new, hard decision. I'd value your advice and support."

The last of any dismay dropped from her. "Losh, no decision to make, no advice or support needed. What's to do but go on—go on and find out?"

"Will you help me? You can hearten them as nobody else could."

Her blue gaze met his and held fast. "I'll help you always, skipper, in any way I can."

Brent and Cleland sat in the second engineer's cabin. It was less individually furnished than others, almost monastic, its principal decoration inactive portraits of his heroes. Currently he was screening Alexander, Charlemagne, and Houghton. A coffeepot stood on the table between the men. They had forgotten about the aroma. Their cups rested half empty, cold.

Brent jabbed a finger at his invited guest. "Extrapolate the data points," he urged. "Every time we stop and take a reading, the traces are more sparse, more closely spaced. Right? Shorter and shorter interstellar passages, fewer and fewer. At this rate, in another month or two we'll register nothing."

Cleland stared beyond him. "And we'll still have two thousand light-years to go," he said dully.

"Yeah. When we arrive, starfaring will be four thousand years dead."

Cleland attempted to square his shoulders. "Unless it's revived."

"How likely is that? What are we going on *for*?"

"To—to learn what happened."

Brent scowled. "We may wish we hadn't."

"What do you mean?"

"Whatever ate that civilization could get us, too. The robots in the cluster— Next time we may not be so lucky."

"It isn't the same situation," Cleland maintained without force. "They have the zero-zero drive yonder."

"Do they yet?"

Brent let the question sink in. Ventilation whirred.

"Well," he said, "I'm glad we've got some weapons." His tone went thoughtful. "And studying the machines we captured, yes, very interesting military potential there."

Cleland winced. "Must you always think about combat?"

"Somebody has to," Brent replied. "Just in case, let's say. And then, when we get back to Earth, what then?"

Again Cleland's look went afar. "Earth," he sighed.

Brent considered him. "You don't really want to continue, do you, Tim?"

Cleland bit his lip.

"You can do your planetology as well a lot closer to home," Brent told him. "Right on Earth, from the databases they must have."

Cleland straightened, met his eyes, and demanded, "Are you saying we should turn back?"

Brent spoke slowly. "Listen. I signed on to get away from the decadence. I thought we'd return with knowledge our race might never otherwise get. With prestige, power. The power to set right what we found that was wrong, and give humans a new start. A long shot, maybe, but I was willing to take it. Now, if all that's ahead of us is the ruins of a dead empire, what can we learn? What's the sense of keeping on? Why not turn back while we can?"

"What difference would that make? W-we've already lost Earth, the Earth we knew."

"It won't grow any less foreign with time. Six thousand years gone isn't as bad as ten thousand." Brent lowered his voice and leaned over the table. "Though the difference to us might be that we save ourselves, save more than our lives."

Cleland blinked. "What do you mean?" he asked once more.

"You should know. Six men, four women. And yours is drifting from you pretty fast, isn't she?"

Cleland bridled. "Wait a minute!"

Brent raised a hand, the peace sign. "No offense, Tim. Think about it, is all. Two years in this Flying Dutchman. In between, five years, if we survive them. What'll that do to our relationships, our morale, our purpose? To us? What'll we be fit for at the end of them?"

"We . . . considered that b-before we set out. Took psych tests, day after day, and got counseling, and— We're educated, mature—"

"And under a stress like nobody else in history. Sure, the doc can prescribe you something that'll make you feel better, but it won't change the causes of the stress. And is it really wise to feel better, when we're running into trouble nobody foresaw and nobody can guess at? Tim, you know me. I'm not panicking. I just ask where courage leaves off and foolhardiness begins. What's the best use for our strength, while we still have it?"

"We promised. We're committed to go on." *Jean is.*

Brent nodded. "So far. Maybe I'm too gloomy. Maybe things will improve. We'll see. Whatever happens, we'll give the ship our loyal service, you and me. But that doesn't mean blind obedience. Keep alert, Tim. Keep thinking."

The meeting had been little more than a formality. All knew beforehand: *Envoy* had passed the last wavefront of light, there was no more spoor of the Yonderfolk ahead, a decision was necessary. Nor was it a surprise when two brought up the idea of turning back—Yu as a suggestion that should be discussed, Ruszek as a profane statement that it was plain common sense. Cleland opened his mouth, glanced at Kilbirnie, and said nothing; he sat hunched. Brent did not bother to speak. Arguments and speculations through the past weeks had eroded any real dispute away. Response was likewise mainly for the record.

Zeyd: "We have a faith to keep."

Dayan: "We need to learn what went wrong. It could be a warning to our kind."

Kilbirnie: "Maybe nothing did. Maybe they've gone on to what's better than aught we know of."

Nansen did not call for a vote. Some things are best left unsaid, however well understood. The gathering dispersed.

Mokoena and Sundaram lingered. The common room felt empty, its color and ornament meaningless, the breeze cold. They stood for a while, side by side, looking into a viewscreen crowded with stars.

"Something better," she said at length. He heard the scorn. "In God's name, what?"

"Perhaps, indeed, in God's name," he answered softly.

She gave him a startled glance. "I beg pardon?"

He smiled the least bit. "Well, it isn't likely a scientific or technological advance, is it? Such as the legendary faster-than-light hyperspatial drive."

She nodded. "I know. I've heard Hanny on the physics of that."

"I should think if it were possible, someone in this vast galaxy would have done it long ago, and we would know."

"They wouldn't necessarily have come to us. Or they might have paid Earth a visit in our prehistory, or be leaving us alone to find our own way, or— Oh, all the old scenarios. Dreams that our race once had. We're awake now. Dreams are brain garbage, best dumped out of memory."

"I don't entirely agree. Never mind. I have proposed another logical point against the idea. You didn't happen to be in that conversation. If faster-than-light travel were developed where zero-zero craft operated, they would immediately be obsolete, and their traces would terminate within a few years. Instead, we have observed a slow dying out."

"Ahead of us. And elsewhere, too, those other far, far scattered regions— as nearly as Wenji and Hanny can tell—" Mokoena took her gaze from the terrible stars. "What do you mean, 'God's name'?"

"Perhaps the Yonderfolk have put their faring behind them, having outgrown it. Perhaps they seek the things of the spirit."

Mokoena shook her head. "I can't believe that, either. I'm sorry, Ajit, but I can't."

"I don't insist on it. Simply a thought."

"Spacefaring *is* a spiritual experience. Selim's right about that. Whatever God there is, if any, we come to know Him best through His works. The grandeur, the wonder—" She shivered. "The hugeness, the inhumanness."

He regarded her soberly. "You are troubled, Mamphela."

"No. Disappointed, but I'll be fine." He saw her head lift athwart the sky. "I came to do science and I will do science."

"Of course. However, what you feel is not disappointment. We have all had time to accept that and carry on. You— I shall not pry."

Now she studied him. The air rustled about them. Reflections off the jewels on the spintree flickered in scraps of color across the bulkheads, tiny, defiant banners.

"You notice more than you let on, don't you?" she said. "More than anyone else, maybe. Do you think I would like to talk? Is that why you stayed behind?"

"I think you deserve the opportunity," he replied. "The choice is yours."

Impulse exploded. "All right. I would. I know you'll respect a confidence. Not that this isn't obvious, probably. It's Lajos. You saw how he stalked out, stiff-legged, his face locked, his fists knotted. He's bound off to get drunk. Not for the first time. Oh, no, not for the first time."

"Is that his way when he is angry or in pain?"

"Yes. Stupid, isn't it?"

"I wouldn't quite say that. He is intelligent, but a very physical man. Among us, he has taken the news the hardest. And he has no one, nothing to lash out at but himself."

"And me. You've only seen him brooding, sulking, foul-tempered. When we're alone in one of our cabins— No, no, never any threat or violence. To me. He hits the metal. He breaks what's breakable, flings it down or crushes it under his heel. He raves and curses till he falls into a snoring sleep. Or he goes slobbery and wants to make love—" Mokoena caught her breath.

"I'm sorry." Her voice had gone harsh. "I shouldn't be angry like this. I should try harder to help him." A plea: "I don't know how. I'm supposed to be the physician, and I can't make him accept any calming medicine. Nor, somehow, can I make myself do it and turn the anger off. It would feel too much like a surrender. So I flare up, and we fight; fight with bitter words and next daywatch with still bitterer silence."

"I daresay his behavior accords ill with your standards."

"Yes." She was objective again. "My upbringing. Not that I've lived by it especially well. In my parents' eyes I was a sinner. That they could forgive me, over and over, made me love them even more. But some of their teaching stayed. Drunkenness has always disgusted me."

"You are not compelled to put up with it."

"No." Her mood went over to sadness. "He is a good man, basically. We used to be happy together, most of the time. Not in love, but we enjoyed each other's company. I shouldn't abandon him. I keep hoping he'll . . . recover. Meanwhile, though, I feel overborne, confined, in a rage."

"Work is often a blessing. How goes your research?"

"Poorly. I can't concentrate. Not that it's anything important. Marking time, maintaining the skills, till we get to where the real work is." A hint of fear: "Will I be fit to do it?"

"I think so. We have months of travel yet. Time for coming to terms with reality, time for healing. You are a good person yourself, Mamphela, and a strong person, and you are able to see things clearly. That is not as common a gift as one would wish. It bears hope with it."

As the slow words flowed, her muscles began to loosen. When Sundaram had finished, Mokoena stood for a minute or two, breathing. Then she said low, with a catch in her tone, "Thank you, Ajit. Already that helps. Thank you."

He smiled. "No thanks are due me. I merely listened."

"You listened in the right way. And— Could we sit down and talk some more? I don't want to impose, but—"

"I shall be honored," he said. His touch on her hand guided her to a chair.

Envoy fared onward, each hour of her nightwatch seven months among the stars.

A park occupied three hundred meters of outer deck circumference. Terraces rose at one end to a flower-surrounded well in the inner deck, on which people lived. Planning, planting, and tending had been the particular, though not exclusive, pleasure of Yu, Mokoena, and Zeyd. To all, the park became a sanctuary.

Fragrance breathed from the well, out into the dim lighting and cool air of a deserted corridor. On the path to it Yu brushed against hollyhocks and lilies gone slumberous. The way down the terraces was broader, moss moist and resilient underfoot. A streamlet wound through rosemary, clover, and pampas grass. It sparkled and trilled where it fell over an edge. Here the overhead illumination was a little more bright than on the upper deck, but still meant for darktime, about like a full Moon above Earth. Glowbulbs set widely apart along the footways gave guidance, muted ruby, emerald, topaz.

The gardens were various, intricately laid out, mostly screened by hedges or vines, so that it was as if a visitor passed from one miniature world to another. Yu chose a track that took her between tall ranks of bamboo to the place she sought: a circle of turf, fringed by the bamboo and by privet and camellias, open to the overhead. At its center lay a pool in which played a fountain.

Yu stopped. A man slumped on a bench. In spite of the dimness she recognized Ruszek's bald head and arrogant mustache—not that she could ever fail to tell her nine shipmates apart. He gripped a bottle.

"Oh," Yu murmured, surprised.

"You, too?" Ruszek called hoarsely. He pondered. "No. You wouldn't come here to get drunk."

"Pardon me." She started to go.

"No, wait," he said. "Please. Don't let me drive you away. I'm harmless."

She couldn't avoid smiling a trifle. "I think I can take your word for that, Lajos."

"I'd like some company. Yours would be very nice. If you can stand it. Though I sus-sus-suppose you came looking for peace and quiet."

"And beauty and memories," she admitted. Compassion mingled with courtesy. "If you wish to talk, by all means let us."

"You are a sweet lady." He beckoned.

She joined him on the bench, keeping well aside. For a span the fountain alone had voice, rushing and splashing, white beneath the gray-indigo false sky. Ruszek held the bottle out to her. She made a fending motion and shook her head. He tilted it and swallowed.

"Forgive me," she ventured, "but is this wise?"

"Who cares?" he growled.

"We do. Your comrades."

"After they've made us gone on to nowhere? And on and on."

"That isn't fair. The nature of our mission may have changed, but they feel it is still our mission."

"Yes, yes. Everybody honest, everybody honorable. Except me. The captain doesn't approve of getting drunk. Mam doesn't. You don't. I've been smuggling flasks out of stores. Bad. Wicked." He glugged.

"Does the new knowledge really make such a difference?"

"You've heard me on the subject. We thought we were bound for another race of starfarers. Now— It'll get skullcrack boring, relics, ruins, tombs, bones. Archeology. Why? We'll never learn anything, not in five years, not in a hundred. And I didn't sign on for archeology."

"It need not be like that at all."

He ignored her rejoinder. "Meanwhile, Earth—Earth may not be completely alien yet. If we went straight home. We might still find taverns and wenches and . . . and bands playing in the street, picnics in the countryside, life not too much changed—if we don't come back too God damn late. But we will. And for what?"

"I am afraid we are already too late."

He squinted at her. "Eh? You've raised the same argument. I heard. I remember how we both tried to convince Hanny Dayan."

Yu shook her head. "You misremember, Lajos. I simply felt that someone should point out the possibility. I know well how faint the hope—even if we started back at once—how faint the hope would be that anything is left of what we knew."

"Your government?" he gibed.

She forgave the cruelty, dismissed it. "Certainly not. It must be extinct, forgotten, like all the troubles that drove some of us to enlist. But so, too, almost certainly, are the things we . . . loved." Staring at the fountain, she folded her hands. The fingers strained against each other. "The land, mountains, rivers, grass, trees, the sea, Earth, maybe they survive. Then they can for another few thousand years. No, we do best to continue."

He rasped forth a sigh. She caught a whiff of gin breath. "The best of a bad bargain. Maybe. At best."

She turned her head to regard him through the deep twilight. "I can imagine why Timothy Cleland and Alvin Brent are less than happy. But you? Frankly, your attitude has astonished me."

"Why? Earth might still be where I could feel—argh, not at home—feel free, able to find my way around and roam and cope, with my enemies gone."

"Was that your reason? Enemies? I thought—you gave us to understand—you joined for the sheer adventure of it, like Jean Kilbirnie."

"Plenty of adventure closer to home. Closer in space and time. Except home got too hot for me."

"You have never said—"

Ruszek drank again. "Nansen knows. I had to explain to him and the board. He was glad to get me. Anyway, he said he was. At least I had space experience, piloting, commanding men, navy and civilian—the Space War— That's why I am the mate, you know. If something happens to him, I won't be the same fine, correct, spit-and-polish kind of gentleman, but I can lead us home. So he used his influence with the directors, and got them to put pressure where it counted, and the authorities didn't bring charges. They stayed quiet. After all, they'd soon be rid of me. Yes, I'm grateful to Ricardo Nansen. In spite of everything, I'll serve him the best way I can." Ruszek brooded. "Shouldn't feel sorry for myself. I'll probably enjoy part of what happens. Maybe most of it. But tonight I want to forget, and Mam will be furious with me and I want to forget that, too."

"You are giving her cause," said Yu sharply.

"I know. And she's giving me cause. She told me, our last fight, if I keep this up, there are other men aboard. For all I know, she's with one of them tonight." Ruszek drank.

"She is a free person. If she does . . . give others some kindness . . . it will somewhat relieve a difficult situation."

Ruszek leered, though he kept his free hand at his side. "You could, too, Wenji."

"We should have been pairs to begin with. But the Foundation had to take whatever qualified persons were available. And it was not a libertine, sex-obsessed era, like some in the past. We ought to be sensible and self-controlled."

Blood had mounted hot into Yu's face. She turned it back to the coolness of the water.

"Later?" Ruszek asked.

Yu hesitated. He had not done or said anything actually offensive, and she didn't want to hurt him. However, this line of thought must stop. She mustered will and sprang to another, stronger question.

"Were you in conflict with the law, then, Lajos? Do you care to discuss it?"

"Nothing crooked!" he barked. "Nothing I'm ashamed of or sorry for."

She recalled her accusers in China. "The self-righteous never regret what they did. I do not say this is true of you. But I do say no man can judge his own case."

"Can a woman?" he retorted. "All right, if you insist. I didn't want to d'sturb anybody. But if you insist."

"I don't—"

His words rushed on, slurred, yet sufficiently organized to show they had long been gestating and now the shell was broken.

"You know my career. Tramped 'round Earth, got into Space Command of th' Western Alliance, got commission, got in trouble, a brawl, broken in rank, got it back, lost it again for in—in-sub-or-dination, didn't re-enlist when my term was up but went to piloting for the Solmetals Consortium.

"Space War broke out, Chinese ship missiled an asteroid base of ours. China not offish'ly *in* war, but I was there, I saw what I saw. Yes, we were shipping out str'tegic materials, but it was lawful. Good friends of mine killed. Couple of them died pretty horribly. Then some of us borrowed an engineering rig and put a big rock on a new orbit. It hit an Asian naval base a year afterward. Demolished it.

"By then Europe had pulled completely out o' the war. The Asians could tell the strike was engineered and'd used European gear. Military denied having anything to do with it. Asians demanded investigation. Europe obliged. Soon whole bloody FN did. My comrades and me, we'd covered our tracks best's we could, but evench'ly we knew they were on our trail. And, yes, we were civilians when we launched that rock.

"We scattered. I got to Nansen and he saved me like I told you. If most of the blame could get shifted onto me, it wouldn't matter, and my friends sh'd get off lightly."

"I am not ashamed!" Ruszek shouted.

Yu shrank from him. "You killed men you never knew," she whispered, "for revenge?"

"It was war. I felt cheerful enough. Even looked forward to this voyage." He sagged. "Shouldn't 'a' said anything, sh'd I? To you espesh'ly. But it happened three thousand years ago, Wenji. Nobody remembers."

"*We* shall."

He nodded, a heavy movement, and spoke more clearly, quietly. "Yes. The news from ahead got me thinking too much, remembering too much. We are all damned to remember, aren't we? They believed in damnation where I am from."

Yu sat silent. The fountain leaped and sang.

"We must forgive," she said at last. "All of us must forgive. We are so alone out here." She rose. "Good night, Lajos." Her tone was gentle. She stroked a hand across the bare head and down a cheek before she left him.

And again two people were in the common room, with another smuggled bottle, this one of champagne and in a refrigerator jacket. Here, too, lay dusk, though lighter, making stars in the viewscreens doubly radiant. Music lilted. Zeyd and Dayan had moved furniture aside to clear a broad space for themselves. They danced over it, an archaic dance that was revived during a wave of historical nostalgia on the Earth of their day, a waltz. As "The Blue Danube" flowed to a close, they laughed aloud.

Disengaging, they looked into one another's eyes. A hint of perspiration shimmered on skin and gave a slight, human pungency. Dayan's hair had become tousled. Half breathless, she said. "We should not be this happy."

"Why not? We celebrate a victory. Foreordained, symbolic, nonetheless a victory."

Her smile sank. "Was it? Not for some of us. And we may be on our way to discovering a cosmic tragedy."

"Maybe we are not," he answered easily. "Who knows? The point is, we will *discover*."

"Yes. That makes up for much."

He bowed. "Not to mention the pleasure en route. The delightful company."

Unable to stay serious, she smiled anew, lowered her head, and gazed up at him through her lashes. "Likewise, kind sir."

Hand in hand they went to the table and refilled their goblets from the bottle, which was already half empty. He raised his. "To us," he proposed. *"Saha wa 'afiah."*

"Mazel tov." Rims clinked.

Sipping, she teased: "You really should not be doing this, should you?"

"You have seen me at dinner. I am not a very good Muslim, I fear."

"But an excellent dancer."

"Thank you, Hanny, dear." He leaned closer. "Dear indeed."

Color came and went and came again across her face. "This nightwatch—oh, it's a night to forget everything else . . . even those stars—"

His months-long siege of her ended as she moved into the circle of his arms.

19.

The clocks in *Envoy* had counted one year and thirty-seven days. By computation she had been under way, including time spent in the normal state, four millennia, nine centuries, fifty-six years, and eight days. Somewhere near the middle of the region she had been seeking, *Envoy* once more halted her zero-zero engine, lowered her defenses, and peered about with every relevant instrument at her command.

Naked vision would have availed little. Stars teemed through crystalline dark. They were no longer in their familiar constellations, though you might have recognized pieces of a few, partial and distorted, in the direction of vanished Sol; but it was hard to pick any array out of such a multitude. The Milky Way still girdled heaven, bayed with the same nebular blacknesses; you had to look closely and remember well if you would find the changes brought by this perspective. Neighbor galaxies glimmered as remote as ever.

Devices capable of registering single photons were soon overflowing with news. When it seemed enough, the ship made a leap of some two hundred astronomical units and repeated the observations. Automated and computer-evaluated, they went quickly. Again she jumped, again, again. Interferometry thus evoked further data. After less than a week, during which some aboard went short on sleep and excitement mounted in everyone, the picture was complete.

Not surprisingly, the region resembled that around Sol. A thirty-parsec radius, the approximate practical limit for the equipment available, defined a sphere containing perhaps ten thousand stars. A thousand or so rated as "Sol-like"—single, main sequence, spectral class from middle F to late K—and therefore prime candidates for closer examination. Fifty-three proved each to have a planet at a distance where it would be reasonable to expect liquid water. Some of those planets were probably giants or otherwise unsuitable. Dayan's team did not spend time on that. Instead, spectroscopy searched out indications of atmospheres in chemical disequilibrium, which ought to betoken life. Identifications were uncertain at greater distances, but within forty light-years it found three.

And this was well out in a spiral arm, where the stars thinned away toward emptiness. Most were crowded close to the galactic nucleus, with a radiation background that made organic evolution unlikely almost to the point of unthinkability. Life must be rare in the universe, hardly ever burgeoning into sentience, and the chance of a high technology vanishingly small.

Notwithstanding, when *Envoy* left Sol humans had found spoor of four spacefaring civilizations, widely separated. More must exist, their traces hidden by the dust clouds around the nucleus—unless all had perished by now. So enormous is the number of the stars.

When knowledge is slight, making every action a gamble, you play the odds, as nearly as you can judge them. One sun with a presumably life-bearing planet was a middle-aged G8 dwarf, less bright than Sol but virtually a twin of Tau Ceti, twenty-seven light-years from *Envoy*'s last stop. With a short burst of plasma drive, she aimed her velocity at it. The interstellar crossing took two of her days.

It ended at a distance of nine astronomical units. She could have come somewhat closer before getting so far down in the sun's gravity well that zero-zero was forbidden. The maneuvers would have been trickier than they were worth. She simply trudged ahead on jets, correcting her vectors as she accelerated toward rendezvous, reversing herself at midpoint and braking. At one-half *g*, a compromise between impatience and reaction-mass economy, the passage took a pair of weeks. Nobody commented on the irony. Well before *Envoy* left home, starfarers had grumbled it threadbare.

Dayan returned from the reserve saloon-galley bearing a tray with a teapot, two cups, and a few cookies. She set it down on a tiny table unfolded at the middle of the cabin and herself on her bunk alongside. Yu already sat on the one opposite. Dayan poured. "Here," she said. "To steal a phrase from an old book I once read, the cup that cheers but does not inebriate. Unfortunately."

"Thank you." The engineer sipped. "It's good."

"Anything would be, wouldn't it, at this stage of things?"

Dayan gestured about her. The low, cramped space held the table, a cabinet, and two curtained bunks tiered on either side. Doors at the foot ends gave on a corridor, barely wide enough for one person to squeeze past another, and on the bath cubicle shared with the men, whose dormitory lay beyond. Except for the captain, the men were worse off than the women, since an extra bunk had had to be fitted in. Again the crew perforce spent most of their waking hours in the saloon-galley, which offered screens, games, and a few hobby materials, or in the exercise chamber, where workouts were possible if they didn't require much room. Such were conditions on the gimballed decks.

"I'm not complaining," Dayan added quickly. "But I am glad we could get together for a while by ourselves, Wenji, and speak our minds without worrying what someone will think." They had done that off and on since Jerusalem.

"I imagine Selim feels restricted, too," Yu remarked, slyly demure.

Dayan laughed. "Yes, poor man. Jean says she's seen him paw the deck and puff steam when I pass by."

"Jean has a lively imagination."

"She calls it second sight. Looking through that suave mask of his."

"I daresay you have grown a little frustrated yourself."

"More than a little, sometimes."

Yu turned serious. "You two do seem happy together."

Dayan glanced away. "Well, he is a—a charming and interesting fellow, as we know. His travels on Earth, his culture and— A first-class lover." Her fair skin pinkened.

"Do you think the relationship will become permanent?"

"I don't know," Dayan answered slowly. "Neither does he. Who can tell—out here? For now, we feel lucky."

"May you always be, Hanny."

The hazel eyes swung back to meet the brown. "And you, Wenji, dear. May you be lucky again."

"I am. I have memories."

Dayan hesitated before plunging ahead. "Will you be content with that, for the rest of your life?"

Yu cradled her teacup as if to draw warmth from it and breath from the rising fragrance. "I may have to be."

"You're over your grief, that mourning you tried to keep hidden. Surely you are. You're a healthy young human being."

Yu spoke mildly, almost matter-of-factly. "But who else is there? With due respect, also for your Selim, Hanny, who among them could I compare to my Xi?"

Again Dayan paused. "Ricardo Nansen?" She sounded half reluctant.

Yu nodded. Light from overhead rippled over her midnight hair. "He is a remarkable person, yes. But he is . . . distant. When he smiles, how often does it come from within?"

"He's the captain. He thinks—I believe he thinks he has to be our impersonal father figure."

"He may well be right."

A rueful smile flitted over Dayan's lips. "Pity. I confess to occasional thoughts of my own."

"Jean has them, too, I suspect."

"I know she does."

"Poor Tim."

"Not inevitably. He's too shy and socially inept, but he may learn better."

"Devotion like his should count for something."

"M-m, that's a handicap, I think. For Jean, it must be like having a large, clumsy puppy always bumbling after her and staring with wetly reverent eyes. He actually has a wide range of interests, you know. I wish they hadn't come to include Al Brent's theories, but that's probably *faute de mieux*," Dayan observed parenthetically. "Tim is quite attractive when he relaxes and is himself. The problem is, he can't in Jean's presence, at least when he's sober. But do you remember our Apollo Day party, when he'd had an extra drink or two, and the songs he got to singing?"

Yu giggled. "How could I forget? I still blush. But they *were* comical."

"If someone seduced him, it might work wonders," Dayan speculated. "It might also make Jean take a new look at him."

The blunt pragmatism embarrassed Yu. She retreated to her cup before she replied, "Who should that be? I like him, but no."

"I, too, of course. Neither of us is the sort who can handle something like that well, especially so as not to leave wounds. Mam?"

"I—I don't believe she would, either, even as a kindness. Lajos—"

"They don't sleep together any longer. No, I have not snooped. That would be practically criminal, here aboard ship, wouldn't it? But I am not blind, either. Nor are you."

"He has stopped drinking heavily."

"Was he? I thought so, but couldn't be sure. That would explain the estrangement. Did Mam tell you?"

"No." Yu did not elaborate. "He is a—a warrior without a battle."

"What Al Brent imagines he himself is," Dayan said tartly.

Yu's tone was more sympathetic. "It may be true. Lajos, however—a man of action, condemned to what he feared would be inaction. And with memories harder to bear than he knew, than he admitted to himself until lately." Dayan refrained from asking for details. "Now, when he may soon have a challenge, a use for his strength, he stays fit to meet it."

"And she may take him back?"

"Who knows? Does she? At any rate, I do not imagine she will choose to do anything soon that would make the situation more tangled."

Yu drained her cup and set it down hard; the tray rattled. "Isn't this ridiculous?" she exclaimed. "Here we are, crossing the cosmos, bound into mystery, and we sit and gossip like village wives about petty sexual problems, things we already know and things we should not pry into. Are we really so shallow?"

Dayan smiled. "I'm not geared to be forever the pure scientist and bold explorer. Every once in a while I want some girl talk."

Yu returned the smile, wistfully. "Well, I also. Humans, apes. We do not groom each other with fingers. We use words. But it is the same instinct."

Dayan nodded. The red locks stirred on her shoulders. "We are what we are. Maybe we do our great things not in spite of, but because of it."

Save for lacking a moon, this planet, even more than the one in the cluster, recalled Earth, blue laced with white clouds, lands ruddy-brown on shining oceans, ice caps whitening the poles. Studies revealed unlikenesses in mass, axial inclination, rotation period, precise atmospheric composition, spectra and therefore composition of vegetable life—on and on, a catalogue that was never completed. They did not lessen the beauty.

They did not lessen the revelation. Down on the ground stood buildings, and artifacts more enigmatic: about a score of groupings spread around the globe, untenanted, often overgrown, like the relics of the other spacefaring age at the other world. These, though, were not wreckage; time had not much gnawed at their clear, strange lineaments.

It was as if an angel had unsealed and opened a book in a language none could read—yet.

Envoy lay in low orbit. Instruments would search and probe, machines descend on sampling expeditions, more machines analyze, computers and brains sift the data for meaning, before any human set foot on yonder soil. None would, were it deemed too hazardous. The crew accepted this. It was standard exploratory doctrine. For the time being, they had ample fascination of discovery, and the space and comfort of their regular decks.

Dayan finished helping Yu prepare an observer assembly and returned to quarters. She found Zeyd at prayer, prostrated toward a Mecca he could not face and that by now perhaps existed only in his heart. Respectful, she waited till he was done. Then, as he looked up, she grinned and jerked a thumb at the bed. He laughed and scrambled to his feet.

Mokoena knelt in prayer of her own. From a simulation of stained glass above the altar in the little Christian chapel, Jesus smiled down at her. She whispered not to him but to the spirits of her kinfolk, should they survive and remember her, using the dear tongue of her childhood. Afterward she walked to the park and worked with the flowers. Poor things, two weeks aslant had not been easy on them, and though robotic service was adequate, they must have missed the touch of living hands.

Brent looked his fill at the planet, sought his cabin, and bioconnected. In full-sensory, interactive simulation, hardly distinguishable from reality if he avoided thinking about it, the program sent him riding and conquering beside Pizarro.

Cleland busied himself in the flood of information. For this while he was quite happy.

Sundaram savored the view of the world outside.

Nansen sat in his own cabin. It was no different from the rest, spacious, with a sliding partition that could divide it in two and a bath cubicle. Furnishings were likewise the same, chairs with lockable gripfeet, bed convertible to double width, built-in cabinets and large desk, viewscreen and computer terminal and virtuality unit and other standard items. His possessions made it his. On the deck he had laid down a multicolored carpet from the *estancia* of his family. Crossed sabers hung on a bulkhead. Framed opposite was a faded photograph of an ancestor, Don Lucas Nansen Ochoa. Picture screens displayed views from parts of the Earth he had known, mostly still although in one grass billowed and trees tossed on the plains of home. Another, currently reproducing Monet's *La Meule de Foin*, seemed no less alive. Shelves held a few mementos from planets where he had walked, together with a codex Spanish Bible. Otherwise the ship's database could provide him with anything he might want to read or watch or listen to. Most of humankind's entire culture as of the year of departure was in it.

He sat at the desk, beneath a small ancient crucifix, fashioning a statuette of a horse. It reared, mane and tail flying. Once he might have gone on to cast it in bronze, but here he must be content with the clay. It gave beneath his fingers, stiffly voluptuous.

The door chimed. "Open," he bade it, and turned around.

Kilbirnie stood clad in shorts and skinshirt. "Hi," she greeted. "Are you busy?"

"Not to notice." He rose and approached. "What can I do for you?"

"Well, I thought I'd be appallingly brutal to a handball. We've been cramped such a long time. But I can't find anybody who wants to play. Are you interested, skipper?"

The wide white smile suggested that she had not tried very hard. He considered for a moment, then said, "I would be delighted. Let me change clothes."

He ducked behind the partition. She wandered about. It was not her first visit—everybody came now and then, for this or that reason—but three of the scenes were newly on display, a Parisian sidewalk café, a toucan perched on a tree she did not recognize, the view forward from the tiller of a sailboat heeling to a hard wind. She gestured at them as he came back. "Are these from your personal life?" she asked.

"Yes, recordings that happened to come out well," he answered. "Souvenirs."

"I have some myself."

He did not respond to the implied invitation. They went forth.

Their game was brisk and merry. At the far end of the gymnasium, Ruszek silently and doggedly lifted weights. To them he seemed askew, for the chamber was so long that its curvature neared the bounds of sight. Markings on the deck, hoops and whirlers on the bulkheads, assorted equipment in the corners, gave a wide choice of exercise or sport.

After a while Nansen and Kilbirnie were ready for a breather. Sweat sheened on her skin, darkened her shirt, and livened the air around her. Beneath a headband, the light brown hair was in elflocks. "What's got Hanny so excited?" she asked out of nowhere.

Caught off balance, he replied awkwardly, which was unusual for him, "Why, what—what makes you suppose she is?"

"I know her. And I saw you and her huddled together, buzzing. You're excited, too, skipper."

He cast a glance toward Ruszek and lowered his voice, though the other man was out of ready earshot. "A . . . preliminary indication. Possibly false. We shouldn't make any announcement before it's confirmed."

She quivered. "Aw, come on. I won't wilt if it turns out negative. Nor will I blather."

"The scientific tradition," Nansen said. "One does not publish until one is reasonably sure of one's results."

Kilbirnie looked aside, as if outward to the stars. She laughed. "Publish, here? Skipper, I've said it before, pomposity does not become you." He flinched just enough for her to see. She touched his arm. Admiration abruptly colored her words. "Yes, you do maintain traditions."

He yielded. "Well, if you promise not to tell or hint—"

"I do. I'd never break a promise to you."

"It is possible—it will take time and effort, given the low signal-to-noise ratio, and it may prove to be nothing more than a normal variation in the background count—it is possible that Dr. Dayan has acquired a nonstellar source of neutrinos. Within this region. But it is only a—it could be only a blip. She has not placed the source, if it is a source, more closely than several arc minutes."

Kilbirnie whistled.

Then she said, "Aweel, maybe no muckle surprise. I didna believe a civilization that went starfaring could die just overnight. I didna care to believe that." She looked up at him. "If 'tis true, will we go there?"

"Of course," he said. "Remember, though, confirmation—or disconfirmation—will take time. Meanwhile we should investigate what is here. If nothing else, it may give us some pertinent information."

"Aye." Eagerness flared. "If only we can land, our own selves!"

"I hope so." Nansen's eyes shifted from hers. He forced them back. "You understand, do you not, in that case Pilot Ruszek goes first? We cannot risk both boats, and he is senior."

"Give him that," she agreed. "He needs it. Just don't keep me waiting too long, please."

"You are patient, Pilot Kilbirnie."

"Not very. But I understand."

"Thank you."

"And you—" It burst from her. "You're a saint."

"What? *Disparate.* Nonsense."

A sudden intensity pressed at him. "You want to go yourself, don't you? The way you once did. Now you're the captain, and the captain does not personally make exploratory flights."

"Well, when we find the Yonderfolk, if we do, that may be different."

Her smile gave way to something like tenderness. "It matters tremendously to you, this, doesn't it?"

"To our whole race," he said. "Otherwise why would I have accepted the mission? Alienation after my few short voyages wasn't reason enough."

Kilbirnie's head drooped a little. "Alienation. When we come back, will they care?"

"I like to imagine they will. That whatever they have become, we'll bring back what will make them care."

"Knowledge?"

"Yes, but more. New arts, new ways of thinking and feeling and living." All at once, though his demeanor stayed calm and his arms remained at his sides, he spoke more passionately than she had ever heard him do. "Creativity was dying in humans, before we left, before we were born. The modes were exhausted. Nothing original was being done. Science and technology were on a plateau, with no higher ranges in sight. Government, political and social thought, was devolving through Caesarism toward feudalism. Yes, one could paint in the manner of Rembrandt or Renoir, compose in the manner of Bach or Beethoven, write in the manner of Tolstoy or Joyce, and many did, but what was new, where were the fresh worlds? Yes, the fractal school sparked artists for a while, but it depended on machines, and it, too, was sinking down into sterile self-imitation. Perhaps colony planets have begotten dynamic civilizations, perhaps humans have met aliens who inspire them, but if not, or even if so, the works of an old and great foreign society would give us a renaissance."

He stopped.

"You've never said much about that," Kilbirnie murmured.

"No, I did not want to lecture." Nansen half smiled. "My hobbyhorse ran away with me. I'm sorry."

"Is enthusiasm unbecoming Don Ricardo, *el Capitán* Nansen? I do wish you'd open up more, skipper."

He eased. "Oh, come, now. I am not—what is the word?—not that standoffish."

"Prove it."

"How?"

"Well," she purred, "you did say something once about teaching me an old South American dance."

20.

Cast free, *Herald* drifted out between the wheels, in the harsh radiance of the sun and soft glow of the planet. When she was safely clear of her mother ship, Kilbirnie swung her into the proper orientation and wakened the jets.

From low orbit she fell swiftly. The globe before her—huge, blue and tawny under marbling clouds, rimmed with night—swelled, was no longer ahead but below, an ocean and a land. A shrilling of cloven air grew into thunders. The boat bucked and shuddered; heat blinded the viewscreens with fire.

Slowed, though still ahurtle, she came through that barrier and her riders saw a mountain range sweep far beneath them and fall behind. Kilbirnie's fingers gave commands. Wings and empennage, folded into the hull, molecularly remembered their former shapes and deployed. Under the wings were two airjet engines. The shock as they hit atmosphere at this speed thudded through metal and bones. "Hee-yi!" she shouted, and started the motors. The boat leaped. Hills, amber with forest, reached after her. The target site rushed over the horizon, a thinly vegetated mesa without too many boulders. Braking in a roar, Kilbirnie turned the nose aloft, extended the landing jacks, and set down with a flourish.

Ears rang in the sudden quietness.

"Merciful God, Jean," Mokoena gasped. "Did you *have* to arrive like that?"

Cleland chuckled. "Her style, Mam. How well I've learned. Don't worry. She and I are both alive yet."

Kilbirnie had already unharnessed. She bounced up. "What are we biding for?" she cried. "Out wi' ye, slowbellies!"

There was indeed no reason to linger. Zeyd, analyzing specimens in his quarantine laboratory, had found no danger of infection; the life, proteins in water solution, was otherwise too different from Earth's. Observation from orbit had revealed few large animals and no sentient inhabitants—only the relics of them. Then Ruszek in *Courier* had shown it was safe to land.

Just the same, explorers had better be careful. Poisonous leaves and stings were simply among the obvious possibilities. The three emerged in boots, hooded coveralls, and gloves. The equipment they carried included firearms and medical kits.

For minutes they stood silent, breathing wonder. Weight was noticeably lessened and the air blew mountain-top thin under a sky of deeper blue than Earth's. It was hot and laden with odors, some spicy, some suggestive of wet iron. The fronded blades that sprang from the soil, a few centimeters high, were yellow. The membranous foliage(?) on the oddly shaped trees(?) that covered the downslope and the surrounding hills was in darker shades of that color. Tiny creatures flitted by, gauzy-winged, bright as burnished copper.

"People could live here," Cleland said at last, as if he needed to break the spell with any banality that came to hand.

"People did," Mokoena replied. "Not our kind, but people."

Kilbirnie brought a portable transmitter to her lips. "We're about to go for a preliminary look," she told Nansen. *Envoy* would soon swing past the horizon, but had planted relays in orbit.

She put the transmitter back at her hip and strode off. "Poor skipper," she murmured. As pilot, she should perhaps have stayed at the boat, like Nansen in the ship. However, she had argued successfully that Ruszek could descend in *Courier* at short notice if need be, and remote-steer *Herald* into space. The contingency seemed remote. Meanwhile, a third member of the scouting party might make a sudden critical difference.

They walked to the rim of the mesa and stared outward. The hair stirred on Cleland's and Kilbirnie's arms. Below them a valley widened off into distance. Through the leafage down there they glimpsed bright hues and sharp edges, walls. Farther off, several scattered towers reared twenty or thirty meters above the forest, iridescent and lacily graceful where ivylike growth had not overrun them. The wilderness was reclaiming what dwellers had forsaken—when, why?

Sonoptics on shoulders whirred, swung to and fro, recording, recording.

"The Cold Lairs," Kilbirnie whispered.

"What?" asked Cleland.

"From an old book the skipper screened for me. Come." She took the lead. He bit his lip and followed. Mokoena brought up the rear, alert for whatever might strike from that direction.

Nothing did. The descent was easy and the woods below free of underbrush; apparently a dense buff turf prevented its growth. Footfalls muffled, the band went on through sun-flecked shade, welcome after the heat in the open, among convoluted trunks that divided into over-arching withes. The flyers dazzled about. Sometimes something croaked or trilled somewhere in the depths.

Mokoena's voice rang startlingly loud. "Hold! Wait!"

Her companions turned. She pointed. Her hand trembled. "Look," she said.

A cluster of shrubs(?) filled a glade. They grew about a meter tall, branching and rebranching, sprouting three-pointed leaves that might have fluttered in the winds of Earth except for the rich red-brown hue. White petals graced many twigs.

"Odd, aye," Kilbirnie said. "But isn't everything, to us?"

"Not like this." The biologist stepped over and fingered a blade. "Nothing like what we have seen."

"Well, a planet, a whole world," Cleland reminded. "You'd expect variety. On Earth you can find, oh, a palm, a cactus, and a mesquite on the same plot."

"Plot. . . . I have a feeling this isn't natural. We must take samples back for Selim, of course, but I suspect he'll discover it isn't native life. Introduced. From the home of the Yonderfolk?"

"Like us planting grass and roses on new planets. . . . Did they?"

"Come along, come along," Kilbirnie urged. "This is very interesting, but what we want is artifacts, pictures, any clues to the builders we can get."

"Life here—a whole evolution, billions of years, and then invasion—" With a wrenching effort, Mokoena set off again after her team.

Cleland stopped next. "One moment," he begged, and scuttled aside. The woman watched him peer at a porous grayish boulder of his own height, run fingers across it, strike off a piece with the geologist's hammer at his belt, and turn it over and over beneath his eyes.

"What's the matter?" Kilbirnie demanded.

He sighed and returned. "That rock," he said. "Looks volcanic, though extraordinarily large for its type, but it's isolated and I'd swear there's been no volcanism in this area for an era at least. I'd dearly love to know how it got here. Some peculiar geological process? This globe's dynamics must be similar to Earth's, but can hardly be identical. Maybe, even, it hasn't had what we could rightly call eras and periods and epochs. . . . Or was this a biological product, like chalk formations at home?"

"I doubt you will ever know," said Mokoena.

He nodded. "Our time here is so pathetically short."

Kilbirnie tossed her head. "Aye, but 'tis a way station for the treasure we do seek. Come along, noo."

Aboard ship they gathered in assembly.

Dayan stood and related, "It seems clear. We have the data, better astronomy than before for this vicinity, indisputable identification of the neutrino flux associated with fusion power plants, and preliminary triangulation. The Yonderfolk, or at any rate *a* high-tech civilization, are in that direction"—her forefinger jabbed at a point on a bulkhead—"about a hundred light-years off. As we get closer, we should be able to pinpoint the location."

Breathless silence, until Sundaram inquired, "Isn't that well off from what was formerly the center of interstellar activity?"

"Yes, rather," Dayan agreed.

"We assumed the civilization would expand outward more or less radially," Yu added. "That was merely an assumption."

"The astronomy we've been doing may well explain the facts," Dayan said. "Late G and early K stars happen to be more concentrated there than elsewhere. That strongly supports the idea of the original sun being of that type, and should narrow our search down considerably. I venture to guess that we'll find it in another month or two, less if we're lucky."

"Hurrah!" Zeyd cheered.

Down in the empty settlement, where a receiver was tuned in, Kilbirnie whooped, "Hallelujah!" and danced on a terrace in front of strange images.

Before Envoy left orbit, her crew festooned the gymnasium with ribbons and ornaments, set up the equipment they would want, and held a celebration. A table stood crowded with potables and canapés; the nanos could replace everything consumed. Folk mingled, drank, talked, laughed. Presently some offered performances on an erected stage. Yu shyly recited a few translations of poetry she had done. Dayan rendered a couple of rousing soldier songs. Cleland and Ruszek joined to give rowdier ones.

Music pulsed and wailed. Clad in archaic costumes which a couturier program had made according to his orders, Nansen and Kilbirnie did a tango. As he watched the sensuous steps and gestures, Cleland's merriment left him.

The rest applauded. Nansen smiled and bowed. Kilbirnie blew a kiss. They rejoined the audience.

The room darkened. The stage alone was lighted, a flickering red and yellow light like flames. Projected on the rear bulkhead, shadowy figures swayed and stamped, ghost spears shook above phantom shields. Mokoena trod forth, plumes on her head, a grass skirt around her waist, lightning-jagged lines of paint white across her skin. The sound of whistles, drums, and deep-voiced chanting came with her. She raised her arms and began to dance as her people had danced long ago. She was the lion, the elephant, the fire loose on a dry veldt, the onrushing horde of lean warriors, the death, and the triumphant scorning of it.

When she was done and illumination returned, her shipmates stood mute for a span before they clapped and shouted. Most then sought the table, much wanting a drink.

Mokoena returned to the deck. Sweat glistened on her face and over her breasts. Brent intercepted her. "Mam, that was superb," he declared.

She stopped. "Thank you."

"The power and the—yes, a lot of subtlety, too— That was a strong culture."

Her expression changed. "You admire strength above all else, don't you?"

"You must yourself, the show you gave."

"It was history. Or romance." Her mood brightened. "I gather you think well of your own ancestors, but would you really like to run through the swamps, dyed blue?"

"No, of course not. But they, and yours, had something our countries have lost—had lost—and sorely needed."

"Strength? Is it, by itself, that important?"

"When you get down to the basics, what else do we survive by?"

"Honor. Kindness."

"They aren't easy. They take strength."

"You have always felt you had to be strong, haven't you?" she murmured. "Strong to stand against disappointment, hostility, loneliness. To go on this ship in a forlorn hope of bringing a destiny back to Earth."

"I'm not convinced the hope is forlorn. Besides, that phrase properly means, meant, a military detachment. South African, in fact."

"You and your military!" Mokoena laughed. "We're in serious danger of getting serious."

He smiled stiffly. "Sorry. Bad habit of mine."

"Let's suppress it." She gave him her arm. They went to the table, poured champagne, and touched goblets.

Later, having changed back to conventional party garb, she led him through several ballroom dances and foolish, funny games. Ruszek joined in, once with her; they exchanged a few friendly words. He seemed cheerful enough and drank, if not quite in moderation, not to excess. The other women found themselves once more enjoying his slightly raffish company. He twirled his mustache at them, paid compliments, told anecdotes that might or might not be true, cracked jokes, all without either person pretending it could lead to anything.

The celebration began to ebb. Sundaram was first to leave, then Zeyd and Dayan went out together. Brent and Mokoena lingered near the door, talking. They had shared more of their lives in the past several hours—nothing very intimate, but more—than ever before.

"This has been a great evening, Mam," he said at the end. "For me anyway."

"Yes," she agreed, "good for everybody." Her lips formed the words, not in English: "Almost everybody."

"Would you, uh, would you like to continue?"

She looked to the corner where Ruszek was in conversation with Nansen and Kilbirnie. Cleland stood aside, unspeaking. Ruszek's glance strayed her way for a second. She brought hers back to Brent.

"No, thank you, Al," she said gently.

His fists doubled. His features tightened. "On his account? You and he've broken up."

To mention something so personal, uninvited, was a bad breach of the tacit code aboard. Mokoena overlooked it. "That is too hard a word. We agreed we'd do best to separate until . . . circumstances change, if ever. For one thing, the relationship was complicating my role as physician. Work goes easier when I am free. Life does." Perhaps she would have been less frank if she had emptied fewer glasses, or perhaps she carefully decided to tell him what she did. He didn't stop to think which.

"Free!" he exclaimed. "Then why not—tonight, anyway?"

"No, Al. I could not do that."

The hope died behind his eyes. "To him?"

"To you," she answered. "Good night." She went away, out into the corridor.

Envoy departed. The weeks of confinement under boost did not seem overly long to most of her crew.

Still, occasionally the mood sobered. Sundaram and Ruszek played a game of chess in the saloon. They were often together these days. The linguist's quiet, unofficious counsel, a few techniques of meditation he explained, or simply his presence had helped the mate back to emotional balance. Ruszek won the game. "I didn't expect that," he confessed.

"You underestimate yourself, my friend," Sundaram said.

"No, I don't. If this had been poker I'd have cleaned you down to your naked bones, but here I just meant to pass the time and maybe sharpen my skill a little. You weren't paying attention."

"Forgive me. My mind does wander. The Yonderfolk—how we shall communicate with them—what happened to their starfaring."

"I wonder more what has been happening at home," Ruszek said.

The monorail set Kenri Shaun and his fellows off at the edge of Kith Town. There the buildings were low and peak-roofed, mostly houses. Clustered together, they seemed dark beneath the towers and lights that surrounded them; it was as if they sheltered night and quietness from the city.

For a minute the group stood silent. They all knew Kenri's intention, but they didn't know what to say.

He took an initiative of sorts. "Well, I'll be seeing you."

"Oh, sure," replied Graf Kishna. "We'll be here for months."

After another pause he said, "We'll miss you when we do go. I, uh, I wish you'd change your mind."

"No," replied Kenri. "I'm staying. But thanks."

"Let's get together again soon. For a game of comet's tail, maybe."

"Good idea. Let's."

Graf's hand briefly cupped Kenri's elbow, one of the Kith gestures that said more than speech ever could. "Well, good night."

"Good night."

The rest mumbled likewise. They stood a few seconds more, half a dozen young men in the loose blue doublets, baggy trousers, and soft shoes current among the local lower class. Folk costume was inadvisable in public. They themselves bore a certain similarity, too, short and slender build, olive complexion, features tending to high cheekbones and curving nose. Stance and gait marked them out even more, nowadays on Earth.

Abruptly their group dissolved and they went their separate ways. Kenri started down Aldebaran Street. A cold gust hit him; the northern hemisphere was spinning into autumn. He hunched his shoulders and jammed hands in pockets.

Kith Town thoroughfares were narrow strips of indurite, lighted by obsolete glowglobes. You wanted to come home to a place as familiar as possible, never mind how outmoded. Houses sat well back, lawns around them, often a tree or two close by. Not many people were out. An elderly officer walked grave in mantle and hood; a boy and girl went hand in hand; several children, not yet ready for bed, rollicked, their laughter chiming through the stillness, above the background rumble of the city. Some of those children were born a hundred or more years ago and had looked upon worlds whose suns were faint stars in this sky. Generally, though, buildings lay vacant, tended by machines. Except for a few permanent residents, the owner families were gone decades on end, only present here between voyages. A few houses would never know another return. Those families, those ships, no longer fared.

Passing the Errifrans residence, he wondered when he'd see Jong. They'd had fun together at such times as their vessels met. The *Golden Flyer* had last set course for Aerie, and should be well on her way Earthward by now. Since the next trip that Kenri's *Fleetwing* made would just be to Aurora, there was a fair chance that the two would take Solar orbit within the same period— *No, wait, I'm staying on Earth. I'll be old when Jong Errifrans arrives, still young, still with a guitar on his knee and jollity on his lips. I won't be Kith anymore.*

It happened that three starcraft besides *Fleetwing* were currently in, *Flying Cloud*, *High Barbaree*, and *Princess Karen*. That was uncommon. Kith Town would see one supernova of a Fair. Kenri wished he could take part. Oh, he could, when he wasn't engaged elsewhere, but he wouldn't feel right about it. Nor would it be wise. The polite among the Freeborn would raise their brows; the uninhibited would say, maybe to his face, that this showed he was and would always be a—tumy, was that the latest word for a Kithperson?

"Good evening, Kenri Shaun."

He stopped, jerked from his reverie. Street light fell wan over the black hair and slim, decorously gowned form of the woman who had hailed him. "Good evening to you, Theye Barinn," he said. "What a pleasure. I haven't see you for—two personal years, I think."

"Slightly less time for me." It had been on Feng Huang, whence *Fleetwing* and *High Barbaree* went to different destinations before making for Sol. She smiled. "Too long, though. Where have you been hiding?"

"A party of us had to boat to Mars directly after our ship got in. Her mainframe navigator needed a new data processor. The Earth dealer told us he'd stopped carrying that type." *We suspect he lied. He didn't want to do business with tumies.* "We found one on Mars, brought it back, and installed it. Didn't finish till today, and then, groundside, we had to go through two hours' worth of admission procedures. Never did before."

"I knew that. I asked your parents why you weren't with them. But I—

they supposed you'd be finished sooner. Didn't you get"—she paused—
"impatient?"

"Yes." Feverishly. For Nivala, awaiting him. "The ship came first,
however."

"Of course. You were best qualified for the job."

"My father's handling my share of sales for me. I don't like that much,
anyway, and I'm not very good at it."

"No, you're born an explorer, Kenri."

Chatter, monkey noises, keeping me from Nivala. He couldn't simply
break off. Theye was a friend. Once he'd thought she might become more.

She continued quickly: "On the surface, things haven't changed a lot
since last I was here. The same Dominancy, the same buildings and technology and languages. More hectic, maybe. Not that I've ventured to see
for myself. I take my impressions from the news and entertainment
shows."

"You're probably well advised. I hear they're clamping down on us."

She flinched. The gladness fled her. "Yes. So far we're being denied
permission to hold the Fair anywhere outdoors. And we have to wear a
badge everywhere except the Town."

Is that what that "special pass" business was about? he wondered. *We
didn't want to make the spaceport official surlier by asking.* Nor did he
now care to inquire, partly because of the tears he saw glint in her eyes.

Her mouth quivered. She reached a hand toward him. "Kenri, is it true?
I've heard rumors, but I didn't feel I . . . ought to ask your parents—"

"About what?" He wished immediately that he hadn't snapped.

"You'll resign? Quit the Kith? Become an Earthling?"

"We can discuss that later." He couldn't hold down the harshness. "I'm
sorry, but I haven't time this evening."

She pulled her hand back.

"Good night, Theye," he said more amicably.

"Good night," she whispered.

He saluted again and strode off, fast, not looking back. Light and
shadow slid over him. His footfalls rustled.

Nivala waited. He would see her tonight. Somehow, just then, he
couldn't feel quite happy about it.

✳

She had stood alone in a common room, looking at the stars in the
viewscreen, and the illumination from overhead had been cool in her
hair. Glimpsing her as he passed by, he entered quietly. What a wonder
she was. A millennium ago, such tall, slender blondes had been rare on
Earth. If the genetic adaptors of the Dominancy had done nothing else,
they should be remembered with thanks for having re-created her kind.

Keen-sensed, she heard and turned about. The silver-blue eyes
widened and her lips parted, half covered by a hand. He thought what a

beautiful thing a woman's hand was, set beside the knobbly, hairy paw of a man. "Oh," she said. Her voice was like song. "You startled me, Kenri Shaun."

"Apologies, Freelady."

Since he had had no reason to come in—none that he could tell her—he felt breathtakingly relieved when she simply smiled. "No harm done. I'm too nervous."

An opening for talk! "Is something the matter, Freelady? Anything I—anybody can help with?"

"No." And, "Thank you," she added. "Everyone is already very helpful." They'd better be, with a passenger of her status. However, these first two daycycles of the voyage she'd been courteous, and he expected she'd continue that way. "It's a sense of "—she hesitated, which wasn't like a Star-Free—"isolation."

"It's unfortunate that we are an alien people to you, Freelady." *Social inferiors. Or worse. Though you haven't treated me so.*

She smiled again. "No, the differences are interesting." The smile died. "I shouldn't admit this." Her fingers brushed across his for a bare moment that he never forgot. "I should have grown used to it, outbound. And now I'm headed home. But the thought that . . . more than half a century will have passed . . . is coming home to *me*."

He had merely clichés for response. "Time dilation, Freelady. People you knew will have aged." *Or died.* "But the Peace of the Dominancy still holds, I'm sure." *All too sure.*

"Yes, no doubt I can take up my life as it was. If I want to." Her gaze went back to the blackness; stars and nebulae and cold galactic river. She shivered slightly under the thin blue chiton. "Time, space, strangeness. Perhaps it's that—I fell to thinking—I'll make the crossing in practically the same time as before, over the same distance, as far as the universe is concerned—except that it isn't concerned, it doesn't care, doesn't know we ever existed—" She caught her breath. "And yet the return will take nine days longer than the going did."

He took refuge in facts. "That's because we're rather heavily laden, Freelady, which *Eagle* wasn't. Our gamma factor is down to about three hundred and fifty." *Not that it ever gets much above four hundred. We merchantmen are not legendary* Envoy. *It isn't necessary for us, it wouldn't pay; and maybe even we Kithfolk have lost the vision.* Kenri put the thought from him. It spooked too often through his head.

For a while they stood wordless. Ventilation hummed, as if the ship talked to herself. Nivala had once wondered aloud how a vessel felt, what it was like to be forever a wanderer through foreign skies. He hadn't actually needed to explain, as he did, that the computers and robots lacked consciousness. She knew; this was a passing fancy. But it stayed with him, having been hers.

Nor did she now resent his pointing out an obvious technicality. She looked at him again. A breeze brought him a faint, wild trace of her perfume. "The time is more frightening than the space," she said low. "Yes, a single light-year's too huge for our imagining. But I can't really grasp that you were born eight hundred years ago, Kenri Shaun, and you'll be traveling between the stars when I'm dust."

He could have seized the chance to pay a compliment. His tongue locked on him. He was a starfarer, a Kithman, belonging to nowhere and to no one except his ship, while she was Star-Free, unspecialized genius, at the top of the Dominancy's genetic peerage. The best he could do was: "The life spans we experience will be similar, Freelady. One measure of time is as valid as another. Elementary relativity."

She cast the mood from her. It could not have gone very deep. "Well, I never was good at physics," she laughed. "We leave that to Star-A and Norm-A types."

The remark slapped him in the face. *Yes, brain work and muscle work are the same. Work. Let the suboptimals sweat. Star-Frees shall concentrate on being aesthetic and ornamental.*

She saw. He had not had much occasion to conceal his feelings. Abruptly, amazingly, she caught his right hand in both hers. "I'm sorry," she said. "I didn't mean to—I didn't mean what you think."

"It's nothing, Freelady," he answered out of his bewilderment.

"Oh, it's much." Her eyes looked straight into his, enormous. "I know how many people on Earth dislike yours, Kenri. You don't fit in, you speak among each other of things unknown to us, you bring wares and data we want and drive hard bargains for them, you question what we take for granted—you're living question marks and make us uncomfortable." The pale cheeks had colored. She glanced down. Her lashes were long and sooty black. "But I know a superior type when I meet one. You could be a Star-Free, too, Kenri. If we didn't bore you."

"Never that, Freelady!"

They didn't pursue the matter and he soon left her, with trumpets calling in him. *Three months,* he thought. *Three ship months to Sol.*

※

A maple stirred overhead as he turned at the Shaun gate, its leaves crackling in the wind. The street lighting didn't do justice to their scarlet. *Early frost this year,* he guessed. The wind blew chill and damp, bearing autumnal odors, smoke from traditional hearthfires, cuttings and soil in gardens. He realized suddenly what had seldom come to mind, that he had never been here during a winter. He had never known the vast hush of snowfall.

Light poured warm and yellow from windows. The door scanned and recognized him. It opened. When he walked into the small, cluttered living room, he caught a lingering whiff of dinner and regretted arriving too late. He'd eaten at the spaceport, and not badly, but that was tech food. His mother cooked.

He saluted his parents according to custom and propriety. His father nodded with equal restraint. His mother cast dignity aside, hugged him, and said how thin he'd gotten. "Come, dear, I'll fix you a sandwich. Welcome home."

"I haven't time," he replied. Helplessly: "I'd like to, but, well, I have to go out again."

"Theye Barinn was asking about you," she said, elaborately casual. "The *High Barbaree* came in two months ago."

"Yes, I know. And we happened to meet on my way here."

"How nice. Are you going to call on her this evening?"

"Some other time."

"Her ship will leave before ours, do you know? You won't see her for years. Unless . . ." The voice trailed off. *Unless you marry her. She's your sort, Kenri. She'd do well aboard* Fleetwing. *She'd give you fine children.*

"Some other time," he repeated, sorry for the brusqueness; but Nivala expected him. "Dad, what's this about badges?"

Wolden Shaun grimaced. "A new tax on us," he said. "No, worse than a tax. We have to wear them everywhere outside the Town, and pay through the nose for them. May every official of the Dominancy end in a leaky spacesuit with a plugged sanitor."

"My group got passes at the spaceport, but we were told they were just for transit to here. Can I borrow yours tonight? I have to go into the city."

Wolden gazed for a while at his only son before he turned around. "It's in my study," he said. "Come along."

The room was crammed with his mementos. That sword had been given him by an armorer on Marduk, a four-armed creature who became his friend. That picture was a view from a moon of Osiris, frozen gases like amber in the glow of the mighty planet. Those horns were from a hunting trip on Rama, in the days of his youth. That graceful, enigmatic statuette had been a god on Dagon. Wolden's close-cropped gray head bent over his desk as he fumbled among papers. He preferred them to a keyboard for composing the autobiography that officers were supposed to bequeath to their ships' databases.

"Do you really mean to go through with this resignation?" he asked.

Kenri's face heated. "Yes. I hate to hurt you and Mother, but— Yes."

Wolden found what he was searching for. He let it lie. Face and tone kept the calm suitable to his rank. "I've seen others do it, mainly on colony planets but a couple of times on Earth. As far as I could learn afterward, mostly they prospered. But I suspect none of them were ever very happy."

"I wonder," said Kenri.

"In view of the conditions we've found here, the captain and mates are seriously considering a change of plans. Next voyage not to Aurora, but a long excursion. Long, including into regions new to us. We may not be back for a thousand years. There'll be no more Dominancy. Your name will be forgotten."

Kenri spoke around a thickness in his throat. "Sir, we don't know what things will be like then. Isn't it better to take what good there is while we can?"

"Do you truly hope to join the highborn? What's great about them? I've seen fifteen hundred years of history, and this is one of the bad times. It will get worse."

Kenri didn't respond.

"That girl could as well be of a different species, son," Wolden said. "She's a Star-Free. You're a dirty little tumy."

Kenri could not meet his gaze. "Spacefarers have gone terrestrial before. They've founded lasting families."

"That was then."

"I'm not afraid. Sir, may I have the badge?"

Wolden sighed. "We won't leave for at least six months—longer, if we do decide on a far-space run and need to make extra preparations. I can hope meanwhile you'll change your mind."

"I might," said Kenri. *And now I'm lying to you, Dad, Dad, who sang me old songs when I was little and guided my first extravehicular excursion and stood by me so proudly on my thirteenth birthday when I took the Oath.*

"Here." Wolden gave him the intertwined loops of black cords. He pulled a wallet from a drawer. "And here are five hundred decards of your money. Your account's at fifty thousand and will go higher, but don't let this get stolen." Bitterness spat: "Why give an Earthling anything for nothing?" He clamped composure back down on himself.

"Thank you, sir." Kenri touched the badge to his left breast. Molecules clung. It wasn't heavy but it felt like a stone. He sheered off from that *Fifty thousand decards! What to buy? Stuff we can trade—*

No. He was staying here. He'd need advice about Earthside investments. Money was an antidote to prejudice, wasn't it?

"I'll be back—well, maybe not till tomorrow," he said. "Thanks again. Good night."

"Good night, son."

Kenri returned to the living room, paused to give his mother a hug, and went out into the darkness of Earth.

※

At first neither had been impressed. Captain Seralpin had told Kenri: "We'll have a passenger, going back to Sol. She's on Morgana. Take a boat and fetch her."

"Sir?" asked astonishment. "A passenger? Have we ever carried any?"

"Rarely. Last was before you were born. Nearly always a round trip, of course. Who'd want to spend ten, twenty, fifty years waiting for a return connection? This is a special case."

"Does the captain wish to explain?"

"I'd better. At ease. Sit down." Seralpin gestured. Kenri took a chair facing the desk. They were groundside on Maia. The Kith maintained offices in Landfall, the planet's principal town. Sunlight streamed in through an open window, together with subarctic warmth and a cinnamonlike odor from a stand of native silvercane.

"After I got the word, naturally I searched out everything I could about her," Seralpin said. "She's the Freelady Nivala Tersis from Canda. An ancestor of hers acquired large holdings on Morgana in pioneering days. The family still draws a fair amount of income from the property, though she's the first of them to visit it since then. Evidently she—or rather, no doubt, an agent of hers—made inquiries at Kith Town and learned what the current arrangements, schedules, were for 61 Virginis."

"Current" is not exactly the word, passed through Kenri. *We're talking about a span of several centuries. But no, that's by cosmic time. To Kithfolk, not very many years. And "schedule" is pretty vague, too, the more so when fewer ships ply the lanes now than once did.*

"You can see how it worked out," Seralpin went on. "Given the existing agreement on trade circuits, she could take *Eagle* here, knowing *Polaris* and *Fleetwing* would call within about a year of her arrival before proceeding to Sol. *Fleetwing* happened to make port first, and she's ready to go, so we'll take her." Seralpin paused. "I can't say I'm overjoyed. However, she'll pay well, and you don't refuse a person of that status. Not if you want to stay in business at Earth."

"Why would anybody like that ever come, sir?"

Seralpin shrugged. "Officially, to inspect the holdings and collect data, with a view to possible improvement of operations. Actually, I imagine, for the thrill and glory. How many in her circle have gone beyond the Solar System? She'll be a glamour figure for a while, till the next fad comes along."

"Um, uh, maybe she's serious, sir. At least partly. She's taking some risk and making some sacrifice. She can't be sure what things will be like when she returns, except that everybody she knew will be aging or dead."

"So much the better," replied Seralpin cynically. "New fashions, new amusements, and new young people. Liberation from boredom. She spent her time on this planet till lately, and only then popped over to Morgana. Now she wants back, though she knows we won't leave for weeks."

"Well, sir, Morgana's not humanly habitable. Those valuable biochemicals can be repulsive-looking, or dangerous, in their native state."

Seralpin grinned. "That's why I picked you to fetch her. You're an idealist who wants to believe the best about his fellow human beings. You should get along with her and not have to swallow as much rage as most of us would." He turned solemn. "Make sure you do get along. Be super-respectful and obliging. She's not ordinary upper class, she's a Star-Free."

Thus it came about that Kenri Shaun piloted a boat to the neighbor planet. At the present configuration, a one-gravity boost took four days. He spent some of the time rigging a private section for the guest, though it left scant room for him, and arranging the minor luxuries that his mother had suggested he lay in. Afterward he was largely at the reader screen, continuing his study of Murinn's *General Cosmology*. He couldn't win promotions if he didn't have that material firmly in his head.

But must he accept it as the absolute last word? True, there hadn't been any fundamental change since Olivares and his colleagues worked out their unified physics. Everything since had been details, empirical discoveries, perhaps surprising but never basic. After all, went the argument, the universe is finite, therefore the scientific horizon must be, too. Where a quantitative explanation of some phenomenon is lacking—biological, sociological, psychological, or whatever—that is merely because the complexity makes it unfeasible to solve the Grand Equation for this particular case.

Kenri had his doubts. Already he had seen too much of the cosmos to keep unqualified faith in man's ability to understand it. His attitude was not unique among his folk. When they mentioned it to an Earthling, they generally got a blank look or a superior smile. . . . Well, science was a social enterprise. Maybe someday a new civilization would want to ask new questions. Maybe there would still be some Kith ships.

He set down on Rodan Spacefield and took the slideway into Northport. The hot, greenish rain sluicing over the transparent tube would have poisoned him. Though its machines kept it clean, a subtle shabbiness had crept into the Far Frontier Hotel. Partly that was because of the plantationers drinking in the lounge. They weren't rowdy, but lives as lonely as theirs didn't make for social graces.

Hence Kenri's surprise approached shock when he entered the suite and found a beautiful young woman. He recovered, bowed with arms crossed on breast, and introduced himself humbly. That was the prescribed way for one of his station to address one of hers, according to the latest information from the laser newsbeams.

"Greeting, Ensign," she replied. Her language hadn't changed a great deal since he had learned it. She got his rank wrong; he didn't venture to correct her. "Let's be on our way."

"Immediately, Freelady?" He'd hoped for a day or two in which he could relax, stretch his muscles, go someplace other than the boat.

"I'm weary of this dreary. My baggage is in the next room, packed. You should be able to carry it."

He managed a smile. At the craft, he managed an apology for her cramped, austere quarters. "That's all right," she said. "The ferry out was no better. I called for a ship's boat for the sake of trying something different."

After they had lifted, settled into steady boost, and unharnessed, she glanced at her timepiece. "Hu, how late," she said. "Don't worry about dinner. I've eaten and now want to go to bed. I'll have breakfast at, um, 0900 hours."

But then she surprised him anew. Having stood pensive a moment, she looked in his direction and the blue gaze was by no means unfriendly. "I forgot. You must be on quite another cycle. What time is it by your clocks? I should start adapting."

"We have four days for that," he replied. "The first breakfast shall be when the Freelady wishes." It was not convenient for him, but somehow he did not now resent it.

Emerging from his berth after a few hours' sleep, he was again surprised by finding her already up. Her tunic would have been provocative were they of equal status. As it was, he merely admired the view. She had started his readscreen, evidently curious to know what interested him, and sat pondering Murinn's text. She nodded at his salutation and said, "I don't understand a word of this. Does he ever use one syllable where six will do?"

"He cared for precision, Freelady," answered Kenri. On impulse: "I would have liked to know him."

"You people do a lot of reading, don't you?"

"Plenty of time for that in space, Freelady. Of course, we have other recreations as well. And communal activities, such as educating the children." He wouldn't discuss the rituals with an Earthling.

"Children— Do you truly need hundreds in a crew?"

"No, no. Uh, Freelady. When we're on a planet, though, we often need many hands." *And all want to travel, to walk on those worlds. It's in our blood.*

She nodded. "M'hm. Also, the only way to keep a family, no? To keep your whole culture alive."

He stiffened. "Yes, Freelady." What business was it of hers?

"I like your Town," she said. "I used to go there. It's—quaint? Like a bit of the past, not virtual but real."

Sure. Your sort come to stare. You walk around drunk, and peek into our homes, and when an old man goes by you remark what a funny little geezer he is, without bothering to lower your voices, and when you haggle with a shopkeeper and he tries to get a fair price you tell each other how this proves we think of nothing but money. Sure, we're happy to have you visit us. "Yes, Freelady."

She looked hurt. A while after breakfast she withdrew behind her screen. He heard her playing a portable polymusicon. He didn't recognize the melody. It must be very old, and yet it was young and tender and trustful, everything that was dear in humankind.

When she stopped he felt an irrational desire to impress her. The Kith had their own tunes, and many were also ancient. Equally archaic was the instrument he took forth, a guitar. He tuned it, strummed a few chords, and left his mind drift. Presently he began to sing.

"When Jerry Clawson was a baby
On his mother's knee in old Kentuck,
He said, 'I'm gonna ride those deep-space rockets
Till the bones in my body turn to dust.'—"

He sensed her come out and stand behind him, but pretended not to. Instead he regarded the stars.

"—Jerry's voice came o'er the speaker:
'Cut your cable and go free.
On full thrust, she's blown more shielding.
Radiation's got to me.

" 'Take the boats in safety Earthward.
Tell the Blue Star Line for me
I was born with deep space calling.
Now in space forevermore I'll be.' "

He ended with a crash of strings, turned his head, and rose.

"No, sit down," she said before he could bow. "We're not on Earth. What was that song?"

" 'Jerry Clawson,' Freelady," he replied. "A translation from the original English. It goes back to the days of purely interplanetary flight."

Star-Frees were supposed to be intellectuals as well as aesthetes. He waited for her to say that somebody ought to collect Kith folk ballads in a database.

"I like it," she said. "Very much."

He glanced away. "Thank you, Freelady. May I make bold to ask what you were playing?"

"Oh, . . . that's even older. 'Sheep May Safely Graze.' By a man named Bach." A slow smile crossed her lips. "I would have liked to know him."

He raised his eyes to hers. They did not speak for what seemed a long while.

✳

Kith Town lay in a bad district. It didn't always. Kenri remembered a peaceful lower-class neighborhood; his parents had told him of bourgeoisie; his grandparents—whom he had never met, because they retired from starfaring before he was born and were therefore centuries dead—had spoken of bustling commerce; before the city was, Kith Town stood alone. Forever it remained Kith Town, well-nigh changeless.

No, probably not forever, the way the traffic was dwindling. Nor really changeless. Sometimes war had swept through, pockmarking walls and strewing streets with corpses; sometimes a mob had come looting and beating; often in the last several Earthside lifetimes, officers had swaggered in to enforce some new proclamation. Kenri shivered in the autumn wind and walked fast. He'd learned that nowadays, except for where the monorail from the spaceport stopped, there was no public transport within three kilometers.

Light became harsh as he entered the Earthling neighborhood, glare from side panels and overhead fixtures. He had heard this was decreed less to discourage crime than to keep it in its place, under surveillance. Vehicles were few. Inhabitants slouched, shambled, shuffled along littered walkways between grimy façades. Their garments were sleazy and they stank. Most of them were loose-genes, but he saw the dull, heavy faces of Normal-Ds among them, or the more alert countenance of a Normal-C or B. Twice a Standard thrust them aside as he hastened on his errand, ashine in the livery of the state or a private master. Then Kenri imagined he saw an electric flickering in the eyes around. Though still ignorant of current politics, he had caught mention of ambitious Dominants who were courting the poor and disinherited. Yes, and the Martians were restless, and the Radiant of Jupiter openly insolent. . . .

But the state should be more or less stable through his and Nivala's lifetime, and they could make provision for their children.

An elbow jabbed his ribs. "Out o' the way, tumy!"

He tensed but stepped off the walk. The man strutted on by. As Kenri went back, a woman, leaning fat and frowzy from a second-floor window, jeered at him and spat. He dodged, but could not dodge the laughter that yelped around him.

Has it gotten this bad? he thought. *Well, maybe they're taking out on us what they don't yet dare say to the overlords.*

The long view gave thin consolation. He felt shivery and nauseated. And the sadness in his father and mother— Though Nivala awaited him, he needed a drink. A lightsign bottle winked above a doorway ahead.

He entered. Gloom and sour smells closed in on him. A few sullen men slumped at tables. A mural above them jerked through its obscenities. A raddled Standard-D girl smiled at him, saw his features and badge, and turned away with a sniff.

A live bartender presided. He gave the newcomer a glazed stare. "Vodzan," Kenri said. "Make it a double."

"We don't serve no tumies here," said the bartender.

Kenri sucked in a breath. He started to go. A hand touched his arm. "Just a minute, spaceman," said a soft voice; and to the attendant: "One double vodzan."

"I told you—"

"This is for me, Ilm. I can give it to anyone I want. I can pour it on the floor if I so desire. Or over you."

The bartender went quickly off to his bottles.

Kenri looked into a hairless, dead-white face. The skull behind had a rakish cast. The lean gray-clad form sat hunched at the bar, one hand idly rolling dice from a cup, scooping them up, and rolling again. The fingers had no bones, they were small tentacles, and the eyes were cat yellow, all iris and slit pupil.

"Uh, thank you, sir," Kenri stammered in bewilderment. "May I pay—"

"No. On me." The other accepted the goblet and handed it over. He put no money down. "Here."

"Your health, sir," Kenri said, emboldened. He lifted the vessel and drank. The liquor burned his throat.

"Such as it is," said the man indifferently. "No trouble to me." He was doubtless a petty criminal of some sort, maybe an assassin, if that guild still flourished. His somatype was not quite human. He must be Special-X, created for a particular job or for study or for fun. Presumably he'd been released when his master was done with him, and had ended in the slums.

"Been away long?" he asked, his gaze on the dice.

Kenri couldn't immediately remember. "About a hundred years." Or more?

"Watch out. They really hate Kithfolk these days. Hereabouts, anyhow. If you get slugged or robbed, it'll do you no good complaining to the militia. You'd probably get your butt kicked."

"It's kind of you—"

"Nothing." The supple fingers gathered the dice, rattled them in the cup, and tossed. "I like having somebody to feel superior to."

"Oh." Kenri set the goblet down. "I see. Well—"

"No, don't go." The yellow eyes lifted toward his and, astonished, he saw tears glimmer. "I'm sorry. Sometimes the bitterness breaks loose. No offense to you. I tried to sign on as a spaceman once. Naturally, they wouldn't have me."

Kenri found no response.

"A single voyage would have been enough," said the X dully. "Can't an Earthling dream, too, now and then? But I realize I'd have been useless. And my looks. Underdogs don't like each other."

Kenri winced.

"Maybe I shouldn't envy you at that," the X muttered. "You see too much history. Me, I've made my place. I don't do badly. As for whether it's worth the trouble, staying alive—" He shrugged. "I'm not, anyway. A man's only alive when he has something bigger than himself to live and die for. Oh, well." He rolled the dice. "Nine. I'm losing my touch." After a moment: "I know a place where they don't care who you are if you've got money."

"Thank you, sir, but I've an appointment," Kenri said. How awkward it sounded. And false, in spite of being true.

"I thought so. Go ahead." The X glanced elsewhere.

"Thank you for the drink, sir."

"Nothing. Come in whenever you want. I'll tell Ilm to remember you and serve you. I'm here pretty often. But don't yarn to me about the worlds out there. I don't want to hear that."

"No, sir. Thank you. Good night." Kenri left most of his drink untasted. As he went out, the dice clattered across the bar again.

✳

While she waited on Maia for *Fleetwing*'s departure, Nivala had taken the opportunity to see the Tirian Desert. She could have had her pick of the colony for escorts, but when she heard that Kenri had been there before and knew his way around it, she named him. Less annoyed than he would have expected, he dropped promising negotiations for vivagems and made the arrangements. An aircamper brought them to the best site. He had proposed that from this base they tour the area for two days, overnighting here in between. She readily agreed, though they'd be alone. Both knew he wouldn't touch her without leave, and to a person of her status scandal was as irrelevant as the weather on another planet.

For a while they rode quietly in the groundcar he had rented. Stone and sand stretched around them, flamboyantly colored. Crags lifted from the hills in fantastic shapes. Scattered thornbush breathed a slight peppery odor into thin, cool air. Overhead the sky arched cloudless, royal blue.

"This is a marvelous world," she said at last. "It's just as well we're leaving soon. I might come to like it too much."

"Aside from the scenery, Freelady, I should think you'd find it rather unexciting," Kenri ventured. "Hardly even provincial."

The fair head shook. "Things here are real. People have hopes."

He didn't know what to say to that.

After a few more minutes she murmured thoughtfully, "I envy you, Kenri Shaun. All that you've seen and done. That you will see and do. Thank you for the data your ships bring. Infinitely better than any fiction or . . . entertainment. On Earth I spent much of my virtuality time playing Kith documentaries—riding along with you like a ghost. You live it."

The wistfulness made him feel he could ask: "Was that why you came here, Freelady?"

She nodded. "Yes. Inspecting the property was an excuse. Worth doing, but an agent, or perhaps even a robot, could have done it better. I wanted the experience. A taste of the reality."

He thought of weeks and months on end in a flying metal cave, of huddling in a groundside shelter while deadliness raged outside, of toil and danger, hurt and death—fleeting days of friendship, and then your friends were gone on their next voyage and you wondered if you'd ever meet them again; sometimes you didn't, and then maybe you wondered how they had come to die. "Reality doesn't always taste good, Freelady."

"I know. Because it is reality. But I didn't quite know how hungry I was till I made this trip."

The words stayed with him. When they returned to camp he suggested that he build a fire and cook their evening meal over it, primitive style. Her delight chimed in him.

The sun set while he worked. A small, hasty moon rose, nearly full, to join the lesser half-disk already aloft, and argency rippled over the dunes. Afar a creature wailed—a hunting song? Warmly clad, they squatted close to the fire. Flamelight and shadow played across her, and her hair seemed as frosty as her breath. "Can I help?" she offered.

"It isn't fitting, Freelady." *You'd make a mess of it.* The filets in the skillet sizzled, savory-smelling. They were natural food, purchased at a waterfarm.

She regarded them. "I didn't think you people ate fish," she said.

By now he knew she didn't intend any condescension. "Some do, some don't, Freelady. You've seen we grow fruits and vegetables aboard, along with flowers, more for the sake of the gardening than to supplement the nanosystems; and we often have aquariums, also mainly for pleasure but sometimes for a special meal. In early days, when ships were smaller, an aquarium would have crowded out a substantial piece of garden for the benefit of a very few. Crews couldn't afford the resentment that would cause. Abstention acquired almost the force of a taboo. Even offship; it was a symbolic act of loyalty. Nowadays, mostly, only older folk observe it."

She smiled. "I see. Fascinating. One doesn't think of the Kith as having a history. You've always simply *been*."

"Oh, we do, Freelady. Maybe we have more history and tradition than anybody else." He considered. "Or maybe it's just that we pay more attention to what we have, study and talk about it more. Another thing that helps hold us together, keep us what we are."

Her gaze dwelt on him through the smoke, above the sputtering flames. "And it's an intellectual activity, isn't it?" she said. "You Kithfolk are a brainy lot."

His cheeks grew warm. He concentrated on his cooking. "You flatter us, Freelady. We're not exactly Star-Frees."

"No, you're more whole." She jumped back toward impersonality; it was safer. "I did do research on you before leaving Earth. Spacefolk always had to be intelligent, with quick reactions but stable personalities. It was best they not be too big, physically, but they must be tough. Dark skin gives some protection against soft radiation, though I suppose genetic drift, happenstance, has been at work, too. Over generations, those who couldn't fit into your difficult life dropped out. The time factor, and the widening cultural gap, made recruitment more and more unlikely, till now it's essentially impossible. And we have the race of starfarers."

"Not really, Freelady," he protested. "Anybody who wants to can build a ship and flit away. But it's a big investment, of lifetime still more than capital, for small profit or none; so nobody does. We, though—we never attempt the kind of voyage they embarked on aboard *Envoy*, before there ever was a Kith." *Does that name mean anything to you?*

*And the profits shrink century by century, as demand shrinks; and so
we do not replace our losses any longer, and our numbers grow less
and less.*

"Small profit or none? No, you gain your lives, the freedom to be what
you are," she said. "Except on Earth— You're aliens there; because the
profit *is* small, you have to set high prices; you obey our laws, but you
don't submit in your hearts; and so you come to be hated. I've wondered
why you don't abandon Earth altogether."

The idea had passed through his mind occasionally. *Veer off. Don't
speak it.* Dangerous, also to his soul. "Earth is our planet too, Freelady.
We get by. Please don't feel sorry for us."

"A stiff-necked people," she said. "You don't even want pity."

"Who does, Freelady?" He laid her meal on a plate and handed it
to her.

✳

Where the slum ended, Kenri found a monorail nexus and took an ascensor up to the line he wanted. Nobody else boarded the car that stopped
for him and nobody else was on it. He sat down and looked out the
canopy. The view speeding past was undeniably superb. Towers soared in
columns and tiers and pinnacles; streets and skyways glowed, phospho-
rescent spiderwebs; lights blazed and flashed in strings, arcs, fountains,
every color eyes could know; scraps of dark sky heightened the brilliance. Was any world anywhere more exotic? Surely he could spend a
lifetime exploring this, with Nivala for guide.

As he neared city center, the car paused to admit four young persons.
They were Frees, he saw, though styles of appearance and behavior had
changed. Filmy cloaks streamed from luminous draperies or skintights;
jewels glittered in headbands; men sported elaborately curled short
beards, women wore twinkling lights in flowing hair. Kenri hunched in
his seat, acutely aware of his drabness.

The couples came down the aisle toward him. "Oh, look, a tumy,"
cried a girl.

"He's got a nerve," said a boy. "I'll order him off."

"No, Scanish." The second female voice sounded gentler than the first.
"He has the right."

"He shouldn't have. I know these tumies. Give 'em a finger and they'll
take your whole arm." The four passed by and settled behind Kenri. They
left three rows vacant between themselves and him. Their conversation
still reached his ears.

"My father's in Transsolar Trading. He'll tell you."

"Don't, Scanish. He's listening."

"Well, I hope he gets a potful."

"Never mind," said the other boy. "What'll we do tonight? Haven't settled that yet, have we? Go to Halgor's?"

"Ah, we've been there a hundred times. How 'bout we hop over to Zanthu? I know a place there, not virtual, realies, it's got apparatuses and tricks you never—"

"No, I'm not in that kind of mood. I don't know what I want to do."

"My nerves have been terrible lately. I think they're trying to tell me something. I refuse medication. I might try this new Yanist religion. It should at least be amusing."

"Say, have you heard about Marli's latest? Who was seen coming out of her bedroom?"

Ignore them, Kenri thought. *They may be of Nivala's class, but they're not of her kind. She's a from Canda. An old family, proud, the blood of soldiers in them.*

A Kithman's not too unlike a soldier.

Their building loomed into view, stone and crystal and light mounting heavenward. Their crest flamed on its front. The depression that had dogged him let go. He signaled his stop and rose. *She loves me,* sang within him. *We have a life before us.*

Pain stabbed into his right buttock, through his back and down the leg. He stumbled, fell to a knee, and looked around. A boy grinned and waved a shockstick. Everybody began to laugh. He picked himself up and limped to the exit. The laughter followed him.

*

Aboard ship he served in the navigation department. Ordinarily one person was plenty to stand watch in the immensity between suns. The room was big, however. With interior illumination dimmed, it became a twilit grotto where instrument panels shone like muted lamps. The viewscreens dominated it, fireballs fore and aft, sparks streaming from them across the dark to melt into a girdle of intermingled keen hues. Air moved inaudibly; it was as if the ship kept silence before that sight.

When Nivala came in, Kenri forgot to bow. His heart sprang, his breath stopped. She wore a long, close-fitting blue gown, which rustled to her stride. The unbound tresses fell over bare shoulders in waves of pale gold.

She halted. Her eyes widened. A hand went to her mouth. "O-o-o-oh," she whispered.

"Weird, isn't it?" was the lame best he found to say. "But you've surely seen pictures and virtuals."

"Yes. Not like this. Not at all like this. It's nearly terrifying."

He went to stand before her. "An optical effect, you know, Freelady. The system here doesn't process photons captured in the instants between zero-zero jumps. It displays the scene during the jumps, when we're moving close to the speed of light. Aberration displaces the stars in the field, Doppler shift changes their colors. Among other things, these readings help us monitor our vectors."

He was suddenly afraid he had sounded patronizing, afraid not that she would be angry but that she would think him a pedantic fool. Instead, she smiled and looked from the sky to him. "Yes, I do know. Thank you for trying to reassure me with a lecture, but it wasn't necessary." Seriousness returned. "I misspoke myself. I should have said 'overawing.' The other face of the universe, and I'm not being shown it, I'm meeting it."

"I'm, uh, glad you like it."

"A passenger, like a child, wasn't allowed in vital sections on *Eagle,*" she said. *And you didn't use your status to force your way in,* he thought. "Thank you for inviting me."

"My pleasure, Freelady. I knew you wouldn't do anything stupid."

"It was good of you, Kenri Shaun." Her fingers brushed his knuckles. "You're always kind to me."

"Could anybody be anything else, to you?" he blurted.

Did she blush? He couldn't tell, in this dusk he had made for her to get the most from the spectacle. She eased him when she said merely, slowly, "I'd be interested to hear what you do at your post."

"Usually not much," he admitted. "The computer handles the data; the navigator's in case of emergency. But need for a human can arise. No two routes are ever identical, you see, because the stars move—not negligibly in the course of centuries. Likewise dark dwarf nebulae, black holes, or rogue planets. They're extremely few and far between, but for that very reason they haven't all been identified, and encountering any would be fatal. Comparing the high-velocity and low-velocity starscapes gives clues to possible hazards ahead—spectral absorption lines or gravitational lensings, for instance. But interpreting them can take more, well, creative imagination than a computer program has. Twice in my time, a navigator's called for a course change. And, oftener, he or she's decided it wasn't necessary, the alarm was false."

"So that's your work here, Kenri Shaun?" She smiled anew. "Yes, I can well picture you, with that funny tight expression, as if the problem were your personal enemy. Then you sigh, rumple your hair, and put your feet on the desk to think for a while. Am I right?"

"How did you guess, Freelady?" he asked, astounded.

"I've thought about you quite a lot lately." She stared away from him, at the lurid blue-white clustering ahead.

Her fists doubled. "I wish you didn't make me feel so futile," she gasped.

"*You*—"

She spoke fast. The words blurred on her lips. "I've said it before. This is life, this is reality. It's not about what to wear for dinner and who was seen where with whom and what to do tonight when you're too restless and unhappy to stay home. It's not about traffic in goods and information, either. The laser beams only bring news from the settled worlds, and only what the senders choose to transmit. You bring us the news from beyond. You keep alive—in some of us—our kinship with the stars. Oh, I envy you, Kenri Shaun. I wish I were born into the Kith."

"Freelady—"

She shook her head. "No use. Even if a ship would have me, I couldn't go. I'm too late. I don't have the skills or the character or the tradition that you took in with your mother's milk. No, forget it, Nivala Tersis from Canda." She blinked at tears. "When I get home, knowing now what you are in the Kith, will I try to help you? Will I work for common decency toward your people? No. I'll realize it's useless. I won't have the stubbornness. The courage."

"Don't say that, Freelady," he begged. "You would be wasting your effort."

"No doubt," she said. "You're right, as usual. But in my place, you would try!"

They looked at one another.

That was the first time she kissed him.

✳

The guards at the main entrance were giants bred, 230 centimeters of thick bone and boulderlike muscle. Their uniforms were sunburst splendor. Yet they were not ornaments. Stunners and fulgurators rested at their hips. A monogrammed plate in the paving between them could withdraw to let a cycler gun rise.

Kenri's pain had subsided to a background ache. He approached fast, stopped, and craned his neck upward. "The Freelady Nivala from Canda is expecting me," he said.

"Huh?" exploded a basso. "You sold your brain, tumy?"

Kenri extended the card she had given him. "Scan this." He decided it was wise to add, "Please."

"They've got a party going."

"I know." *When I called her confidential number, she told me. I'd have waited till tomorrow, but she insisted this is actually a chance we should seize. Don't hang back, Shaun. She's counting on you.*

The titans exchanged a glance. He guessed their thoughts. *Could it be a stunt, a farce for the guests? Or could he be a secret agent or something? If he's lying, do we arrest him or pulp him here and now?* The one who held the card put it in a scanner. The screen came alight. He read, shook his head, and gave the card back. "All right," he grumbled. "Go on in. First ascensor to your left, sixtieth floor. But watch yourself, tumy."

It'd be pleasant, later, to summon him and make him crawl. No. Why? Kenri passed under the enormous curve of the doorway, into a vaulted reach of foyer where murals displayed bygone battles and honors. Most of that history had happened within his lifetime. Uniformed

Standard servants goggled at him but drew aside, as if from his touch. He stepped onto the ascensor and punched for 60. It lifted into the shaft through a stillness beneath which his heartbeat racketed.

He emerged in an anteroom of crimson biofabric. More servants struggled not to gape. An arch gave him a view of motion, dance, a blaze of color. Music, talk, sporadic laughter bubbled out. As he neared, a foot man mustered decision and blocked his way. "You can't go in there!"

"I certainly can." Kenri flashed the card and walked around him. Radiance poured from faceted crystals. The ballroom was huge and thronged. Dancers, waiters, performers— He stopped in confusion.

"Kenri! Oh, Kenri, dearest!"

Nivala must have been keeping herself nearby, alert for his arrival. She ran straight to his arms. He wondered for a second whether that was shamelessness or ordinary upper-class behavior these days. Then they were embraced and kissing. Her misty cloak swirled about them. Her perfume smelled like roses.

She drew back. Her smile trembled away. He saw that she'd lost weight, and shadows lay below the silver-blue eyes. It struck him in the gut: *This past couple of weeks, since* Fleetwing *took orbit, were worse for her than for me.* "Maybe I'd better go," he said.

"Not now," she answered, stammeringly urgent. "I—I hoped you'd land earlier, but w-we have to meet them sooner or later, and a bold stroke— Come." She caught his hand and tugged. With forlorn gaiety: "I want them to see the man I've got me."

Side by side, they advanced. The dancers were stopping, pair after pair, awareness spreading like a wave from a cast stone, turning faces and faces and faces around. Voices choked off. The music persisted. It sounded tinny.

Nivala led Kenri to a dais. They mounted it. A troupe of erotic performers scampered aside. She lifted her head and beckoned to the amplifier pickup. Her voice rang as loud as the voice of some ancient storm goddess. "Stars and Standards, kindred and friends, I . . . I wish to announce—to present my . . . my affianced, . . . Lieutenant Kenri Shaun of the starship *Fleetwing*."

For a time that dragged, nobody moved. At last someone made the ritual bow. Then someone else did, then all the rest, like jointed dolls. No, not all. A few turned their backs.

Nivala's thunder went shrill. "Carry on! Enjoy yourselves! Later—" The music master took his cue and activated a bouncy tune. Couple by couple, the guests slipped into a figure dance. They didn't know what else to do.

Nivala looked back at Kenri. "Welcome home." She had forgotten the amplifier. Her words boomed. She guided him off the dais and around the wall.

"It's been too long," he said for lack of anything else.

A doorway gave on a corridor. It ended in a room screened off by trellises where honeysuckle climbed, a twilit room with a screen playing a view of moonlight on a lake. The music reached it, but faintly, not quite real.

Again she came to him, and now they had no haste. He felt how she shivered.

"This is a hard situation for you, isn't it?" he said when they stood holding hands.

"I love you," she told him. "Nothing else matters."

He had no response.

"Does it?" she cried.

"We, uh, we aren't alone on our private planet," he had to say. "How's your immediate family taken this?" The call in advance had amounted to endearments and the invitation.

"Some howled. But the colonel curbed them. My uncle, the head of us now Father's gone. He ordered them to behave themselves till they see what happens." Nivala gulped. "What happens will be you'll show them, you'll show everybody what you're worth, till they boast about your being one of us."

"One of you— Well, I'll try. With your help."

They sat down on a biopadded bench. She nestled close. His right arm was about her, his left hand closed over hers, and he breathed the sunniness of her hair. From time to time they kissed. Why did his damned thoughts keep straying?

I'll try—what? Not to plan parties or purvey gossip or listen politely to idiots and perverts. No, that's not for her, either. What can we do?

A man can't spend all his waking hours making love.

They'd talked about it aboard ship, though he realized now how desultory the talk had been. He could join a trading firm. (Ten thousand pelts from Kali recd. pr. acct., arrange with Magic Sociodynamics to generate a vogue for them, and lightning flared above those wild hills. Microbes, discovered on Hathor, their metabolism suggesting certain useful variations in nanotechnics, and the jungle was a geometrics of mystery. Intriguing customs and concepts recorded on a recently discovered world, and the ship had raced among foreign stars to a fresh frontier.) Or perhaps the military. (Up on your feet, soldier! Hup, hup, hup, hup! . . . Sir, this intelligence report from Mars. . . . Sir, I know the guns aren't to spec, but we can't touch the contractor, his patron is a Star-Free. . . . The General commands your presence at a banquet for the Lord Inspector. . . . Now tell me, Captain Shaun, how *really* do you think they'll handle those rebels, you officers are so *frightfully* closemouthed. . . . Ready! Aim! Fire! So perish all traitors. Long live the Dominant!) Or the science centers. (Well, sir, according to the text, the formula is—)

"Otherwise, how do you like being back?" he asked.

"Oh, it's, aside from the family trouble, it's, oh, cordial." She smiled uncertainly. "I am a romantic figure, after all. And finding my way around in the new generations, that's a challenge. You'll enjoy it, too. And you'll be still more glamorous."

"No," he grunted. It was as if his tongue spoke on its own. "I'm a tumy, remember?"

"Kenri!" She stiffened beneath his arm. "What a way to talk. You aren't, and you know it, and you won't be if you'll just stop thinking like one—" She drew up short. "I'm sorry, darling. That was a terrible thing to say."

He stared at the lake view.

"I've been . . . reinfected," she said. "You'll cure me."

Tenderness welled in him. He kissed her again.

"Ahem! I beg your pardon."

They pulled apart, dismayed. Two men had entered. The first was gray, gaunt, erect, his night-blue tunic agleam with decorations. After him trailed a young person, pudgy, gaudily clad, not overly steady of gait. Kenri and Nivala rose. The Kithman bowed, arms crossed on breast.

"Oh, how nice." Nivala's voice had gone thready. "This is Kenri Shaun. Kenri, my uncle, Colonel Torwen Jonach from Canda, of the Supreme Staff. And his grandson, the Honorable Oms." Her laugh jittered. "Fancy coming home to find you have a cousin twice removed, your own age."

"Your honor, Lieutenant." The colonel's tone was as stiff as his back. Oms giggled.

"You will pardon the interruption," from Canda proceeded. "I wished to speak to Lieutenant Shaun as soon as possible, and must leave tomorrow for an . . . operation that may take many days. You will understand that this is for the good of my niece and the entire family."

Kenri's armpits were wet. He prayed they wouldn't stink. "Of course, sir. Please be seated."

From Canda nodded and lowered his angular frame to the bench, beside the Kithman. Oms and Nivala took opposite ends. "How 'bout we send for wine?" Oms proposed.

"No," from Canda told him. The old man's eyes, winter-bleak, sought Kenri's. "First," he said, "I want to make clear that I do not share the prejudice against your people. It is absurd. The Kith is demonstrably the genetic equal of the Star families, and doubtless superior to a number of their members." The glance went briefly to Oms. Contemptuously? Kenri guessed that the grandson had tagged along, half drunk, out of curiosity or whatever it was, and the grandfather had allowed it lest he make a scene.

"The cultural barrier is formidable," from Canda went on, "but if you will exert yourself to surmount it, I am prepared in due course to sponsor your adoption."

"Thank you, sir." Kenri felt the room wobble. No Kithman had ever— That *he*— He heard Nivala's happy little sigh. She clutched his arm.

"But will you? That is what I must find out." From Canda gestured at something unseen. "The near future will not be tranquil. The few men of action we have left shall have to stand together and strike hard. We can ill afford weaklings among us. We can absolutely not afford strong men who are not wholeheartedly loyal."

"I . . . will be, sir. What more can I say?"

"Better that you ask what you can do. Be warned, much of it will be hard. We can use your special knowledge and your connections. For example, the badge tax on the Kith is not mainly to humiliate them. The Dominancy's treasury is low. This money helps a little. More importantly, it sets a precedent for new levies elsewhere. There will be further demands, on Kithfolk as well as subjects. You can advise our policy makers. We don't want to goad the Kith into forsaking Earth."

"I—" Kenri swallowed a lump. It was acid. "You can't expect—"

"If you won't, I cannot compel you," said from Canda. "But if you cooperate, you can make things easier for your former people."

It surged in Kenri: "Can I get them treated like human beings?"

"History can't be annulled by decree. You should know that."

Kenri nodded. The motion hurt his neck.

"I admire your spirit," the colonel said. "Can you make it last?"

Kenri looked down.

"Of course he can," said Nivala.

The Honorable Oms tittered. "New tax," he said. "Slap a new tax on, quick. I've got a tumy merchant reeling. New tax'll bring him to his knees."

"Hold your jaw," from Canda snapped.

Nivala sat straight. "Yes, be still!" she shouted. "Why are you here?" To her uncle, desperately: "You will be our friend, won't you?"

"I hope so," said from Canda.

Through rising winds, Kenri heard Oms:

"I got to tell you 'bout this. Real funny. This resident merchant in Kith Town, not a spacer but a tumy just the same, he lost big on a voyage. My agent bought the debt for me. If he doesn't pay, I can take his daughter under contract. Cute little piece. Only the other tumies are taking up a collection for him. Got to stop that somehow. Never mind the money. They say those tumy girls are really hot. How 'bout that, Kenri? Tell me, is it true—"

Kenri stood up. The room around him lay as sharp as if he saw it in open space. He no longer heard the music. A metallic singing filled his skull.

He did hear Nivala: "Oms! You whelp!" and from Canda: "Silence!" The sounds came from light-years away. His left hand caught hold of the tunic and hauled the Honorable Oms to his feet. His right hand made a fist and smote.

Oms lurched back, fell, and moaned where he lay. Nivala quelled a scream. From Canda leaped to his own feet.

"Arrest me," Kenri said. A detached fraction of him wished he could speak less thickly. "Go on. Why not?"

"Kenri, Kenri." Nivala rose, too. She reached for him. He saw at the edge of vision but didn't respond. Her arms dropped.

Oms pulled himself to an elbow. Blood coursed from his nose. "Yes, arrest him," he squealed. "Ten years' penance confinement. I'll take everything he's got."

From Canda's shoe nudged his grandson in the ribs, not gently. "I ordered you to stay quiet," he said. Oms whimpered, struggled to a sitting position, and rocked to and fro.

"That was reckless of you, Lieutenant Shaun," stated from Canda. "However, it was not unprovoked. There will be no charges or lawsuit."

"The Kith girl—" Kenri realized he should first have said thanks.

"I daresay she'll be all right. They'll raise the money for her father. Kithfolk stick together." The tone hardened. "Bear in mind, you have renounced that allegiance."

Kenri straightened. A hollow sort of peace had come upon him.

He remembered a half-human face and eyes without hope and *A man's only alive when he has something bigger than himself to live and die for.* "Thank you, sir," he said belatedly. "But I am a Kithman."

"Kenri," he heard.

He turned and stroked a hand down Nivala's hair. "I'm sorry," he said. He never had been good at finding words.

"Kenri, you can't go, you mustn't, you can't."

"I must," he said. "I was ready to give up everything for you. But not to betray my ship, my people. If I did that, in the end it would make me hate you, and I want to love you. Always."

She wrenched away, slumped onto the bench, and stared at the hands clenched in her lap. The blonde tresses hid her face from him. He hoped she wouldn't try to call him tomorrow or the next day. He didn't know whether he hoped she would take treatment to adjust her mind-set or wait and recover naturally from him.

"We're enemies now, I suppose," the colonel said. "I respect you for that more than if you'd worked to be friends. And, since I presume you'll be shipping out and we'll never meet again—luck to you, Lieutenant Shaun."

"And to you, sir. Good-bye, Nivala."

The Kithman passed through the ballroom, ignoring eyes, and through the anteroom to the ascensor. *Well,* he thought vaguely on his way down, *yes, I will be shipping out.*

I do like Theye Barinn. I should go around soon and see her.

The time felt long before he was back in Kith Town. There he walked in empty streets, breathing the cold night wind of Earth.

22.

After her last zero-zero leap, *Envoy* paused a while, some seven astronomical units from her goal. Again Dayan and Cleland took instruments out onto the hull.

The destination sun glared as bright as Sol at the orbit of Saturn; it was a K0, with about two-thirds the luminosity. Already the searchers knew that eight worlds attended it, that the second was in the zone of habitability and indeed had an oxynitrogen atmosphere, and that thermonuclear power plants operated not only on it but at several other sites around the system. Now they gathered more data, more precise, for forecasts and warnings.

For a long span, however, their attention was on a point where eyes found nothing but the dark. Meter readings computed numbers, graphic displays bore them the tidings. Their hearts knocked.

"Yes," Dayan said, "there's no more doubt. A pulsar, within one-third parsec of us. And it has planets."

No mere white dwarf like Sirius B—a neutron star, self-compressed remnant of a giant that burst itself asunder, clinker still shooting its furious radio beams into space with no message but its own ferocity—Unless ships from Earth had traveled well beyond Sol's neighborhood since *Envoy* left, humans had never before been this close to one.

"Wouldn't the supernova have sterilized the planet here?" Cleland saw immediately that his question was stupid, blurted in excitement.

Dayan's head shook, shadowy behind the helmet. "No, it wasn't near at the time. High proper motion; it's only passing by. I've detected an expanding nebulosity yonder." She pointed at another object which distance made invisible. "If it's from the eruption, then that happened about a thousand light-years off and ten million years ago."

"Only ten million? M-my God, those planets must still be re-evolving!"

Dayan's own voice quivered. "Yes, and the pulsar itself probably hasn't reached a steady state yet. The physics—" She set about directing instruments to more urgent concerns. "I imagine the Yonderfolk can tell us about it," she finished a bit harshly.

Envoy proceeded inward at a full g, ignoring economy, to cut the passage time down to a week. Her people were impatient.

"Look at that," Kilbirnie breathed. "Just *look* at that."

"Apa Isten." Ruszek did not seem to notice he had crossed himself.

The ship was passing within twelve million kilometers of the third planet. Her crew had gathered in the reserve saloon-galley to see what her optics could screen for them. Magnified and enhanced, a thick crescent stood ruddy, mottled—and silver-spotted with seas. Air slightly blurred the limb and softened the edge between day and night. Clouds, elongated and patchy rather than marbling, shone less brilliantly white than Earth's; but they shone. Three firefly sparks glinted against the blackness beyond, satellites. Instruments had found at least a dozen more.

Only a third again as big as Mars, receiving at its distance no more light from the weaker sun, the globe should have been a similar desolation, its atmosphere almost as thin. But: barely discernible as a shimmer where sunlight struck at particular angles, a transparent shell enclosed it, twenty-odd kilometers greater in radius. A few of the travelers thought they could make out one or two of the pillars upholding the structure. Spectroscopy showed the air within to be thicker than Earth's, and as warm. It was carbon dioxide, nitrogen, water vapor, traces of methane and other gases, nothing to sustain creatures with lungs. Nevertheless waters and land gave reflection spectra of complex organic materials. Life-stuff?

"Those satellites are neutrino radiators," Dayan said. Not everyone aboard had yet heard of her newest discoveries. "Thermonuclear reactors. I think they're beaming energy down to the planet, heating it. And there are areas of violent activity on the surface. The waste heat from them contributes." Awe underlay her dry words.

"The Yonderfolk are terraforming," Mokoena marveled.

Sundaram smiled, less calmly than he was wont. "Not precisely 'terra,' Mam."

Cleland spoke confidently, in his element. "It can't be that simple. I daresay they brought in ices from comets, and roofed everything in to keep volatiles from escaping. Probably the shell also filters out excessive ultraviolet and screens off hard radiation. The planet's not massive enough to have much of a magnetic field for protection, if any. But neither can it have plate tectonics. How do they propose to maintain the carbonate-silicate cycle and the other equilibria necessary for life to last? For that matter, transforming raw gases into breathable air and rock into soil takes huge amounts of energy. Which means time—geological time."

"Perhaps the Yonderfolk think that far ahead," Yu said low.

Nansen's gaze brooded on the image. "All that time, all that effort," he murmured, "when they have zero-zero—or did—and could go find new worlds. Why this?"

"We'll learn, skipper," Kilbirnie said.

"And learn how they're doing it." Zeyd's enthusiasm drove off the momentary chill.

Brent's eyes smoldered at the burning moonlets. "The power," he said, deep in his throat. "The power."

Envoy took orbit around the world of her quest.

It glowed as beautiful as expected, royal blue with a tinge of purple, wreathed and swirled with white. To adaptable human vision, the sun disk seemed well-nigh homelike.

Differences abounded. The planet was darker than Earth, of lower albedo, for only half was under water, there were no polar caps, and the vegetation covering most of the land ranged from red-brown to almost black. A single moon, small but close, showed a disk one-seventh the familiar width of Luna, like a tiny gold coin; scars had been smoothed over, and magnification revealed curious shapes scattered across the surface.

The humans' attention was wholly on the planet. Rapt at their instruments and screens, they beheld forests, fields that clearly were tended, buildings that curved and soared, vehicles that skimmed and floated and flew, creatures walking about who must be the dwellers. Settlement was dispersed, with few concentrations, none comparable to a terrestrial metropolis. Much seemed to be underground, including fusion power plants, though most energy was evidently generated on the moon and beamed down via half a dozen artificial satellites.

"A clean nuclear cycle," Dayan said when the neutrino spectrum had identified it for her. "Extremely high transmission efficiency. But nothing like the gigawattage at home. The population must be much less."

"And less greedy?" wondered Sundaram.

The ship's exocommunicators rolled through band after band, visible, infrared, radio, calling, calling.

No more than three breathless hours had passed when Nansen's command rang through the wheel: "All hands to emergency stations. A spacecraft is approaching."

His hands poised over the control console of the weapons. He expected no hostility, he prayed for none, but who could tell? After the robots in the star cluster, who could tell?

The vessel converged at a fractional *g*. It must have risen from the ground, for nothing like it had been in ambient space when *Envoy* arrived. Torpedo-shaped, coppery-hued, some fifty meters in length, it maneuvered as smoothly as an aircraft into the same orbit. There it took station, three kilometers ahead.

"N-n-no jets." His crew had never before heard Nansen stammer. "*Dios todopoderoso,* how does it boost?"

"We'll learn," Kilbirnie called once more.

Silence stretched.

"They are probably scanning us," Nansen said.

"Wouldn't we do the same with surprise visitors?" Zeyd replied. "I think we can safely go back to our proper work, and be more useful."

Nansen hesitated a bare second. "Yes. Engineers and boat pilots, stand by. The rest may leave their stations."

"No, let me go outside," Ruszek proposed. "Give them a look at one of us."

Nansen considered. "That may be a good idea. Proceed."

"Damn you, Lajos, you spoke first," Kilbirnie lamented.

Before the mate had his spacesuit on, receivers awoke—visual flickers, audio clicks and glissandos; response from the Yonderfolk.

The quickness was not overly astonishing. Although it could not be expected that equipment would be compatible, scientists(?) should soon analyze what was coming in and devise means to send back the same kind of signals. Thereafter the humans could explain how to make audiovisual sets that would work together with their own. Best do it thus; the Yonderfolk undoubtedly had more resources, on a whole planet vis-à-vis a single spaceship from five thousand years ago.

Envoy's database contained the work of many bright minds who had dreamed about exchanges with aliens. Programs were ready to go. After the simple initial flashes, messages became binary, describing diagrams on a grid defined by two prime numbers. By showing such easily recognizable things as the black-body curve of the sun and the orbiting of its planets, they established units of basic physical quantities, mass, length, time, temperature. The Yonderfolk replied similarly, with refinements—for instance, the quantum states of the hydrogen atom. Not everything was immediately comprehensible on either side, but computers sifted, tested, eliminated, deciphered, electronically fast. Nature herself was providing a common language.

The time seemed long aboard ship—where nobody slept well or ate with any appreciation of the food—but it was not really—until circuit diagrams crossed the gap, and circuits were built, and pictures and sounds began to pass to and fro.

Nansen chimed Sundaram's door. It opened. He entered the cabin. Austere furnishings revealed little that was personal other than some views and mementos from the India that had been. An incense stick sweetened the air. Sundaram sat studying a recorded image. He would activate it for a few seconds, then stop it and think.

"Good evenwatch, Captain," he greeted absently. "Please be seated."

Nansen took a chair. "I'm sorry to disturb your concentration," he said, "but I do need to know how your work is progressing, and you didn't want to discuss it openly." Sundaram had practically sequestered himself.

"Not yet. Too early in the game."

"I understand. I wouldn't have asked for this meeting, except that— Well, Zeyd has now examined those biospecimens the others shot over to us from their spacecraft, in that capsule full of containers. The quarantine conditions were unnecessary, he's found. Not that the aliens would mean to harm us. If they did, they could blow us apart with a nuclear warhead." Nansen seldom spoke superfluously. He was under stress. "No hazard of disease. The biochemistries are too unlike. Mokoena confirms. I daresay the others have reached the same conclusion about the material we sent them. So, how soon can we communicate well enough to take the next step, whatever it may be? Can you give me some hint? Lying idled like this is beginning to fray people's nerves."

Sundaram gestured at the screen. Although by now Nansen had often seen what it showed, and pored over similar images for hours, a tingle went along his spine.

A being stood unclad against a background of enigmatic apparatus. The first word aboard for it had been "centaur," but that was like calling a man an ostrich because both were bipeds. It stood on four stout legs with four-toed, padded, spurred feet. The body was likewise robust, lacking a tail and any obvious genitalia. Its back rose in a shallow ridge. The torso in front did not rear very high above. Two long, sturdy-looking arms ended in hands around each of which four nailless fingers were symmetrically arranged; they seemed flexible, boneless, like an elephant's trunk.

The head was big, round, high-browed, a lipless mouth in the blunt muzzle but no nose. Apparently the being breathed through two slits, somewhat resembling gills with their quivering protective covers, in the neck under the jaw. Above the muzzle, two elliptical eyes—presumably eyes—were set close together, while two large circular ones flanked them on the sides of the head. The inner orbs were black, the outer green, and none had whites, nor pupils resembling the human. From the brow rose two short antennae crowned with clusters of cilia. Pointed earflaps stood a trifle higher than the head, hairless, thin, and yellowish; Mokoena had guessed that that was the color of blood, or blood's equivalent.

Neck and shoulders were blanketed by a mane of small, leaflike growths, of the same hue, like a kind of ivy. They were constantly astir, as if winds blew changeably through them. Otherwise a velvety pelt decked the skin, dark brown on this individual, on others it had been seen to vary from black to pale green.

From direct observation the humans knew that they—adults, at any rate—ranged from about 130 to 140 centimeters long and stood about as tall: the height of a child some ten years old, though with more mass. They moved gracefully, sometimes quite fast.

"They shall have to take the initiative," Sundaram said.

"Can we do nothing?" asked Nansen. "We did send the first keys to language."

"That was the easy part." Sundaram leaned back, bridged his fingers, and looked straight at his visitor. "On ancient Earth and in the Age of Discovery, explorers found people new to them, speaking languages unrelated to theirs. They could soon talk to each other. But you see, they shared the same world, the same body pattern and needs and instincts; they could point, they could pantomime, and be understood. Here we begin with separate origins and evolution of life itself, from billions of years ago."

"Yes, I've heard that discussed, of course. But still—*bien*—"

"They have voices," Sundaram said. Nansen nodded, recalling whistles and rumbles. "However," the linguist went on, "I am beginning to think their language is only partly vocal, perhaps only in minor part. It gives me the impression of being principally a body language, employing especially the countless possible configurations of those leafy, erectile manes. And what other elements does it have? How do they write it? The eyes suggest that they see the universe differently from us. What are their pictorial conventions? No, we will not quickly be able to speak in their manner. I doubt we ever will be."

Nansen sighed. "I suppose we are just as weird to them."

"Well, now, there the situation may not be quite so difficult. That is why I believe they will take the lead. Their ancestors went to hundreds or thousands of stars. They doubtless have a far larger database to work from than we do."

"Do you mean they can retrieve parallels to us? I wonder. How many intelligent races, primitive or civilized or—whatever else—did they ever find?"

"That is one thing we have come here to learn."

"Let's begin, then!"

"Give us time. They appear to be willing, interested—"

"As well they might be."

"We may see some action reasonably soon." Sundaram spoke into Nansen's sudden hopefulness: "But as for proper communication, you must give us time."

"Us." He includes the Yonderfolk. Already he feels a kinship across all foreignness.

The crew were gathered. Nansen spoke straight to the point.

"It went better than we anticipated. Icons, animations— We're invited to come down and settle in."

Ruszek's hand shot up. "First landing!" he roared.

"Again?" Kilbirnie said. She shrugged. "Aweel, if you must. There should be lots more, shouldn't there, skipper?"

"We still have details to work out," Nansen cautioned. "First and foremost, I suppose, the actual landing site."

"They ought to have one in mind already, given their experience in the past," Mokoena said. "Selim and I have established that the biology and biochemistry here are the same as in the anomalous plants we collected at our previous stop." This, too, though not unexpected, was a new announcement; knowledge had been leaping forward. "And the architecture— That *was* a colony of theirs. They *are* the Yonderfolk."

Nobody asked why that world lay forsaken. They had raised the question wearisomely often. Nevertheless, for a moment it spooked around them.

Cleland pushed it aside. "Uh, this may be silly," he ventured, "but have you found out the name of this planet, Ajit?"

Sundaram smiled. "Silly but natural," he replied. "No, of course not. Perhaps we never will. It may have many names in many distinct languages. Whatever they are, I doubt we can ever pronounce any, if pronunciation is even appropriate—and if the Yonderfolk bestow names."

Zeyd half rose from his seat, sank back, and declared, "We want one to use among ourselves."

Yu nodded. "We have talked about this also."

"We should decide. You know what I propose. Tahir."

"That seems fitting," Nansen said, "and out in these parts we don't have to go through registration procedures. Shall we agree on Tahir?"

Assent murmured around the half-circle.

"Well," Nansen said gladly, "we can start planning and preparing for descent, and thinking what to do down there."

"Five years," Brent growled.

Eyes went toward him. "What?" demanded Dayan.

He glowered back. "You know. The contract, the ship's articles. We are not obliged to stay more than five Earth years after we've reached our goal. Which we have."

"We may be at the start of the real, the greater search," Sundaram said.

"Five years," Brent insisted. He looked around from face to face. "Then we can go home if we choose. Wouldn't you like to be back where you can dare have children, before you're too old?"

23.

Year one.

The site was a broad opening in an expanse of woodlands on the eastern seaboard of a northern continent. A stream flowed through, clear and pure although the human palate sensed a slight pungency. A stand of trees screened an area that had been paved overnight to provide a field for spacecraft and aircraft. When violent weather was on its way, as happened not uncommonly, a flexible sheet extruded from one end, arched over to form a transparent dome, and grew rigid. It opened for you wherever you approached, closing again behind. After the storm was past, it softened and withdrew. Otherwise the Tahirians had prepared nothing, and raised no objections to whatever their guests did.

On clear days the land lay darklingly rich beneath a deep blue sky. Growth was nowhere green, but ruddy-brown, chocolate, black, maroon, damask, countless shades, lightened by petals white or colorful. The effect was not gloomy; there was so much life, leaves rippling and soughing in sunlight, odors as of strange spices. A mossy turf seemed to play the basic role of grass. Trees, shrubs, canes, brachiated more or less like Earth's; to that extent had two evolutions happened to run parallel. Wildlife abounded, from tiny things that could incorrectly be called worms or insects, on through swimmers, runners, and wings multitudinous in heaven. Cries, whistles, bellows, trills sounded through the glades.

Tahir rotated once in nineteen and a quarter hours, with an axial inclination of thirty-one degrees. Though the irradiation was lower, the atmosphere, slightly denser than Earth's, joined with albedo to maintain a planetary mean temperature three degrees higher. However, climates

varied tremendously from region to region, weather still more, through a
year seven-tenths terrestrial length. This was in considerable part due to
an orbit as eccentric as Mars's—northern summers longer and colder,
northern winters shorter and warmer, than southern. All factors considered, the place granted the humans might well be the best possible
for them.

A gravity 9 percent above terrestrial added about five to eight kilos to a
person's weight, depending on mass. It was evenly distributed, and the
crew soon hardened to it; as well as resetting their circadian rhythms—
with pharmaceutical help. The work of settlement kept them busily and,
most times, cheerily occupied. Ruszek and Kilbirnie ferried down load after load of equipment, supplies, and prefabricated parts. Robots helped,
but hands found plenty to do. A storage shed rose; a building for a power
plant and other facilities; a third for meeting, cooking, dining, recreation,
celebration. At last individual cabins replaced the two temporary shelters
that had separately housed men and women.

Although the Tahirians did not seem to have closed the region off,
none of the nuisances appeared who would have come swarming on
Earth, journalists, curiosity seekers, salespeople, cranks, politicians. Three
or four visitors were frequently present, arriving and departing in small,
silent aerial vehicles of teardrop shape and iridescent hues. They observed and recorded, with exotic apparatus, except for those who worked
with Sundaram. They let the humans stare and record in turn. Otherwise
they kept to themselves.

"It suggests a very controlled society," Dayan remarked.

"Or a very alien one," Cleland said.

Abruptly that changed. While speech was not yet possible, sign language had steadily improved. It took the form of animated cartoons
displayed on a portable screen. The figures were simplified and conven-
tionalized to the point of grotesquerie, but usually comprehensible. One
day a Tahirian ran off a sequence that made Kilbirnie shout, "Harroo!"
and dance across the sward.

The newcomers were invited to go on tours.

"They've decided we know enough by now and are harmless," Nansen
guessed.

"Not necessarily harmless," Brent said.

"Who made the decision, and how?" wondered Yu.

Evidently the Tahirians gave priority to scientific and technological rap-
port. Was that because those were the least difficult subjects? They tried
to explain what kinds of establishment they offered to show, on trips of a
few days' duration. Nansen divided his people accordingly. It made more
sense than going in one herd. Nor did he want the camp left empty. For
the initial jaunts, he assigned just two parties. The rest would stay behind until another time. He took the worst jealousy off that by including

himself. When the aircraft took off, swiftly vanishing, Kilbirnie saw him bite his lip. She swallowed her own disappointment and slipped over to stand beside him.

Mokoena and Zeyd entered into magic.

They landed at a cluster of structures, low shapes of complex, pleasing geometry around a filigree tower. Their guide showed them to a chamber with soft pads on the floor and an adjoining bath and sanitor copied from the humans'. Obviously this would be their lodging. They stowed the food, bedrolls, changes of clothing, and personal kits they had brought along and turned eagerly back to the guide. The little being led them straightway to a descent and down a spiral ramp, down and down.

"Does he feel how our curiosity burns?" Zeyd asked.

"I think curiosity must be universal to intelligence," Mokoena replied, "though it may not always express itself in the same ways."

The laboratory(?) in which they ended was long and wide, a hemiellipsoid out of which poured illumination. Several benches(?) were vaguely familiar, though no drawers were visible; did they extrude on command? The paraphernalia on top and standing elsewhere was unrecognizable.

Three more Tahirians waited. All had been in the camp from time to time. They gave their guests a few minutes to look around. Thereupon one stepped forward. His(?) leaf-mane waved. He uttered a few piping notes. Arms and tentacular fingers wove through a series of gestures. A sweet smell drifted into air that otherwise hung warm and quiet.

"A polite greeting?" Mokoena hazarded.

Zeyd bowed. "*Salaam,*" he responded. His companion raised a palm.

The being trotted off. They followed. He stopped between tall cabinet-shaped devices on three sides of a square. An associate operated controls. A screen of some kind slid out to make the fourth side.

A three-dimensional image of the scientist appeared in it. "Holographic projection," Zeyd muttered. "*Limatza*—why?"

Skin vanished from the image. The watchers beheld muscles, unlike theirs but serving the same purposes. After a minute this was gone and they saw deeper layers, vessels through which ran fluid, pale streaks of a solid material. . . . "Tomographic fluoroscopy," Zeyd said unevenly. "Why don't they just show us anatomical models?"

"I expect they wish to use it on us, and are demonstrating it's safe," Mokoena opined.

"*Allah akbar!* That skeleton—modular trusses—"

Mokoena gasped. She had dissected small animals that Ruszek and Brent shot. This, though, was a different line of evolution, even a different phylum, if "phylum" meant anything here.

"See, see," she breathed. The view moved inward. "That big organ, does it do the work of our heart and lungs? It could be how they inhale and exhale, in spite of the rigid body—"

"Ionic and osmotic pumps?"

"Oh, Selim, revelation!" She caught his hand and clung.

"Well, they have bowels," he said, as if prosaic words could fend off bewilderment. "What those other things are—"

The view went back outward, step by step. The humans focused their attention on the head. A brain was identifiable, however peculiar its form. Instead of teeth, convoluted bone ridges extended from the flesh of the jaws, presumably regenerating continuously. The fernlike shapes of four tonguelets, two above and two below, suggested they were chemosensors, perhaps among other functions. Indeed, Tahirians generally kept their mouths partly open.

"What do the antennae do?" puzzled Zeyd.

"I'd like to know more about the eyes, too," Mokoena said. "So far we've only guessed the inner pair is chiefly for day vision, the outer for night."

"And for peripheral."

She glanced at him before her gaze jumped back to the screen. "Yes, of course, but why do you make it sound so important?"

"This was a dangerous world in the past. Life developed ways to cope with it."

"Every world is dangerous."

Zeyd spoke in a rapid monotone. They both kept watching the screen. "Here more than most. Tim and I were talking about it a few days ago. He pointed out that a planet this size must go through bouts of enormous volcanic and seismic activity, with radical effects on climates. The core and spin give it a strong magnetic field, but the field will vary more than Earth's and in some geological periods the background count goes high. The moon is too small to stabilize the axial tilt, like ours. Chaotic variations must cause still more ecological disasters. I said to Tim that all this must have bred many different biomes. Probably ancestral Tahirians often wandered into territories where animals and plants were unknown to them. They needed a wide sensory field."

"And range? I hope you can explain the biochemistry of those eyes to me."

"What?"

"I've been noticing things. Don't you remember that wall panel in the aircar? An inscription on it, slashes and squiggles and— Red on red. Very hard to read. It has to be easy for them. That implies better color vision than ours. More than three receptors, I would guess. Not incredible. Shrimp on Earth have seven. If 'receptors' is the word I want."

Zeyd chuckled. "Please. This is too much for a single hour."

"I know. It's like being a child in a toy shop. What shall we play with first?"

The image became that of a complete Tahirian. It blinked out.

Exhilaration brought levity. "Isn't sex more interesting than eyes?" Zeyd japed. "Did you get any idea of how they reproduce?"

"No. It's still as baffling as those dissections of mine." Mokoena grinned. "Perhaps they'll show us some explicit scenes."

"Or enact them?"

She sobered. "Let's hope for no serious misunderstandings."

The screen retracted. The scientist emerged, approached, beckoned. He was gray-pelted, though presumably not aged, and wore a pouched belt around the torso. "What comes next, Peter?" Zeyd asked. As they began to tell individuals apart, humans had given them names, because humans need names. Zeyd could as well have put his useless question in Arabic, but Mokoena was listening.

Snaky fingers reached up to pluck at clothes. "Are we supposed to—to undress?" Zeyd exclaimed.

Again Mokoena's teeth flashed white in the dark face. "They may be thinking about the same subject we were."

"A demonstration?"

"I trust not!"

They looked at one another. Laughter pealed. They removed their garments. For an instant they could not hide enjoyment of what they saw. Then the four Tahirians crowded around to examine them, peering and sniffing(?), touching and feeling, gently but with unmistakable fascination, prior to putting them in the tomograph.

"Do they wonder if we're separate species?" Zeyd speculated.

"As our good captain would say," Mokoena answered, *"viva la diferencia."*

In a vast, twilit chamber, shapes bulked, soared, curved, coiled, phantasmagoria reaching beyond sight. Some moved, some whirred. Lights danced and flashed in changeable intricacy, like fireflies or a galaxy of evanescent stars.

"Beautiful," Dayan said, "but what is it?"

"I don't know," Yu replied softly. "I suspect the beauty isn't by chance, it's there for its own sake. We may find we have much beauty in common, we and they."

The two were at the end of a tour. They had walked through twisting kilometers with their guides, and had stood looking and looking without understanding, but their daze came less from an overload of the body than of the mind.

The frustration in Dayan broke through. "We won't make sense of any of this till they can explain it to us. Can they ever?" She gestured at the nearest Tahirian. "What has Esther, here, really conveyed, today or back at our camp?"

As if to respond, the native took a flat box with a screen out of her(?) pouch belt. Such units were the means of pictorial communication. Fingers danced across control surfaces. Figures appeared. Yu leaned close to see. Minutes passed. The other hosts waited patiently. Dayan quivered.

Yu straightened. "I think I have a hint." Her voice rejoiced. "The symbols we have developed— I think one of these assemblies, at least, is a cryomagnetic facility for studying quantum resonances."

"Don't they already know everything about that?" Dayan objected. "These people were probably starfaring before Solomon built the First Temple."

"I suspect this whole complex is a teaching laboratory."

Dayan nodded. "That sounds plausible. It would be the best for us." She paused before asking, "Do they do any actual research anymore?"

"What?"

"Would they? They gave up starfaring long ago. We may be the first newness they've encountered for thousands of years."

Yu pondered. "Well, did not the physicists on Earth believe the ultimate equation has been written and everything we discover hereafter will only be solutions of it?"

Scorn replied. "*They* believed. What about those jetless flyers here?"

"That may be an application of principles we know in ways we have not thought of."

"Or maybe not." Dayan's mettle forsook her. "You will doubtless find out," she said wearily. "Technological tricks. The science underneath them is something else."

Surprised, Yu said, "No, the basic laws will come first. They are far simpler."

Dayan shook her head. "Not without a proper vocabulary, verbal and mathematical. We won't reach that point soon, will we? Newton's laws, yes—but the Hamiltonian, Riemannian geometry, wave functions? Not to mention Navier-Stokes, turbulence, chaos, complexity, all the subtleties. It'll be years before we even know whether the Tahirians know something fundamental that we don't. What shall I do meanwhile?"

Yu touched her hand. "You will help me. If nothing else. No, we shall be partners."

"Thank you, dear Wenji."

The warmth was short-lived. Dayan looked off into the dusk. "Technology, your work, interesting, vital, yes," she said. "But the mysteries—"

Sundaram sat in his cabin. The interior resembled his own aboard ship, except for the windows. They gave on a wild autumnal rain. Wind yelled. Before him on the floor, legs folded, torso upright, rested the Tahirian whom humans called Indira, because this happened so often that an Indian name felt appropriate. He was coming to believe that Indira was not known among her/his/its kind by any single symbol, but by configurations of sensory data that changed fluidly according to circumstances while always demarking the unique individual.

Computer screens and a holograph displayed sketches, diagrams, arbitrary figures, pictures. With illumination turned low, reflected light set

Indira's four eyes aglow. Sundaram spoke aloud, not altogether to himself.

"Yes, I am nearly certain now. Yours is primarily a body language, with chemical and vocal elements—characters and compoundings infinitely, subtly variable. It causes your writing to be ideographic, like a kind of super-Chinese hypertext. Is this correct? Then Wenji can make a device for expressing the language we create, the new language our races will share."

Winter brought snow, glistery white and blue-shadowed over the ground. Icicles hung like jewelry from bare boughs; many Tahirian trees also shed their leaves. Cold air laved the face and stung the nostrils. Breath smoked.

Kilbirnie, Cleland, Ruszek, and Brent came back from a walk. Taking their turns as caretakers at the settlement, they had grown restless. The outing roused Kilbirnie's spirits from boredom. She dashed around to look at things, threw snowballs, tried to make her companions join in a song. Only Cleland did, halfheartedly.

Leaving the forest, they saw across the openness that huddle of buildings their crew had dubbed Terralina. Kilbirnie stopped. "Oh!" she gasped.

One of the great, rarely seen creatures they knew as dragons swept overhead. Sunlight streamed through wing membranes and broke into rainbow shards. The long, sinuous body gleamed beryl green. Her gaze followed the arc of flight until it sank below the horizon.

The others had halted, too. "Pretty," Ruszek said. He sounded reluctant to admit that anything could break the monotony of these days.

"More than bonnie," she crooned. "Freedom alive."

Cleland's glance had stayed on her. "You really do feel caged, don't you?" he mumbled.

"Don't we all?" Brent said. His words ran on almost automatically. "Yeah, it was fun at first, the novelty, the jobs, and then traveling around, but what are we now except tourists, once in a while when his high and mightiness Nansen lets us go? The scientific types, sure, they've got things to do that matter. Are *we* supposed to spend the next four years yawning?"

"Stop whining," Ruszek snapped. "You've overworked your self-pity."

Brent glared. "I don't take orders from you. Not planetside."

Ruszek snarled and drew back his fist.

"Hold, hold!" Kilbirnie protested. She grabbed his arm. "We dinna need a fight."

The mate gulped. His hand lowered. The flush left his cheeks. "No," he yielded. "We've been shut in, our nerves frayed. I . . . didn't mean offense, . . . Al."

"Okay," Brent replied sullenly. "Me neither."

"We will get out and rove, every one of us," Kilbirnie vowed. "We've talked of what we want to do. 'Tis but a matter of learning enough that we can make reasonable plans to lay before the skipper. Hanny has a thought—" She broke off. That hope was unripe, confidential. "Wha' say now we make hot toddies? Big ones."

Ruszek managed to smile. "The best idea I've heard in weeks."

"She's full of them." Cleland's expression showed what idea he wished she would get.

Ruszek's and Brent's eyes went the same way. Briefly, the cold seemed to crackle. Yes, crewfolk were honorable, respectful of their mates; no sane person would dare behave otherwise; there were the soothing medications if desired; there were the virtuals, and nobody asked what interactive programs anybody else chose; nevertheless—

Kilbirnie broke the tension. "Or shall it be hot buttered rum?" She bounded ahead. The men followed more slowly, none venturing to overtake her.

24.

Year two.

As aboard ship, beds in the cottages were expansible to double width. After half an hour, the cedary odors of lovemaking had faded from Zeyd's. He and Dayan had begun to talk, sitting up against the headboard. Their mood was less bright than earlier.

"It's been far too long," he said.

She nodded. "Yes."

He stroked his mustache and attempted a leer. "We must do something about that."

The hazel eyes challenged him. "Can you?"

He looked the question he neither needed nor wanted to speak.

"You are the one always away," Dayan said. Her tone regretted but did not accuse, and she did not add that his absences were with Mokoena.

"Research," he defended. "The environments, the ecologies, the laboratories. All over the planet."

"Of course. You know how I envy you that."

"Do you still feel idled? I thought you were happy enough, working with Wenji." It was not quite true. He was an observant man. He had left some things unsaid in hopes they would improve by themselves; and she was not given to complaining.

She nodded, red locks sliding across pillow. "It is interesting. But—"

He tensed. "Yes?"

She had gathered resolution. "There is real science screaming to be done."

"What?"

"The pulsar. Some of us have quietly discussed it. We'll soon be ready to present a plan for an expedition."

"No!" cried shock.

She smiled a bit sadly and stroked his cheek. "If it happens, I'll be sorry to leave you forsaken. I'll look forward to coming back." She turned implacable. "But go I will."

The device that Yu held before Sundaram fitted on her upturned left hand. It had the form of a thin forty-centimeter slab bent at right angles, the vertical part twice the length of the horizontal. A control board, a continuous touch-sensitive surface with a grid of guidelines, covered the top of the lower section. Screens filled both sides of the upper. As the fingers of her right hand gave directions, characters came and went across the screens while a speaker produced melodious sounds.

"I hope we may consider this the finished model," she said. "The Tahirians who have tried it seem to like it well."

She gave it to Sundaram. He experimented. Even the randomness he got entranced him. "Magnificent," he praised. "It will require practice, of course, to master, but— I have been thinking about it. Let me suggest we call it a parleur. A voice across the abyss between two utterly different kinds of communication."

"You still must create the mutual language."

"It progresses. I suspect that with this tool progress will rocket. But I will need your help—what you can spare from your technological studies—I will need your help more than ever."

"How?"

"I imagine that programming your nanocomputer demands a special talent." He shrugged, with a rueful smile. "Under the best conditions, I am not a good programmer."

"You have no reason to be."

Sundaram blinked. "I beg your pardon?"

Yu regarded him levelly through the muted lighting in his cabin. Rain roared against the windows, a savagery of silver.

"Your own genius is too big," she said. "It crowds other things out."

"Oh, come, now, please. I am simply overspecialized."

"It grows lonely, does it not?"

"Can you collaborate?" he asked in haste. "Have you time?"

She lowered her eyes and bowed above hands laid together. "Certainly. I am honored and delighted."

"The honor and delight are mine, Wenji," he let out.

Nansen took a group of Tahirians on a tour of *Envoy*. They flitted up in a native spaceboat. Considerable preparation had gone beforehand, while people of both species struggled to explain things and outline procedures; thus far, they had little more than their diagrams and cartoons to talk with. In the course of it, he gathered that nearly all space activity was robotic. Sometimes minerals were brought to Tahir, or finished products whose manufacture on the surface would harm the biosphere. However, this was seldom. The planet's economy seemed to be as close to equilibrium as the laws of thermodynamics allowed.

Then why does so much material, energy, effort go to the world they're transforming? he wondered for the thousandth time. *What became of the ships that once plied among the stars?*

On its drive that he did not understand, the boat glided up toward his vessel. Wheels and hull swelled before him, homelike athwart these constellations. Docking facilities were incompatible. The tube that extended to mate with a personnel lock was an engineering improvisation. Air pressure had equalized en route, and the party passed through to the interior. The Tahirians were less awkward in weightlessness than untrained humans would have been, but evidently appreciated the help Nansen gave them.

Approaching, they had studied the external fittings of the plasma drive, as they doubtless had done before. Now their first concern was the zero-zero engine. Having led them to that section, he anxiously watched them and their instruments swarm over it. Though they did no damage, it was with relief that he finally decided he could blow the whistle hung around his neck, an agreed-on signal. "We should get you settled in, and all take a rest," he urged. "You can have as much time here afterward as you like. But aren't you also curious about how we lived, on our way to you?"

English, he noticed. *Out of habit. It might as well have been Spanish or Hebrew or Chinese or anything.*

They packed their apparatuses, gathered their other belongings, and accompanied him to the shuttle. It crossed to the forward wheel. Weight mounted as a railcar whisked them to the inner deck. He led them down a passageway. They peered right and left, busily conversing, although he heard few sounds, none of which his throat could make. "I wish you could tell me how you feel about this," he said aloud, for his own comfort. "Is it splendid, primitive, pathetic, or frightening?"

In a common room gone echoey he did what nobody had managed hitherto. Humans could not yet operate the Tahirian equipment that would have provided a representation of the galaxy. Here he could spread one over a four-meter screen, shining in blackness. Of course, only the most gigantic stars appeared singly, and the display included only what his race had known when *Envoy* departed—a skeleton galaxy, half empty on the far side of the central clouds. A scale along the bottom was calibrated in units already standardized.

Nansen manipulated the keyboard. A spark sprang to life, an arrow pointing at it: the sun of Tahir, hue precisely correct for the extraordinary Tahirian color vision. He sent the pointer back along a signified five thousand light-years. Where it came to rest, another spark jumped forth, whiter, Sol.

Mostly he watched his guests. He thought he captured a sense of emotions and attitudes. A sound that purred or trilled added overtones of pleasure to a statement; a growling or piping note was less favorable. When the leaves of a mane rose and fell, a smooth wave through them bore a different meaning from the same sequence proceeding jaggedly. The code of odors was as subtle as the movements of a fan in a woman's hand had anciently been, or more so, and an integral part of the language.

The languages?

Reactions exploded. Two of the beings bounded forward and hugged him, a gesture they had perhaps learned by watching humans. Others kept aside, manes ashiver, as if whispers went between them. Dubious? When Nansen made arrows expand outward from either star, trying to propose future voyages and meetings, he wondered whether what he saw on some was horror. Smells certainly got sharp.

He blanked the screen. "Well," he said in his most soothing tone, "let's go to your quarters, and then eat," in the wardroom, separate foods. He smiled lopsidedly. "May the day come when we can drink a toast."

A score of buildings, small, curved, delicately tinted, clustered among trees in the middle of a burgeoning hillscape. The tropical sky arched cloudless, the air below lay hot and pungent. Zeyd thought this was less likely a village than a node in a global city.

A large structure stood a hundred meters aside, surrounded by well-tended sward. Waiting nearby, he had ample employment. A score of Tahirians had gathered about him. Three were newly parents, infants clinging to the dorsal ridge with the help of their spurs. All knew more or less what he wanted, and were willing.

One after the next, he held his instrument near a pair of antennae and activated it. A magnetic field extended. The antennae stirred, following its variations with a sensitivity equal to that of the built-in meters, or better. He replaced it with an electrostatic field. The Tahirians cooed. Their manes dithered. Puffs of scent blew from glands in the skin.

He nodded. "Yes," he said to himself in his mother tongue, "these organs are surely compasses and, I suspect, much else. Manifold are the works of God."

The building clove. Mokoena came out, accompanied by Peter and a couple of other scientists. Zeyd forgot his experiment. "Ha, at last!" he called. "What did you get in there?"

She drew near him and halted. Her eyes were wide, her voice low. "They showed me their act of love."

He caught his breath.

"Two adults performed it," she told him, with a reverence he had seldom heard from her. "A holocinema, and anatomical diagrams on a flat screen, ran concurrently. They've finally learned how to do visual presentations that are comprehensible to us."

"How—"

"A pair meets, mouth to mouth. They embrace, they speak with their manes, they kiss with their scents. Once I understood, I saw it was beautiful. It went on for—eleven minutes by my timer."

"And the . . . reproduction?"

Mokoena stood silent, bringing herself back to mere science, before she replied in a more nearly academic voice. "I think both partners have to be in arousal. Pheromones . . . courtship, love. . . . Fluids flow between them, both ways, driven by sphincters and the tonguelets, which must be centers of sensation. The gonads release—gametes—that swim down the streams and fuse in the mouths. Then the zygotes swim up the other stream to a—womb? There are many of them, but only a single spot where one can attach and grow. Gestation takes about a Tahirian year. We've noticed what we supposed was a . . . birth outlet . . . on everybody. It is. At first the parent nourishes the young by regurgitation."

Mokoena paused again. "I don't know why they didn't let you in too, when we've generally been together working with them," she said. "Were they afraid of alarming you? They know nothing about how unlike we may be, inside as well as outside, and—I do have a vagina."

Zeyd nodded. "It must make for a strange psychology, having the sex organ in the face. Where the newborn feed, too. And hermaphroditic—"

"That's not the right word. We need a word for *their* sex."

"Could this be why we haven't seen any behaving like married couples?"

"I don't know. How would a Tahirian married couple behave? It varied over Earth, you remember." *You remember.* Mokoena went on quickly: "I can guess at communal or group rearing of the young."

Zeyd reached for lightness. "Aren't they curious about our methods?"

Mokoena relaxed and laughed. "Oh, my, yes! I have a feeling our pictures of it leave them puzzled. It's too weird."

Scantily clad, she stood with sweat running agleam down a frame that gravity stress had brought back to well-rounded slenderness, panther-dark, joyful. He deepened his voice. "The wondrousness of two sexes—"

"They would doubtless like to know the chemistry as much as we would like to know theirs."

"We should give them a demonstration."

"Who will volunteer?"

He grinned. "Well—"

She met his look head-on. "I don't care to put on a show myself, Selim, not even in the interests of science. Perhaps especially not in the interests of science."

He kept his composure. "Pardon me. No offense intended. But aren't you free-spirited?"

"I never did anything that did not mean something more than fun. Good friendship, at the very least. And I never came between two others." She turned from him to address her guides as best she could.

25.

From high above and afar, after the planetary shell opened a cleft to let the Tahirian spacecraft through and closed again behind, the spectacle was awesome enough. White steam and black smoke roiled in upward-rushing winds where sometimes flame flared. Below sprawled and reared a step pyramid the size of a small mountain, bearing towers, battlements, portals, keeps, roadways, trackways, kilometers-long tubes of mighty bore, forms as alien to human eyes as functions were unknown to human minds. Around it spread a forest of lesser structures, dense near the center, thinning out with distance until empty desert framed the edge of vision. They bore many different shapes, but dominant was something like a metal tree with an intricate mesh between the leafless boughs. Lights flashed throughout, a tumbling, bewildering shift from moment to moment, so that the men caught illusory half-glimpses of fireworks, waves, a maelstrom, a thing that danced. Machines scuttled about or clustered to do some task. Here and there moltenness welled up, seethed sullen red, rolled slowly down channels until it congealed into dark masses. There the machines were at their busiest.

"Jesus Christ!" Brent rasped. "What *is* that? Like the middle of hell!"

"I—I think I can guess," Cleland said.

"Better wait till we have had a closer look," Nansen advised. The spacecraft sped onward and the titans' workshop sank below the horizon.

A number of the third planet's fifteen-hour days passed before the three visitors saw the sight again. Then they were not sure whether it was the same one; there were several, distributed over the globe. Although they and the Tahirians could now communicate slightly, most things remained obscure, occasionally even the interpretation of a map. This particular uncertainty didn't matter. They had already encountered more astonishments than they could sort out.

The tour began at an enclosed headquarters where air was breathable, with imagery of the original work. Comets had not contented the builders; to win the stuff that was to become atmosphere and hydrosphere, their machines also dismembered an icy moon of a giant planet and put the pieces on a collision orbit. Centuries later, when things had somewhat quieted down but not much gas had yet escaped back to space, they roofed the world. Thereafter they tapped its own buried reserves of ice, though that was a minor contribution.

"Tremendous!" Brent said. "We've *got* to learn the engineering. What we could do with it—"

"I wonder," mused Nansen. "Will humans ever start anything that will take millions of years to finish? It's a rare man who tries to provide for his grandchildren."

"He can't," Cleland replied. "Human affairs are too, uh, chaotic. Everything's bound to change b-beyond recognition in less than a thousand years. Nothing's predictable. The Tahirians, they've achieved a . . . stable society. And any, uh, profit motive is irrelevant, when self-maintaining, self-reproducing robots do the work."

"Um, why was the work ever begun? What need for it?"

"Never mind now," Brent said. "I'm thinking what we could do, we humans, for our purposes, with power like this."

"We may well find it waiting for us when we return," countered Nansen.

"Or we may not. Or if we do—we won't arrive helpless."

A pillar, one of those that upheld the enclosing sky, was in many ways still more numinous. No plain shaft, it rose organismically intricate, responsive, well-nigh alive. Its interplay with strata and height, ground tremors and winds, not only kept it standing but acted on them, was a force in the development of the planet. The ascent and descent of it, in a bubble that climbed, with stops to go inside for an uncomprehending look, became a voyage in itself.

The waters teemed with microscopic life. Some had begun to aggregate: patches of scum, ragged mats. Crumbling shorelines revealed where germs gnawed rock down to the motes that would go into soil. The life had not arisen naturally, nor was its evolution driven by blind chance and selection. An underlying, interweaving set of mechanisms—biological and nanorobotic together, Cleland speculated—would hold it on the many roads to its destiny, which was to prepare this world for the kind of life that lived on Tahir.

"Everything guided," he muttered. "Accelerated. Maybe half a billion years will serve. Maybe less. Though if they want what they've made to last as long as that—" He stared before him. "Yes, I believe I'm right about what those monster establishments are for."

And at last their guides, the Tahirians they called Emil and Fernando, brought them to one.

They stood a long while by the aircar, trying to grasp a sight so huge and strange that their eyes did not know how to see it. At their backs reached the barrens, red dunes, black rock, scudding dust. On the right a pillar lifted white over the horizon, made thin by distance, sheering and narrowing until it became a point thrust against the violet heaven.

Ahead lay the forest, metal boles, skeletal limbs, glimmery webs from end to end of vision. Shapes hunched among them, low domes, pentagonal upthrusts, helices, congeries. Robots moved between, some like giant beetles, some like dwarf war machines, some like nothing describable. The forest thickened farther in until it became a shadowy mass. Beyond loomed the central pyramid, its terraces saw-toothed with walls and spires. Smoke and vapors hazed it to blue-gray. Everywhere blinked the light-sparks, over the metal trees, tangled in their meshes, all hues, chaotic in complexity, the lunacy of a million intermingled meanings. A rumbling noise filled the air, a bass that stole into the bones. Now and then the ground boomed and faintly shuddered.

Nansen brought his glance back to the Tahirians. Emil made a forward gesture. Evidently it was safe to proceed on foot. They started. Human pulses beat high.

In a gravity less than two-fifths terrestrial, the men did not feel weighted down, although they were well burdened. Elsewhere it had sufficed outdoors to wear a breathmask attached to a tank of oxynitrogen, ordinary field garb, perhaps a canteen and food pouch, and whatever scientific equipment seemed appropriate. Here it became helmets with regenerative units, full coveralls, gloves, and boots. The air was noxious from upwellings and ongoing chemistry. The Tahirians wore similar protection, though theirs was mostly transparent and flexible, films enclosing the little four-legged bodies. Fernando carried what must be a locator. A magnetic sense was of scant avail on this planet, and the forest would screen off signals from their vehicle.

Minutes and meters passed. A machine composed of joined modules crawled into view. Emil spoke. Sonic amplifiers conveyed a whistle and purr; the mane shook.

"I wish I knew what en just said," Cleland sighed. Sundaram had invented the pronoun for members of the race. "That caterpillar— It's maddening, these scraps of pidgin technicalese we've got."

"We've added some vocabulary on this trip," Nansen reminded. "And Ajit does promise a real language soon." He grinned. "Of course, then we'll have to learn it."

"Meanwhile, though— And we can't ask what all these lights are for."

"I can guess," Brent said. "Whatever else they do, I'm pretty sure the trees make up a sensor-computer network. The blinks are a code, mainly issuing orders to the mobile machines."

Nansen nodded. "M-m, yes, that sounds like a very Tahirian idea."

"I wish it weren't," Cleland complained. "Confusing. Makes everything seem to jump around. Do you hear a buzz?"

Nansen listened. Only the noise ahead, as of a gigantic kettle aboil, reached him. "No."

"Imagination. I'm getting sort of dizzy, too."

"Yeah, can't say I feel comfortable here," Brent admitted.

Nansen scowled at the stiff shapes that surrounded them. "Nor I, quite. Perhaps we should turn back. . . . No, we'll continue for a while."

The growling and seething waxed. The group came in view of the source. Cleland jarred to a halt, stood for a moment agape, and uttered a yell. "It is! I was right! It's got to be!"

They had entered a broad open space, a black and jumbled lava waste. Near the middle squatted a sooty shell wherein power labored. Before it, smoke and steam eddied above a ten-meter pool that glowed red. Even at their distance and through their suits and helmets the men felt its heat. It bubbled, spat gouts and sparks, roared in its fury. A channel bore the molten rock off, to congeal after a while into slaggy masses. Several robots quarried these as they cooled, loaded them into a great open-bed vehicle that rested wheelless above the ground. Metal trees lined the channel. Their lights blinked through the same intricate rhythms, over and over.

Steady state, Nansen thought. *Repetition, except when something goes wrong and the robots make repairs. A full carrier takes the freight away and dumps it, while another arrives for more. Through millions of years?*

The din hammered in his skull. He felt suddenly as if he were falling down a chasm. Tensing every muscle, he hauled his gaze free of the hypnotic *flash-flash-flash.*

Cleland's word's clattered. "Yes, yes, the pyramid, it holds the magma pump, electromagnetic or however it works, but here's one of the outlets, and maybe before the stuff's left to weather the pyramid processes it for calcium, phosphorus, potassium, or maybe erosion and biology do that well enough, but here's the thermostat, safety valve, renewal—"

He doesn't sound like himself, Nansen thought vaguely. *What's the matter with him?* He recalled the planetologist's controlled excitement of days—weeks?—ago:

"Plate tectonics keeps Earth alive. It frees the elements that life locks up in fossils, and releases others like potassium. It raises new rock to take up carbon dioxide as carbonate, and takes the old rock down below before the carbon dioxide is too depleted. This planet the Tahirians are converting, it's got to have that cycle or the atmosphere will never be right for them, but it doesn't have subduction. Also, I suppose, with a shell enclosing it, they don't want enormous shield volcanoes. But then they've got to bleed off the core energy; and they can use it for more of the geochemistry they need, eventually for stabilizing the air and regulating the greenhouse. I think they're making a start on doing all this artificially, and in the long run making it natural, self-operating for the next couple of billion years. They've drilled clear down to the core. The mills of God!"

Today:

"Science in action," Cleland chanted at the lava well and the machines. The ground drummed, the wind hissed, the lights flickered and flickered. "Oh, what's to learn!" He rocked forward across the stone field.

"Something's damn wrong," Brent groaned. "I've got a headache to kill me."

"And I—*vertiginoso*—" Nansen looked to Emil and Fernando. They stood calmly, innocently, untouched.

Cleland kept going. Did the Tahirians show concern? They glanced from him to the captain. Leaves stood stiffly in their manes. They twittered.

"Cleland!" Nansen shouted. "Come back! That's dangerous!"

The planetologist tripped on a lump. He fell, rose, lurched on toward the channel where the trees flashed.

"Hey, is he out of his head?" Brent cried. A fire fountain leaped briefly up from the pool.

"I . . . don't know—Cleland, Cleland!"

We're giddy, muddled, like drunks. What to do, what to do? "Go get him," Nansen begged the Tahirians. They stared back, obviously worried but baffled, unwilling to take action . . . because the man must know what he was doing. . . .

He doesn't.

The knowledge burst over Nansen. He swung around, seized Brent by the shoulders, wrestled the engineer about until they both stood sidways to the lava stream. His brain still gibbered, but it became an undertone. "Listen," he said fast. "Those lights combine to flicker frequencies that cause something like an epileptic fit—in humans. I remember reading about it. He's lost all judgment. He's going for a close look, and probably he'll fall into the channel, the lava. I can't explain to our friends and ask them to go after him."

"Shit in a whorehouse!" Brent exploded. He pulled away from Nansen's grasp. "I'll fetch him."

"No. I will."

Brent glared. "Like hell. You're our captain."

"Yes, I am." *And the commander sends no man into danger he would not enter himself.* "But you work with machinery. You can better gauge distances and angles. I'll go blind, eyes shut. Else the lights might take me, too. You call directions. Don't look at them more than you absolutely must. Can you do that, Mr. Brent?"

The other man snapped to attention. "Yes, sir."

"Very well." Nansen wheeled. Before the lights could touch him again, he had squeezed his lids together.

Cleland was already near the channel bank. He slipped and stumbled in the chaos of scoria. It got worse the farther he went.

Nansen strode. "Left about ten degrees," came Brent's voice, faint beneath the thunders. Nansen tuned up his amplifier. The well brawled. The formless blobs of blindness floated before him.

But his mind was clearing. Out of the racket he sifted words: "Right just a tad. . . . Watch out, you've got a boulder in your path. . . . No, Tim's veered off. Bear left about fifteen degrees. . . ."

He's the hero—Brent. He clings to his sanity and forces his judgment to function, while the lights flash, flash, flash.

Could there be something else, some inductive effect on our brains from the computers everywhere around, making us this vulnerable, Tim the most? I don't know. I hope we'll live to know.

Nansen tripped and fell. Pain jabbed through knees and hands. He picked himself up, he groped onward. Heat washed around him and smote through his helmet.

"Sir," amidst the tumult, "he's climbing onto the bank. You'd better turn back."

"No."

"But you might go over, yourself, into the stream—"

"Guide me, Mr. Brent."

"Sir. Left, ten degrees. No, a little more right. Careful, there's a heap of junk ahead. . . . Better go on all fours."

Nansen obeyed. The heat in the rock baked through clothing and gloves.

Dimly in the roar: "You're nearly to him. He's on the rim, staring down. You could knock him over, if he doesn't fall on his own account first."

Nansen opened his eyes. He saw the lava up which he crawled. And two boots, ankles, shins— He surged to his feet. "Come back with me, Cleland," he said into the noise and the scorching.

The enthralled man made no answer. He swayed where he stood above moltenness. Again the lights attacked Nansen.

He laid hold. Cleland moaned. He struggled. Nansen got a lock on his arms, a knee in the small of his back. He wrenched him around.

The lights were behind them. Nansen saw only stone, the forest that was merely befuddling, Brent and the Tahirians at its edge. Emil and Fernando stood stiff—suddenly realizing what had almost happened? Nansen frog-marched Cleland down the bank and across the waste.

"Hey!" Brent shouted. "We did it! By God, we did it!"

Cleland slumped. "Wha—wha's uh matter?" he wailed. "I was—I don't know—"

Nansen released him but kept an arm around his waist. "You'll be all right. Come along. And never look back to where you were."

"Cap'n—Cap'n, was I crazy or, or what—?"

"It will be all right, I say. We simply met another thing we did not know."

26.

Besides his research notes, which he entered in the general database, Sundaram kept a journal. At first it was for himself, later he shared it with Yu. In it he set down subjective impressions, tentative ideas, ruminations, remarks, speculations, the raw stuff of knowledge.

"Now that we and the Tahirians have developed the basic structure of Cambiante"—the common language, with the parlours its means of expression—"and are rapidly increasing and refining its vocabulary, we can try to explain what we are to each other," he wrote one day. "This may well prove the most difficult task of all, perhaps not entirely possible, but we must try, for it is the ultimate purpose of *Envoy*'s journey.

"Herewith a fragmentary rendition of what I believe our collocutors have been attempting to tell us.

"Their species evolved to cope with the changeable, often harsh, occasionally murderous environments on this planet. Omnivorous but largely vegetarian, they lived in groups with a dominance hierarchy. However, alpha, beta, etc. obtained their ranks not directly by strength and aggressiveness, but by contribution to the group. Thus, in a jungle the primitive alpha might be the strongest fighter against predators, while in a desert en might be the best water finder. This appears to have helped drive the evolution of higher intelligence. The primal psychology persists, cooperative, with solitary individuals rare, usually pathological cases. The normal, optimal ordering of a Tahirian society appears to be an interaction between what I may very roughly call clans, the ultimate units, as families are the ultimate human units.

"Inevitably, clashes occurred between bands, cultures, ideologies.

However, they were always less ferocious than among humans. Empathy is too natural when so much of language is somatic and chemical. Civilizations did rise and fall, with accompanying ruination. I suspect that more often than not the causes were environmental catastrophes, perhaps triggered by misguided agricultural and industrial practices.

"Be that as it may, Tahirians are no more born to sainthood than humans are. When a society no longer works smoothly, respect for the established order decays, the underlying mystique disintegrates, and chaos and suffering follow. This world, too, has known dark ages.

"When science opened a way to the stars, it gave the race unprecedented opportunities, but also enormous challenges.

"Probably in us humans the basic motivations for most of what we do, including science and exploration, fall into two general classes. One is the hope of gain, whether wealth, power, fame, freedom, or security. The other is the need to make sense of the universe, a need that expressed itself originally in myth and religion. I imagine corresponding urges are present in the Tahirians, but not in the same degrees and ways, and more for the group than the individual. To them, I think, science is as much communion as discovery. One shares findings and achievements with one's society, thereby enhancing it as well as one's own standing in it. Let us remember that science is itself creative art.

"Thus, I think—in the most vague and general terms, subject to endless qualifications and exceptions—the Tahirians went forth more in search of newness, inspiration, spiritual refreshment, than profit. And for thousands of years their ships traveled among the stars.

"Why, then, did they go no farther? Why did their voyaging fade out as their colonies were abandoned?

"I can only guess. Rather, we can, for our crew has discussed the riddle over and over. Let me list a few considerations.

"The sheer number of stars. Granted that most planets are barren, and most of the living ones bear little more than microbes, still, the variety, the puzzles, the possibilities, within just a few light-years are overwhelming. Data saturation begins to set in.

"As for going farther, one reaches a radius where nobody on the mother world will live long enough to hear about one's discoveries. Motivation flags.

"The economics is, at best, marginal. Interplanetary enterprise saved human civilization by bringing in material and energy resources that Earth could no longer supply, as well as industrial sites outside the biosphere. But given a recycling nanotechnology, how much is a cargo hauled across light-years worth?

"Planets where people can settle—without needing an investment in life support that goes beyond feasibility—are very rare.

"Will such limitations close in on humankind? Have they already? We do not know.

"Nor do we know whether they were enough by themselves to bring about the extinction of Tahirian starfaring. We have hints that, early on, Tahirians encountered yet another interstellar civilization, which lost heart and gave up for reasons of its own. We also have clues to something else the Tahirians found, something terrible, to retreat and hide from; but this is barely an intimation, and I may be quite wrong about it. We shall have to learn more, pebble by pebble.

"Suffice it now that the Tahirians have long since recalled their colonists, ended their voyagings, scrapped their starships, and settled down into stability. Their clans are globally coordinated, population and economy are steady-state, they do not seem to fear the future. Indeed, they plan on continuing essentially as they are for as long as imagination reaches. By the time, perhaps a billion years hence, that their aging sun has grown so hot that Tahir is uninhabitable, the third planet will be ready for them. No doubt they look beyond even this. Humans could not. Tahirians are not human.

"How they reconcile such an endlessness, which is also such a narrowness, with what I believe is an instinctual need for a hierarchy with meaningful functions, we do not yet know. I suspect that multisensory electronic communications are necessary for dynamic equilibrium. Are they sufficient? Beneath the calm surface, are there tensions and contradictions, as there surely would be in humans?

"We must continue our investigation."

Sundaram keyed off, leaned back in his chair, and blew out a breath. "Enough for today," he said. "Tomorrow I will make it into a lecture for the troops."

Yu came up behind him. "Must you?" she asked. "You work too hard."

"Well, true, they know most of it already, but in bits and pieces, unsystematic. Perhaps a synthesis will provoke fresh ideas."

"Meanwhile," she said, "what you need is some nonscientific meditation, followed by tea and a bite to eat and what else goes with having a good night's sleep." Her fingers closed on his shoulders and began to massage, firmly, lovingly.

It was late fall at Terralina when Ruszek returned from space. He had fared about with a pair of Tahirians, partly to see something of robotic mining in the asteroids—if "mining" was the word for extraction and refining processes largely on the nano level—and partly to learn some of the practical characteristics of a Tahirian spacecraft. There might be useful hints for human engineers, and even a clue to the mysterious driving force.

He found the settlement abuzz. Nansen was absent, visiting a historic and artistic center, perhaps a kind of Florence or Kyoto. That was not tourism; with the help of his guides, he would bring back a rich store of referents to enlarge and strengthen the Cambiante language. The others greeted Ruszek cordially.

Yet he could not make complete sense out of what he heard from them. Sundaram was preoccupied with the latest semantic bafflement he had come upon, Yu with the improvement of scientific-technological vocabulary. Dayan, Kilbirnie, Cleland, and Brent were in their various ways so enthusiastic about their wish that Ruszek lost patience with sorting out what struck him as babble. Zeyd was analyzing his latest biochemical acquisitions. That left Mokoena. She was busy, too, working up her notes, searching deeper into the patterns of Tahirian life. But she was willing to take a break.

He wanted to get her aside anyway.

Dressed against chill, they walked out into the woods. A game trail had become familiar to the humans; their passages had widened it till two could go side by side. Trees and undergrowth walled it in. The bronze, russet, amber foliage was now mostly gone, though, the walls left open to the wind. It whittered, boughs swayed and creaked, a pale sun in a pale sky cast fluttering shadows. From the damp soil rose a scent as of an oceanside on Earth, early decay, nature's farewell.

The two were silent for a while, awkward after apartness. When at last Ruszek spoke, it was of the least personal matter. "This about the pulsar," he said roughly. "Can you explain it to me?"

"Why, you've heard. They've made their proposal public. To go there and study it."

"Halál és adóok!" Ruszek exploded. "Why? We're supposed to have a good, useable language in another year or less. Then the Tahirians can tell us everything about it, down to whether it takes cream or sugar in its coffee."

"That is the point," Mokoena said. "They can't. I see this wasn't made clear to you." She smiled. "Well, everybody talking at once, and also wanting to hear what you had to tell."

"They can't?" His stride missed a beat. He stared at her. "When it's next door?"

Mokoena gathered her words as she walked. The wind shrilled.

"Ajit and Wenji have inquired into this lately, at Hanny's request," she said with care. "They have learned— Yes, the Tahirians were there more than once, thousands of years ago. When they stopped starfaring, they left robots to observe and beam back the data. But the robots wore out. Radiation, electronics degraded, I don't know. Either they weren't meant for self-repair and reproduction, or the materials are lacking in that system. The Tahirians haven't sent more."

"Are they that petrified? Those I've been with haven't acted like it."

"I don't know," Mokoena sighed. "None of us does, yet. I have an impression that their ancestors . . . recoiled from everything to do with starfaring. They didn't *want* reminders. So curiosity died in them."

Ruszek shook his head. His mustache bristled against the wind. "That just is not true. I deal with them. They're fascinated."

"I likewise," she replied. "And, in fact, the plans for a pulsar expedition include several Tahirians. But we—naturally, we see the most those who are interested, who're glad of us." Her voice sank. "I have a feeling that other Tahirians wish we'd never come to rouse forgotten emotions from their graves."

"An expedition, why? There are space observatories. I've seen them."

"Well, Hanny and Tim say the system, neutron star and planets both, must be in very fast, early evolution, and the instruments here aren't adequate to track it properly. At least, a close look should provide data that'll make the local observations a great deal more meaningful."

Ruszek grinned. "Mainly, they want to go see."

"Scientific passion." Mokoena lowered her voice further. She gazed ahead, in among the bare, tossing boughs. "Also, what better have they to do?"

If flared in Ruszek. "*Isten,* what a jaunt!"

Mokoena laid a hand on his arm for a moment, the merest touch. "I'm afraid you shall have to forego it, Lajos," she said gently. "The captain would never let both our boat pilots go, and Jean has already spoken for that berth. Hanny, the physicist; Tim, the planetologist; Al, the engineer and general assistant—it cannot be more. We don't dare."

Ruszek's mouth twisted. "I wasn't alert enough. Ah, well."

"Besides," Mokoena said, "perhaps you didn't understand it in all the cross talk, but the captain opposes the idea. He says it can't justify risking our ship."

Ruszek narrowed his eyes against the bitter air. "Hm. I should think— we do know a lot about pulsars, this one especially, don't we?—we could program *Envoy* so she can't endanger herself."

"We don't know everything. We can't foresee every hazard."

"Nor can we here. I'll speak to Nansen when he returns. He should at least let us vote on it."

Mokoena gave Ruszek a long look. "Although you can't go?"

He shrugged. "I am no dog in the manger. And I do now have plenty to keep me out of mischief."

The wood opened on a glade where turf grew thick and soft, still deeply red-brown. A spring bubbled forth near the center, to rill away into the forest. In summer it was a favorite spot for humans to seek peace and, sometimes, human closeness. Man and woman stopped. Slowly, they turned toward one another.

"You've become a happier man than you were," she said.

"I'm doing something real again, and enjoying it," he replied. "Like you."

"I'm glad, Lajos."

Her eyes were very bright in the dark face. His words began to stumble. "You—us— I asked if we could go for this walk so we could talk alone—"

"I know." Sudden tears glimmered. "I'm sorry, Lajos."

His countenance locked. He spoke as nearly matter-of-factly as he was able. "You don't want to try again, we two?"

"I—" Mokoena swallowed. "Lajos," she said in a rush, "I am not casual. Whatever you may have supposed, I am not."

"You mean you have somebody else in mind."

"I mean only— No, Lajos, we'll be friends, God willing, but only friends."

After a bit, he shrugged again. "Well, I said I have enough to keep me busy."

Impulsively, she caught his hands. "You are more than a man, Lajos. You're a gentleman. I could almost wish—"

He disengaged. "No harm if I hope, is there?"

With the suddenness of the seasons in these parts, the first snow fell soon afterward and the land lay white when Nansen returned. He had stayed in radio contact; his folk were waiting to greet him as he stepped out of the Tahirian aircar. One by one the men shook his hand, then one by one the women embraced him—Yu shyly, Mokoena heartily, Dayan with eagerness and a long kiss while Zeyd went impassive, Kilbirnie unwontedly hesitant. As they left the landing field, the car took off.

A banquet was ready in the common room, as there had been for Ruszek earlier. Any occasion for a celebration was to be seized. Business could wait. News took over the conversation, gossip, small talk, babble and cheer, drinks clinking together. After dinner they set music playing and danced for a while. As she swayed in Nansen's arms, Kilbirnie whispered, "Could we talk alone later?"

His pulse jumped. "Why, of course."

"I'll leave soon and meet you under the lightning tree."

She could visit my office tomorrow, but we might be interrupted, or we might not have time afterward to mask ourselves. Or she could come to my cottage tonight, or I to hers, but that might be too intimate; it might confuse whatever she has to say. The thoughts and questions tumbled in him. He became rather absentminded company for the rest of the evening.

Finally he could say good night, don his thermal coverall, and go. Snow glistened crisp, scrunching beneath his shoes. The settlement huddled black by the dull sheen of ice on the river. Air went keen into his nostrils and streamed forth ghostly. The moon was full but tiny; nearly all light fell from crowding stars and argent Milky Way. It blanched the leafless boughs and towering bole of the tree he sought. The scar from which it had its name stood like a rune on high.

Kilbirnie trod from its vague shadow. Nansen halted where she did. They looked wordless into eyes that gleamed faintly in half-knowable faces.

"We missed you, skipper, we truly did," the husky voice said low.

"Thank you. I missed you." He smiled. "But that was personal presence. I continued as bossy as ever on the radio, didn't I?"

"Nay. Ye're a guid leader, the kind who trusts his followers to think and do for themselves."

He saw what was coming, he had guessed it beforehand, but to help her he asked, "What did you wish to talk about now?"

"Surely you know." She gestured at a point in the glittering sky. "Yonder wild star."

"I've heard the arguments to and fro," he said. "We'll repeat them at a formal meeting. Is this the place for any?"

"Not the technical questions, no, like whether we can indeed program *Envoy* to keep herself safe—"

"Probably we can," he interrupted. "But we can't program you."

Her grin flashed. "Och, I'll be canny. We all will who go. We like being alive."

He decided on a blunt challenge. "Do you, here?"

"Always and everywhere." She plunged ahead: "But we can be part alive or fully alive. Ajit and Wenji, Mam and Selim—you and Lajos, among these planets— The rest of us want something real to do, too."

"You can help," he urged. "We need your help. *Dios mío,* have we not mysteries everywhere around us?"

"It is less than we could be doing. Fakework, often, which a robot can handle as well or better. Hanny and Tim think we may learn what we'd never otherwise know, yonder. And those Tahirians who want to come along—what might we learn from them, and about them?"

"Also," he said slowly, "you would cut a couple of years off your time of service before we turn home."

She straightened. "Aye, that's at the core of what I wanted to speak of tonight, skipper. The technical matters, the public matters, we've chopped them over and over, and will over and over again, like making a haggis. But what it . . . means."

Nansen waited.

She looked down at the snow. "Naught I'd care to say in a meeting." The words came out one by one, in small white puffs. "What it means to me."

He waited.

She looked back at him. Her tone steadied. "I'll be away half a year, or thereabouts, more or less as much time as we'll allow ourselves there. For you, two and a half years."

He nodded. "Yes. And you'll send your messages to us, but they'll be almost a year old, and we won't know—"

"Whether the ship that's to bear you home is safe."

"Whether you are."

Silence shivered.

"Aye, 'tis much to ask," Kilbirnie said.

"I have to think about more than safety. What will this do to morale?"

Her smile caught the starlight afresh. "You've a high-hearted crew these days, skipper. Make them more so."

"Yes," he said harshly, "if I let this come to a vote, we both know how the vote will go. But may I?"

Her reply was soft. "I understand. The responsibility is on you. And we *are* being selfish in a way, we four. We'll not be those who suffer a long span of fear for us."

"A long separation," escaped him.

She was mute for a while in the frost. When she spoke, it stumbled. "Skipper, that's what I—I hoped to say—that it is unfair to you, Ricardo Nansen."

He rallied. "But you feel that forbidding it would be unfair to you."

"Not me, not too much. Hanny and Tim—and, yes, poor, lonely Al— and those Tahirians who long to go starfaring . . ."

"And perhaps the star itself," he conceded. "It does offer some fantastic opportunities . . . almost as if God is being generous—" He pulled loose from abstractions and returned to her. Breath had caught in stray locks over her brow and frozen to make starlit sparkles. "You burn to go, don't you?"

"I could stay—aye, quite happily—if . . ."

"But you would always wonder what you had missed, wouldn't you, Jean?"

Her eyes widened when he said her first name. He hurried on: "And your points about the others, and what it could all mean to the mission, yes, they are valid." *I can give you this gift, Jean, if I can bring myself to it.*

"Always the man of duty, no?" He couldn't tell whether she admired or reproached or tenderly mocked. On Earth he would soon have found out, but this wasn't Earth.

"Let me think further," he said. "Meanwhile, the hour's grown late, and we're tired and cold."

"And you're heavy burdened. Aye, let's go to our sleep."

27.

Year three.

Envoy had been a star, hastening through night heaven to vanish in the planetary shadow, emerging to sink toward the eastern horizon. Now it was gone. For a while people found themselves glancing aloft before they remembered. At first they were glad of the undertakings that kept them occupied. Later, one by one and more and more, they were troubled.

A hurricane formed in midocean. On a previous trip, the Tahirian he called Stefan had shown Ruszek the energy projectors on the little moon. With animated graphics—using conventions lately developed, mutually comprehensible—en had explained that focused beams, precisely aimed, changed the courses of such storms; they veered from coastlands where they could wreak harm. Now en and he boarded a robotic aircraft, among those that were to monitor events from within. "You're really learning to read our feelings, aren't you?" Ruszek exulted.

The teardrop sped through the stratosphere. Ruszek kept his instruments going, recording whatever they were able to. Eventually he might accumulate such a stack of information that Yu could make something of it, maybe even figure out how the jetless drive worked. He suspected the principle was quantum mechanical, and a starship's engineer was necessarily a jackleg quantum physicist. At least, when Dayan got back—

The teardrop plunged. The weather loomed black ahead. He recalled

Nansen's story about flying through stuff like this, once . . . but that was five thousand years and light-years away. . . . The boat slammed into the dark. Wind raved, lightning flared. Forces shoved Ruszek brutally back and forth against a safety web improvised for him. "Ha!" he bawled, and wished he were the pilot.

But the pilot was a machine. Its purpose was not to have fun but to collect data and shoot them up to the moon. Harnessed nearby, Stefan stared at a crystalline ball en clutched. Glints danced in it, barely visible to the man. *Another kind of instrument,* he guessed while his skull rattled. *Keeping track of . . . velocities, pressures, ionizations, a barrelful of shifty rages. Why? The robot must have full, direct input. Does Stefan want to follow along? Does en want to share the stress, effort, risk? Did any Tahirian do anything like this, before we arrived from beyond?*

Stefan gestured. The fuselage went opaque. Interior lighting went out. Ruszek sat tossed about in a blindness that shuddered and howled.

Enjoy, he told himself, and did.

Light returned. This was no place to use a parleur, but Stefan fluted notes that were perhaps apologetic while looking with ens middle eyes at Ruszek, touching the globe, and waving at the lightnings.

En needed total darkness to take a delicate reading, Ruszek deduced. *No . . . not total. Just no background. We've wondered if Tahirians can see single photons. Why not? Humans almost can.* A coldness crept up his spine. *Yes, I think that's so. And . . . all the chaos while they evolved—let the science gang chew on the idea—but* I *think they think more naturally in quantum mechanics than we do. What does that mean for the way they understand the universe?*

Wind ramped, rain and hail struck like bullets, the aircraft flew onward.

It was not clear to Nansen and Yu why the Tahirian Emil asked them to come with en, or took them where en did. The mutual command of Cambiante was, as yet, too limited. The scope of the language was. Probably in many ways it always would be.

Its creation, which was still in process, had been comparable to the great breakthroughs in physics. Without computers to generate possible approaches, try them, discard them, and generate better ones, it would doubtless have been impossible—certainly within a lifetime, let alone a pair of years. Sonics would not do. To a Tahirian, a vocable by itself was a signal—an alarm cry, for example—but not a word. Indeed, en did not converse in what humans knew as words, but rather in mutable concepts that shaded into each other. Straightforward writing was equally insufficient. A man or woman found Tahirian ideographics hopelessly complex, while to a Tahirian any human system, even Chinese, was bafflingly rigid.

The races had evolved separately, they experienced the world differently, and thus their minds were unlike. The most fundamental thing they had to work out was a mutual semantics.

A parleur screen displayed three-dimensional hypertext. Changes in any part of it, especially cyclic or to-and-fro changes, added a fourth dimension. Learning to write this would have imposed an intolerable strain on memory, but the nanocomputer rendered what a party entered, within the logico-grammatical rules, into agreed-on symbols. With diligence and patience, one could master these.

From either viewpoint, Cambiante was a restricted language, functioning best when it dealt with scientific and technological matters, poorly or not at all in poetics, faith, or philosophy. However, by now it could generally convey practical statements or questions reasonably well. As users discovered some of the cues in tones, attitudes, movements, even odors, they added to the vocabulary, both written and connotative.

Whatever one person understood another to be saying would scarcely ever be quite identical with the intent. But they improved.

The site was an upland, wind-swept and stony, where turf clung in crannies and the few trees were gnarled dwarfs. Seen from above, the country showed signs of former habitation: roads, levelings, excavation where communities had been, occasional rubble heaps. Yu shivered. "Bleak," she said.

"I suppose, as the axis of rotation shifted, it got too uncomfortable here to be worth bothering with," Nansen suggested prosaically.

"Abandonment. A millennial necessity. What do they do when the obliquity becomes extreme?"

"Well, they seem to keep the population at half a billion or less. It will never overcrowd whatever lands are suitable. They can move gradually. We know they plan ahead much further than that."

"Humans would never be able to. We aren't . . . sane enough. Is it really easy for Tahirians?"

The laboratory where the aircar set down was isolated, small, with sparse facilities. Although it and associated buildings were well maintained by robots, everything stood long unused. Such amenities as heat and running water must be restarted. The guests had been told to bring their own sanitary unit and whatever else they would need.

Two who were strangers to them waited outside. With Emil, they hustled the newcomers along, barely letting them unload their baggage in a house before conducting them to the laboratory. "No time for a cup of tea?" asked Yu, only partly in jest.

"Plain to see, they're in a hurry." Nansen frowned. "Do they want to make sure they accomplish what they have in mind before anyone else finds out?"

Once inside, the two other Tahirians were straightaway busy at control boards. Emil faced the humans. "(We wish to convey certain information,)" en spelled out. "(At the present stage of communication, it is best done through graphics, using a larger screen than a parleur's.)"

"But why just here?" Nansen muttered in Spanish. Yu trembled, mainly with eagerness.

Imagery appeared, drawings and numbers, symbolizations meaningful to the watchers.

A sun that exploded, blown-off gas ramming outward to shock against englobing nebulosity—

The remnant dwindling and dwindling, as if downward into nothingness—

Against the background of the stars, a sphere absolutely dark, save for a fiery ring of matter whirling inward—

Close-up of the rim, and the sky behind it eerily distorted—

"A black hole," Yu breathed. "A supernova greater than the one that made the pulsar. Collapse beyond the neutron stage, in past an event horizon, falling forever."

The image receded in sight. A map of local star distributions replaced it. A marker ran from a dot marked with the sign for Tahir's sun, unrolling a distance scale behind it. When it stopped, Nansen read, "About five hundred light-years away. That's as of today. Obviously it was farther when the eruption happened, or this planet would have suffered badly. But what has it to do with us?"

"Hush," Yu murmured. "There's more."

They peered and puzzled. The characters were mostly unknown to them. "I think that's the 'organism' radical," Yu said, pointing. "But why are those quantum physics symbols attached?"

Emil trod back in front of them and fingered ens parleur. "(Life)" en declared. "(Intelligence.)"

"*¿Qué es?*" ripped from Nansen. "No!"

"How?" Yu whispered. "It . . . seems . . . impossible. But—look, the big display—something about quantum states. . . . I can't quite understand it. I don't think Hanny could, either. Not yet."

Emil whistled what they had come to recognize as a note of warning. "(Do not reveal this until further notice,)" en said.

Nansen steadied the parleur in his grasp. "(Not to our shipmates? Why?)"

"(It is dangerous.)" Emil paused. "(If you must tell any, be sure they will let it go no further.)"

"Someone doesn't want us to know," Nansen said.

Dismay shook Yu's voice. "Factions, among these people?"

"I've been getting strong hints of it. We shall have to be careful," *when we cannot now escape to the stars.*

"I can't believe they would be violent. I won't believe it."

"I would rather not, myself. But sometimes there are worse things than violence."

Emil observed them. "(You are weary and perplexed,)" en said. "(The sun is low. Best you take refreshment, rest, and thought. We will resume tomorrow morning early.)"

"That means a short night's rest." Nansen chuckled a bit. "Well, I don't expect I'd sleep much in any case."

"Nor I," Yu agreed. "Not when this is waiting."

The walk across to their quarters was through a chill wind. They didn't feel it. Emil left them at the entrance. The dilation closed behind them. They were in a curve-walled, rosy-tinted room, bare except for his outfit, their food and drink, and a glower to warm the rations. She had taken the adjoining chamber. Eyes looked into eyes.

"Don't worry," Nansen said. "Our friends must know what they're doing—whatever it is."

Yu shook her head. The bobbed blue-black hair swished past the high cheekbones. "No fear. The wonder of it! Something utterly strange, I don't know what, but something we could never have foreseen if we'd stayed home— Oh, Rico, we haven't come this whole long way for nothing!"

"*Ay, sí.*" Upborne together, they embraced. It became a kiss.

He let go and stepped back. "Forgive me," he said unevenly. "That won't happen again."

"I helped it happen." Her laughter drained away into sobriety. "You are right, it had better not again. We must be careful about more than secrets."

He smiled. "Agreed. Permit me only to envy Ajit Sundaram a little in my heart, as well as respect him and you."

"You have a hard time ahead," she answered. "May it end happily." She hunkered down at the supply pile. "Come, let's put this in order and have that cup of tea before we eat."

The island was beautiful

There could be no real knowledge of the life on a planet unless that knowledge included the life in its seas. Once this desire had been expressed to them, some Tahirians brought Mokoena and Zeyd there. Robotic boats came and went from a dockside building full of investigative equipment. It was probably a monitoring station rather than a research laboratory. The civilization must have catalogued every species but be concerned with maintaining a healthy ecology.

At the end of a hard day's study the humans felt ready for some recreation. Walking across a wooded corner of the island, they emerged on a strip of turf, beyond which a beach lay dazzling white under a clear sky and long sunbeams from the west. The air was warm but laden with fresh sea smells. The ocean rolled deeply blue. Although tides were less than Earth's, at this point the conformation of the bottom made breakers high and thunderous.

Mokoena clapped her hands together. "What a surf!" she whooped. "I'm going in."

"Not alone, please," Zeyd cautioned. "The undertow may be bad."

"Well, I appoint you my lifeguard," she laughed.

Her mood captured him. "Why not your partner?"

"Why not indeed?"

For an instant they hesitated, but only an instant. After all, they had stripped before. Clothes fell off. They ran over the sand and into the waves.

The water brawled and surged. When they plunged, it slid sensuously around them, a pulsing whole-body caress. They frisked and frolicked like seals.

Still, they remembered not to get beyond their depth. A comber broke over their heads. They collided, caught at one another, found footing, and sank their toes into shifting grit. The wave rushed on past. Chest deep, Zeyd gazed down into Mokoena's face. Her lips were parted, her breasts thrust against him as she snatched for breath. He kissed her. She responded.

Letting go, they saw the next breaker coming at them, taller yet, a glassy cliff maned with foam. They turned about, jumped clear of the bottom, swam, caught the onslaught, and rode it in.

As it receded they scrambled to their feet and waded ashore. "Hoo," Mokoena panted, "that beast tumbled me!"

He looked her over. "It had the right idea," he said.

She stopped. He moved closer. She lifted her hands and pushed at him, not very hard. "No." Her tone wavered. "Hanny—"

"She's away. For two years and more."

"I won't go behind her back."

"*We* won't. Mam, Hanny and I were—are—friends. We never owned each other. If we did, she would not have left. She told me again and again, as the time approached—the last night, too—she told me she won't be jealous and you are her shipsister."

"I don't know—when she returns—"

"That will depend on you, Mam. You and no one else."

She quivered. "Selim, if you mean that—"

He pulled her to him. "A lovely setting, this, for a lovely woman."

"And a—lovely man . . ."

They hurried to the soft sward and sank down upon it.

Afterward, happily, she murmured, "I wonder if our friends have us under observation."

He grinned. "Then they got their demonstration. Do you mind?"

"Not too much, now."

Before Dayan left, Yu had traded cabins with her so that she might be next to Sundaram's. He and she no longer slept apart.

They sat in the unit that had been his, among relics and keepsakes they had mingled, sipped wine, and gravely talked about their research. It was among their highest pleasures.

"No," he said, "I do not think we can properly call this a conservative society, like old China or old India. That is too weak a word. I think it is posthistoric. It has renounced change in favor of a stable order that apparently provides universal peace, plenty, and justice."

"Or so they tell us, if we understand them rightly," she replied. "A majestic vision in its way. Like a saint reaching Nirvana, or a stately hymn at the end of a Catholic mass."

"But how can we explain it to our shipmates? I fear several of them will find it ghastly."

"Really? Why?"

"Because it may forecast what will happen to our own race."

She considered. "Would it be tragic, actually? Not an eternity of boredom or anything like that. The riches and beauty of the world, the treasures of the past, aren't they new to every newborn? A lifetime isn't long enough to know and savor them all. And there can still be new creations. Ancient, fixed modes, I suppose, but new poems, pictures, stories, music."

Sundaram smiled ruefully. "I doubt that the likes of Ricardo Nansen or Jean Kilbirnie will agree. For that matter, I doubt that every individual Tahirian is content with things as they are. I have an impression, almost a conviction, that some of them look at the stars with longing."

She nodded. "That may be one reason the race ended its starfaring. Deliberately, as a policy decision. It carried the danger of bringing in something new and troublesome." She winced. "What effect are we having? Is it for good or ill?"

His smile warmed. "You have an overactive conscience, my dear."

She smiled back and teased, "Have you none?"

He went serious again. "Oh, I feel my occasional qualms. But I don't have your—tenderness, beneath the tough competence. I am too detached."

"Nonsense. You are the kindest man I have ever known."

"And you—" He leaned forward in his chair. They clasped hands.

Less than two shipboard hours after she had gone zero-zero, *Envoy* arrived at the pulsar.

28.

Year Four.

Nine-tenths of a light-year distant, the sun of Tahir stood lord among the stars. But it was another point of light that vision sought, nearly as bright as Sirius in the skies of Earth. Enhancing every other stellar image, the screen mildened this one, for it would have burned a hole in the retina of a naked eye.

"One millionth Solar luminosity," Dayan said like a prayer to a pitiless god, "shining from a body ten kilometers in diameter. Therefore nineteen thousand times the intensity; and that's just in the visible spectrum."

Her companions could well-nigh hear the thoughts prowling through her. *The core of an exploded giant sun, a mass almost half again Sol's, jammed down by its own gravity till it's that small, that dense, no longer atoms but sheer neutrons, except that at the center the density may go so high that neutrons themselves fuse into something else, hyperons, about which we know little and I lust to know more. An atmosphere a few centimeters deep—incandescent gaseous iron? What storms go rampant through it, what quakes rack the ultimate hardness beneath, and why, why, why? A spin of hundreds per second, a magnetic field that seizes the interstellar matter and whips it outward till it nears the speed of light, kindles a radio beacon with it that detectors can find across the breadth of the galaxy. O might and mystery! Out of the whirlwind, God speaks to Job.*

Cleland's voice trembled. "How close dare we come?"

"The ship will decide," Dayan answered, her tone flat, her mind still at the star. "Not very, I think. It's blazing X rays, spitting plasma and neutrinos—lethal."

"Besides," Brent put in dryly, "we're at about two hundred AU now. Another jump in that direction, and we'd certainly fry."

"But we're no so far frae the planet we ken, are we?" Kilbirnie cried. "We'll tak' our station 'round it, no?" *And explore it,* said the glance she exchanged with Cleland.

Of the three Tahirians, Colin and Fernando stared as raptly at the object of the quest—and beyond it, into the cold cataract of the Milky Way? Leo stood aside, ens mane held stiff. The powers on Tahir, whoever they were and whatever their power meant, had required that a person whom they would pick come along to observe.

The spaceboat was not intended for humans. There was no way *Envoy* could have carried it or any of its kind on her expedition. Not only the hull docks but the entire control system would have had to be rebuilt, which would have caused dangerous instabilities elsewhere in the robotic complex that she was. Improvised facilities—for security, sanitation, nourishment, sleep—enabled humans to go as passengers in the boat. Lately Yu and the Tahirian physicist Esther had jerry-rigged circuits that allowed a skillful human to act as pilot—temporarily, under free-space conditions with plenty of safety margin.

"Hoo-ah!"

Ruszek tickled the board before him. The craft leaped. Nonetheless, weight inside held steady. The moon loomed enormous in sight, a sweep of smooth-fused stone studded with structures, curving sharply to a near horizon. Ruszek cut the drive. Zero gravity felt like an abrupt fall off a cliff. The three aboard had learned to take it as a bird does. The boat swung low around the globe on a hyperbolic hairpin and lined out for the great blue crescent of Tahir.

"That will do," said Yu from aft. "Let us return."

"*Járvány,*" grumbled Ruszek. "I hoped for more of this." His tone was genial, though, and a smile bent his mustache toward his brows.

Harnessed beside Yu, Esther asked, "(Did you record the data you need?)" En quivered and fluted; sweet odors wafted from the skin.

Yu nodded. "(I believe so.)"

"What's the result?" called Ruszek, whose back was to them.

"Excellent," Yu replied. "I think once I have analyzed these readings, with Esther's help, I will know how the field drive operates."

"You don't? I mean, uh, you told me before, you're sure it's a push against the vacuum."

Yu sighed. "An interaction with the virtual particles of the vacuum," she corrected. "Energy and momentum are conserved, but, loosely speaking, the reaction is against the mass of the entire universe, and approximately uniform. What I referred to was understanding the exact, not the general, principle."

"Uniform? Don't they adjust the field inside a hull? Weight's the same during any boost."

"In quantum increments, obviously." Yu paused. "Compared to this drive, jets are as wasteful as . . . as burning petroleum, chemical feedstock, for fuel once was on Earth."

"What *I* like is the handling qualities. How soon can you and your computer design a motor for us, Wenji?"

"Not at all, I fear, until we're home. Besides, we couldn't possibly do so radical a retrofit on *Envoy*, or even her boats." Yu's voice lilted. "However, I think, with Hanny's help when she gets back, we can devise a unit that will compensate for linear acceleration and keep the vector in the wheels constant."

"Do you mean, when the ship's under boost, we won't have to cram like swine onto those manhater-designed gimbal decks?" Ruszek waved clasped hands above his shining pate. "Huzzah!" he bellowed.

Esther looked at ens friend. "(Does he rejoice?)" en asked; or so Yu thought en asked.

"(It is no large matter,)" the engineer replied. "(What I think we have really done, at last, is break some dams of misunderstanding. Now you and I can add a proper language of physics to Cambiante, and have it ready for Hanny Dayan when she returns. Before then, you should be able to explain some things to us. Hints of a strange, tremendous truth—)"

Her gaze went ahead, to the planet, where spring was gusting over Terralina.

Envoy rode as at anchor, circling a world of steel.

Cleland and Kilbirnie stood before the spaceview on a screen. Already their shipmates were busy. Robots would flit out to place instruments in orbit; Tahirian probes with Tahirian field drives would plunge toward the pulsar, wildly accelerated, bearing other instruments; preparations filled every waking hour and haunted many dreams. These two alone had little to contribute. Their yearnings reached elsewhere.

In the light from the heavens, the globe was barely bright enough for the unaided eye to search. Its plains were like vast, murky mirrors, mottled with ice fields. Gashes broke them here and there. Mountain ranges and isolated peaks thrust raw-edged. The limb arched slightly blurred against the stars.

"Mass about half Earth's, diameter about seventy percent—given the mean density, more or less the same surface gravity." Cleland was repeating what they had both heard a dozen times, as humans will when the matter is important. "Thin atmosphere, mostly neon, some hydrogen and helium retained at this temperature. Other volatiles frozen out, including water. Paradox, paradox. What's the answer?"

"What do you mean, Tim?" Kilbirnie asked. It was chiefly to encourage him—she had a fairly good idea—but she hoped for thoughts he might have had since the last general discussion. *God is in the details,* she reflected. *And so is the devil, and the truth somewhere in between.*

When he was into an enthusiasm he spoke fluently. "Look, we know this has to be the remnant of a bigger planet. The supernova vaporized the crust and mantle, left just the core and maybe not all of that. The loss of star mass caused it to spiral out into this crazy orbit it's got now. Meanwhile, taking off the upper layers released pressures—expansion, eruption, all hell run loose. It hasn't stabilized yet, I suspect. What's going on? Theoretically, it should be a smooth ball, but nonlinear processes don't pay much attention to theory, and so we've got rifts, grabens, highlands. How? Where did it get the atmosphere and ice—outgassing, cometary impacts, infall from the supernova cloud, or what? Oh, Jean, a million questions!"

She gripped his hand. "We'll go after the answers," she said, "yonder."

No doubt Dayan, the acting captain, would object, and still more would *Envoy*'s robotic judgment. Kilbirnie's thought coursed about in search of arguments, demands, ways to override opposition: anything short of mutiny. She had not come this far, leaving her true captain behind her, to sit idle in a metal shell.

Summer heat lay on the settlement like a weight. Forest stood windless, listless beneath a leaden overcast. Thunder muttered afar.

Windows were not opaquable, but Nansen had drawn blinds over his and the air conditioning worked hard. In the dusk of the living room, a crystal sphere, a Tahirian viewer, shone cool white. Within it appeared the image of a being. Nansen leaned close. The form was bipedal, slanted forward, counterbalanced by a long, thick tail. From beneath a scaly garment reached clawlike hands and a hairless, lobate, greenish head. The effect was not repulsive, simply foreign.

"(I show you this,)" wrote the parleur of the Tahirian he called Peter, while attitudes and odors gave overtones he was beginning to interpret, "(because somehow, in your company, command flows through you. Later we will talk, and then you can decide what your others shall learn.)"

"(Everything,)" Nansen replied. *I can't explain about tact, discretion, timing, especially when four of us are off beyond reach. (Jean, what are you doing as I sit here, how do you fare?)*

He sensed grimness. "(Yes, you are free with information, whatever the hazard. Most of us would have kept knowledge of the black hole from you, for fear of what reckless things you may do. Too late.)"

Inevitable that that incident become known, I suppose. No mention of punishment. Emil and the rest go about as freely as ever. A consensus society? What are the sanctions?

Maybe none were needed, only the slightest social pressures, until we came. The powers that be don't know how to handle us.

As if en had read the thought, Peter said, "(Yours is the second starfaring race we have encountered. Now that communication is acceptably clear, I will tell you of the first.)"

Nansen steadied his mind.

"(Their nearest outpost was about three hundred light-years from Tahir, their home world twice as far,)" Peter said. "(As with you, the trails of their ships inspired our scientists and called our explorers—although for us the development took much longer than yours did. Already those trails were dwindling away. By the time we arrived, the beings had ended their ventures and withdrawn to their parent planet.)"

Nansen felt a chill in his flesh. "(Did you find out why?)"

"(We believe we did. Communication with such alien mentalities was slow and difficult. Your resemblance to us, however tenuous, is greater by orders of magnitude. They are communal creatures, descendants—we theorize—of animals that dwelt together in burrows, in large numbers, with just a few breeders of the young-bearing sex.)"

That experience might account for the Tahirians' eventual grasp of the roles of men and women, Nansen reflected. He also noted that Peter had not used the symbol for "female." Doubtless the analogy was not exact.

"(Their whole culture, identity itself, resides in the kin group,)" Peter went on. "(It is remarkable that they finally achieved a global civilization. We think electronic data processing and communications made it possible.

"(Over time, starship crews and even colonies proved insufficient to maintain it. Numbers were too few for mental health, contact with other nests too weak and sporadic for social ties. Madness(?) ensued, cultures twisted, destructive, evil(?). Some went extinct, through internecine conflicts that destroyed their basis of existence. One lashed out across interstellar space, and a continent was laid in radioactive ruin. Finally the sane core of the race succeeded in quelling the mad and recalling the survivors. Slowly they settled down into the peace that still prevailed when our last expedition visited them.)"

Peter blanked the view, as though the sight was too painful, and stood motionless. Nansen sank back in his chair, shaken. Thunder rolled closer.

"Trágico," the man muttered, for Cambiante had not yet found an utterance for that concept and perhaps Tahirians had never had it. He turned to his parleur. "(They were unfit for starfaring.)"

Peter's mane bristled more than was needful to convey ens feelings. "(In a sense, every race is. We have seen several other, more distant signs of it fading. A new one has sprung up in the past three thousand years, but we expect it will likewise prove mortal.)"

"(Why?)"

"(Probably always the cost becomes too great for the gain. The nature of the highest, least bearable cost may well vary from race to race, but in the end, either necessity or wisdom will call a halt, and starfaring will have been no more than an episode in the history of a planet's life.)"

Nansen's grip tightened on his parleur. "(Ours will not.)"

"(It should, on moral(?) grounds alone. What we have learned of your past, the cruelty(?) and slaughter, fills us with horror. Best for you as well as for the cosmos that you retire and study how to live with yourselves.)"

Nansen bit his lip but responded with the calm that this mode of discourse usually enforced. "(Are you afraid of us? We would never threaten you. How could we, across the gap between? Why should we?)"

"(You are already a threat. By your very existence.)"

"(I do not understand.)"

"(You have made some among us eager to travel anew, regardless of the infinite danger. The sane wish you would go away.)"

Nansen hesitated before asking outright, "(You cannot simply kill us, can you?)"

Peter flinched. A rank smell, like acid on iron, blew from en. "(That you can imagine that exemplifies the horror.)"

"(Have you and those who think like you absolutely never even considered it?)"

Peter seemed to draw on some inner source of composure. "(It would be counterproductive, an act almost as destabilizing as your presence.)"

So Tahirian society isn't as perfectly balanced as it seemed, Nansen thought.

"(Only go away,)" Peter said. "(We ask it of you, who have not treated you ill.)"

The plea touched Nansen and eased him a little. "(We plan to leave in another three (Tahirian) years, you know.)"

"(Will you? And what of those who may come afterward? What of your whole ruthless(?), willful race?)"

"(We few cannot speak for all.)" *All who are to live after us.*

"(Yes, that is part of what makes you terrible.)"

Resolution rose. Peter's torso drew erect. The middle eyes speared Nansen's. "(It is well, it is like providence(?), that wherever starfaring has begun, in a cosmically short time it has died,)" en said. "(The causes are surely many; but through them, does reality preserve itself?

"(I cannot now say more. You would not believe me. I am not versed in the subject. First, under proper tutelage, you must learn how to read the mathematical proof. You shall. Then your voyage here will have been not for harm but for good. You will bring a message back to your people and make them, too, call their ships home forever.)"

29.

Optical amplifiers turned the stars into a sphere of dazzlement, bright ones become beacons, thousands upon thousands more leaping into visibility, the Milky Way a river of frozen fire, the Andromeda galaxy a glowing maelstrom. Only the pinpoint neutron star was dulled, lest it sear eyes that strayed in its direction. Ten kilometers distant, the boat *Herald* gleamed like a splinter off a sword.

Dayan and Brent gave the splendor no heed. Their attention was on the bulky nexus of a metal spiderweb, five kilometers wide, slowly spinning, its concavity always facing the pulsar. Spacesuited, they floated before the mass, touching a gripsole to the extended lattice whenever they needed to correct a recoil-drift, plying tools and meters with hands that power joints and tactile contractors made as deft as if bare. Nonetheless it was a demanding task. Each heard the breath of the other loud through radio earplugs, and recycling did not fan away all smell of sweat.

Finally Brent nodded. "Yep, what I suspected. Imbalance in the main data reducer. That program's gone abobble. Not much, but enough. No wonder the input you were getting stopped making sense."

"At first I thought we might have stumbled on some wild new phenomenon—" Dayan laughed. "No, this is better. We've more mysteries pouring in on us already than we can handle." Her mirth thinned out into the light-years around. "How soon can we have this unit working right? The gravity waves from the starquakes—what they have to tell about the interior—"

"We can replace the whole module right now. The robots keep spares

of everything, don't they? The question is, will we get the same problem
again soon? What mutated the program?"

"I've been thinking about that since you first suggested the possibility." Dayan started plucking her implements from the lattice where
they clung and securing them to her harness. It was a near-automatic
task; her gaze went afar, her voice meditative. "We did record a partial reflection of the southern pulsar beam off something—seemed to be a
drifting molecular cloud, maybe a remnant of the eruption—and it may
well have happened to strike the reducer here. That'd probably be plenty
to scramble a few electronic configurations. A weird accident, sheer bad
luck, but we have to expect weirdness. . . ."

His look dwelt on her. The spacesuit muffled the curves of the small
body, but clear within the helmet stood large eyes, curved nose, full lips,
fair skin; the amplification gave just a hint of colors, but he knew the
bound hair was flame red and could fall loosely down over her shoulders.

"So the stupid robots couldn't figure out what the trouble was, and
hollered for us," he said.

"They're only as good as their programs, Al, and the programs are only
as good as our knowledge and foresight."

"Yeah. Well, let's get this fixed and head home for *Envoy*."

Every array that the expedition deployed had its machine attendants,
to monitor and maintain. Brent snapped an order.

Waiting, there alongside the great web, among the stars, Dayan regarded him for a silent while. "I'm sorry if this has inconvenienced you,
Al," she said.

"Huh?" She had not before seen him taken quite so off balance. "In-
convenience? Why, no, no. I thought you were impatient to get back. Me,
I'm, uh, happy to do anything useful. That's what I came along for."

"And to shorten the time for yourself till we go home, not so? Nothing
wrong with that. We all miss Earth."

"Well, but—" He cleared his throat. "Hanny, working like this, together
with you, it's special. I'm almost sorry we'll soon be done. Anytime you
want—"

A blackness crossed the Milky Way. "Here comes the repair robot."
Dayan sounded more relieved than the event called for.

The shape—octopuslike, starfishlike, machine—approached on thin,
invisible jets. The humans saw a flash of its optics. It passed within meters, seemed to wobble for a second or two, and moved on, shrinking
into the heavens.

"What the fuck?" Brent shouted. "Come back, you bastard!"

"Something's wrong," Dayan said fast. "Its program's deranged, too.
Same cause?" She grabbed a radar gun, aimed, squinted at the reading,
put it aside and took an ionoscope. "It cut jets off as it came near. Safety
doctrine. But then it didn't maneuver to dock. It just stayed on trajectory.
It's falling free, bound for infinity."

"And it's got the module. I'll go after it." Brent took hold of the lattice and swung himself around.

"No!" Dayan said. "Not safe. Too much momentum there for your suit drive to handle."

"I'll match vectors, lock on, decelerate—"

"No, I say. You're not outfitted for any such operation."

"Damn it, Hanny, we don't have a proper replacement for that robot, and the module it's carrying— Don't you want this rig fixed?"

"Not if it risks a life."

Kilbirnie had been listening throughout. Her voice purred on the radio. "Dinna fash yersel's. I'll fetch yon runagate."

"What?" Dayan cried. "No, Jean, the parameters—too high, too uncertain—you could end with the boat stove in."

Kilbirnie's tone jubilated. "Aye, 'twould be nice to have one of those slippy-slidey Tahirian hookers, but I'll barge guid auld *Herald* around handily enough. Guaranteed."

"No! I forbid—"

"Hanny, aboard *Envoy* you're acting captain, but piloting my craft I am in command of her. You shall have your module back, to plug in by yourself, and your robot back to fix, and may Clerk Maxwell bless your science. Colin," they heard Kilbirnie say to the Tahirian who had most avidly accompanied them, "pay attention, now, for the day may come when you take this helm." Probably en caught her gist. They had become rather close.

A fire streak, faint even when amplified—the plasma drive was efficient—shot *Herald* across the star throngs. She drew nearer, swelled in sight, a barracuda hunting. Fire; rotate along three precise axes; fire; at the end, quantumlike delicacy of pounce and drift. A cargo hatch opened. The robot glided in as if borne on a springtime breeze. The hatch closed. "We've got our fish," Kilbirnie called.

"W-w-well done," Dayan perforce said.

"Och, 'twas nowt. I hope it showed what I can do. And now I ask for my reward, Hanny, that I may take Tim down onto the planet for his own work."

Autumn did not flame as in remembered lands on Earth. Colors went wan, sometimes gray, oftener dun or fallow. Some leaves held fast, some died and blew away on the wind. Yet skies pulsed with migratory wings, forests rustled with migratory feet, cries resounded, and in the country where Terralina lay the rapidly shortening days were mostly brilliant and the chill tingled in human blood.

Nansen and Yu strode to and fro across the meadow. He had received her in his cottage, which doubled as his office, but the hoped-for report she brought had immediately made them unable to sit still. Though they were not far from the settlement, it appeared small against its backdrop of woods, beneath scudding clouds whose shadows raced over the ground. Wind whistled, rumpled their hair, laved their cheeks like a glacial river.

"Yes," Yu said through the noise, "it is quite clear. Ajit has determined the meanings beyond any further doubt."

Nansen smiled down at her. "He didn't do that entirely by himself."

"Oh, I handled the physics, of course. But the interpretation of—of what goes beyond any physics we know—that was his. There is definitely life at the black hole. Intelligent life."

"How?"

"Emil and his friends still haven't been able to convey any explanation. We are not sure whether the Tahirians themselves have more than . . . an educated guess. They don't think in the same fashion as us. They express their science in different ways. For example, do you remember the dimensions they use?"

"In what sense of 'dimensions'?"

"The basic quantities of their dynamics are not mass, length, and time, but energy, electric charge, and space-time interval."

"Oh, yes. That."

"It was one reason the texts they prepared for us were so incomprehensible, until Hanny deduced what the situation must be. And that example is almost trivial. If she were here, we'd make faster progress. I can only gnaw my way ahead."

He laughed. "I'd call you a very effective little rodent. You've found out enough about the field drive that you can build one for us—"

"No, no, please. I have explained that we can't retrofit *Envoy* or her boats. They are too integrated with their existing systems. I do think we can add a unit that will make us more comfortable under acceleration, but any real shipbuilding must await our return to Earth."

"Where they may already long have had such craft." Nansen glanced at her again. "Didn't I understand you to say you have also something new about the zero-zero drive?"

She nodded. "It is not the happiest discovery. The Tahirians found, long ago, that there is a random possibility of quantum gate malfunction. The Bose-Einstein condensate goes unstable and the energy from the substrate is not returned through it in full. The differential is slight, but apparently ample to cause destruction. They believe such accidents account for a number of disappearances in their starfaring days, ships that set forth and were never heard from again."

Nansen scowled. *"¡Ay!"*

"Oh, the probability is minute, and decreases with quantum gate capacity. Given our gamma of five thousand, the danger to us is negligible. Even lesser ships are far more at risk from the ordinary hazards of space."

"However, it may have helped discourage the Tahirians."

"I doubt that. Would we humans let it deter us? I think Ajit must be right in his opinion, the society went more and more conservative for a variety of reasons. Although—"

The wind shrilled. "Yes?" prompted Nansen after several seconds.

"I don't know." He heard the trouble in her voice. "Something else in the equations—what they imply—Emil says en doesn't know. It's obviously not common knowledge, at least not in this era. As if—as if it is so terrible that none of those who do know care to speak of it."

Nansen recalled the hint that Peter had refused to clarify. "Something not obvious to every theoretical physicist. Something we probably wouldn't take on faith. I think we can—you and Hanny can get help, however, in working it out yourselves."

"I have an impression the Tahirians learned it at the black hole, perhaps from the beings there."

"And fled from it?"

"We are not sure, Ajit and I."

He thrust uneasiness from him. "*We* can go and learn."

"Perhaps," she said with care. "I think we would also need Tahirian help in dealing with them, the Tahirian . . . feel . . . for quantum mechanics. Surely this . . . life . . . is a quantum-level phenomenon."

"Oh, we'd have Tahirians happy to sign on. Emil, Esther, Fernando, Colin, Stefan, and more. We've infected them with dreams of a new age of discovery." Nansen smote fist in palm. "*Dios mío,* what a discovery yonder! It could change our whole *perspectiva* on—on everything. If science finds life is not purely material— Oh, Wenji!"

He stopped in the middle of the field. She did, too. He whirled about and embraced her. A shadow flew across them. It went past and the sunlight struck blindingly.

He let go and stepped back. "I beg your pardon and Ajit's," he said. "Once again I do."

She smiled. "What, shall the captain never show his feelings? Don't freeze into that armor of yours, Ricardo Nansen. Stay ready for your own time."

Seen by enhanced starlight, the planet on the ground was black, gray, white, here and there a steely blue shimmer. Cleland and Kilbirnie rode over a valley buried under two kilometers of ice, a landscape riven, pocked, often tilted up in great blocks. Afar reared a conical mountain. A few kilometers behind them, a murky escarpment cut off the opposite horizon. Atop it *Herald* sheened tiny against the unnaturally brilliant constellations. A shelter dome had been erected nearby. Aboard the boat, scanning through its optics, Colin followed the humans' progress— enviously?

The pair sat on a carrier robot. Gear secured to it hid most of the long body. A balloon bobbed overhead at the end of a three hundred-meter cable, bearing instruments to study the ghostly atmosphere, like a grotesque moon. The thud of the robot's six feet, conducted through its metal, was the only sound that came to the riders.

They had said little since they left camp. Cleland was occupied with his visual recorder, surveyor, gravitometer, and whatever else he could wield in the saddle, or simply with gazing around. Kilbirnie lacked his professional appreciation, but the country was interesting, unique, in its stark fashion. Besides, conversation had become a bit difficult. There was a certain new tension between them, unexpressed, not unfriendly; two people and one nonhuman alone on an entire world. . . .

Yet when at length Cleland spoke into his radio transmitter he sounded nearly cheerful. "Whoa, Dobbin." He touched controls. The robot stopped. Twisting his neck to see her, he said, "You can get off now and stretch your legs."

"Whoosh! Best word I've had since 'Breakfast's ready.' " Kilbirnie dismounted, trotted ten or twelve meters over the rough surface, and began to do limbering exercises as well as possible in a spacesuit. "Why here?"

Cleland had descended, too. "Several considerations. We don't want to go beyond sight of the boat or ready return to her. This is a promising spot to take what measurements we can, seismic, isotopic analysis, the works, and a core down to the rock."

"How can you tell?"

He smiled shyly at her through his helmet, across the ground between under the stars and the swaying false moon. "A hunch, based on experience. We may get some notion of where these volatiles came from. And, of course, what's going on in the solid body. Solid liquid, I should say. To judge by what I've been able to observe and guesstimate so far, the molten component of the core is huge."

"Not so huge as my thirst for beer will be when we return to camp. Aye, let's get busy." Kilbirnie ceased her motions and started back to assist him.

The glacier rumbled, as if the sound going through it were a giant machine. A shock threw Cleland off his feet. He staggered up, to see the wave of ruin rush across the valley. Ice split, sundered, spun aloft in flinders, crashed down, and shattered into dust that glittered like tiny stars.

He saw it gape open at Kilbirnie's back. She lurched and went over the edge, out of his sight.

Quake! Shouldn't be! And just here, just now! "Jean!" he screamed. A grinding answered.

He stumbled over frozenness that still trembled, to the verge of the cleft. Six meters wide and fifty long, it plunged into sudden gloom. He dropped on all fours and stared over. *Ten meters down,* he gauged in a part of his mind not lost in nightmare, ten meters down to a bottom covered with broken chunks. In amplified light the sides shimmered an outrageously delicate blue. Kilbirnie was a blot of shadow and glints. "Jean!" he yelled again.

"Aye," he heard. The mass had screened off their radios.

"Are you hurt, darling?"

"Not badly. I didn't fall, I slid and rolled."

"I'm coming." He moved to crawl over the edge.

"No, you gowk!" Her shout knifed his eardrums. "Not both of us! Too steep. We canna climb back."

Another quake growled and shuddered. It was less violent than the first, but pieces of ice cracked off and rattled into the depths. "I'll call Colin—"

"No! En's only learned to lift the boat into space. Trying to land here, he'd crash her. Go get a line and come haul me out."

Numbed, he backed off. "Colin," he said idiotically, "hang on. Tell 'em when *Envoy* comes over the horizon. Wait for me."

The ground shook anew. More lumps broke free and fell. Riding the robot at full, reckless tilt, he'd take at least an hour to reach the scarp, climb it, and fetch a cable. And another hour to return. How much turmoil did the planet have left? It shouldn't have had any. A molten metallic ball should quickly have reached equilibrium and spent the next few billion years quietly cooling off. But—currents in it, differential congealing, unsettled crust?—he had come here hoping to do real science, hoping to find surprises.

He ran toward the robot. The glacier groaned underfoot. The balloon swung on high against darkness at the end of its tether.

"Yes!" For a second Cleland's vision blurred, tears of joy.

No time to waste, though. He started the winch. While it reeled in the line, he got out a small ion torch. It was intended for assembling parts of the geophysical observatory he had meant to establish here. Too bad. No, glorious. He thanked the God in Whom he did not believe.

Ten meters, make it twenty to be sure, don't stop to pull in any more. The torch flared, wire glowed white and parted; the balloon wobbled off, trailing a tail of the rest. The equipment it bore away— *An offering for Jean's life,* he thought. *Superstition? Never mind, if it works.* He uncoiled what he had retrieved, slashed it free of the winch, looped it around his shoulder, and headed back.

Again the valley shook, and again, and again. Lumps tumbled into the crevasse. A few struck Kilbirnie, glancing blows that sent her asprawl. She bounded up at once, for the wreckage on the bottom was shifting about as the temblors rolled, grabbing like jaws that could bite armor and bone in two. She danced for her life upon them, across them. She wolf-howled, half in defiance, half in glee. She was too busy for terror. But she could know that in this moment she was totally alive.

Cleland fought his way to the rim. He laid the cable down, made a loop at one end for a stirrup, secured it with a quick torch blast. "Do you see me?" he called. "I'm lowering a line to you from here. Can you find it?"

No response. The last quake ebbed away. He lay on his belly, helmet over the edge, and peered, frantic. A sob caught in his throat. She was there, crawling over the chaos in his direction. He payed out the cable, felt it slither along the ice walls and knock on the chunks below. She reached it and took hold. He backed a short distance off for safety's sake, rose, threw a bight over his waist, and began to haul, hand over hand. It went slowly, friction and weight allied against him. He gasped. Should he have brought the robot and its winch? He'd been in too big a hurry to stop and think, and it was too late now. His arms ached, pain cut into his hands through the gloves. Still he hauled.

Over the top!

He kept stance till she had crept well clear of the gap. Then he let go and rushed to her. Once he tripped and fell. She rose as he did. He saw that her radio antenna was gone, doubtless the whole set bashed out of commission. But she stood there, swaying a bit, grinned at him through her helmet, and opened her arms to give him a hug.

A rapid star lifted over the scarp. Cleland set for relay via *Herald*. "She's okay!" he cried to *Envoy*. "Do you hear? She's all right!"

The ride back to the boat was not entirely silent. They exchanged some words by touching helmets together. Mainly she assured him that no bones were broken. However, she wasn't unhurt. Though a spacesuit resisted impacts, shock was transmitted. Also, she'd been thrown down and tossed about more than once. He rigged a harness to keep her in the saddle behind him. As they rocked along, he felt her slump forward against him, asleep.

The jolting climb up the cliff roused her. When they stopped at camp and he dismounted to help her off, he saw how she set her jaw against pain. Colin stood anxiously by in ens own suit, clasping a parleur. Kilbirnie took it from en and wrote a message. Cleland couldn't see what it was. The Tahirian seemed to protest. Kilbirnie made an emphatic gesture. Colin yielded—nonplussed?—and set to work unloading the robot. Kilbirnie tugged Cleland's arm and pointed at the shelter.

She leaned on him, limping, as they made their way to it. Here the ground was naked dark metal, some places jagged, some almost mirror-smooth, under the fantastic stars. *Herald* stood upright on her jacks, a shining watchtower. Beyond lay the dome of the shelter and the adjacent squat housing of its power unit—laboratory, workshop, and home for the three living creatures on the world. While they waited for the airlock to exchange atmospheres, he and she felt in their faces the infrared light that baked the skins of their spacesuits free of a cold their flesh had better not touch.

They passed through to the cramped, crowded interior. Its brightness turned viewports into circles of black. Three flimsy partitions marked off the sections where she slept, he slept, and they took care of personal hygiene. Colin's arrangements were out amidst the assorted apparatuses; privacy was irrelevant to en, here, and maybe not even a Tahirian concept.

The humans took off their helmets and breathed warm, sweet-scented air. "Ahh," Kilbirnie sighed. " 'Tis like coming in from the final exam for a pilot's commission to a friendly pub."

Despite the jest, her voice had been ragged. "How—how are you?" Cleland stammered.

"Bruised, battered, thirsty, and bluidy damn glad," she laughed. "Also overdressed, both of us."

"Yes. Let me help you—"

She accepted, though the outfits could be donned and doffed single-handedly. Sweat plastered her skinsuit to the lean body. He stared at darker stains. "You're . . . wounded," he said. "Oh, Jean, Jean."

"Bumps and abrasions, no worse." The blue gaze speared him. "Before you start beating your breast over how this is your fault, Tim Cleland, remember what a supersonic boom I trailed in my rush to come along. I thank you for my life. Now shuck your gear so you can be useful."

While he scrambled free of his suit, she went to the cooler, snatched a beer, and drained it in three gulps. "Ah-h-h, *la agua verdadera de la vida*." She saw him wince. "But how are you, Tim? Are you hurt?"

"No. No, nothing worth mentioning." Except by hearing the Spanish from her.

"Good, oh, very good. Well, I do ache and twinge and creak. If we'd not have me disabled tomorrow—and we flinking well want to pick up our science again, don't we?—best treat it richt the noo. First a hot shower. Meanwhile, lay out the medicines, will you?"

Kilbirnie disappeared behind the bath partition. He heard water gush from overhead tap to recycler tank. Steam eddied forth. He racked their outfits and sought the medical cabinet. Topical analgesics, hemolyte, cell-repair promoter— He arranged them on the table off which they ate their meals, mechanically, his head spinning. Over and over he read the instructions, as if he didn't know them by heart as any spacefarer must, while the water pounded and steamed.

It stopped. A hot airstream brawled.

She emerged. The bruises were just beginning to show. Mostly, she glowed. Still damp, the brown hair clung to her head, and droplets glistened between her thighs. She laughed aloud. "Och, the look on ye! Be practical, man. I've contusions in places where I canna slather on the salves myself. You may as well do them all. Enjoy."

"You, you c-c-could have asked Colin," he said through the roar in his ears.

"Clumsy, explaining where and how with a parleur." She raised the tumbler of water he had filled and swallowed two of the internal medications.

"The—the general painkiller and, uh, sleeping pill . . ." he reminded her.

"Not yet. If at all. Numbness is so boring. Come, don't stand there like a geological specimen."

He put some ointment on his palm and stroked it between her

shoulderblades. "Well, that's a start," she purred. "Harder, though. And now here." She arched her back beneath his hand. "Rr-r-r-r, excellent. You're a quick learner."

The injuries were actually rather few, on shins, elbows, knees, hips, arms. He was soon done. "Ah, thanks. It's like little hotpads." She took his hands in hers. "Now wipe the rest of the stuff off, so it doesn't get where it's not wanted." She rubbed his palms over her sides.

"Jean, Jean," he croaked. "I don't—"

"What I told Colin," she said, "was to be a good fellow and bunk in the boat this nightwatch. You might have felt embarrassed." She led his hands to her breasts. The nipples stood straight. Her arms went around his neck. "This brushing by death, it wakes up quite a wish for life."

"I—Jean, I . . . I'm filthy, I stink—"

"You smell of man. Come along, now."

Much later, when they had told the lighting to turn off and lay on the pallets they had dragged together, she murmured in his ear, "You do understand, don't you, Tim, dear? I'm fond of you, but this is only something that happened." His even breath replied; he did not stir in his sleep. "I suppose it should keep on happening while we go around this star," she sighed into the dark. "You are such a sweet lad."

30.

After an inspection tour of operations at the giant planet, Ruszek wanted some outdoor recreation. The woods around Terralina were too familiar, too peaceful. His Tahirian guide, whom he called Attila—a perfectly respectable Hungarian name—felt likewise, and suggested a subtropical island en knew. It "sounded" like Hawaii, surf and forest and mountains together. Ruszek happily agreed.

The number of visitors at any given time was restricted, so as not to overstress the environment. "Typical of this race," he grumbled to himself. However, Attila made some kind of deal with somebody who had a reservation, or what corresponded to it, and soon they could flit there.

Accommodations were at the seaside, modest structures overgrown with colorful vines, scattered among trees and shrubs. Occupants prepared their own food. No shops, restaurants, or anything of the kind were on hand, merely a sort of ramada where parties could gather if they chose. A boathouse by a jetty offered watercraft, diving gear, and the like, rent-free. "(The purpose is to experience the nature,)" Attila said.

"(A pretty solemn holiday,)" Ruszek remarked.

He had learned that a certain ripple pattern in the mane was like a chuckle. "(One makes liveliness for oneself, especially if one is young.)"

Given the equipment and rations the human had to deploy, they did nothing on their day of arrival but settle into their cabin and go for a stroll at evening. Air lay warm, perfumed, stirred by the *hush-hush-hush* of waves. Where purple in the west shaded to sable in the east, the first stars blinked. They did not seem like furious great suns strewn through a waste of space; they were little and friendly, almost close enough to touch.

Ruszek woke at sunrise. Breakfast could wait on a swim. Unclad, he and Attila took a footpath to the beach. Dunes stretched in a huge white arc. The water tumbled and rumbled, green, streaked and maned with foam, darkening horizonward to blue and indigo. It was cool, salt, sensuously aflow. The pair frolicked for the better part of an hour.

As they waded back ashore, Ruszek laughed, "Grand! Just one thing wrong, *barátom.* You're not a beautiful woman." He must needs jape when he let himself think about that. *Well, once we get back to Earth— or maybe, even, when* Envoy *returns—* Attila wouldn't have understood without a parleur, and probably couldn't have anyway.

A number of Tahirians had meanwhile come down to the beach. They seemed to be largely clan groups, two or three adults with several children ranging from half-grown to infants borne on the back. Clearly, the human took them by surprise. They stared. Manes shivered, arms gestured, legs pranced, noises and odors blew about on the sea breeze.

Ruszek stopped halfway up the strand. Some of the Tahirians were now moving slowly toward him and Attila. "Let's get acquainted with our neighbors," he proposed, though his stomach clamored. Everybody must know about the visitors from beyond, but few had actually seen a live one. These people didn't crowd in the monkey fashion of his.

Emboldened, a couple of youths galloped his way. Smaller siblings merrily followed their example. They encircled Ruszek, manes and antennae dithering, hands held out. They buzzed, trilled, and gusted scents. Fingers touched him and retreated. He spread his arms wide. "Go ahead," he invited. "It's safe, seeing that you are *not* beautiful women."

Elders hastened to the cluster. Voices snapped, manes erected, smells grew sharp. Attila exchanged a few "sentences" with them. Ruszek scowled, aware of the sudden tension. After a minute, obviously reluctant, the youngsters trudged off. Their parents followed. The backward glances were—wary?

"What the flaming hell?" Ruszek exclaimed. "Come on, let's go where we can talk."

In their cabin he grabbed his parleur and demanded an explanation. Attila hesitated before replying.

"(They are not hostile to you personally.)" Or so Ruszek interpreted it; Cambiante was still riddled with ambiguities, and doubtless always would be. "(They wish to protect their children from your influence. Best we avoid contact during our stay.)"

The man spat an oath. Then he composed a civil question. "(What harm in our company? Most humans would be overjoyed to meet anyone from a different world.)"

"(As I was, and those who think like me. Many do not. They fear unrest, the impact upon this stability our ancestors painfully achieved. Your arrival dismayed them.)"

"(I see.)" Ruszek's head nodded lead-heavily. Preoccupied with investigation, and sometimes his personal difficulties, he had not thought much about the subtleties that Sundaram, Nansen, and others said they had encountered. He had supposed vaguely that a privileged class didn't want changes that could threaten its status. But if Tahir had no privileged classes— "(If your race got seriously interested again in starfaring, new information and new ideas would pour in, and what might become of your planetary preserve?)" For the last word, he wished he had a way to render "paradise."

"(The conservatives do not want to maintain things as they are merely for the sake of maintaining them,)" Attila answered. "(Life is a rare and fleeting accident in this cosmos, civilization as fragile as blown glass. Think of what you met in the star cluster you entered. Think of the horror that starfaring brought on that other race we found. Our ancestors deemed their own gains not worth the costs and risks. Indeed, lately there go rumors of some infinitely great peril—)" En stopped. Presently: "(They determined to end the spreading thin of effort and resources. Instead, they would fortify this home of ours against time. That meant creating a society which would endure, adaptable when necessary but always true to itself.)"

"(Humans couldn't.)" *I think. Might they try?*

"(So some among you have told some among us, I 'hear.' Forgive(?) my saying it, but certain Tahirians wonder if your race is basically sane.)"

"(Maybe we aren't. By your standards, at least.)" Ruszek's mustache bristled. "(We are what we are, whatever it may be, and I'll stand by that.)"

"(It is not a simple either-or matter.)" Did Attila's posture, tone, earthy odor, signify earnestness? "(Individuals vary within both our species. You know how your coming has caused persons like me to look back to the stars and sense in them a future more dangerous but more rich than anything our careful planners ever imagined. Naturally, it is us with whom you have had most to do. But we are a minority.)" Again en paused. "(Our opponents may be right. For the time being, I and those like me will continue to assume they are the ones mistaken.)"

"(They don't want us touching off dreams in others. Very well, you and I will keep to ourselves here,)" Ruszek said. "(Now let's make some breakfast,)" he added, although his appetite was not what it had been.

An hour before midnight the common room lay quiet, lighting subdued, mobile adornments in stasis, air cool; but Brent had started some music, very softly, a piece that most of his fellows would not have recognized but that would speak to the same emotions in all, *"Là, mi darem la mano."* He stood clad in a blue uniform-like tunic and trousers, hands clasped behind his back, looking out a viewscreen at the stars.

Dayan entered. He turned about and touched his brow, a quasi-salute. She stopped more than a meter from him and stood as if watchful. Her garb was plain to the point of drabness, which was not usual for her, but even in the dusk her hair tumbled vivid to the shoulders.

"Good evenwatch," she said tonelessly.

"Thank you," he replied. "For coming here. This late."

"Well, you asked me to. I can sleep a bit extra in mornwatch." Her slight smile faded as her glance drifted to the stars. "What do our clocks matter, here?"

"I need to say something to you, Hanny, in private."

She looked back at him. "Why not my office?" Another forced smile. "I am supposed to act like a captain."

"You might have . . . misunderstood . . . in that setting."

She waited.

"Though you've probably guessed," he said. Fast: "I love you, Hanny."

She nodded. "Yes," she answered gravely, "I did expect this."

"And—"

The hazel eyes locked with his brown. "Al, be honest. Is it love or lust?"

He reddened. "Both. Sure. You're a—a marvelous woman."

"The only one available within a light-year."

"All right!" he burst out. His hands lifted, though he kept them close in. "And I'm the only available man. Why not? What harm? We'll both feel better. We'll function better."

Her voice stayed level. "Will we really? And what when we return to Tahir?"

"We'll worry about that then." He cleared his throat. "But you don't believe Selim's spending these two and a half years alone, do you? It was plain already before we left, him and Mam hot for each other."

She frowned. "Please—"

"And now, here aboard ship, Tim and Jean making like minks." Seeing her reaction, he lowered his hands and stood nearly at attention. "Oh, I've learned self-control. I've had to, my whole life. But if you would—" He wrestled his pride to the deck. "If you would be kind—"

She shook her head. "I'm sorry, Al," she said, most gently. "I truly am. But no."

"It wouldn't commit you," he argued. "I won't pester you afterward if you don't want. I'd do my best to make you want, but it's your choice. We're shipmates, Hanny, a long ways from a home that's a long time gone."

"I'm sorry," she repeated. "No."

His lips writhed. "You don't like me. Is that it?"

"Wrong. I'm simply not casual."

"I'm not, either. I said I love you. That doesn't count, huh? Not when it's me."

"Al, stop that. You're brave and able. You're charming when you care to be. I don't agree with some of your ideas, but as an Israeli and a soldier's daughter I understand them better than most of our crew, and I share many of your feelings."

"But I'm not worth a few hours in bed," he rasped. "Not like Selim Zeyd. Or Ricardo Nansen, if you get a chance at him."

Her countenance froze. "That will do."

"All right," he said dully. "Sorry. No offense intended."

"None taken." She failed to conceal that that was not quite true. However, once more she spoke mildly. "I regret this meeting wasn't more . . . cordial."

"Me, too."

"We'd better end it on that note. It won't make any difference between us if we leave it here."

He jerked a nod.

"Good night, Al." Dayan went out.

He stood motionless till she was gone. "Yeah," he muttered. "A really, really good night."

Through the hollow passageways he sought his cabin. Standing amidst portraits of conquerors, he called the Tahirian quarters on the intercom. "Leo," he said. "Brent. Can you come to me?" The others had learned a few English phrases. For his part, he recognized the sibilance that meant "Yes." He paced until the door chimed and he let the being in.

"(Thank you for coming,)" he said with his parleur. The irony impaled him. "(I trust I have not disturbed your rest.)"

"(No,)" Leo replied on ens own instrument. "(We have not attempted to adjust to the twenty-four-hour cycle you keep aboard ship. Moreover, I, personally, welcome any distraction.)"

"(Of course.)" Leo was not along to participate in the science or the adventure but to observe it and report back to ens faction on Tahir. Brent had been tempted to think of en as a political officer or secret police agent, but realized that was nonsense. "(I wish I could give you refreshment.)"

"(You can give me discourse. You must have a purpose.)"

Brent gestured en to lie down and took a facing chair. His fingers marched and countermarched across the touchpanel. "(What do you make of our activities here thus far?)"

"(They disturb me profoundly.)"

"(Too dangerous?)"

"(Too successful. Colin and Fernando tell me that knowledge is being gathered which is new to our race as well as yours.)"

"(And you fear it will stimulate Tahirian starfaring.)"

"(By itself, scarcely,)" said Leo in the methodical, academic fashion that Cambiante tended to impose. Ens tone, mane, muscles, and pungencies belied it. "(The information is interesting, and not in itself revolutionary. Indeed, an improved database in stellar dynamics and evolution may prove useful to our long-term planning. What I fear is that the success will cause your people to abide among us longer than you had intended.)"

"(And we'd continue endangering your social order.)" Brett tensed. "(Why don't you command us to go? Why haven't you already?)"

"(Why do you ask? You must know that no organization exists to make or enforce such a policy. The need was not foreseen.)"

"Uh-huh," Brent murmured. "You've never thought in terms of sovereignty or military strength, have you?"

"(Our race has always possessed establishments like that,)" he said.

"(It appears to be in your nature.)" The smell turned rank. "(If some of you told us to leave against our will, others would reply that we should stay. This could be disruptive. Your people are not accustomed to strong disputes.)"

"You don't have the instincts for them we do," Brent added under his breath. "So you'd have a lot more trouble containing any that did break out. And just getting together some killers—unthinkable. Too bad . . . for you."

"(You and I and associates of yours such as Peter have touched on these matters before, of course,)" he said. "(What I want to make clear tonight is that certain of *us* don't wish to stay. I want to start your side and mine thinking how to bring departure about.)" *Never mind why I picked this exact time for it.* "(This begins with uniting in our purpose and agreeing on what will be acceptable.)"

"(Can we prevail over your dedicated scientists?)"

"(I believe so, if we have important things to bring back in this ship. Then lingering will become—)" No word for treason. "(—an actual disservice to our race.)"

Leo sat sphinx-alert. "(I suspect what you have in mind.)"

"(Yes. Your science and technology. The mighty capabilities of your planetary engineering. The field drive.)" To go with the robots captured in the star cluster. Study of them had by now revealed potentialities that Brent did not discuss.

"(It has been observed before that humans may well have developed these things for themselves.)"

"(Perhaps, perhaps not. You have your own viewpoint on the universe. Besides, your desires have conditioned the research and engineering you have done.)"

"(True. I have heard of superiorities you possess, notably in artificial intelligence and in . . . lethal instrumentalities.)"

"(Capabilities mean power.)"

The mane flattened. "(More ships of yours could seek us out.)"

"(Not if a leader forbade, a leader with power. He would have better things for his followers to do.)"

"(Stability, enduring purpose, does not appear to be possible to your race.)"

"(We shall see. At the very least, if you get rid of us you will have fourteen thousand of your years in peace; and first I could suggest defenses, safeguards, to you.)" Brent leaned forward. "(I want to make liaison with your group. We'll find ways to work together. We'll bend the future to our will.)"

A rainstorm turned evening into early night. Water dashed against windows and sluiced shimmering down them. Wind skirled. Sometimes lightning flared and thunder crashed. Interior illumination focused like an antique lamp on the desk where Sundaram studied his notes, as if he sat in a cave. It helped him concentrate. He needed the help.

The door opened. He looked up. Yu stepped through, closing the door behind her while a gust tried to seize it. Sundaram sprang to his feet. "Wenji!" he cried gladly. "Where have you been? Two days without a word—"

He went to her. She stood where she was. Water dripped off the hooded poncho, down to the floor. She did not look straight at him, but beyond. "With Esther." Her tone was flat.

"The physicist? I was becoming worried about you." He attempted geniality. "Well, you were in fascinating company, I'm sure."

She remained silent. He looked beneath the hood at her face. Dim though the light was, he saw that the drops along her cheekbones were not rain. "What is wrong?" he whispered.

"I have solved the equation."

"Equation?"

"With Esther's help. En led me through the mathematics. I had to go through it. In mere words—" Her voice broke. "How could I have believed? I wouldn't dare. Esther was appalled, too. She had not realized, either. It is not something that is taught to students."

He regarded her for a moment longer. The wind hooted. "Come, darling," he said low. "Sit down. Rest." He helped her doff the poncho, hung it up, and guided her to the table where they shared meals and played games when they were alone. Passive, she took the seat he drew back for her.

He flicked a thumb at the culinator. "I have a pot of tea there," he offered. "Or would you prefer something stronger?"

Now she met his eyes. A kind of tenderness trembled in her speech. "Just you. Please come be with me."

He brought his chair around beside hers and lowered himself to it. When he took her hand, it was colder than the weather outside. He cradled it.

As if drawing strength from the clasp, she told him quietly, "We are a menace to creation."

Seldom before had she seen him amazed. "No, how? The universe? We, less than dust motes?" Lightning set a window ablaze. Darkness clapped black down. Thunder went like monstrous wheels.

She drew breath and now talked rapidly, as if rattling off a litany. "You recall the theory. When the universe formed, the big bang, that first great quantum leap was not to the lowest energy level, the ground state. It stopped higher up, like an electron falling into one of the outer possible orbits around a nucleus. The unspent energy, the substrate, we borrow from it for our zero-zero drive."

"Yes, yes," he said. "But the state is metastable, isn't it?" He shaped a smile. "After all, billions of years have gone by, and we are still here."

"The state can change. Collapse, fall down. Spontaneously, randomly, at any time, any point." Her voice went thin. "A sphere of nothingness, expanding from that point at the speed of light, swallowing stars, galaxies, life—blotting them out—the past itself annulled, and we not only cease to be, we never *were*."

"It hasn't happened yet," he said as soothingly as might be.

"It may already have happened somewhere. It may be on its way to us. We'll never know."

"Darling," he argued, desperately reasonable, "Olivares explained this five thousand years ago. I have read that for a while there was a certain amount of hysteria about it. But the probability is so tiny. Isn't it unlikely to happen until long after the last star has burned out? Or, yes, if I remember rightly, the last proton has disintegrated?"

She clenched her teeth. "We raise the chance," she said.

His grip slackened. "I was afraid of that. My chatter—" He sighed. "I was trying to stave the sentence off. I am a coward."

Warmth surged in her. "No! You're as brave as anybody, Ajit, more than most, brave enough to be serene."

"I can grow terribly afraid for you. . . . Say on."

She had become able to talk evenly. "The grand basic equation of the Tahirian physicists isn't quite identical with ours, even after all the terms have been translated. And this particular solution of it is not at all obvious. It is what Hanny would call very tricky. But the result is that exchange of energy back and forth between substrate and universe—the zero-zero process—is destabilizing."

"No, surely—" he protested. "How many millions of star crossings have there been, in how many billions of galaxies?"

Her tone grew weary. "Oh, yes, the change in probabilities is minute. I haven't learned the measure of it. But I have learned that starfaring increases the danger. It's one reason the Tahirians stopped. That was so long ago, and the point is so esoteric, that few today have ever heard of it, and they shun discussion of it even among themselves. It's as if they have a sense of ancestral guilt."

He sat mute. Rain slashed, wind keened.

"Can we take the risk on ourselves?" he wondered at last. *"May* we?"

"That is the question."

"How certain is this?"

"I don't know. I'm at the limit of my mathematics and physics. If Esther has a better idea, it's not something en can make clear to me. We'll have to wait till Hanny gets back and follows the proof herself." Bleakly: "If that isn't the voyage that triggers the downfall."

"It won't," he declared.

"It mustn't." She shuddered.

He released her hand and laid his arm around her shoulders. "You've had a downfall of your own, dearest," he murmured. "A dreadful intellectual shock. Let me get some food into you, and a sedative to sleep on. Things will look brighter tomorrow."

"I hope so. The stars—life, beauty, love, meaning—"

She clutched at him. They held each other close, taking what they could while they could.

31.

<u>Year five.</u>

The first snow lay crisp around the landing field. It sparkled white, blue in its hollows, broken by shrubs which it dusted with diamond. Air rested cold and still. The folk at Terralina could not see *Envoy* as a spark in orbit through this dazzle, but they clustered at one edge of the pavement, and when another gleam appeared above them, they cheered.

The Tahirian spaceboat bearing the returned explorers descended smoothly. Cleland and Kilbirnie could stand in a compartment, shut off from the world, hearing merely a low thrum, feeling merely a faint shiver.

"Well," he ventured after silence had become unendurable. Then he could not go on.

He heard the sympathy: "I'm sorry, Tim. I know what you mean to ask, and I have to say no."

"Not even . . . a good-bye time . . . just once, after all these days in the d-damned gimbal dorms, crawling along on jets?"

"I told you at the outset how it would be."

His shoulders slumped. "Yes, you did."

"Maybe I should have said it oftener."

"No, I was glad you didn't. I could pretend." Cleland raised his head. "Well, let me thank you for what you gave me."

"I wish I could go on giving it."

"But."

"Yes, but."

After a while, she said, looking straight at him though he kept dropping his glance and lifting it again: "I should have been stronger, Tim. I should have curbed myself that first time. Or if it had to happen, I should have stopped straightaway afterward. But I couldn't bear to hurt you. Now I must, and beg your forgiveness."

He achieved a smile of sorts. "I hope you weren't just being kind to me."

She smiled back. "I enjoyed it." Sober: "I even wondered if something more might grow between us. But the expedition was all we shared, really. You deserve better." She took his hands. They lay passive in hers. "Fare you always well."

"And you," he mumbled.

She kissed him lightly, stepped back before he could respond, and felt the slight thud as the boat set down. Her smile flashed full. "Now, my fere," she said, "let's go out and put a good face on things. You did conduct one glorious explore. I'm sure you'll do your next one likewise."

Slipping out into a passage cluttered with gear and people, she grabbed her personal bags. He stayed behind, in no hurry to debark.

A gangway extruded like a tongue from an open airlock to the ground. Kilbirnie bounded its length and over the paving. Nansen stood ahead of his crew. "Welcome home!" he called.

She dropped her load and dashed to him. "Oh, skipper, what you radioed to us inbound—might we go on from here? To more discovering?"

"We might." The sky was less blue than her eyes. "You'd like that, wouldn't you?"

"I'd love it, skipper. And so would you."

Hands linked and tightened. They stood where they were. The others held back, forgotten.

Nor did anyone immediately seek Dayan when she went down the gangway. Her gaze traveled over the group and came to rest on Zeyd and Mokoena, side by side. Very slowly, Mokoena nodded. Zeyd seemed half abashed. Dayan waved at everybody. Thereafter Sundaram, Yu, and Ruszek met her. She exchanged a hug with the engineer, handshakes with the men. Ruszek took her bags. She went over to Mokoena and Zeyd. A few words passed. Dayan threw an arm around either and held them for a minute.

Cleland and Brent descended together. They said the greetings and received the good wishes. When all were walking toward the settlement, Brent drew Cleland aside.

"Tim," he muttered, "we've got to talk, first chance we get at some privacy. This lunacy about the black hole—"

"I don't know anything except what was in the captain's message to us." A minim of life roused in Cleland. "It's like a scientific miracle."

"If it is a miracle," Brent said, "then it's the kind that could make me believe in Satan."

Piece by piece during the sojourn, the dwellers in Terralina had decorated their meeting hall as they had done their common room aboard *Envoy*.

Tonight the bright colors, mural panels of Earth scenes, and kinetic figures were obscured by festoons and spangles. Music rollicked from speakers. The robots had set a table with white napery, crystal, and the noblest menu in their programs. After a time of rest, recollection, and reacquaintance, this was the reunion celebration.

It became a curious mingling of festivity and formality, moodiness not always quite concealed, mirth not always quite restrained. There were toasts, little speeches, and the songs that had gotten to be traditional on special occasions. Although complete reports lay in the database and individuals had talked with each other, viewshows followed. Zeyd presented the most attractive scenery and interesting life-forms encountered on Tahir; Nansen showed views from its sister planets and the engineering works upon them; Dayan discussed her astrophysical findings, with spectacular images of the pulsar, taken by robots that would continue to transmit for many decades; Cleland doggedly described the world he had studied.

(He did not dwell on the near disaster there, and made no mention of its aftermath. But, *"Dios misericordioso,"* Nansen whispered to Kilbirnie, seated beside him, "we almost lost you," and, "I almost lost you," she whispered back.)

Things livened when the program was over, the robots had cleared away the table, and it was time to dance.

The four women duly circulated among the six men. Presently Dayan joined Ruszek. That number was the swirl, for separate couples. They undulated across the floor, one hand clasping the partner's, his other on her waist and hers on his shoulder. The music sang low and easy, composed for intimacy.

"Ah-h," she murmured, "I appreciate this, Lajos. You're nimble on your feet."

He beamed. *"Köszönöm szépen.* Thank you very much." His glance flickered to Cleland and Brent, with whom she had gone the previous two rounds. They stood at the sideboard drinking and desultorily talking. Remarks would have been tactless. He did attempt modesty. "You're better, though. And, uh, I hear the captain is an expert."

She didn't deny that, but neither did she look toward Nansen and Kilbirnie where they dreamily circled. Her smile quirked rueful. "He's busy this evening. I expect he will be for some while to come."

Ruszek chuckled. "He has much lost time to make up. It took two and a half years away from her to break down his propriety."

An underlying darkness tinged her voice. "Let them be happy while they can."

He was not too surprised. They had seen considerable of each other since she came back. Mostly it had been in the company of two or three more, swapping accounts of experiences. But twice she had taken him off to inquire about his dealings with Tahirians and his impressions of them; and this had touched on the personal, however indirectly.

His hold on her strengthened. "You're not happy yourself, are you?"

"Nonsense." The red head tossed. "I'm fine. Magnificent immediate past, incomparable prospects."

"You don't mind about Mam and Selim?"

"Not if you don't."

"Well, nobody is anybody else's property."

She grinned. "Lajos, you're as subtle as a crashing asteroid."

His steps faltered. "*Sajnálom*—I'm sorry—"

She led him back into the rhythm. "It's all right. In answer, no, I'm pleased, and not surprised. They were falling in love before I left. I think it's become solid."

"They are . . . fine people. But you, Hanny, you are, *nos,* you have trouble in you."

"Why should I?" she demanded.

"Is it this business about the zero-zero drive? The danger to the universe? I doubt that is everything."

They trod another measure. She regarded him, bald head, sweeping mustache, blouse open on hairy breast, a slight male odor of sweat. "You're more perceptive than you let on."

"Is the risk to worry about?"

"I don't know. I've barely glanced at the math yet." Determination clanged. "At worst, the probability is very small. It can't—even morally, I'd say—keep us from going home. Or from first going to the black hole."

Again his steps failed. They stood halted, ignoring the music and the other couples. "Do you truly want to do that? An extra thousand years?"

"Something is there we thought was impossible." Ardor mounted in her. "A whole new vision—" She hauled at him. "Oh, Lajos, come on, let's dance!"

Only once as they swept onward did her look seek Nansen and his Kilbirnie.

The last good nights rang through the frost, across the snow. Stars in their myriads gave light to see by. Dayan walked with Ruszek, leaning on his arm. Much music had played, much wine had gone down, nobody was drunk but it was as if the sky still sang.

"The wonder of it," she said. "Something utterly strange, I don't know what, something we could never have foreseen if we'd stayed home— We haven't come this whole long way for nothing, Lajos!"

They stopped between two cottage walls. Shadows hid them, but overhead stood constellations unknown to Earth. Blindly impulsive, they embraced. It became a kiss, which went on while hands roved.

"Hanny," Ruszek said in her ear—a cold and delicate coil between cascading locks and sculptured cheekbones— "Hanny, I've wished, you're so beautiful—"

She laughed aloud under the stars. "It's been a long time for us both, hasn't it? Tonight we'll make free!"

32.

Heavy snowfall and the silence it brought laid an air of solemnity on the meeting room. Colors and ornaments seemed unreal.

Nansen took stance before the semicircle of chairs. His gaze ranged briefly over his crew. He had come to know them as well as he had known parents and siblings on the *estancia*, who were dust these five thousand years; but how well does one human being ever really know another?

Kilbirnie met the glance and joy flamed up in hers. A quieter happiness wrapped Yu and Sundaram like a shared cloak. Mokoena and Zeyd were as content as ever. Dayan and Ruszek were—well, friendly, anyhow, he perhaps more than that.

Grim Brent and haggard young Cleland remained. Poor devils. Maybe things would have been simpler if two of the persons who applied and qualified for berths, so long ago, had chanced to be homosexual. Or maybe not.

"The meeting will please come to order," Nansen said. He insisted on formal procedure at gatherings like this, for the same reason he insisted on proper attire whenever they ate supper together. Ritual was a bulwark against chaos in the spirit.

And obviousness could soothe, thereby helping clear the mind to think about what might not be obvious. "It may seem absurdly unnecessary. Haven't we talked and disputed enough? But I repeat what I have often said before, we must present our positions in an orderly manner, both for the record and because it is prudent. I trust those of you who wish to speak have prepared their words with care. Furthermore, some new and important information has come to my attention, which you should all hear.

"After our discussion we'll take a preliminary, nonbinding vote on whether to return to Earth at the end of this terrestrial year, if not a little sooner, or set our contract aside—as it provides we may—and first make an expedition to the black hole. You know I personally favor the expedition—"

"Cheers, skipper!" Kilbirnie shouted. "What've we come this weary way for, if not to explore?"

Nansen frowned fondly at her. "Order, please. I'll be as impartial a chairman as I can. To begin with, for the log, let us declare our opinions, though there will be no surprises. Will those in favor of a black hole venture please raise their hands?"

Kilbirnie's shot up. Dayan's was nearly as quick. Sundaram's came after in more deliberate fashion. Then Yu's and Ruszek's rose. *Reluctant, those two,* Nansen understood, *but loyal to their lovers.*

"Opposed?" Brent and Cleland responded at once, Mokoena and Zeyd slowly. "Thank you. A well-reasoned presentation may change somebody's view. Dr. Sundaram, I believe you wish to speak." *For the record, the database, the history that perhaps no historian on Earth will get to write.*

The linguist nodded, smiling at first, soon gaining a fervor they had rarely seen in him. "As you say, Captain, what can I say that has not been said among us a *lakh* of times? This is an incredible opportunity. The physics of black holes is Hanny's department, and conceivably humans will have observed several in person when we return. Or conceivably not. The apparent limitations and mortality of interstellar connection do suggest that they will not have done so. But in all events, the life, the intelligence at this one may well be unique. From it we may receive a revelation as profound as any that our species has ever been vouchsafed. I feel more than curiosity, I feel a moral obligation to learn what we can."

"Hear, hear!" sang out Kilbirnie.

"Dr. Dayan, you have something to add, don't you?" Nansen prompted.

The physicist nodded. "Yes. It concerns the possibility that a zero-zero drive, borrowing substrate energy, may kick the universe out of its metastable state and set off an expanding sphere of annihilation. The probability is exceedingly small. I can't give you a number, because I'm still at work trying to acquire the theory. The Tahirians seem to have developed a concept of probability that denies it can ever be zero. There is always a minimal chance of an event, finite though tiny. I think of it as the Planck probability."

"Get to the point, will you?" Brent grumbled. Nansen frowned, but before he could reprove, Dayan continued.

"Well," she said, "inframinuscule though the chance of any given voyage bringing on destruction is—the likelihood of a quantum gate malfunction wrecking just a single ship is immensely greater—nevertheless, a few of you, like some Tahirians, question whether anyone should make any trips. Is our duty not to go straight home, bearing this news, and do what we can to end human starfaring, too?"

She looked around. "My word today—so far I've only told the captain—is that the Tahirian theorem doesn't feel quite right to me. I don't grasp the mathematics fully enough yet to identify a mistake, and perhaps there is none. Call this a hunch, and remember that hunches are wrong more often than not. However, the fact is that the theorem is based on things the Tahirians learned at the black hole. They did not go back there more than twice. I suspect, and Captain Nansen agrees, this was in part because they were so horrified. They never established more than rudimentary communication with the aliens. Therefore, it's possible that the math is correct but a premise or two are false, that the Tahirians misunderstood something or obtained poor data, and the danger does not exist.

"We can only find out by conducting our own investigation. I may add that Colin, who's a physicist enself, is afire to go."

Dayan gestured to signify that she was done. Ruszek patted her back. She smiled at him and laid a hand on his thigh.

Yes, they are doing well together, Nansen thought. *As well, at least, as two such different souls can. Or so I suppose. Maybe the well-being is what let her go through that mathematics as fast and brilliantly as she did.*

However that is, the exchange of mates with Mam seems to have worked for them. Outright promiscuity might help others— No, it's not in most of these natures. Certainly not in mine. I still have to resist resenting, just a little, what happened before Jean and I—

He quelled that recollection and responded to Dayan's speech. "A number of Tahirians are. If anything, we'll have a problem choosing among them. But let us hear from the opposition. Mr. Brent?"

The second engineer jumped up, stepped to the front, and stood like a military officer addressing his troops. His tone, though, flowed now angry, now patient, now amiable, now rising with controlled passion. He was much the best public speaker of the ten.

"Oh, you've heard it. What I can't figure out is why you don't see it. Look, we've found plenty here, biology, planetology, a whole civilized race and a lot about another, and why a civilization that spans the stars is too damn likely to decay. Plus wonderful technology, the field drive, moon-sculpting ion beams focused by a giant planet's magnetic field, geological forces put to work—and what we got at the star cluster—all those powers that our race could make such use of. Yes, maybe people at home have invented everything for themselves. But maybe they haven't, and that's my guess. Certainly they know nothing about Tahir. That knowledge might well show them how to keep their interstellar travel alive.

"Dr. Dayan has just told us that this business about ships threatening

the whole vast universe isn't proven. That's a service to humankind."
Odd, how grudging his praise sounds, Nansen thought. "It bears out
my gut feeling. I believe that what the universe is about is not self-
destruction, but destiny.

"However, be that as it may, I must disagree with your proposal,
Dr. Dayan. We can't risk losing what we've gained, everything we've got
to give our race, on a crazily dangerous jaunt for no guaranteed prize
whatsoever. Our duty is to bring the treasures back, including some hard-
won wisdom."

A point, Nansen conceded. *Although I think he sees himself as coming
to Earth like Moses down from Mount Sinai, prophet and leader.*

"It—it is full of danger, the mission," Cleland croaked. "Everything we
know about b-black holes says so. And how much don't we know? And
we're tired, we've been n-nearly six of our years gone, we're not . . . not
fit to deal with it. For God's sake, let's go home! The damned black hole
can wait another ten thousand years."

Brent nodded approval and returned to his seat. *I know why you
want an end to our voyage, Tim,* Nansen thought with pity. Mokoena
raised her hand. He recognized her.

"Everybody knows Selim and I would personally prefer to start directly
homeward," the biologist said. "The black hole sounds fascinating, even
to a physical-science layman like me. The risks are real. But I think if we
decide to go there, we will be able to cope—"

"As well as God allows," Zeyd murmured.

"—and this *is* a fantastic chance, which may well never come again.
Ten thousand years are insignificant cosmically, but historically it's a very
long span. Yes, biologically, too. Whole new species have evolved in
shorter periods. Here we are. Who knows what they will be like on Earth
when we tell them?"

"What Mam means," said Zeyd, "is that she and I are persuadable in either direction."

"These are factors for us to take into account," Nansen agreed. "As you
are aware, but for the record, there is another. The Tahirians. We would
need some of them along, for their special knowledge and their intuitive
grasp of quantum mechanics. It could make a critical difference."

Kilbirnie laughed. "We've already noted we'll have no dearth of volunteers. They think their world has been stagnating quite long enough."

"I wouldn't call it stagnant," Cleland argued. "I'd call it, uh, stable.
That's how most of them see it."

"How the reactionaries among them do," Dayan snapped.

"Please, no swear words," Yu said gently. "Let us call them the
conservatives."

"Exactly," Brent declared. "We shouldn't make more trouble for these
people than we already have. Let's go and leave them in their peace.
We're human. Starfaring is in our nature, not theirs. It's a birthright we've
got to secure for *our* race."

"I wonder about that," Yu said. "How many cultures in Earth's history ever actually bred explorers?"

"Order, order," Nansen called. "We're drifting from the issue. Dr. Sundaram, do I see your hand?"

The linguist spoke with his wonted care. "The question is not irrelevant, Captain. The Tahirians face the basic problem of balancing an instinct for the hierarchy that challenge evokes against the threat to hierarchy that radical change poses. They have solved the problem by creating a remarkable combination of incentive and dynamism, especially in the arts and entertainment, with a system of negative feedbacks that keeps society, population, and global ecology in equilibrium. But although it has endured for centuries, that equilibrium is vulnerable. I think this was a strong factor in their decision to terminate interstellar travel. Certainly many of them fear that a revival of it, with all the input that will entail, may undermine this society their ancestors built."

"And many just don't want to be bothered with new ideas," Kilbirnie snapped. "I'll wager that's predisposed them to suppose starships are a menace to everything."

"Jean, that is unfair," Yu said. "Most are sincere, I'm sure. And we know a growing number welcome us and actually want a future that will be different from the past."

"Isn't this another side issue?" Zeyd asked.

"Not really," Nansen replied. "I have news of my own for this meeting. We've all formed our impressions of what the Tahirian attitudes are. Probably the impressions are biased because, in the nature of the case, we've mainly been with those who are glad of our presence. I have been 'talking' more systematically, these past several weeks. Meanwhile, Tahirians have been making decisions of their own.

"The conservatives—let's use that word, and never mind now whether they're a majority or a minority or such concepts mean anything to them—the conservatives demand, if we go to the black hole, we take representatives of theirs along, as *Envoy* did to the pulsar."

"Yeah, I knew that," Brent said. "I've been 'talking' around, too. Your friends Colin and Fernando, my friends Leo and Peter. But we aren't going if I can help it."

"*Can* you help it, Al?" Kilbirnie purred.

Nansen lifted his palm. "No bickering, please. The fact is, spokespeople for the conservatives have been quite frank with us. They won't allow us and the, um, adventurers of their race to set out for the black hole unless several of them do, too. They can enforce this. We do need Tahirians with us, and not even the boldest will defy the, hm, moral suasion. This is a consensus society, after all, and they have to live in it after they return."

"The requirement is not unreasonable," Sundaram said. "Their group is entitled to full information about events, to use in arguing their case for the status quo."

"I didn't mean it's unreasonable," Nansen answered. "I only meant it's another factor to take into account."

"But—Jesus Christ," Cleland choked, "isn't anybody taking th-the extra time into account? Five hundred light-years to there, five hundred back to leave the Tahirians off—if we survive the . . . the damned escapade— another thousand years before we see Earth!"

An added two and a half months of voyage, for us, Nansen thought. *Worse is the time we'll spend at the black hole, doubtless at least a year, probably more. All the while, Tim, you will see Jean every day, and cannot have her again.*

I wonder if you hate me.

Kilbirnie was laughing, "What difference does that make by now?" while Zeyd mused, "Set beside the discoveries we can hope for—" Nansen foreknew what the final tally of votes would be.

33.

After all the while since last they trod the decks of *Envoy*, to do so felt less like a homecoming to Mokoena and Zeyd than like entering a house—a labyrinth—long forsaken and half forgotten. Cabins lay empty. A whisper of ventilation only deepened the silence in the passageways.

Yu proceeded more matter-of-factly. Her involvement in designing an acceleration compensator had already brought her aboard several times. The biologist they called Peter trailed along, impassive in ens foreignness.

A larger number of Tahirians than had gone to the pulsar would fare to the black hole. Expanding quarters and facilities for them meant more than simply clearing out another storage compartment or two. Zeyd had quipped that the spaces under consideration bore no obvious relation to the stars.

"As for the occasional magnetic stimulation they need for comfort and long-term health," Mokoena said, "I suggest that this time, instead of a special cabinet, we provide a field in their new gymnasium."

Yu frowned. "That great a volume?"

"Oh, in a corner, as part of the exercise and recreation equipment."

"It will still take massive superconducting coils."

"Which must not pass too near their food synthesizers, wherever we locate those," Zeyd pointed out. "Induction effects would interfere with the nanos."

"My, my," Mokoena laughed, "this is a jigsaw puzzle, isn't it?"

Peter trilled. They turned to en and reached for the parleurs slung at their belts. *"Duìbùqì,"* Yu apologized. "I'm sorry. We left you too much out." Before she could put it in Cambiante, Peter's screen was flickering while ens voice growled.

"(On an expedition as lengthy as this one may become, conditions that were tolerable for a limited time are so no longer. The reduced weight compensates to some extent for the differences in atmospheric pressure and composition, and the previous travelers grew accustomed (resigned?) to the foul odors. They also adjusted to the circadian cycle. However, over a period of more than a year, the lack of weather will prove unendurable.)"

The humans recalled wild shiftings from month to month or day to day, and the geologically swift climatic changes under which this race had evolved. "(Are the variations in our ship too bland?)" Yu asked. "(We shall certainly do something about that. What do you propose? Virtual-reality programs? Your people must have had an answer in their own starfaring era.)"

Peter's mane erected stiffly. They caught an acrid whiff. "(Everything would be unnecessary if you would go away. Go home. Never seek our world again.)"

Yu winced. "(You know that won't happen until we have been to the black hole. Besides, no few among you want to accompany us.)"

"(Unnatural desire. When they return, their kin will be centuries dead.)"

"That may be worse for them than for us," Mokoena murmured.

"No, they'll have the same society waiting for them," Zeyd said as quietly. "We won't."

"Let star travel start up again, and soon that won't be true for them, either."

"(We gave our promise to those who wish to go,)" Yu reminded Peter.

"(And therefore some who are sane must go with them.)" Unspoken: Abandoning our beloved forever. Because of you. "(Ill fortune. I almost hope the expedition will be ill-fated. Then the race can abide in its peace.)"

Yu stood her ground, trying to phrase friendliness. Zeyd and Mokoena moved closer together.

"But why me?" Cleland asked, dumbfounded. "I'm no engineer or machine operator or—or anybody who'd be useful in this."

"You're handy enough with your own professional gear," Brent replied, "and what counts for more, you're experienced in free space, including work on the outside of the ship. What you don't know, I'll teach you."

Sunlight and a breath of forest streamed through an open window into his cabin. Cleland looked around, as if the equipment-crowded machine shop in *Envoy* were somehow hidden behind these walls. "Uh, well, I'll try my best," he said, "but, really, the compensator is Hanny's and Wenji's design, and they ought to oversee the project"—it's construction and installation.

Brent grimaced. "They will, from time to time. However, they're busy elsewhere. Mainly, they'll just keep track of us."

"And as for an assistant, Al, if you need a human to help you, besides the robots, well, Lajos is far better at that sort of thing than I am."

"He'll be busy, too," Brent snapped. "They'll all be working with the Tahirians to make the orbiting observatory station."

"I happen to know Lajos won't be called on very much for that." Cleland flushed. "Al, you aren't co-opting me for this job to give me something to do—because you feel sorry for me—are you?"

Brent smiled rather grimly. "No. The fact is, you can handle your share of it, given some training and supervision, and I don't care to work alongside Lajos Ruszek. Or Hanny Dayan."

Cleland gaped. "What?"

"Never mind! My business. We won't say any more about it, okay?" Seeing the younger man's discomfiture, Brent yielded enough to add: "Look, everybody needs to keep a civil tongue in his head, or the crew'll tear itself apart. I don't want to overstress my self-control. You and I, we get along fine."

"Well, yes—but—"

Brent changed to his persuasive mode, though it was steely, like a commander talking to his troops on the eve of battle: "And we have the same purpose. I know how you want to go home, Tim, an end to this voyage of the damned. Me, I want it so bad it's like a slow fire in my bones. All right, we are committed to the stinking black hole, and we'd better make ready to survive it. But you and I, we can think beyond. We can keep alert for any chance that comes to improve the situation, and keep the guts to grab that chance."

"I'm . . . not sure what you mean. Yes, I'd rather head straight back from here. Still, the science, the discoveries— I'll make the best of it I can. Won't you?"

"Of course. The expedition's crazy. But I do have to admit the technology we're developing for it here has potential I can barely guess at— for Earth, for our race. And maybe we'll even learn something more where we're bound, not abstract knowledge but something with real-life possibilities. This is the kind of information we have got to make riveted certain we bring home, in a form human experts can deal with. The right experts."

"You don't suppose they already know, back there?"

"I wonder if they do. We've already doubted they'd duplicate every Tahirian idea and invention. What's being created now, a joint human-Tahirian thing—it's instrumentation and control intended for absolutely freak conditions. People in Sol's neighborhood may well never have met any such. There may not be a black hole in whatever radius they've reached, or if there is, it may be different somehow. In that case, they've had no reason to develop systems like these."

"Then what good will it do them?"

"Things have a way of finding uses. Fireworks became guns and the first spacecraft. Nuclear physics showed how to make nuclear weapons and power plants. I can see applications of this stuff—especially if it's linked with robotics from the star cluster and the Tahirian engineering. . . . Power." Brent stared before him. "Power."

The planet hung beautiful at quarter phase, a purple-blue scimitar flecked with rust that was land and banded with silver that was cloud, laid along the dark velvet cushion of nightside. Closer by, though toylike at her distance, the wheels of *Envoy* flung sunlight back in flashes as they spun about their axle the hull.

Kilbirnie sat harnessed, weightless, at the pilot board of the boat *Herald*. The Tahirian Colin crouched in the seat beside her, clinging with spurs. Aft of them Dayan and the physicist she knew as Esther floated free at a recently rigged console.

Dayan flicked a switch. From a launching rack outside, also lately built, sprang a slim torpedo shape. It shot off under field drive, diminished into remoteness, became one of several sparks that flitted far-scattered athwart the stars.

After a while Esther nudged her. Red hair waved as she looked about. "(I, too, should practice with this model,)" said her colleague.

Dayan took her own parleur. "(My regrets. I forgot. You are no more familiar with these devices than I am.)"

"(Centuries have passed since my ancestors dispatched any.)"

And into strange conditions, Dayan refrained from answering, since it was needless. *Special vehicles carrying uniquely special instruments. Granted, they will be directed by computers, from the inner station we'll orbit. But we have to have knowledge of them ourselves, how they behave, what their capabilities and limitations are, as soldiers need knowledge of even their robotic weapons. Space around the black hole will be our implacable, unforeseeably treacherous enemy.*

She concentrated on monitor screens and data readings. Her peripheral vision traced what the flexible Tahirian fingers did.

Kilbirnie and Colin had nothing to occupy them meanwhile except talk. "(I wish I could practice my job the same way,)" she said.

"(You have done it in simulation,)" Colin pointed out.

She sighed. "(Virtuals. In decent, ordinary space there is no proper substitute for the actual doing—let alone the region where we are bound.)" A crooked grin. "(But for that, we will only learn to swim by jumping into the water.)"

"(The simulations are as good as the ancient data allow.)"

"Och, aye," Kilbirnie said. "Nightmare good." Radiation, infalling matter, electromagnetic pulses, a gravitational field that waxed monstrous as you neared, until space itself, yes, time itself, got twisted beyond recognition. Not that any living creature could come so close and remain living. But the station from which the probes would operate must be guided into orbit. And later, who knew what might be required?

She laughed. "(I suppose I am impatient,)" she signed. "(However, I do think the simulations should include more sudden, unexpected fluctuations in things like the accretion disk and the electromagnetics.)"

"(I have suggested that, and been told it would be pointless, precisely because we know little about those events. Our data leave obscure the very causes of much of what was observed to happen.)"

"(I should think you Tahirians could deal with such matters more handily than us. Your sense for quantum mechanics, your instinct for coping with chaotic changes.)"

"(Like you, I look forward to our effort to learn more. But I think you humans have gifts of your own. Between us, we may accomplish what neither could do unaided.)"

"(We will try.)" Kilbirnie shivered in a rush of delight. "We will give it a bluidy great try." Impulsively, she stuck out her hand. Colin entwined ens with it. They shook partnership.

Presently Dayan called, "Enough already. I'm getting too tired. And Esther."

"It has been a long session," Kilbirnie agreed. "Aye, we'll take a break and a night's sleep. Strap in, folks, and hang on while I retrieve our beasties."

When everybody was secured, she tickled controls. The boat leaped. To and fro she jetted. "Harroo!" the pilot cried once. Robotic arms on the racks snatched missiles on the fly.

Having collected them, she whooped back to *Envoy*, made a contact that by rights ought not to have been as smooth as it was, and cut power. "Don't bother neatening inboard," she said. "We'd promptly make a new mess tomorrow. I'm for a cold beer and a hot shower." She led the way into the hull, through it, across to the forward wheel, and onto the railcar.

As usual, Nansen waited in the common room to receive them. He was conversing with the Tahirian they named Indira. Sundaram's close collaborator had come along on this visit to study the layout. It would influence the technical arrangements by which they hoped to communicate with the dwellers yonder.

The captain was not paying much attention. Perhaps for that reason, the semantician had begun to set forth elementary facts. "(. . . Do you realize how scant the earlier contact with the aliens was? We do not know if we can re-establish it on a regular basis, or at all. If we do, that will be the commencement of our true difficulties. We are ignorant of their nature . . .)"

Kilbirnie stopped in the doorway, so as not to rudely interrupt. Dayan caught up with her. They could read Indira's screen from there, hear ens voice and watch ens stance. "Yes," the human physicist said low, "I do believe the Tahirians of that time were afraid of what they might learn. It could overthrow the whole philosophical basis of the Eden they were building at home. That may have predisposed them to conclude that starfaring is a threat to everything."

Kilbirnie shrugged. "Myself, I've always felt grateful to Eve, that she succumbed. Eden strikes me as an unco dull place."

Nansen grew aware of them and turned on his heel. "Jean!" he cried.

Kilbirnie entered. "Dinna look so terrified, skipper, my jo. I was a good girl today. I flew strictly within the safety rules."

He frowned. "I followed your maneuvers on the 'scopes before I came down here. You pushed the envelope so hard that it crackled."

"Well, I need practice with more than routine. Wha' when we reach the black hole?"

His face went bleak. "Yes, what then?"

"Och, there I'll be vurra, vurra canny. It will make my recklessness for me."

"We'll have to talk about that."

"Richt the noo?" She stood before him, disheveled, sweaty, smiling her wide white smile. "Aweel, as you like. I can postpone my shower." She glanced at the others. "If ye will excuse us till dinnertime?"

Nansen reddened, harrumphed, and said quickly, "We don't seem to have anything more to do till tomorrow mornwatch. And I'm sure everyone would like to rest awhile before we meet this evening."

"Oh, yes," Dayan replied, flat-voiced. Her gaze trailed the captain and the pilot as they went out, side by side.

When she looked back, she saw Esther's parleur signaling. "(Why did those two leave abruptly?)"

"(They wish to be by themselves,)" Dayan said.

"(What is their motivation?)"

Sometimes speaking with a nonhuman through a device made frankness all too easy. "(She is a desirable person. He is the best man in five thousand light-years. Or maybe anywhere.)"

34.

Once in the primeval galaxy, soon after the first burst of starbirth, a blue giant sun came to the end of its short and furious life. It exploded, the stupendous violence of a supernova. Briefly, it outshone its whole island universe. The gas it blasted out into space held elements heavier than iron, which could have formed no other way: nickel, copper, silver, tin, gold, uranium, and more. Some of this would later enter into the nascence of newer stars, together with hydrogen, carbon, nitrogen, oxygen; and around some of these would arise living creatures.

The wreckage did not collapse to a neutron globe. The sun had been too great, its eruption too mighty. Any planets were vaporized. A remnant mass, ten times that of the Sol that did not yet exist, fell in on itself. So huge did the gravitational force become that it overwhelmed all resistance, and the mass contracted without limit. Beyond a certain point, even light could not break free. Therefore nothing could that was drawn in. The star took on the aspect of a sphere absolutely black, 185 kilometers in circumference.

You could not calculate a radius from this. In the distorted space-time geometry within, as the mass approached the pointlike state of a singularity, such concepts lost their familiar meanings. Nor could you have discovered what was going on inside; whatever information the matter had borne was lost. There was only that black, slightly flattened sphere, the event horizon.

The body did retain properties of angular momentum, corresponding to a wildly fast spin, and magnetic field, immensely strong. It could also keep an electric charge, though slight, because ions and electrons from the interstellar medium effectively neutralized any. Through these, and the gravity of its mass, it still interacted with the outside cosmos.

At the event horizon, space and time were deformed, twisted, virtually dragged along by the whirling. Now and then, one of the nuclear pairs that seethed in and out of existence in the vacuum happened to appear in just such a position that a single member was captured while the other flew off, energized. In this fashion, the black hole evaporated, radiated— but insignificantly while it was its present size, so slowly that the last red stars anywhere would burn out before it was gone.

Atoms and dust sucked in from the environs kindled the real fire. Gathering velocity as they streamed inward, they began colliding near the blackness. Energy shot off as photons. The forces drew much of the plasma into an accretion disk, a maelstrom gyring about the black hole, to plunge at last down the throat of the vortex. Matter was also carried to the north and south magnetic poles and there hurled in beams back across light-years.

Without a companion star to strip, this body did not appear spectacular. Its luminance, X rays, was weaker than the X-ray band of all but the dimmer red dwarf stars. Through a telescope the eye saw the disk as a small, flickery ring of wan blue-white. The beams were only visible to radio receivers. But the intensity of either shining would be lethal to any traveler who came within tens of thousands of kilometers.

The maelstrom did not quern steadily. Waves billowed through, clashed together, flung flares like spume; great coils flamed forth, arching a million kilometers or more until they sleeted back; magnetic convulsions made the plasma shudder across still wider distances; and chaos, less well understood than these unforeseeables, wreaked havocs stranger yet.

Envoy took orbit at ten million kilometers' remove.

In the launch control center, Yu and Emil worked silently, deftly together. The Tahirian had learned well how to operate human devices. Instruments and consoles filled the rest of the cubicle. Nansen, come to watch, stayed in the entrance.

He heard nothing but breathing, felt nothing but a ventilation current on his cheek and his weight under spin. Suddenly, however, a new shape appeared among the stars in the viewscreen before him. Slim and sleek, faintly ashine by their light, it dwindled fast to his vision, accelerating. A second followed, a third, a fourth.

"Bravo!" he exclaimed. "They're well off, no?"—the first scientific probes.

Momentarily, as often in the recent past, he wished for more craft than these with the efficient field drive. But it had not been feasible. Except for adding the Yu-Dayan acceleration compensator, any retrofit of *Envoy*, the sole starship on hand, would have been an impossibly long and complex task, and what came out of it would not have been reliable. Likewise for the boats. *Envoy* was designed for *Herald* and *Courier*. The facilities for launching, docking, housing, and synergy with the ship could not be modified without affecting the entire integrated system. It was not even practicable to carry along a Tahirian boat secured to the outside of the hull. The Tahirian probes had been specially made to fit in the missile bays—arrows of peace, he prayed.

Well, Jean and Lajos are used to what we have anyway, Nansen thought. *As I was once.*

He forgot about it when Yu turned to look at him and reply quietly, "Yes." As their gazes met, the weariness of the journey seemed to drop from them. "May they go safely and make many discoveries."

Emil took up ens parleur. En had learned some English, but Tahirians were nonetheless apt to say the obvious over and over to humans, evidently unsure whether a meaning had gotten across. *How much do we to them?* wondered Nansen. "(This is entirely preliminary, you know,)" en said. "(The probes will simply confirm what the ancient expeditions found, and possibly report changes in conditions since then.)"

Nansen nodded impatiently.

"(They will also give us experience prior to the main effort,)" Yu reminded. To respond with an equal truism had somehow become polite, as relationships developed between the races.

Emil's mane stirred. Ens antennae quivered. "(I could almost wish I were one of the new robots we will dispatch at that time,)" en said. "(To sense these marvels directly—)" En broke off. Cambiante did not handle emotions well.

What an un-Tahirian feeling, even for an astronomer, Nansen thought. *Or is it? * Envoy *and what she does have been transforming them.* He harked back to Fernando, Stefan, Attila, all who had been eager to go, left behind and . . . grieving? But when six Tahirians was as many as the ship could reasonably provide for, and when the conservative faction made their demand stick that three of their own number be included— *At what personal sacrifice to* them, *who hate the whole idea? How devoted they must be. Or fanatical?*

"Well done," he said aloud. "Now let's be about our other business."

If only everyone aboard had some.

The station that was to orbit closer in, base and proximate command center for machines more powerful and sophisticated than the probes, had arrived dismantled. Robots could take most of the parts outside and assemble them, with Yu or Brent keeping an eye on progress from within the ship. But the core components, brain and heart of the entirety, required joining and testing in space by physicists—Dayan and Colin. Ruszek went along to assist. His former work among the asteroids of Sol qualified him uniquely.

It was an exacting task. Undiffused lamplight cast deep, sharp-edged, confusing shadows. In weightlessness, any slight blunder could send objects bobbing away. Usually, gloved hands must control manipulators, which had more sensitivity and precision, while a helmeted head strained against a microviewer. The humans needed frequent breaks. The Tahirian seldom did, although Ruszek muttered in English that en handled enself sloppily. Dayan replied that few of that race had had much practice in space. Besides, after hours with no sense of a magnetic field, en was not quite comfortable.

He and she agreed on a pause, one certain hour. They racked their tools and strolled off, around the curve of the hull. Boots swung to and fro, alternately in gripping contact. Safety lines unreeled, slack trailing loosely, as if rippled by some phantom wind. When the two stopped, shielded from lamps, they regained dark vision. Stars and Milky Way appeared to them like an epiphany, frosty, regal.

They had posted a small telescope at this spot. A bit of amateur astronomy was relaxing. This time Ruszek aimed it at the black hole. Through the eyepiece he made out a vague glimmer, no larger or brighter than a nebula his unaided sight had found in the same part of the sky.

Straightening, he sighed, "I have trouble believing. That monster—is that *all* we can see?"

Dayan spread her palms. "The nature of things," her radio voice answered.

He grinned sardonically. "Well, I've always said God has a sense of humor."

Her mood was more serious. "I wonder about that. As I wonder about His benevolence. Life, the universe, they can be dreadful."

"Practical jokes, maybe."

A cry cut into their earplugs. They twisted about where they stood. Flailing, Colin's form tumbled from the hull. No line followed it.

"*Vér és halál!*" Ruszek roared. "Damned clumsy fool—"

The Tahirian drifted outward, toward the whirling after wheel. "Colin!" Dayan wailed. She gauged speeds and distances, crouched, sprang free, and soared.

"No!" Ruszek bawled too late.

A jetpack was ready at the workplace. He hadn't time to go for it. Nor could he grab her line and haul her back. It was already out of his reach. He made his own swift estimate and leaped.

Dayan neared Colin, overshot, tried to check herself and swing sideways by a tug on her line. She wobbled, and still the cable unreeled.

Ruszek passed in arm's length of the Tahirian. He clamped a hand on a leg. They lurched onward together. "Stop squirming, you," he grated. He had judged his vectors well. He didn't quite encounter Dayan, but his free hand laid hold of her line.

By now he and Colin were on the same trajectory. He could let go and yank her tether. She jarred to a halt relative to him and rebounded back. The wheel was close, enormous, each spoke a club that would smash a spacesuit and the body within asunder.

Ruszek braced himself. "Hang on to me, Colin," he ordered. Whether or not the Tahirian understood the words, en got the idea and clung to his right calf.

Dayan bumped into him. He laid an arm around her. "You hang on, too," he said. She had not panicked. She clutched at the biounit on his back. He gathered a bight and gave his cable the kind of tug that locked the reel at the other end. Thereafter it was to pull himself and the others along, back to the hull.

"Bloody stupid safety features," he growled. "Leashes should be too short to reach a wheel. But then some jellybrain would find some different way to— Argh."

They thudded against the ship. Boots clung. Colin crouched low. Dayan stood shaking. The lights that drowned out stars made the sweat sheen on her face.

Ruszek seized her by the shoulders. "*Isten*—God damn it, you could have been killed," he choked. "Didn't you expect I'd go after this idiot here?"

"I—I'm sorry," she stammered. "It was so sudden. I didn't stop to think—"

"No, you did not. Idiot number two."

She straightened. He saw the abrupt chill upon her. "If you please," she said.

Instantly contrite, he dropped his hands and backed away a step. "*I'm* sorry. I didn't mean that."

"I hope not."

"It seemed like—like I might lose you, Hanny—"

She thawed. "I did act recklessly. It won't happen again. Shall we leave it at that?"

"If you want," he mumbled.

She had not said that she might have lost him.

He guessed that she didn't appreciate how close the brush with death had been, as quickly as she calmed. Helping Colin rise, she led the Tahirian over to their parleurs to inquire about the cause of the trouble. Ruszek heard later that ens line, floating about, had gotten in the way of delicate manipulations, until en unsnapped it. Then when en tried to shift a loosely secured cabinet—weightless, but with inertia unchanged— and didn't take proper care about footgrip, reaction flung en free.

Nansen could not give en a suitable tongue-lashing in Cambiante, but Dayan got one, and the captain suspended work while further precautions were devised.

At the moment, the mate struggled to regain his own equilibrium. Thereafter he resumed the relatively unskilled task she had assigned him. *I do still have her,* he thought.

* * *

Three little Tahirians seemed lost in the wide, high human gymnasium. Several of the machines outbulked them. And yet to Cleland they dominated the space, filled it from end to end and deck to overhead with their alienness.

And with what they stood for?

He stopped in the doorway. "I don't understand, I tell you," he protested. "Why this rush?"

Hand to elbow, Brent urged him onward. "It's a chance that won't come again. The other three are playing in their gym. Ivan fixed that; he's a clever customer. And I've been watching, listening, made sure all our breed are elsewhere. We can talk privately. If somebody does happen to see us, it won't seem as odd as if we were crowded together in a cabin."

Cleland shuffled ahead. "Talk? What about?"

"What do you suppose?"

Cleland stared at the trio who waited. Leo, Peter, and the—social technologist?—they called Ivan gave him back his gaze out of their multiple eyes. Ripples went through their manes, antennae trembled, he caught metal-sharp odors.

Stopping in front of them, he said, "Uh, yes. The . . . opposition," agents of that party on Tahir which did not want a revival of starfaring to trouble their world's millennial calm.

"Right," Brent replied. "Now that we know how the situation is shaking down here, we can start planning."

"Planning?" Cleland asked.

"Contingency plans, of course," the crisp voice told him. "Nothing's certain. But we can lay out ideas, arguments, tactics, whatever might bring an early end to this dangerous misery."

Hesitation yielded to bleakness. "I see. Our ship does seem to have become a Flying Dutchman, doesn't she?"

"And not even guaranteed eternal punishment. That thing out there can *kill* us, Tim."

"All right." A flick of humor twitched Cleland's mouth. "The loyal opposition will please come to order."

Brent remained grim. "Loyalty can be misplaced."

"I'm thinking of, well, survival. Everybody's."

"Me, too. I wish Nansen and his gang would."

Brent unslung his parleur and addressed the Tahirians: "(Our common purpose is to stop this undertaking, bring you home, and ourselves turn homeward. Let us consider ways and means.)"

Ivan responded. "(If no signs of intelligent beings become manifest, presumably the effort will cease before long.)"

Peter spoke in ens body language and harshened tones. Perhaps Leo translated, perhaps en commented: "(That is nothing we can count on.)"

"(I have been considering how we could see to it,)" Ivan said.

Cleland tautened, shocked. "Sabotage?"

"Would it be so bad a thing to do?" Brent demanded. "Against the scientific ethic, no doubt. But wouldn't it be better, more moral, to get us home alive, and soon, not after five more years in orbit around that hole into hell?"

The Tahirians had been conferring. Peter spoke for them. "(It scarcely seems feasible.)"

"(I cannot think of a way, either,)" Brent admitted. "(But we can give thought to it, among other approaches. Something may occur to us.)"

"P-persuasion," Cleland said. "Maybe, whatever happens, we can . . . persuade the rest."

"I doubt that. Christ knows we tried, back on Tahir."

"Conditions, events, they, uh, they may make people change their minds."

"Maybe." Brent spoke to the Tahirians again. "(What about Simon?)" He did not use the human-bestowed name for the linguist who replaced an Indira too old to travel, but the Cambiante symbol set identifying en.

"(Simon is only mildly in favor of this venture,)" Ivan said.

Brent nodded. "Ha, yes, I know," he muttered. "That must've been real sweet politicking they did, to get en aboard instead of another gung-ho dreamer." He went on as if to himself, retracing a well-worn trail. "And Mam and Selim aren't much for it. Nor Lajos, though now that Hanny's got this new toy—" His throat thickened. "Maybe the toy will turn out not to be such fun," he spat. "Damn near didn't, already."

"We don't know," Cleland said. "We can't foretell."

"No, we can't. That's why I want us to think what we *can* do, plan for every possibility we can imagine."

Cleland winced. "We may find . . . when the reality comes along, we can't d-do anything about it."

"I am not going to take that attitude," Brent stated. "Nor should you. Men, real men and women, they don't tamely whine, 'Thy will be done.' They fight back."

After their many talks through the years, Cleland heard the implication. "Fight—literally?" cried horror. "Out of the question!"

"Quiet." Brent glowered at him. "I didn't mean that. I certainly hope never. But I can imagine extreme emergencies, when nothing but quick action will save us. One thing we can do here and now is work out a drill for getting at the guns."

"No!"

"I agree, it'd be a desperate act. But you said it, we can't foretell. Maybe we will suddenly find ourselves desperate, with no time for arguing with fools. Survival knows no law."

Cleland's fists clenched at his sides. "It does. It can be too dearly bought—"

Brent's tone softened. The resolution within it did not. "Yours, maybe. Or mine, or any individual's. But not everybody's. Nor this whole ship and the treasures in her, what they'll mean at home in the way of power. Tim, we're responsible for the future of the human race."

"That's far-fetched—"

Brent gestured for silence. Cleland glanced back at the entrance. Nansen and Kilbirnie passed by, hand in hand.

"Damn," Brent said low when they were gone. "I thought they were already in bed screwing." He paused, made a thin smile, and went on in a normal voice, "Well, they don't seem to have noticed us. I guess they wouldn't. Let's continue our session while we can."

Cleland's face had blanched. "Yes," he said. "Let's."

35.

The robot in its spacecraft plunged toward doomsday.

At slightly less than five thousand kilometers out, instruments perceived the black hole as a disk of total darkness, a third again the width of Luna above Earth. X-ray fires blazed around it, from it. To a human the inrushing gas was only luminous from afar, seen as a whole through its entire thickness. Here he would have sensed merely the death that it dealt him. But to the robot it was an incandescent storm, shot through with sudden savage riptides. Magnetic field lines writhed like snakes millions of kilometers long. Gusts of plasma raged by, alive with lightning. There was no sound, but receivers heard hiss and shriek so loud that they must tune themselves down lest the noise shatter their circuits. Every protection, armor, insulation, field, came under attack. Metal members began to bend. Tidal force had reached four Earth gravities and was mounting ever faster with every inward centimeter.

The robot was seeking a stable orbit. The path it had won to was excessively eccentric. It fought to circularize at an endurable distance. Flung through a circuit of thirty thousand kilometers in a pair of minutes, buffeted, blinded, the orbit more and more crazily precessing and nutating, it failed. Each swing brought it nearer, and metal groaned under the stresses.

Still the spacecraft transmitted, sending the data it gathered on beams that could pierce the chaos. Null-one-null-null-one . . . forces, gradients, energies, densities, compositions, velocities, such stuff as reality is made on. It would report until the black hole destroyed and devoured it.

Abruptly the sendings changed. Responsive no more to their computer programs but to mind and will, electronics shuttled in new dances, weaving new signals—messages.

Nansen and Kilbirnie lay in his cabin, pillow-propped against the headboard. The bed was expanded to double width and the bedclothes rumpled. Odors of love lingered. On the bulkhead opposite them a screen played a view from Earth, of a summer sea rolling blue and green to lap around a great rock that Monet knew, beneath a summer sky where gulls and curlews winged. Mendelssohn's "Violin Concerto in E Minor" was reaching its joyous conclusion.

They had shared a beer, and lapsed into companionable silence while the restfulness flowed out of them and a new tide flowed in. As often, his thoughts wandered widely.

"I wish   " he sighed at last. The words trailed off.

Kilbirnie turned her head toward him. "You wish what?" she asked. "Maybe I can oblige."

"*Nada.* Nothing."

She snapped her fingers. "Oh, foosh, I had hopes about your wish."

"I didn't mean—"

The narrow, vivid face laughed into his eyes. "I ken vurra well wha' ye didna mean, laddie. And, truth, ye've no had a reasonable time to rest, yet." She snuggled close. "What is it you wish?"

He looked away again, at the image without seeing it, a furrow between his brows. "I've said it before. I wish we were home."

"Already?"

"Yes, yes, everything we knew as home is gone. But Earth—or any planet fit for human beings, even Tahir—"

"Aye, Tahir has grand sentimental value," Kilbirnie murmured reminiscently. "But Earth will be better. Whatever's happened meanwhile, we'll make our home there when we're ready to settle down, and, by God, make it the way we want it to be. Children—and I'm not a bad cook, skipper. You'll find I have as good an idea of breakfast as a Scotchwoman. Not surprising, that. But I'll wean you from your miserable coffee and French roll in the morning, see if I don't."

He wanted to fall in with her mood, but could not. "Until then, however, you, locked in this metal shell for no one knows how long."

She ruffled his hair. "Locked in wi' you, wha's wrong wi' that?"

"And I with you—"

He ended the kiss.

"But you are a free spirit, Jean, *querida,*" he said unhappily.

"And you're too serious, *querido.*"

"I was thoughtless. I should have foreseen. Now that we are here, in—in this everydayness, I worry about how you'll come to feel, how much it will hurt you, being always idled and confined." His fist doubled on the sheet.

"D'you suppose I gave the matter no beforehand thought myself?" she retorted. "I knew how badly you wanted to go—"

"Should I have wanted it? I could have swung the decision the other way."

She laid her palm over his mouth. "And you know how I wanted it," she finished. "Who says I'll be idled? We've a whole system to explore."

"No planets. If the star ever had any, it lost them when it blew up."

Passion leaped. "The beings, the life!"

He bit his lip. "I'm afraid the contact will be purely intellectual, if we make it." Quickly: "Of course you'll be as interested as everybody else, yes, and have suggestions for it. But is it enough for you, month after month, perhaps year after year?"

"Why, there'll be missions to fly regardless," she said. "You know that. What robots can do is limited. For a beginning, we'll put the command station in orbit. That will be a tricksy little devil!" Her tone and glance sparkled.

He sat straight and glared at her. "Wait! Not a job for you."

She took it coolly. "Indeed? Why not?"

He had avoided bringing the subject quite out into the open. Soon he must. He might as well start now. "It's too hazardous," he said as calmly as he could. "Ruszek is ready, willing, and able."

"Me, too."

"We can't risk both our pilots. He will take that mission."

"You have spoken?" she purred.

He nodded stiffly. "I have."

She smiled and fluttered her eyelashes. "Aweel, 'tis sweet o' ye, if misguided. Maybe I can get ye to unspeak."

Her hand went under the covers and roved shamelessly.

"You realize," Nansen said with difficulty, "you cannot change my mind."

"Belike not. Ye're a stubborn gowk." Kilbirnie slid her free arm under his neck. "But I can have fun trying."

In a room crammed with the disorder that gathers when concentration is complete, Sundaram and Simon stared at a screen.

Nothing moved there but dots and dashes, white on black. A screen alongside flickered through mutable figures as a computer program applied scheme after scheme—mathematical relationships, prime-number arrays, stochastic formulas, anything, anything that might give the binary inflow a pattern, the germ of a meaning.

Sundaram heard a whistle from the Tahirian. Unwashed, disheveled, he bent his head around and read on the parleur: "(Undoubtedly contact. The ancient databases record signals like these. Minds have taken over Probe Three and are calling to us.)"

"This early," the human croaked.

"(It happened thus before, equally fragmentary. As you know, the ancestors never succeeded in extracting much intelligibility.)"

And so at length, for that reason among others, they gave up, Sundaram thought for the hundredth time. *I don't believe we will. This abstract kind of communication suits the human mind better than the Tahirian.*

Half vision, half anguish: *What might we do together, all we different thinking beings in the universe, if we could find the will to keep traveling until we have bridged the distances between, to learn from and inspire each other, to reach and achieve what none of us alone can imagine?*

Chill struck. *But perhaps every voyage endangers existence. Too many, and the senseless random accident will happen, the cosmos and its glories lose the energy that has upheld them and fall into an oblivion that annuls the very past. Can it be the act of a Providence that nowhere does starfaring go on for very long?*

And then. *But how can I be afraid at this moment, this triumph? When Simon and I proclaim the tidings, it will be as if* Envoy *herself rejoices.*

The receiver screen blanked. The analyzer screen continued hunting.

"(I think the probe has come too close to the black hole, as we knew it would,)" the Tahirian observed—calmly?

Sundaram rose. Muscle by muscle, he flexed resilience back into his body. Hope blossomed. "We will send more," he said in English. "And once the station is ready, in orbit, we will truly begin to learn."

Dayan shared Ruszek's cabin, but kept hers very much for herself. Nobody else was present when Kilbirnie came.

Here there were a few constancies, a family portrait, a picture of her parents' home, a framed cloth hand-embroidered with the Star of David and "A good journey to you, Hanny, beloved" in Hebrew. Otherwise screens evoked images from the ship's database, changed weekly or oftener. On this daywatch an old man in a Hiroshige drawing looked across at a dynamic color abstraction, while an electron diffraction pattern, curving white on black like a surreal galaxy, glowed on the rear bulkhead of the room. She had made tea, and its aroma tinged the air, but as talk went on, both women had become unable to sit. Kilbirnie paced back and forth, Dayan stood warily by her desk.

"You can do it, Hanny," the visitor said. "You can make him do it."

The physicist frowned. "I don't like the idea," she answered, as she had already done.

Kilbirnie halted to face her. Hands spread out in appeal. "But for my sake, would you? A birthday present for me. My fortieth. You know what that means to a woman, Hanny." Tears trembled in the blue eyes. The voice stumbled. "Let me take that flight and—and I can laugh at time."

"Well— But is it fair to Lajos? He's like a boy again, looking forward."

"Och, he'll have his chances later. You can make this up to him. He loves you. I think he never loved anybody the way he loves you."

Dayan stared down at her feet.

"I'd not presume on our friendship," Kilbirnie said unevenly. "But it has been close, and—if you could, if you would—"

After a while that lengthened, Dayan looked up. "Well, since it's you, Jean—"

She got no opening to qualify or set conditions or say anything further at all. Immediately she was in Kilbirnie's arms. "Thank you, thank you!" the pilot half laughed, half sobbed.

They flopped back into their chairs, wrung out. Dayan drained her cup of now cold tea, refilled from the pot, and mused, "A gift for you, on your day. Yes, he is chivalrous, in his fashion. I don't like . . . using him." Well-nigh under her breath: "More than I do." Louder, raising her head: "However, I'll try."

"You'll succeed," Kilbirnie said with a flitting grin.

She grew serious. "But don't you or he tell how it's for that birthday of mine. We've never celebrated such aboard." They were too reminding, more than holidays. "It would be bad to start playing favorites. He can explain how he's thought the matter over, studied our two records, and decided I'm a wee bit better for this particular mission. Which is true, and will show how large-minded he is."

Just in case, she had surreptitiously adjusted the personnel database. Launch date was nowhere near her birthday and she was two years shy of her fortieth. Nansen knew it.

"The skipper can't override that!" she exulted.

Nansen's door chimed. He lifted his gaze from the reader on his lap. The text was *Elogio de la sombra*. Those austere verses gave comfort, saying that neither his wishes nor his griefs were unique, alone in space-time. "Enter," he said.

The door slid aside for Cleland and shut again behind him. He walked not quite steadily. His face was haggard, hair unkempt, eyes red, and he didn't seem to have been out of his clothes for the past daycycle.

Nansen smiled as best he was able. "Sit down," he invited. "What can I do for you?"

The planetologist came over to stand above him. "You can—can stop your . . . heartless . . . lunacy," he rasped.

Nansen rose. Cleland's breath stank. "What do you mean?" the captain asked, most softly.

"You know niggering well what."

Nansen went expressionless. He had heard bawdiness from Cleland once in a while, but never before obscenity. The rage went on: "Sending Jean to the black hole!"

"And you know it wasn't my idea and is not my desire," Nansen said. "When Ruszek deferred—"

"If he's lost his nerve, Colin can pilot!" Cleland yelled. "En's going anyway!"

"Nonsense. You know, too, no Tahirian can handle a human craft with any real skill. And Ruszek isn't afraid. This is his professional judgment, for the good of the mission. Couldn't you hear, couldn't you see how reluctant he was?" Nansen let his mask dissolve a little. "Do you suppose I'm glad? I had no choice."

"You do! You can order him to go!"

"No. That would be interference for no other reason than my personal preference."

"Then cancel the launch!"

"That would ruin our whole enterprise. We'll never get clear communication without the proper equipment, closer in than we or any other robots we have can go. Not to mention research on the black hole itself."

"Orbit the damn station by remote control."

Nansen continued patiently repeating common knowledge. "Across thirty-three light-seconds, into that unpredictable inferno? We'd too likely lose it altogether. Then we'd have made the voyage here for nothing."

"We should never've made it. Your cold craving—" Cleland gulped. "You don't care about her. She's been a—a convenience in your bed. Now she's a convenience in your boat. The boat you're too cowardly to fly."

Nansen's tone sharpened. "That will do, Cleland. You're exhausted, overwrought, and drunk. You know perfectly well that none but she or Ruszek can cope with those conditions. And you know—you must know—" Agony broke through. "If I didn't believe it was safe—reasonably safe, as far as we can tell—yes, I would terminate this and order a return . . . rather than—"

"If she comes to harm," Cleland snarled, "I'll kill you."

Nansen grew rigid. "Enough hysterics," he said. "Dismissed."

"You son of a she-swine!" Cleland screamed.

His fist swung. Nansen blocked it with a forearm. At once the captain clapped hands on the other man's tunic, wrists crossed, and pulled the fabric together. Cleland staggered in the choke hold. Nansen let go, hauled him around, yanked an arm of his around his back, and gripped at very nearly the angle to break it.

"Out," he said. "I will keep silence about this if you conduct yourself properly from now on. If not, I will have you restrained and sequestered. Go."

He released his prisoner. Cleland reeled toward the door. He sobbed and coughed.

36.

At the hour of departure, all but Yu, Brent, and Emil were gathered at the wheel exit. Those three were in launch control. The humans stood mute, avoiding one another's eyes, Nansen almost at attention, Cleland apart from the rest. The Tahirians talked together in their own group, signals and attitudes and subdued buzz or trill.

Kilbirnie arrived last. She skipped into the bare chamber, singing.

> *"Farewell and adieu to you, fine Spanish ladies,*
> *Farewell and adieu, all you ladies of Spain!—"*

She halted, looked them over, and laughed aloud. "Och, what long faces! Just bid me bon voyage, will ye no? For bonnie 'twill be. And nob-but two, three days."

"We worry," Ruszek croaked. "I worry. About you."

She danced over to him. "Noo, laddie, syne ye're wise and dear enough to gi' me this, dinna ever feel guilty. Ye're wonderful."

She kissed him heartily. Cleland shut his eyes.

Kilbirnie went about shaking hands. Cleland's lay limp in hers. When she let go, he stared dazedly at it.

For Nansen, at the end, she had a kiss that went on. He kept his arms at his sides. To him passion was a private thing.

"Adiós, amante," she breathed. "We'll do this right when I get back." She stepped from him and made for the exit, waving. "Good-bye, good-bye," she called, reached the ladder, and went from their sight. Her voice came down to them: "Ahoy!"

Colin followed.

After a minute the humans made their way to their common room, to watch the launch on its big screen. Such was not in Tahirian nature. For a while the image was merely of stars. Then *Herald* appeared, floating away until clear of the wheels, jetting briefly to take station, at that distance a bright dart.

The station lumbered into view. It seemed grotesque by contrast, a twenty-meter spheroid warty with turrets and bays, bristly with masts and webs. It moved off under field drive, at low acceleration. The boat maneuvered to match. Slowly they shrank into the screen, down to a pair of sparks in heaven, down and away into darkness.

"Resume your duties," Nansen said, and left the room.

When they were properly vectored, the vessels cut their drives and dropped inward on Hohmann trajectory. It would take them half a day to reach a million-kilometer orbital radius. This part of the transit was easy, and robots could readily handle it.

It fell short of the goal. Calculating from theory, old Tahirian findings, and data sent by their probes, the expedition's physicists had decided the station should circle within a quarter million kilometers. That was still too remote for relativistic and quantum mechanical effects of the black hole to be significant. But it did seem that the closer in a transmitter was, the more clearly the aliens could send; the signal-to-noise ratio increased, while the signal itself would become more than sporadic flashes. Furthermore, from there the station could dispatch sophisticated small spacecraft deeper in, perhaps even to skim the event horizon, with a fair chance of remaining able to control them, receive from them, and retrieve a few of them. Who knew what it might discover?

That last stage of the journey would be through ever worsening savageries. They had wrecked all probes thus far—if not on the first mission, then on the second or third. Heavily shielded, heavily loaded, the station was less agile than they were. It responded slowly to its drive, you could say awkwardly. Its computers and effectors were not programmed to cope with everything they might encounter; nobody could imagine everything, and it was the unforeseen that had slain the forerunners. A question to *Envoy* would be more than half a minute on the way. The response would take as long, or longer—for the black hole would be whipping the station around at well over a hundred kilometers per second. Time lag could prove fatal.

A command vessel must needs go along, prepared to shepherd, prepared if necessary to plunge in, lay alongside, grapple fast, and correct the course before speeding back toward safety. Kilbirnie steered *Herald*.

On the half day of the inward fall she hovered over her instruments, hummed, sang snatches of song, looked out at the stars, raised memories in her head and smiled at them. Colin sat for the most part wrapped in ens Tahirian thoughts.

"Uh-oh. We got trouble."

For a moment Kilbirnie's glance left the pilot console and flicked to the forward viewscreen, as if she could see the wrongness happening. Only stars and a restless blue-white blur that was the accretion disk, images enhanced against interior lighting and exterior night, were visible to her, there where she swung in orbit. The station had left her hours ago, boosting to its new path.

"¿Qué es? What's the matter?" rapped Nansen's voice.

"Radar tracking shows sudden deviation. We don't know why, but it doesn't look good. Hang on."

Data poured in. Colin toiled at ens computer.

Presently en took up a parleur. Kilbirnie leaned around in her seat to read the writing, as well as see, hear, and smell the other components of Cambiante when used by a Tahirian. A human could only supplement with sign language, though that included several facial expressions. "(Apparently the station passed near a large mass,)" Colin said. "(The gravity flung it off course. It will plunge much lower than we planned before rounding periastron and receding.)"

"God! What—" She reached for her own parleur. "(What can the mass be? A wandering planet, sucked in by sheer chance at the exact worst moment for us?)"

"(Possibly. We know such objects exist in interstellar space. The radar indications were unclear, and it is now hidden on the farther side. But you may recall that we have often observed knots, temporary concentrations of plasma, form in the disk. We do not know what the mechanism is, although I have speculated about shock-wave resonance effects. They may create plasmoids in the huge flares we frequently see, reaching far beyond the disk before falling back. Such a plasmoid could be held together for a while by its self-generated magnetism, and might have the mass of a large asteroid. If it came close to the station, the event, although unfortunate, was not unbelievably improbable.)"

However academic the statement, Colin's body shivered in ens seat, the fur stood stiff, the mane tossed like gale-blown leaves, a brimstone reek gusted out.

Kilbirnie nodded, her neck as stiff as her mouth. "Simple bad luck. And the unknown, which we can't ever provide against." Her fingers asked, "(What is the situation, then?)"

"(The radar is collecting data.)" Colin returned to ens work. Kilbirnie reported to *Envoy*.

Time wore away. She wasn't hungry, but forced herself to go aft, take a few bites of dry rations, swallow a half liter of water. It helped more to do a set of limbering exercises. The Tahirian didn't seem to want anything but information.

Shortly after she came back, en told her: "(The station's new orbit has now been computed. It is highly eccentric and will rapidly decay.)"

"Well, let's get that changed." Kilbirnie saw no reason to put it on the parleur. This was her department. She bent herself to the task of establishing direct laser communication with the command computer yonder.

The station was outward bound for the apastron of its shortened and cometary path. The maximum acceleration of which it was capable, properly applied, ought to work it into a safely broad ellipse. "And then we try again for the right one," Kilbirnie said with a lopsided grin.

Envoy kept quiet, not to bother her and her partner. *That must be hard on the skipper,* she thought. *My poor jo.*

Computation. Result. Directive. *Apply this vector three hours, eighteen minutes; thereafter run free, standing by for further orders.*

Power surged in the station, sensed and followed by instruments elsewhere; eyes still saw only stars and the distant disk-fire.

Shock. "Wha' the bluidy hell—"

"(The acceleration is insufficient,)" Colin said from ens meters and readouts.

"(That is clear. Let us find out why.)"

Computerized telemetric systems operated swiftly. Within minutes Kilbirnie could say, "(We have damage to the station's superconductor grid. Deformation. Evidently tidal forces warped it when it passed so near the black hole. The field drive is functioning at barely 27 percent of rated maximum. Can we do anything useful with that?)"

Colin calculated. "(It cannot raise the apastron enough. At best, we can delay the irretrievably close approach and the subsequent engulfment by two orbits. That gives us a total of approximately ninety-six hours. Can the repair systems restore full function within this time?)"

Kilbirnie shook her head. "(I am not familiar with the station and its machines in detail, but with what I do know, I can be sure it will take considerably longer.)"

"(Have we then lost the station?)"

The bleakness in Kilbirnie fled from her sudden laughter. "Nay!" she cried. "We've a rescue to do. D'ye think we can claim salvage rights?" She explained: "(Our boat should be up to supplying the additional boost. Compute the parameters.)"

Almost, Colin shrank from her. "(Is this advisable?)"

"(Work up the numbers and find out,) damn it!"

The figures were soon on hand. Kilbirnie studied them, smiled, and turned to the outercom. "*Herald* to *Envoy.* I've news at last. I daresay you're almighty tired of listening in and wondering what the devil we're at."

A minute went by while her words flew outward, a receiver undid

Doppler effect, and Nansen's came to her. She sat weightless, admiring the heavens. Rounding the black hole in some fifteen hours, the boat pointed her bow at other stars than earlier. But here all constellations were strange.

"Our own observations suggest what the problem is," Nansen said, carefully impersonal. "Give us your details, please."

Kilbirnie transmitted the figures while she told their meaning in English. "We can handle it," she finished. "If we rendezvous, grapple, and apply full thrust in coordination with what's left of the field drive, we'll free the station. In fact, we'll put it directly on trajectory for the orbit we intended. And we'll have ample delta v left for ourselves. But we have to do it on this pass, setting out in just a few minutes. Next time around, the decay will already have progressed too far, plus whatever further harm tidal stress may have done."

Pause. Ventilation hummed. Colin sat quiet. She had an impression that the mintlike scent from en betokened meditation.

"That is . . . very unsafe," Nansen said. "The disk is going into an active phase. It's spitting more and more flares, and they are getting bigger. Quite possibly a plasmoid concentration did bring on the trouble. Diving closer in, you, too, could be caught. Abort. Return to us. Nobody will blame you or imagine you were frightened. You have no right to be reckless."

"I've considered it," Kilbirnie answered. "The odds are long in our favor. If a flare reaches us, it'll hardly include another fat mass. That would be ridiculous. Anyhow, the worst a mass can do, if it doesn't actually hit us, is throw us off course, and we can recover from that. The flare itself is ions and electrons, which'll be famine-thin by the time they get to where we are. Our screens and shielding will fend off the radiation."

She smiled at him, unseen amidst the stars. "Dinna fash yersel', skipper. Of course we'll skyhoot for home and mother if anything truly nasty comes at us." Her tone firmed. "But in my best judgment, here on the spot, we can safely do it, and our duty is to make the effort."

Waiting.

"Duty— I must accept your judgment, Pilot Kilbirnie," Nansen said, word by heavy word. "Take every due precaution. Proceed."

"Thanks, love." Kilbirnie blew him a kiss. "I do love you," she whispered.

Turning to Colin: "(Have you understood? I mean to go save the station. But you have your life, too. Are you willing?)"

The Tahirian lay calmed. Ens middle eyes met hers, ens side eyes contemplated heaven and the vessel that they shared. "(Yes. It will be your task, but is for all of us, and I have confidence in you.)"

"Thanks," she said again, more moved then she had expected.

Then it was to get busy.

Herald jetted. Weight tugged. Stars wheeled in view for a moment, steadied, and gleamed dead ahead. Among them the disk slowly brightened. Kilbirnie began to see the ripples and flickers of tempests within it.

The station hove in sight, ugly, lame, futureful. Kilbirnie lost selfhood, became one with her boat, with instruments, computers, controls, and the flame that drove them onward. Delicately as a stalking panther, she maneuvered in. Speeds were above a hundred kilometers per second; it would not take much of an error to smash her. Match vectors, draw closer, extend grapnels. Guided by their sensors, the arms reached for contact. It registered. They took hold and folded. Hull met hull. The impact was gentle, but rang through *Herald* like a great bell.

Make full linkage with the command computer in the station. Take fresh data. Recompute flight plan. Enter. Apply lateral jet, slewing around a trifle till oriented just so. Now, *blast.*

The acceleration was low, about a quarter gravity, for the boat was helping move a mass considerably larger than her own. Still, give it time and it would be enough, it would serve.

Kilbirnie sagged back under it, into her chair. She wiped a hand across her brow and tasted sweat, salt on her lips. "Whoosh!" she breathed. "I want a drink. Improvident, bringing nowt along stronger than coffee."

Her remark flew on the beam to *Envoy.* "You have to stay alert," Nansen cautioned. "The disk is churning and spouting, worse every minute."

She touched for a view in that direction and magnified. The gas was indeed in upheaval, waves and gouts of fire, a storm in the maelstrom. She was not sure whether she could make out a point of infinite night, the black hole.

"We'll keep watch," Nansen went on redundantly. He had put his ship in a canted orbit for an overview through instruments more powerful than any in the boat. "Be prepared to cut and run upon warning."

"I told you, skipper, we should be fit to ride out whatever the thing may throw at us," Kilbirnie replied. "But of course we're no heroes, we two. Nothing so stupid. I've plenty of living left to do . . . with you," she finished low.

Colin had been occupied at the keyboards. "(I have reset the appropriate systems to monitor ambient space,)" en announced. "(They will provide us information additional to what we obtain from the ship.)"

"Good." Kilbirnie's nod, smile, and brief stroking of the fur conveyed it. She and a few Tahirians, en among them, had come to that much friendship and understanding over the years. She yawned and stretched. "I could do with a nap. And do and do."

She had no immediate job. Boat and station steered themselves. It was a straightforward operation, applying thrust on a line gyroscopically fixed. In this region, nearing apastron, no unusual velocity change was needed to alter orbit radically. Three hours would bring it about. Thereafter, released, the station ought to curve away and fall into the path around the black hole that its builders wanted. This far from the monster mass, the ordinary laws of celestial mechanics kept faith.

Kilbirnie unbuckled, went aft, secured herself on a bunk, and drifted into dreams. Colin stood watch. Perhaps en dozed a little, or the Tahirian equivalent of it; perhaps en was too nervous to rest. It had been long since any of ens race last challenged the universe.

Kilbirnie dreamed of flying. . . .

A yell woke her. She unsnapped her belts and tumbled to her feet. It had come from the outercom speaker. "—danger," Nansen cried. "Respond, *Herald*! Danger!"

She leaped along the deck and vaulted into her seat. A glance at a clock showed that two hours had passed. Colin huddled beside her, mane erected, a harsh smell around en. "*Herald* to *Envoy*," she said while her hands fastened the safety harness. "What's the trouble?"

Wait. Colin gestured at the instrument displays. She could not interpret them at a glance.

"A giant flare has erupted," Nansen said, now iron-cool. "The leading edge will reach you in about fifteen minutes. Abandon the station and boost the hardest you can."

Clearheaded, more exhilarated than alarmed, she replied with the same levelness, "Not necessarily. We couldn't outrun it in any case. And there are no clots or other special hoodoos, are there? We'll take some readings ourselves and report back."

She turned to her companion. Colin raised ens parleur. "(The spectrum shows an extremely energetic volume of gas, largely plasma. It is attenuating as it advances and spreads. Our screens will deflect the particles, and no more hard photons will penetrate our shielding than may perhaps cause us to take a prophylactic cell treatment at the ship.)"

"(I thought so. We stay.)"

"(As is to be expected, the magnetic field is strong and fluctuant, with transients of high local intensity. I cannot obtain quantitative data. This is a chaotic phenomenon, beyond previous experience.)"

"(We can cope, though. Correct?)"

"(Lacking precise measurements and applicable equations, I cannot offer better than a guess. I think we can remain. I am willing.)"

"(Then we do.)" Again she caressed en.

To Nansen: "We can handle it, and besides, we wouldn't gain much if we fled. Don't fear for us."

Wait.

"If this is your decision," Nansen dragged forth, "I will not pester you."

"Save that for when we're together," Kilbirnie suggested.

Wait.

"*Vaya con Dios,*" said her skipper.

And it was to wait, while the linked spacecraft fought their way toward freedom.

The flare poured over them.

Nothing showed to eyes, nothing crackled in ears or prickled in skin. Viewscreens depicted stars gleaming changeless. Only meters told of the rage seething around. Kilbirnie peered unwinkingly at them. That shift-

ing, twisting magnetism, borne outward in the electric torrent, did pose a
threat to her reaction drive. It could divert the plasma stream, even start
ruinous waves of resonance. The boat's collimating fields compensated.
Should they be overwhelmed, they had a fail-safe. Nevertheless—

Abruptly the sky was gone from the screen before her. White flashes
blinked and staggered across blackness. Colin recoiled in ens seat. Kilbirnie's hands clenched her chair arms. "What's this?" she heard herself
gasp. Unreadable, the pattern fairly screamed urgency. "A warning—frae
them, the aliens—?"

The stars reappeared. She saw needles and numbers go wild. Weight
fell to a fraction of what it had been. A synthetic voice stated: "Magnetic
flux was at the point of overriding the screen fields and disrupting jet
control. Thrust has been stopped. No significant damage has occurred."

The nightmare whirled through her, the jet forced aside, slashing
at the lattice of its accelerator, perhaps with a backlash into the hull, a
lethal burst of radiation, but air would already have exploded from the
wound . . . at best, her boat crippled, an object passive in orbit, falling
back to swing through the deadly disk while the tides ripped at structure
and flesh. . . .

"What has happened?" Nansen called.

"I'd like to know, myself," Kilbirnie rejoined. "Hold on."

She conferred with Colin.

"All right," she said. "It's clear." She described the disaster that had
been averted. "The flux has declined. We can resume thrust. We will."

Wait, while breath and blood went in and out.

"You'll cast loose first, of course," Nansen said raggedly. "And—forgive
me, I can't teach you your business, but—as nearly as we can tell, the
flare is full of magnetic line concentrations. More will probably sweep
over you. You'll have to escape by fits and starts."

"That, aye," Kilbirnie conceded. "But no sense in forsaking the station.
It's not yet at a point where it can work into any kind of survival orbit.
We'll stay with it, tugging when we can, till it's ready."

Wait.

"Abort, I say. Return to us."

"No. We've too bluidy much invested in this. Colin and *Herald* and I,
we can save it."

Wait. Kilbirnie began running her new computation. It was elementary; she didn't need help.

"Abort at once," Nansen said. "That is an order."

Kilbirnie sighed. "You're captain where you are. I'm captain here."

Wait. Numbers and graphics arrived. She keyed a command. Weight
came back as it had been, like a hand laid upon her.

"I beg you—"

"Don't. Just wish us luck."

Wait. The fire disk waved and wavered.

Dios santissimo—" Stoicism clamped down. "Proceed, Pilot."

"Carry on, my darling."

The minutes moved through the last hour.

An alarm shrilled. The boat shuddered. Weight plummeted anew.

"A magnetic pulse of very high power seriously interfered with plasma collimation before the shutoff could respond," stated the computer. No fear was in its voice. Not being alive, it could not die. "The jet deviated and burned through the sternmost coil. Maximum available thrust has been correspondingly reduced, by twelve percent."

Kilbirnie took her parleur, to make sure Colin understood.

"Now will you abort?" demanded Nansen.

"We'll decide," she answered. "I think not. We're too nigh victory."

She recomputed. "(This adds thrust time,)" she said to her partner. "(In twenty more minutes we can let go, if all goes well, which it may not. What do you think?)"

"(It is a risk,)" the physicist replied. "(I have noticed in the past, from the ship, that flares and the forces they carry reach a peak shortly before they cease. However, in my opinion it is worth continuing.)"

"(Agreed.)" *How I wish I had the language to say what this means and what you are, Colin. But maybe I couldn't anyhow. We humans are too often shy about speaking such things.* "Skipper, we are not going to quit. We'd leave our hearts behind with the station." *Tahirians don't exactly have hearts. But they have spirit.* "Please keep quiet. We've work to do."

The injured vessels struggled on together. The flare streamed invisibly around them.

And— "Harroo!" Kilbirnie shouted. The prosaic readouts before her spelled glory. "We've done it!"

She inactivated and retracted the grapnels. A nudge of impulse sent the boat drifting clear of the station. It appeared in her screen, a lumpy globule, now under command of its own computer, retreating against the Milky Way.

"This is—is wonderful," Nansen stammered. "Praise be to God." His tone steadied. "You still have to secure your escape, of course."

"Of course," Kilbirnie caroled. "And drink and dance and be outrageous. Well, that's for back aboard *Envoy*."

The two spacecraft were not yet completely free. They had reached a point where either one, even with a lamed motor, could assume any orbit—essentially, go anywhere. But they must *go*. Their present paths remained cometary. If they did not act, they would fall into the nearness of the black hole and it would wreck them.

The station was boosting. Eventually it could stop and coast into the region where it belonged. *Herald* should linger until then, in case of further trouble. First, though, *Herald* had better liberate herself, climbing to a track of much lower eccentricity much higher in the gravity well.

"Gang awa', lassie," the pilot said, and wakened the jet. Weight seized. The boat sprang.

The alarm shrieked. Readings and readouts went crazy. She floated in her harness, falling free, and heard: "An extraordinary magnetic surge has caused the destruction of coils nine through five and the disablement of coil four."

The words tolled away into silence.

"Oh, damn and damn," Kilbirnie said through it. "I'm sorry, Colin."

"What is this?" Nansen called across space. "Your jet, your acceleration—"

"Hold on till I can tell you."

Her fingers, running over the keyboard, and her brain, interpreting what came out, might as well have been machines themselves. She had not yet had time for feelings.

"Bad news," she said flatly. "Our drive is blown. We don't have but a wisp of thrust, not near enough to break loose. If we rejoined the station, it couldn't help, either. We'd simply force it to ruination with us. Whatever we tried, we're bound through the inner part of the disk."

They had already passed apastron and were downward bound.

"No," Nansen pleaded. "Ruszek is ready. He'll come take you off."

"The numbers say he can't reach us till way too late. Wait a minute, darling dearest. I have to talk with my partner."

And presently: "We're agreed. We'll no hae yon thing raddle us wi' radiation and pluck us apart bit by bit. We'll use what's left us to dive straight in."

Kilbirnie swung her boat around and took aim.

"Oh, Jean, Jean."

"Hush. I'm not glad to leave this life, but I'm glad for what it gave me. Fare ye all well, shipmates. I love ye, skipper."

Kilbirnie switched the outercom off. She restarted the motor. The acceleration, the weight, was low and erratic. Yet if a magnetic nexus did not strike *Herald* again—and, really, that was unlikely—speed would mount. In about an hour she and her friend would pass through the gate of death, too fast to sense it.

They joined hands and looked forth at the stars.

The station took final orbit without requiring further assistance. It began activating its systems, to receive, explore, and relate.

37.

Nightwatch laid stillness on the corridors of *Envoy*. When Nansen's door chimed, he looked up in surprise.

He had dimmed illumination in his cabin to a twilight. A stubby candle, one of a number newly made for him by the nanos, burned on his desk below the old crucifix. He sat gazing at the flame, no longer really seeing, though somehow it was like a small sun around which awareness circled through silence, until the door recalled him.

"Come in," he said. *The captain is never free.*

For a moment the fluorescence outside dazzled his eyes. He saw the newcomer as a black hole in it. She stepped through, the entrance closed, and the candle cast his shadow vague over Dayan.

She stopped, herself half blinded until vision grew used to the dusk. He rose. "What is the matter?" he asked wearily.

She caught her breath in a gulp. Her words stumbled. "I'm sorry. This is very late. And I knew you'd rather be alone." *As often as possible.* "But I thought—at this hour we could talk . . . privately."

"Yes, of course. Please be seated." He resumed his chair at the desk and swiveled it around to face hers.

For a while they were mute. She stared down at the hands clenched together in her lap. Finally she got out: "This is . . . hard to say, but—" She raised her head toward him and finished in a rush. "Are you planning any kind of service, memorial, anything for Jean? And Colin," she added dutifully.

"No," he replied.

"Some of us . . . expected you would."

"My fault. I should have made an announcement."

"We'd like to say good-bye to her."

His flat tone gentled. "I understand. But don't you see, there's too much emotion, too much bitterness—in certain of us. It would be disruptive to meet this soon for that purpose."

She regarded him. With the candle behind, his expression was hard to make out. "Do you truly think so?"

"I don't know," he sighed. "I can't read the souls of people. It is my guess. For most of us, me too, a service would be comforting. But I can't very well tell those who look on me as a murderer that they mustn't come."

"Oh, Rico!" She half rose from her seat, reached toward him, and sank back down.

"That is my guess," he repeated. "I could be wrong, but I dare not risk it. Thank you, though, for reminding me. I'll tell them tomorrow, everybody is welcome to . . . pray for her, wake her, whatever feels right, . . . by themselves, or with their near friends."

"You are mourning alone, aren't you?"

"That seems best."

"You are always alone. In your heart, since she went away. Unless you are with your God."

"I am not a very good believer, I fear," he said regretfully. "But one can try." In haste, not to reveal more: "Why have you come here, Hanny?"

He could see how his use of her first name helped her gather courage. "I have a great favor to ask of you. Maybe too great."

"Yes?"

"Let me join in saying good-bye to her. In praying for her."

His eyes widened with surprise. It took him a brief span to respond, most softly, "May I ask why you wish this?"

Tears caught in eyelashes and captured faint flamelight. Her voice harshened. "I need— I am guilty, Rico. I connived with her. She got me to . . . seduce Lajos into giving her the flight—" She lowered face into crook-fingered hands.

"I wondered about that."

"If I hadn't—"

He squared his shoulders. "Then probably Lajos Ruszek would be dead. You could not have known. I did not." The calm broke. "Over and over I tell myself I did not."

She looked anew at him. "And you didn't, Rico."

"Nor you."

"But I—what we feel, what I wish had happened—my horrible thoughts—" She swallowed a breath.

Having regained self-control, he gave her a wry smile. "You're unjust, Hanny. Well, I've heard that Jews are too prone to self-accusation."

"Were," she corrected him in a whisper. "I suspect I am the last Jew. And a woman and an unbeliever, but the only vessel the heritage has left."

"And I am the last"—he shrugged—"whatever it may be."

Dayan became able to speak quietly. "Jean, though, what she was, her kind of spirit, can't we hope it is still alive at home?"

"Thank you for saying that," he gave her.

"Could we remember her tonight—just for a few minutes?—we two? It would help me."

"You do me honor," he replied.

The candle thew dim, shadow-flickery light up over crucified Christ. Nansen knelt and folded his hands in orison. She stood beside him and said Kaddish.

Cluttered, devoid of any outside view, the work center seemed closed off from the stars. But as Sundaram and Yu watched what appeared on a screen before them, awe reached in through metal and coursed through marrow.

"Already?" he wondered.

Those were no longer vague, short pulses. Sharp and clear, a curve undulated through changes of form while simple-looking symbols altered correspondingly but kept the same basic array. The adjacent screen showed its computer's quick interpretations, equations rendered in Arabic numerals, Greek and Roman letters, international signs for mathematical operations. Through analytical geometry, a language was beginning to unfold.

"Yes," Yu said hushedly, "I assumed they would need time to trace out our circuits. Now I think they can . . . move electrons, alter quantum states, directly"—and thus use the enormous bandwidth of the station's transmitters to send pictures . . . and what else, later?

"Intelligence speaking to us. Out of where, out of what?"

"Surely not from the black hole or its immediate environs"—its hell. "But perhaps they . . . draw on those extreme conditions . . . somehow . . . to make something possible."

"Something too strange for us to imagine."

She touched his brow. "We will, in time. You will."

"We shall want Hanny's advice, above all, at this stage. How to interpret, how to respond. Later, as we grow beyond mathematics and physics, Simon's. And at last, everyone aboard?"

From the ship's data hoard Mokoena had summoned some of the music Kilbirnie loved. She was leaning back, eyes closed, listening to "The Flowers of the Forest" and trying to understand that idiom, when Zeyd entered her cabin. She heard, rose to greet him, and signaled the player for low volume. Pipes and drums became background, like wind wailing along a seacoast.

"You look grim," she said.

Her tentative smile died before his face. "I feel grim," he said. "I have been talking with Al Brent."

"Must you?" She attempted a little humor. "I have learned to dodge aside when I see him coming."

"Yes, he is obsessive. But what he has to say, right or wrong, we cannot continue hiding from."

"I suppose not," she said dully. "Hiding, that may be why the mess and the common room are so cheerless"—with strained silences broken by intermittent conversation about meaningless matters.

"Then should we not bring it into the open and have done?"

"Of course. It's only—we're afraid to. The wound is too fresh."

"To stay here in spite of everything, or give it up and go home. A simple question."

"It isn't. Even between you and me." This was in fact their first recent touching on it. "Scientific values versus—what?"

"Survival, perhaps. And the science isn't yours or mine."

She rallied from sadness. "How can you be sure? Those beings, or that being—not life as we know it, but . . . maybe we'll learn things about our own kind of life, too, that we never knew."

"And maybe not. In either case, there'll be nothing for a chemist to do."

Her eyes implored him. "How can you be certain? Besides, you're more than a chemist, Selim. And as for going home, what does that mean any longer?"

"Enough," he snapped. "You're talking general principles again. We have been over that ground until it's trampled bare."

"But Jean's death—"

"Yes, that has changed things." Zeyd began to pace, up and down before her. The music ended. Without it, his tones sounded machinelike. "Doubtless this isn't logical. But people aren't. Al is right. We must meet soon and decide. I will put it to the captain."

"And others will," she foresaw. Pause. "If it comes to a vote, will you be for leaving?"

"Yes."

"And I will be for staying." She drew close to him. "We mustn't let this divide us."

"You are too late," he said. "The crew is already divided." He took her hands. Tenderness welled up. "But we two, Mam, we will not let that happen, will we?"

In Ruszek's cabin the same disagreement took another turn.

"If you hadn't honeyed me into giving her the mission—" he grated.

"I'm sorry, I'm sorry, but how could I have known?" Dayan cried.

They had left their seats and stood stare against stare in the middle of the room. Apart from the furnishings, it was well-nigh empty; he had few possessions. A vase of flowers she had brought was withering. With several drinks under his belt, blood flushed his cheeks, sweat sheened on the bare scalp, the mustache bristled.

"Sorry? Would you rather it was me dead?"

Her glance fled from his. "No, oh, no."

"I can't feel thankful to you. It was blind luck."

"Of course."

"*Evil* luck. For me also."

"Then why are you angry?"

"The senselessness of it."

"Your God—"

He ignored her essay at peace. "And the senselessness of hanging here. You know Nansen won't let me fly. He'll cancel the other manned explorations we planned. Mustn't risk the last boat. But the pilot can sit and rot, after you get your way."

"Please, Lajos, no." She met his eyes afresh and spoke levelly. "We will find work for you, outside observations, interior refitting—"

"Sops, while you scientists have your fun and games. Sops. Or the damned stupid virtuals, no better. I spit them out!" he roared. "I say we go home before we lose more lives!"

"We won't."

"Do you know that? Are you a witch, to know that? And we *will* lose lives, years out of our lives, thrown away, waiting for what? Nothing worth the cost. I say go home."

She braced herself, the red head high. "And I say stay."

He lifted a fist. She stood where she was. His arm dropped. He snarled, turned on his heel, and stamped out.

She remained there a few minutes before seeking her private quarters.

At parade rest before his people in the common room, Nansen saw them seated apart, Sundaram, Yu, and Dayan on the right, Brent, Cleland, and Ruszek on the left. Mokoena and Zeyd were side by side in the middle, as if to bridge what lay between.

Talk had been ragged until Yu now said, "Jean Kilbirnie should not have died for nothing."

"I am sorry," Nansen told her, and meant it, "but that is out of order. We stipulated beforehand that there shall be no emotional declarations at this meeting."

Brent leaned forward. "Then what is there to say?" he flung back. "Are you a man or a robot?"

"We cannot let certain things, such as hostility, go free," Nansen replied to the assembly. "They feed on themselves. If discipline, morale, and common purpose deteriorate, the black hole may quite possibly kill us. The meeting will confine itself to rational arguments."

"We've heard them," Ruszek growled. "They were old before we left Tahir. What's crazy is to keep going over them."

"And the rational thing to do is consider our feelings," Brent advanced. "Most of us can't take much more. If we don't leave soon, that's what will destroy us as a crew."

"No," Zeyd put in. "I disagree. I prefer an early return. But regardless of what the decision is, we should have the brains and backbone to carry it through."

"Or don't you believe you have them, Al?" gibed Dayan.

Our half hour together seemed to calm her, Nansen thought. *But something has her on edge again.*

"That will do," he reproved. "If the meeting cannot proceed in orderly fashion, I will adjourn it."

"What was the point of calling it?" Brent demanded.

"To clarify our thinking."

"W-we know where we stand." Cleland's voice firmed. "Captain, I call for a vote."

"This is not a voting matter," Nansen said.

"Please," Sundaram ventured. "With respect, the articles of the expedition can be interpreted as meaning that after five years at the original destination, which are past, policy decisions will be made democratically."

Nansen looked into the brown countenance. "You want to stay, don't you?" he asked.

"With all my heart. But I am trying to be fair. Logical, as you requested."

Nansen smiled a trifle. "You would." Louder: "A vote is futile in any event. Counting myself, we have five who want to stay," *plus Jean, were she here,* "four who want to go."

"Y-you're forgetting the Tahirians," Cleland said. "Ivan, Peter, Leo— make seven. Emil is for you, I admit. But still, it's seven against six."

"Simon is neutral," Brent added. He spoke truth, they knew. Scientific curiosity was seldom a strong Tahirian motivation, at least in the one Tahirian culture still in existence. Simon had served ens race and clan by enlisting, with the personal sacrifice that that entailed. Whatever came of it, en would be an alpha at home. "Seven to six, Nansen."

"We will not count ballots," the captain stated. "Voting is not a Tahirian concept."

"What?" Cleland yelled. "They're not free, thinking beings?"

"They are. But they never signed our articles. They agreed to take part in our expedition for its duration, which they knew was unpredictable. It was a human idea, this is a human ship, and humans will decide."

Nansen raised a hand to quell protests. "The poll stands at five to four, if anyone insists on a poll. Logic and equity are the real considerations. Everyone accepted—some of us reluctantly, but we accepted—that this new journey was for the purpose of carrying out research on the black hole and making contact with the intelligences. We have barely commenced. Our whole aim, our pledge to our race, who gave much to send us, has been to try to find meaning in the universe. We may be on the verge of doing so. If we cannot stay loyal to that promise, how can we cope with space, or with an Earth that will be alien to us?

"If we continue the work, we can depart at any time: when we have learned enough, or when it does really seem foolhardy to linger. But once we turn back, then psychologically and morally—for we do have our Tahirian shipmates to consider—that is irrevocable.

"Pending such a change in circumstances, we will keep station here. I expect that everyone will work in good faith for our mission and for the general well-being.

"The meeting is ended."

He strode out. His listeners sat wordless. After a while they began to stare at each other.

Cleland could not stay seated for long at a time. In his quarters, where things lay chaotically strewn and every display screen was dark, he poured whiskey for Brent and himself, and wandered around in front of his guest, talking in fragments. The engineer waited the spell out.

Finally he could say from his chair: "Yes, you and I know, Tim. The others don't. They're afraid to face the fact. Even Lajos—I think he and Dayan have quarreled over this, and I've tried him, hinted, but he hangs back. Probably he hasn't yet shed his old dog-grateful attitude toward Nansen. So setting things right has to start with us two. We know."

The low-pitched intensity caught at Cleland. He halted and looked into eyes that smoldered up at him. "What do you mean?" he asked thinly.

"We're dealing with a madman."

Cleland's hand clenched around his tumbler. "A monster, at least. Doesn't give a curse—about Jean— Did he ever in his life shed a tear?"

"A madman, I say. Maybe not by clinical tests, but for all practical purposes, like Mao Zedong in his later years. Lost in his fever dream of a scientific triumph. As if anything anybody could find here can ever matter to humankind, the way the knowledge and power we can bring will. He'll gamble those, and us, to chase his fantasy—down into the black hole."

"He . . . he did say . . . we can always leave if it—it's not working out—"

"He lied." Brent gestured. "Sit down and listen." Jerkily, Cleland obeyed. "You know he lied. When will he admit it? After how many more deaths?"

"But what can we *do*?"

"That's what you and I have got to talk about. And later with Ivan, Peter, and Leo."

"What do you mean?" Cleland begged again.

Brent's voice tolled. "Law, from when men first put to sea, and our ship's articles, and plain common sense, all say there is a right and duty to override a master whose insanity endangers his command."

Cleland gasped. "Mutiny?"

"I don't believe a board of inquiry, or whatever we'll meet when we come home to Earth, will regard it that way. I think we'll be exonerated, because we had no choice, and heroes, because of what we saved—brought back for humankind."

"B-but—"

Brent's manner grew downright practical. "I've given this a lot of thought. It can be done. And without loss of life."

"Just the two of us? Come on, Al!"

"Once it's done, the others will accept. They'll soon see how right we are. But no, not just you and I. Also our Tahirian allies."

Cleland shook his head, as if it had taken a blow. "I think—the whole idea of violence—it'd appall them."

"I tell you, we don't need violence, if we organize the operation and do it right. Nobody has to get hurt."

"Emil wouldn't go along," Cleland protested. "Nor Simon, especially if—if en gets fascinated."

Brent nodded. "That is a problem, yes. Not only recruiting our Tahirians, but keeping it from those two. That body language of theirs makes secrecy unnatural to them." He formed a taut grin. "However, people, including Tahirians, can learn things that never were in their nature. What else is civilization? And this, it'll add to the surprise, come the day. I have some ideas about how. I imagine you'll have some good ones, too, Tim."

"I don't know—really—"

"My God!" Brent exploded. "Nansen sent Jean to her death, and you don't want to see justice done?"

38.

Emil looked shyly around. Humans and Tahirians seldom visited each other's quarters, and en had never been in Cleland's cabin before. The permanent pictures—his mother, the planetologist who had been his mentor, the camp at Valles Marineris on Mars, where he did his first real work—and the screenings—currently a female nude and an abstract pattern—were as foreign to en as the chairs or the bottle of cognac or the laundry tossed into a corner.

"(I daresay you and I feel equally restless, frustrated, unfulfilled,)" Cleland said, approximately, through his parleur.

"(You have your illusions to occupy your mind,)" the guest replied. "(That is not a Tahirian invention. I wish it were, or that your equipment for it were usable by us.)"

"(It soon becomes unsatisfying. Reality is best, and remembered reality second best. That is why I invited you here. I thought we might enjoy talking about what we have experienced, screening images, sharing memories.)"

"(Conversation between us is very limited.)"

Yes, Cleland thought, from a Tahirian viewpoint Cambiante was an impoverished language. Also from a human viewpoint. The richness of an evolutionary history was lacking, instincts, tastes, drives; and of one's civilization, the countless factors both huge and subtle that had formed one's self; and of the other, the individual, appearance, ways, tones, gestures—how Jean cocked her head and glanced aside when something she heard roused a thought, the wide white grin, the archaic dialect she revived now and then, mainly for merriment's sake, but in her it wasn't an affectation—

"(However, this should at least be an interesting diversion,)" Emil continued. "(Yes, let us begin with recalling our mutual expedition to the pulsar.)" The small form folded legs and lay expectant on the carpet.

Cleland sat down there, too. He would have preferred a chair, but being at more or less the same level would make discourse easier and thus perhaps prolong it.

Inwardly he prepared himself for pain. He didn't want to dwell on memories of being with Jean; and today they'd be retrieving views of her, and of her and him together, from the database. He did that only when he was alone and had had several drinks. But if this was how Emil chose to start, he must endure. En couldn't read on his face or hear in his voice what it was costing him.

Simon was working with Sundaram, toward comprehension of the alien sendings and construction of return messages. They would doubtless be occupied for hours. Cleland's part was to keep Emil busy, so that Brent could meet with the three Tahirians who wanted an end of all voyaging.

They had not outfitted their common room like the humans'. For one thing, the wheel's capacity being limited, it had to double as their gymnasium. Exercise machines of exotic design stood about, including a sort of long treadmill on which two persons could gallop for hours. Live turf from home, moist and springy, covered the deck, and shrubs grew in planters. Their odors mingled spicily with those that bodies gave off. Visual screenings decorated the bulkheads and provided entertainment on demand, but what they showed meant essentially nothing to humans, untrained in the artistic conventions and blind to many of the colors.

Standing before Ivan, Leo, and Peter, Brent told them: "(Our purpose is the same, to terminate this bad state of affairs, soon and decisively.)"

"(It is leading to fundamental new knowledge,)" said the biologist Peter.

Ens mates registered . . . disapproval? The three conferred, or argued, in their own language. Manes made wave patterns, fingers undulated sinuous, stances shifted, tones twittered and shrilled, smells gusted rank or sweet or sharp. Brent waited, sweating.

Ivan addressed him. "(The science is a minor consideration. We simply need to clarify our consensus,)" in the usual Tahirian style.

"(You need not depart forever,)" Brent reminded them. "(Your people live ten times nearer the black hole than mine do. Should they wish to, they can readily come back and resume the research.)"

"(That is still a long journey, a long time to be gone from society,)" Leo said.

Probably their dialogue in Cambiante was meant for an explanation to the man, reciting the obvious as so often before to make certain that it really was obvious. "(A stable society must think far ahead,)" Ivan declared. "(Best will it be if we return to Tahir immediately and you then proceed to your home. If our people are to assimilate basic new information, they should first further strengthen their institutions.)"

"I doubt they'll ever elect to go after the new information, if we don't bring them more than we have right now," Brent muttered. "They'll stay put forever. Your breed isn't really venturesome." On the parleur: "(Then we four agree, this expedition shall end in the near future.)"

"(How can we bring that about?)" puzzled Peter.

Leo's mane quivered. Ens middle eyes glowed at Brent. "(You have a plan,)" en said. "(I have come to know you.)"

Brent nodded—from habit, though they had learned what it meant. "(I do. It requires your resolute help. You shall have to obey instructions without questioning or hesitation.)"

Ivan seemed to grow dubious. "(This is like something out of the distant, primitive past)"—when Tahir, like Earth, spawned occasional abnormal cultures, incompatible with the innate nature of the species, and horror followed.

"(We will have need for forcefulness, yes,)" Brent admitted. "(And we must catch the opposition unprepared, as carnivores ambush prey.)"

"(Simon and Emil are of that opposition,)" Ivan said. A rustling sigh went among the three. Regret? Apprehension? When did their race last know serious conflict?

"(Correct,)" Brent said. "(They might well reveal the plan to Nansen. Therefore we will keep them ignorant of it until the thing is done.)"

Dismay? The Tahirians parleyed again, almost frantically.

Yet, shocking though the thought was, it could not have been altogether unawaited. These beings must have disputed among each other, politely but with a bitterness underneath that perhaps grew as great as in any human.

They steadied and turned back to Brent. "(How can we avoid their sensing that something is afoot?)" Ivan asked. "(They will inquire what it is. If we three are less than candid, or refuse outright, they will become suspicious, and report their misgivings to the Nansen group.)"

Brent shivered with a momentary thrill. "(I have considered this,)" he replied. "(Let me convey to them your request that they avoid you for a number of daycycles while you develop a stronger argument than hitherto in favor of aborting the mission.)"

Over the years he had learned enough Tahirian psychology to know that that would not appear unreasonable. The mere presence of an opponent was an emotional and semantic distraction: if nothing else, by involuntary scent emissions, which had the effect of loud heckling or even of interference that distorted the meaning of an utterance. It could rouse anger that might in time go out of control. No wonder the culture set such a high value on consensus.

"(I can arrange new, separate quarters for them, if all five of you tell Nansen you desire it,)" Brent went on. "(Simon is busy with Sundaram, and Cleland, our ally, will keep Emil engaged, so neither ought to feel offended or deprived. Nansen cannot forbid you to think and speak freely under the conditions that best suit you.)" Besides, that idea wouldn't likely occur to the captain.

Ivan made a sound and gesture that apparently corresponded to a human "Hmm." En stood for a while, thoughtful, before saying, with a possible touch of humor, "(Furthermore, settled together apart from the rest of us, they may well develop a mating urge, which would keep them still more preoccupied.)"

Peter expressed an objection in Cambiante. "(No young should be born out here.)"

"(Absolutely not,)" Leo agreed. "(All the more reason to hasten our return.)"

Ivan moved a pace closer to Brent. "(Tell us your proposal,)" en said.

With Sundaram and Simon already there, Dayan and Nansen crowded the workroom. Ventilation overburdened, the air quickly grew thick and hot. Necks craned, eyes squinted at the enigmas on the screen. But the physicist needed to see as well as be told, and she had insisted that the captain deserved to share the revelation. As it burst upon them, discomfort fled from their awareness.

"Yes, you are not merely welcome on this team, Hanny, you are vital," Sundaram assured her. "Communication has been progressing incredibly fast. We have reached a point where the computer programs are no longer adequate to deduce meanings. I believe you alone can modify them, as well as make a unique personal contribution."

Pressed against Nansen, she trembled. "I've gathered you're starting to . . . hear . . . what the beings are?" she asked rather than said.

"Yes. I do apologize for not keeping everyone au courant, but we are overwhelmed with input and— I have sufficient physics background to see that what is being described to us is not molecular, atomic, or—I think—nuclear, not any kind of material configuration, but sets of quantum states. Beyond that, Simon and I are lost."

"Quantum states of what?" wondered Nansen. "The plasma in the accretion disk?"

"That doesn't sound likely," Dayan replied. "Unless it has more structure, more complexity, than I expect is possible. If only Colin were here! Two ways of looking at reality, two different concepts of it—"

His hand touched hers. "Don't underrate yourself, Hanny."

Gazing at the symbols, sight sinking into the depths of the screen, she murmured, "I have speculated a little lately, since you dropped a few hints, Ajit. Quantum states in the vacuum, the sea of virtual particles . . . under the conditions of convoluted, changeable space-time near the black hole. . . . A quantum state can hold and carry information as well as matter can. Maybe better. . . . What is life if not information? . . . But how strange are we to them?"

"Perhaps not entirely strange." Nansen's voice shook. "Perhaps we will discover not just what they are, but what we are. *Dios mío,* what this could mean! Surely now everyone aboard will want to see it through."

The machine shop was spacious but well filled; its equipment, mostly robotic, some nanotechnic, might have to make a variety of things. An area offside was reserved for handwork. Brent sat on a stool at a bench, fitting together items that had been produced for him. Electronic parts from stock lay waiting. A computer displayed the diagram that guided his hands.

Chancing to have an errand there, Yu spied light beyond the big shapes. She wove her way between lathe, drill press, and drop hammer to see what it meant. Brent heard her and looked around.

"Good daywatch," she greeted. "What are you doing?"

He smiled the smile of his that charmed. "Occupying my time. Usefully, I hope."

She glanced at the bench. A cylindrical frame, about three centimeters by fifty, rested half assembled. It was clear that after the circuitry and powerpack were installed, the frame would be completed, an organometallic skin attached, and a stock with a grip fitted. "What is this, if I may ask?"

"Well, I didn't plan to say anything till it was ready, but no reason not to tell you. It's nothing startling. The computer easily designed it to my specs. Check the program if you like. I'm cobbling together a prototype to test how the hardware behaves in practice. It's a short-range radionic override for simple cybernetic systems—for instance, doors, locks, cooling fans, gas filters, conveyors."

"You want to be able to take over control of them? Why?" she asked, nonplussed.

He laughed. "Not I! But the station—" He laid down a spot catalyzer, turned toward her, and spoke earnestly. "The black hole's thrown a lot of surprises at us. They cost us several probes, a boat, and two lives. What's next? What might it derange in the station, given that close orbit? A small but critical item could suddenly go wild or inoperable. Something like a stuck flowgate, maybe. Under the wrong circumstances, that could bring on a disaster."

She frowned in skepticism. "The station's well-built for homeostasis and self-repair, you know."

"Oh, yes. But what harm in one more emergency backup? If this thing seems practical, we can transmit the plans and have the machines there make a few for the maintenance robots to use if it's ever necessary."

"If."

"It gives me something to do," he said.

Sympathy answered: "I understand, Al. Yes, carry on."

"Not makework, either. Not quite. It could prove helpful. Unlikely, but it could. Having gotten the idea, I'd feel remiss if I didn't develop it."

She regarded him. "That is good of you."

He smiled again. "Considering that I'd rather we go straight home? Well, since the decision went against me, I'll do my best for the ship and the mission." In a near whisper: "Jean and Colin's mission."

Her tone softened further. "We have misunderstood you, Al."

He shrugged. "Or maybe I've misunderstood me. Anyhow, call this a gesture, if nothing else." He paused. "Please don't tell anybody. I'd like to spring it as a surprise."

"When we are all together," she proposed. "In the wardroom. Turning a mess meal into a feast of reconciliation."

"Aw, that's too fancy a word."

"I'll help you arrange your surprise," she offered.

The medical center consisted of an office and, behind a door, a sick bay as well equipped as most hospitals had been on Earth. Mokoena found Cleland there. He rose.

"I'm sorry I'm late, Tim," she said. "Hanny caught me, and I couldn't break away. It was too important. Too fascinating, to be honest. You'd told me your problem isn't urgent."

"N-no harm done. What was the, uh, distraction? Something to do with the aliens?"

"What else?" Ardor radiated from her. "Quantum life— She wants me to list whatever analogies I can with organic biology. No, not analogies. Correspondences? Basic principles? Oh, Tim, we're at the dawn of a revolution like nothing since they identified DNA!"

"We can't stay here forever," he groaned.

"No, no. Just long enough to—" She stopped and looked more closely at him. He stood clean and properly clad, in his careless fashion. But the face was haggard, with a tic in the right cheek, and the hands shook slightly. "Never mind," she said. "Here, sit down." He resumed the edge of his chair. She settled behind her desk. "What is your trouble, dear?"

"I'm feeling worse and worse. Jitters, insomnia, nightmares when I do sleep."

"It shows. I've been more and more worried about you. And you're off alone with Emil so much of the time. Nothing wrong with that, but you hardly have a word for your fellow humans."

"I feel trapped."

She nodded. "I know. Listen. Selim Zeyd has accepted the situation. He's adjusting to it, making the best of it. Al Brent seems to be doing likewise. You are whipping yourself to pieces. Tim, you must change your attitude."

"Easier said than done."

"Well," she told him briskly, "you did have the sense to consult me before I hounded you into it. We'll do a physical examination today. If your ills are psychosomatic, as I expect, I'll put you on a euthymic. And we can talk, of course, anytime you wish."

He tried to meet her eyes. "I think, uh, I think it'd help if you explain to the others   I'm not being unfriendly, I simply can't handle sociability."

"Withdrawing into your shell is no medicine."

"Why not? Till I, uh, get my thoughts sorted out. Actually, I'm, uh, fairly at ease with Al."

"M-m, yes, you two always have been close. Complementary personalities? Well, if he's adapting, maybe he can teach you something." Mokoena rose. "Come, let's start that examination."

In this wise Cleland got the excuse he wanted, to be absent from mess or other gatherings whenever he chose, to shun conversation and evade questions, to prefer the company of Brent or a Tahirian, without arousing suspicion.

Nightwatch; stillness in empty passageways. Brent stood with Ivan, Leo, and Peter before the arms locker.

His device unsecured the door. It slid aside, the alarm silenced. Light fell in on racked, darkly gleaming barrels. Boxes and powerpacks filled shelves, like hunched beasts.

His companions were tensed. A smell of fear blew from them. "(These are not for us,)" Ivan spelled.

"(They should not be for anyone,)" Brent said. "(I have explained that we brought weapons in case of unforeseeable dangers. Nuclear missiles for the ship; small arms against ferocious wild animals or something equivalent. We here must make sure they are not used on sentient beings.)"

Peter's mane bristles stiff. "(Could they be?)"

"(Yes.)"

"(How innately violent and irrational is your species?)"

"(Some of us are, some are not. For most, it depends on upbringing and circumstances. Once Tahir, too, knew bloodshed)"—though never on the scale that Earth did, again and again and again. "(Now let us work fast. Quietly but fast.)"

Brent stepped into the locker and passed the weapons out. His fingers lovingly stroked the first several. The Tahirians loaded them onto a cart.

Having closed the door, he would conduct them to the shuttle docked on this side of the gap, and they would conceal their booty inside it. Come mornwatch, the Tahirians would do what they had arranged with Nansen, cross over to the hull. Ostensibly it would be to fetch biotechnic gear of their own stowed there, they having decided to run experiments on terrestrial bacteria for the sake of science and to pass the time. They would indeed bring the stuff back. But first they would have carried the weapons to a hiding place Brent had shown them on a display of the ship's plan.

It was probably needless, but a strategist should provide for all contingencies he could imagine. The hour might come when he was glad the Tahirians, too, had no ready access to an arsenal.

They saw him emerge from the gun-empty locker with a twin-load machine pistol and a box each of disabling and killing cartridges. "(What do you want those for?)" Ivan demanded.

"(To make certain,)" Brent said, tucking them under his cloak.

Certain that he would have the sole firearm.

Daywatch and evenwatch followed.

Cleland led Emil and Simon to the Tahirian section. He had sought them out earlier and asked them to meet him at this time. He would accompany them back to their fellows, he said, and act as human representative while the new arguments for termination were presented to them.

It was pathetically easy to deceive Tahirians. They had such vague notions of deliberate falsehood; and they could not read any nuances of human expressions, intonations, body language, only the most stereotyped attitudes and the bald Cambiante.

Ivan, Leo, and Peter promptly surrounded them. Cleland stood by to help in case they resisted. It trumpeted in him: he was no longer passive, a victim; he was taking action.

Illumination fell gentle over white napery and shining tableware. Yellow, lavender, and purple clustered in a centerpiece of chrysanthemums from one of the gardens. Bottles stood open, cabernet sauvignon breathing, to go with the roast whose fragrance drifted out of the galley—synthetic, made by the nanos, but identical with the original, and no creature had had to die. It was Nansen's turn to select background music, and Vivaldi's "Concerto in G Major" danced for whoever cared to listen.

At this hour the captain felt its lightheartedness was no mockery. Since the tremendous news of quantum-level intelligence broke, moods had soared. Mostly.

His glance went down the table. No garb quite matched the formality of his blue dress uniform, but everybody was in good clothes. On his right, Ruszek chatted with Mokoena and with Zeyd beside her—not exactly cheerfully, yet it was more than the mate had done for a number of daycycles. On his left Yu and Sundaram glowed in their mild way. He wished Dayan, beyond them, were at his side; she had thrown off her own depression and talked enthusiastically whenever she got an opening, about the research and everything else that came to mind.

Maybe she and Ruszek would repair their relationship, maybe not. Nansen didn't know just what had gone amiss, and recoiled from prying. What mattered immediately was that she was herself again, and Ruszek in the course of becoming himself. Though he kept stealing looks at her. . . .

Empty chairs. He had ordered Kilbirnie's put in storage. "Where is Mr. Brent?" he asked "Does anybody know?"

"He told me he had something to show us," Yu said. "He must be preparing it. I am sure he will come in a few minutes."

"And Dr. Cleland called me with word he is indisposed and will stay in his cabin. A shame." *But we* are *better off without his gloomy presence,* confessed that which Nansen kept imprisoned, rebellion against having to be always the captain.

"Too bad." Ruszek reached for a bottle. "Let's pour."

Nansen offered him a smile. "Impatient?"

"Thirsty, damn it." The mate filled his goblet, drank barbarically deep, but then spoke across the table in civilized style. "Any more wonderful discoveries today, Ajit?"

"No, unless they lie somewhere in the flood of input," Sundaram replied. "We have been composing our own next messages. Communication is—a two-way street, do the Americans say? But it isn't easy."

"Describing our kind of life, matter life," Mokoena added. She nodded to her right. "We are going to need you, Selim, very much."

"And I, poor lorn physicist, struggling to see how any of this can possibly be." Dayan was joking; blood beat high under the fair skin.

"You will," Nansen called low.

"Drink to that." Ruszek raised his goblet. Others moved to charge theirs.

Zeyd, who had acute hearing, turned his face toward the entrance. "Footsteps," he said. "Al is here." He laughed. "Excellent. I am starved. Bring in the soup."

The second engineer trod quickstep into sight. He carried an object somewhat like a small, clumsy rifle. And—Nansen stared, narrowed his eyes—was that a pistol at his hip?

From the passageway, Brent pointed the device. It buzzed. The door, which was the single exit from the wardroom, galley, and sanitor complex, drew shut.

Nansen sprang to his feet. "Open!" he shouted. Already he knew it would not, and the manual control was frozen.

Ruszek bellowed. His chair clattered to the deck behind him. He plunged, shoulder foremost. Impact thudded. He lurched back, pale, and sagged to the deck.

"That was unwise," Nansen said flatly. "You only gave yourself a bruise, if not a dislocation. Dr. Mokoena, see to him. Hold back, everyone else. Quiet, quiet. Stand by till we know what is happening."

39.

In helmet, gauntlets, and apron, Brent stepped to the wardroom door. He aimed a large ion torch. Flame hissed out, blue-white. Cleland kept his eyes away from the actinic glare. Brent played the fire along first the right edge, then the left. Sparks showered. Metal glowed, sagged, coursed in thick rivulets, and congealed. "There," he said after a few minutes. "No matter how they may gimmick the lock, they aren't going anywhere without leave."

He narrowed the jet. Lightning-sharp, it cut straight through. He drew a rectangle, about ninety centimeters wide by fifteen high, some 180 centimeters off the deck. When it was almost finished, he reached with an insulated glove, caught a slumping edge, and tugged it toward him. Thus the piece clattered down on his side.

Setting the torch aside and shedding his protection, he moved closer. The rim of the hole was still hot but not molten. "All right," he said. "You can come talk. Just don't touch anything till it cools." He had told the captives over the intercom what he meant to do.

Nansen's face appeared, stiff as a winterscape. Ruszek scowled beside him. The others pressed at their backs. "Very well, Mr. Brent," the captain snapped. "Now will you explain the meaning of this?"

Brent returned his look. "You know it," he said. "I've taken command. We're going home."

"Are you insane?" Nansen's glance went to Cleland, behind and offside from the second engineer. "Are *you*?"

The planetologist clenched his fists. His mouth writhed.

"You are," Brent stated. "You, the great Ricardo Iriarte Nansen Aguilar, monomaniac, megalomaniac, egomaniac." His voice mildened. "Hanny,

Mam, Wenji, Ajit, Selim, Lajos, we're acting on your behalf. Yours and humankind's." The tone went harsh. "He'd have kept us in this orbit of the damned year after year after year, till one way or another the black hole destroyed us. It would have, the ghastly thing. Jean died to warn us. But no, Ricardo Nansen would not heed. We'd have died, and everything we've won, every treasure of knowledge and power we have to give our race and keep it forever starfaring, all would have died with us. For nothing but to serve this man's self-grandeur."

"And so you've sealed us in here," snarled Ruszek. "You brother-buggering swine, let me out and I'll serve you rightly!"

Nansen lifted a hand. "Quiet, Lajos." The use of the first name emphasized the order.

Yu called past him: "You plotted, you two. You deceived us."

"We had to!" Cleland yelled.

"You betrayed your ship and your shipmates."

Cleland shrank back.

Brent turned and clasped his shoulder. "Steady, Tim. They're just swearing. They were bound to."

Sundaram spoke levelly. "You overlook the fact that a majority of us wish to stay."

"By now, all of us in here," Mokoena said.

Nansen made another hushing gesture. "What of the Tahirians?" he asked.

"They have their own arrangements," Brent told him. "We'll take them home as promised. Then we'll set course for Sol."

"Do you two shitbrains suppose you can conn the ship by yourselves?" Ruszek roared.

"*She* can by *her*self," Brent answered. "Personnel only have to instruct her where to go and how fast. I'll study up before leaving orbit, but already I know, if I keep maneuvers simple and straightforward—back to Tahir's sun, back to Sol—*Envoy* will do it."

Ruszek sneered. "How do you expect to make planetfall? On your ass?"

"We probably won't need the boat," said Brent, unperturbed. "Tahirian spacecraft will rendezvous with us in their system. At Sol—we'll see what we'll see. But we'll have had a year en route to learn the boat's operation and practice with virtuals and test flights. It's mainly robotic, too, after all. Piloting's not hard if you don't attempt anything risky." A whipcrack: "Like what you made Jean do, Nansen."

"Please," Cleland begged. "We want to be your friends. We *are* your friends."

Ruszek spat at him through the slot.

"Lajos, no," Nansen said. He pushed slightly at the mate, who took the hint and moved aside. "What are your plans for us?" the captain demanded.

"That depends on you," Brent replied. "Each of you. Listen. You have a washroom, sanitor, and galley in there. I've cut this opening so servitors can bring you food, medicine, whatever you need. Sorry about your having no bunks, but they'll push expansible mattresses through. You can dump your dirty stuff out, and it'll be cleaned and returned. You've got a screen for entertainment, education, the ship's database, the whole culture of Earth—which we're going to enrich and uplift."

Zeyd advanced to the slot. "Each of us, eh?" he murmured.

"Your choice," Brent said. "You can come home prisoners, to trial, or free and heroes."

"Trial?" Yu exclaimed from the rear. "What makes you imagine—"

"Hold, please, Wenji," Zeyd said. "Captain Brent, if I may give you that title, I would like to hear more, privatcly. You know I have always wanted an early return."

Brent laughed aloud. "Nice try, Selim. But I've watched your mind changing as the news came in." Starkly: "The news from hell. I'd sooner trust"—his voice warmed—"you, Lajos. You're honest. And you've hated every minute here. You long for Earth, blue sky, green grass, women, children, freedom. Think about it, Lajos."

"I'm sorry, I'm sorry." Tears blurred Cleland's eyes.

"Then make amends," Nansen said.

"That will do," Brent clipped. "The servitors will bring your mattresses, collect your garbage, and transmit me your requests. Meals will arrive at our usual times. Or just food will, if and when you prefer to do your own cooking. Behave yourselves, and think."

Dayan came forward. "Tim," she said, "we thought better of you."

"It's for you!" Cleland cried.

"That will do," Brent repeated. "Don't listen to her, Tim." To the rest: "I'll look in on you daily or oftener, and I'm willing to talk with you here or on the intercom, if you don't abuse the privilege. At reasonable hours and in reasonable style, okay? Shipmates, think how this one man, Nansen, has forced this to happen. Think hard. Good night."

He turned to go. Cleland hesitated. "Come," Brent ordered. "Pick up the torch and that chunk, and come along."

He strode down the corridor. Cleland slouched after.

Nansen gathered his people around the table.

"First and foremost," he reminded them, "we must keep control of ourselves. Anger and anxiety will wear us down without leaving a mark on these bulkheads."

"What can?" asked Sundaram.

It was as if they were closing in. The bright murals on them had become scornful. Air felt chill.

"Suggestions?" Nansen invited. "Engineer Yu?"

"Nothing comes to mind," she sighed. "I will keep trying."

"Don't bother," Zeyd advised. "This is a mental problem. Can we work on Brent?"

"I don't believe so," Mokoena said. "Of course, I had no inkling he would go this far. But in my opinion, nobody will persuade him, now that he's in motion. He's utterly intense, driven, fearless."

"Unstable?" wondered Nansen.

"Not really, I think." Mokoena's manner became clinical. As the physician, she was also the psychologist. *Though what matters most is how nature endowed her with a feeling for others,* Nansen reflected. "He is insane in a way," she said. "The stress in him has snapped whatever restraints he had. But it's an emotional imbalance. He projects his traits on you, Ricardo. Otherwise he's rational. His plot and the bold, flawless execution show that."

"Those ambitions, those expectations, you call them rational?" Dayan demurred.

"He is taking a wild gamble, yes. He knows it. For him the prize is worth the stake—power, adulation, his name written huge in history."

"How?"

"It's plain to see, by hindsight. Remember how often he spoke of what we can do at Earth, armed with the technology we've acquired from the star cluster and the Tahirians. It does have tremendous military potential, doesn't it? But we'd not likely ever permit such use of it. Meanwhile, in his eyes, we have kept him here, unemployed, empty-handed, caged, while we hazarded his life for the sake of more knowledge; knowledge of nothing but academic interest. Oh, he understands full well that what he'd bring to Earth may prove puny and irrelevant. But down underneath he does not accept that understanding. For a chance at destiny, he'll risk, he'll sacrifice, anything and anyone."

Nansen nodded. "It sounds right. Earth has known many like that."

"Too blood-drenching many," Dayan said between her teeth.

"Well," Zeyd proposed, "if we can't influence him, what about the Tahirians?"

"To begin with," Nansen pointed out, "we have no parleur. And Brent has undoubtedly brought them under his authority. I wish I knew how. Poor Emil, poor Simon."

"Poor all of them," said Sundaram.

"Tim, then," Zeyd pursued. "We heard him, we saw him. He's bewildered, fighting his conscience. We can talk to him."

"Get him close to the slot," Ruszek rumbled. "I'll reach out and grab his throat."

"That would not unseal the door," Nansen said.

"Brent wouldn't surrender anyway," Dayan added. "If we get unruly, he can starve us into submission. My people learned long ago how that works."

"Argh!" Ruszek's fist thundered on the table.

"Lajos, no," Sundaram urged.

Ruszek looked at the linguist as if in appeal.

"That injured shoulder is giving you much pain, isn't it?" Sundaram continued. "If the company will excuse us, I think you and I should retire to the galley for a time."

After that door had closed on the two men, their comrades heard the low sound of a mantra.

"We all need some inner peace," Nansen said. "Tomorrow we'll organize. Establish an exercise program, for one thing. Now we should try to rest."

They had not thought to ask for night clothes, other changes of garb, towels, toothbrushes, or anything else, nor did anyone now feel like putting in the request. Tomorrow would do. There was barely enough unoccupied space on the wardroom deck, if mattresses were laid side to side and end to end. With illumination quenched, though light streamed relentless in through the hole, bodies stretched out and strained to lie quietly.

Nansen heard Dayan breathing on his right. He stole a look. Her eyes were shut, her countenance quiet amidst the loosened red mane, but he wondered if she really slept. Himself, aching with weariness, skull filled with grit, he could not. These, his crew, his trusty folk who trusted him, how might he help them endure? How keep them what they were? Confinement as cramped and hopeless as this bred cancers of the spirit, rage, spite, selfishness, at last hatred. . . . Lovers, what about them? And those who had no lovers. . . . Mokoena, if she kept her jollity, perhaps could provide a little fun. Sundaram's serenity might help more persons than Ruszek. Given the screen, they could hold classes, learn from each other. . . . But always they would be gnawing on the dream of escape. . . . He had to get to sleep. He had to say alert and capable. It was his duty.

The servitors had set up a table in the common room. Until another galley was constructed, food must be prepared in the reserve unit on the gimbals, and would be uninspired. Nanotechnic recycling produced first-class materials but did not cook them. However, the victors were no gourmets; and first-class champagne remained unlimited.

In this triumphal hour, on the evenwatch after the coup, two bottles stood in their cooling jackets before Brent. Beethoven's "Eroica" soared from the player, on whose screen a color abstraction leaped and whirled in time with the music. An ozone tang livened the air, as if a rainstorm were drawing near.

Cleland shambled in. Brent, who sat crisply uniformed, cast him a hard glance. The planetologist was unkempt, his garments rumpled and not very clean. A smell of sour sweat hung around him.

"Attention!" Brent barked.

Cleland halted. "What?"

"You've gone slovenly again. It won't do. We're two men on the most important expedition ever made, with nine desperate prisoners to keep and a starship to bring home. We won't survive without discipline. That begins with self-discipline."

"Sorry," Cleland mumbled.

"And don't take that sullen tone, either. Nansen was right about the necessity of maintaining form, rank, respect. I am your captain, Cleland."

"Yes, . . . sir."

Brent eased. "Okay, enough. A word to the wise. We do need a little shakedown time. You don't have to go back and clean up." He smiled. "We'll pretend you did. Sit down, help me celebrate, drink to our future."

Cleland obeyed, filling a goblet, clinking it against Brent's, and sipping without enthusiasm.

"What have you been doing today, anyhow?" Brent asked.

"Wandering around," said Cleland dully. "Trying to rest. Trying to think. I didn't sleep a blink's worth after we, uh, after we'd secured them."

Brent frowned. "I'm going to have you take medication."

Cleland stared. "Can you prescribe it?"

"I can read a medical database and use a medical computer program, same as any other kind." Brent spoke sternly. "I've begun studying— plans, operating instructions, the captain's and chief engineer's logs. You should have. You will tomorrow. I'll prepare assignments for you. Yes, the ship can run entirely robotic, *if* no surprises hit along the way. We've got to be prepared. You've got to get into shape."

A servitor entered bearing a tray. It deposited the dishes between the place settings and rolled back out. The men helped themselves. Brent took a hefty bite of pork loin. Cleland picked at his vegetables.

"Eat, man," Brent said. "Keep up your strength. You'll be wanting it, and wanting your brains in working order."

Cleland drank before chewing further. Brent savored the symphony. After a while Cleland ventured, "Uh, I did call on the Tahirians. To see how they're doing. They aren't happy."

"I knew they wouldn't be," Brent replied. "This whole business goes against their grain. Can't be helped, and our three allies recognize that. But the sooner we deliver them to their planet, the better. Also our own prisoners."

Cleland's fork dropped to his plate. "Huh?"

"I haven't quite decided yet," Brent said. "But they're a dangerous lot. Smart, tough, and outraged. I wouldn't care to bet they can't find some stunt to pull on us in the course of a year."

Cleland swallowed twice before he could ask, "What . . . do you . . . intend to do?"

Brent shrugged. "What would you? Keep them penned, clear to Tahir and then to Earth? Fourteen months at least. Not humane, is it? And, as I said, certainly dangerous."

"You promised— We can t-try to persuade—"

Brent nodded. "Between here and Tahir, I suppose we may as well, though we'd better plan our arguments first. But suppose they, or any of them, agree, how can we be sure they don't mean to turn on us once they're out, first chance they get?"

"One or two at a time, under guard. Cut a hole for them, reclose it when they've passed through?"

"Risky. And how can we tie ourselves down, guarding them every minute of the daycycle? No, right now my idea is, and I expect I'll stay by it, is to have the Tahirians take them over when we arrive there. The Tahirians will, if we press our case. They can land the crew someplace isolated, an island or wherever, and leave them."

Cleland gasped. "What?"

"They'll be okay. The Tahirians aren't cruel. They'll synthesize Earth-type foods and such. Their scientists will be interested, after all. But I imagine otherwise they'll leave the humans strictly alone—not to have any more of their disturbing influence—till everybody's peacefully dead of old age."

"No—"

"Don't worry about children. We won't reverse any sperm immunities."

"But this is their ship, too!" Cleland shouted.

"No." Brent's voice rang. "It's humanity's, under my command. Taking them back with us would add a completely unnecessary complication. We'll have plenty to do as is."

Cleland shuddered. "Without witnesses against us."

"Witnesses who at best misunderstand the truth. Or at worst will lie, perjure themselves, for revenge. We can't have that. It'd be treason to everything we mean to the future."

"Treason—"

"Eat, I say!" Brent exclaimed heartily. "Drink!"

"And be merry?"

"Why not? Listen, I'm open to argument. I'll welcome any better ideas you may come on. Just not tonight, please. Tonight we celebrate. We've won, we're free, we're going home."

To Cleland's surprise, later to his faint pleasure, the next hour or so passed agreeably. Brent took the initiative. Liveliness sparkled in him. His conversation ranged from witty to serious, discussed diversions and occupations for the voyage, touched on his past rather tenderly, drew hitherto unshared memories from his tablemate, speculated with considerable imagination about what they might find on Earth and what they might accomplish but avoided loftiness, recited stirring passages from literature that most people had forgotten centuries before *Envoy* departed. It was as if he sought to evoke what had been best in his civilization and his species.

Meanwhile, though, he drank, goblet after goblet. That was not his custom. After dessert he ordered brandy and more champagne. Cleland, not wishing to fall asleep where he sat in his own exhaustion, held back, more or less.

With alcoholic suddenness, the mood mutated. Beethoven had left the room. Brent was with Shakespeare.

"—For, as thou urgest justice, be assur'd
Thou shalt have justice, more than thou desir'st."

The words jarred to a stop. He looked before him, past the other man. His grip tightened on his goblet. He threw what it held down his throat. "Justice," he said. "Yes, Nansen, you'll get justice."

Whatever calm he had won drained out of Cleland. "What?"

"Simple justice, marooning Nansen. Give him his little kingdom. Let him rule over his little bootlickers."

"Do you . . . really hate him that much?"

Brent shook his head. "No. Or maybe yes. I tell you, I want to give him justice. A tyrant, a murderer, a menace to the race. But mainly, he can't see. He *won't*. He is a strong man, like me. I respect that part of him. . . . Hate. Justice. Yes," Brent said slowly, "that Dayan bitch, she deserves more than marooning."

Cleland's voice cracked. "Hanny?"

Brent glowered at him. "She humiliated me, the slut, deliberately, and ever since then I've felt her gloat, oh, yes. Oh, yes. Hanny, dear," he purred, "you've got a lesson coming."

"What—what—"

"When we reach Tahir. The Tahirians who take the prisoners off, they'll cooperate. They'll do whatever we ask. They'll even help. For all they know, I'll be bidding her a sweet farewell."

"No, no," Cleland wailed.

Brent grinned. "And cute little Wenji and hot big Mam, how about them, eh? How'd you like a piece of that for yourself? Hey? It'd be a lesson to the men, too. Justice."

Cleland sat dumb.

Brent observed. "Uh, just a thought," he said quickly. "Just a notion. We've a lot to do, a long way to go, before the question rises. . . . Rises," he snickered. He refilled his goblet. "Come on, we'd better drink up and turn in. A hard day's work ahead of us."

"If . . . I can sleep—"

Brent summoned a degree of sobriety. "If you can't, I'll fix that tomorrow. Trust me. Follow me, and I'll lead you further than men ever went before."

Nightwatch yielded to mornwatch. Cleland sat in his darkened cabin. The only light was from the screen in front of him. He had evoked a close-in image of the black hole. Around and down into its absolute night swept the tidal vortex of fire.

"Jean, Jean, forgive me," he whispered. "When you died, on top of everything else, I—I don't know. It seemed like I had to lash out somehow. And Al was my friend, my last human friend—I believed—"

He bit his lip. Blood trickled. "No. Now I'm feeling sorry for myself. Again."

Air stirred, a barren tiny noise among the shadows.

"What to do, Jean? What would you have done?"

Odd, how soon the answer came.

40.

In the dead of nightwatch he arrived at the wardroom. The subdued light of this hour glittered faintly off the scars on the door. The open wound in it yawned black.

Cleland laid down the equipment he bore and leaned close. Sounds of unrestful sleep, warmth, and odors of crowdedness rolled out at him.

"Wake up," he called as low as could be heard. "Wake, but keep quiet. I'm here to help you."

Stirrings and grumblings began to trouble the dark. "Quiet, quiet," Cleland implored. He heard Nansen's soft command, "Silence. Stay where you are." The noise sank to little more than thick breathing.

The captain's face appeared at the slot, etched across shadow. "Quiet," Cleland whispered. Nansen nodded, expressionless.

The vigor that a stimulant forced spoke to him: "I—I'm going to cut you free. Brent's armed. If he hears before you're out, that's it. I didn't use the intercom because he may have a tap connected to an alarm in his cabin."

"Good man!" Nansen gusted in the same undertone. He stuck a hand forth. Cleland took it, a hurried, awkward gesture. "I hoped you'd prove what you are."

"No time. Stand back. Keep them quiet."

Nansen retreated from view. Cleland scrambled into apron, gloves, helmet. He lifted the ion torch and took aim. A blade of flame hissed forth. Sparks flew. Metal glowed white. Cleland cut from the slot on the left side, almost to the deck. He brought the blaze diagonally to the right corner and guided it back downward.

Brent leaped into sight from the curve of the corridor. A pistol belt girdled his pajamas. The weapon was in his grip. "Hold!" he yelled.

Cleland cast a look at the gorgon face and kept his torch going.

The pistol barked. A slug whanged off a bulkhead and ricocheted along the passage. Brent sped nearer, slammed to a halt, slitted his eyes against the actinic glare, and took aim. "You Judas," he rasped, "didn't you think I'd rig a monitor?"

"Break out!" called Nansen from within.

Cleland swept the flame around at the other man. It didn't reach, but, head-on, it dazzled. Brent fired, once, twice, thrice. Cleland staggered. He dropped the torch. It died. He toppled. Blood pumped from him.

Mass crashed against the door. Parted on three sides, weakened across the middle, struck with full force and high turning moment, metal buckled. A jagged tongue of it lapped outward. Nansen and Ruszek burst through the hole, Zeyd at their heels.

For an instant, Brent stood fast. He snapped two more shots. Still half blind, he missed. Ruszek bellowed and plunged at him. Zeyd followed. Brent whipped about and ran. Moving downspin, weight lessened, he needed about ten seconds to disappear where to the eye the deck met the overhead.

"Stop!" Nansen shouted. "Stop, Lajos, Selim!" Zeyd heeded. Ruszek pounded on. Nansen sprinted, overtook him, grabbed him by his sleep shirt, and pulled. "You'll get killed. No sense in that."

The mate obeyed. "We've got to smash him," he panted. "He has that gun."

"If necessary, one or two of us can get killed later," Nansen said. "But we don't want it to be necessary."

They returned. Mokoena squatted at Cleland's sprawled form. She had removed helmet and apron and rucked up his shirt. The blood had spread impossibly far, impossibly bright, before outflow ended. Heedless of it, the others stood close and pale. "How is he?" Nansen asked.

"Gone," Mokoena said.

"Revival?"

She pointed to a gap in the right temple and the gray material spattered opposite. "No." She closed the eyes in the wet red mask. "Goodbye, Tim." She rose.

Nansen signed the cross. Ancient words trembled on his lips. "He was one of us," the captain finished.

Then, tone gone steely: "Brent's loose, armed and frenzied. God knows what he'll attempt. He may even try to destroy the ship."

"*Götterdämmerung,*" Dayan whispered.

"We should have a short grace period while he finds a hiding place, recovers full vision, and thinks what to do. After that, we have to capture or kill him. Is everybody in active condition? We can do nothing for Tim till later. But take a moment to wash off his blood, if only because it'd leave tracks, and change clothes if you need to. Then we'll arm ourselves."

*   *   *

Hollowness met them at the gun locker.

"I am a fool," Nansen groaned. "I should have known he'd clean this out before he acted."

"You couldn't be sure," Dayan said. "We had to verify it."

"Where the fuck did he take the things?" Ruszek snarled.

Nansen grew thoughtful. "I would have hidden them well away. That Tahirian trip over to the hull. . . . Yes-s-s. . . ."

"Do the Tahirians hold the arsenal?" Zeyd asked sharply.

"I doubt that. Not designed for them, not in their psyche, and not something Brent would want them to have on hand. No, almost certainly, they stowed them in the hull for him. We'll stop at the machine shop and collect whatever can double as a weapon."

"Pardon me," said Sundaram, "but could not Brent meanwhile cross over and take possession of the munitions?"

"*¡Jesús Cristo, sí!*" Nansen exclaimed. "I *am* a fool."

"You're a strategist, darling, and never knew it," Yu told Sundaram. Laughter crackled half hysterical from a few throats.

Nansen regained decisiveness. "The command center, it is critical. Hanny, Lajos, come with me there. The rest of you to the machine shop. If he gets into it, he can work every kind of mischief. Mam, Selim, proceed from there to the command center with stuff we can use for fighting; knives, crowbars, pipe wrenches, anything. Wenji, Ajit, stay behind, armed likewise. Keep the door closed and barricaded. If he tries to break in, call on the intercom."

Sundaram hesitated. "What of the exocommunications room?" he asked.

"He could wreck it out of pure malice. That would be a pity, but we can rebuild it once we're safe. Move!"

Viewscreens showed stars, the minute, hazy blaze of the accretion disk, the frosty galactic river. Instruments and controls filled most other bulkhead space, marshaled like sentinels against the dark. Nansen went immediately to a certain panel.

"The shuttles are still in place, one on either side," he read from the meters. "Excellent." His fingers worked. "Now neither of them will go anywhere without new orders from here. We have him in this wheel."

He took a seat at the observation board. Ruszek joined him on the right, Dayan on the left. They divided the task and began operating interior monitors. Scene after scene flashed before them, passages, rooms, parks and gardens whose flowering was suddenly pathetic.

"Look here!" Dayan cried.

The men leaned over toward her screen. It was as if they saw the Tahirian gymnasium from above. Five figures clustered amidst the exercise equipment. She centered them in the field and magnified.

Ivan and Leo crouched on the turf in the attitude of slumber. Peter lay awake, a miniature sphinx. Emil and Simon were asleep too. Tethers connected a leg of each captive to an immovably heavy machine. Within reach stood an object that must be an improvised sanitary box. Sonics amplified the sound of breath. It was different from human, sucked in below the jaws by the heart-lung pump, noiselessly and odorlessly expelled at the rear. Manes stirred, antennae twitched. Did all sentient beings throughout the universe need recurrent oblivion, broken by dreams?

"So that's how they treat their prisoners," Ruszek muttered.

"Gently, kindly," Dayan said.

"I don't know. Tying them like that—"

"They aren't used to being jailers. This was the best they could think of."

"Search on," Nansen said.

And at last: "Not a trace."

"He's probably in a cabin," Dayan suggested. Nobody's living quarters had a scanner.

"Or in a locker," Ruszek grunted. There had been no obvious reason to make those observable from outside.

"If he stays where he is, we'll find him by ransacking," Nansen said. "But I'm afraid he won't."

Mokoena and Zeyd came in, burdened with iron objects, which they dumped clattering on the deck. The trio joined them. Mokoena picked up a long pry bar with a sharp edge on the end and hefted it, seeking for the balance point. "Not an assegai," she murmured, "but it will do."

Dayan smiled bleakly. " 'Tis enough, 'twill serve,' " she said, and bent down to rummage.

"Ha!" Ruszek had carried the ion torch here but set it aside. He grabbed a maul, short-handled, heavy-headed, and swung it. They saw him wince and heard him snatch for air. He straightened and stood firm. Nobody stopped to think how his shoulder, now bashed against that door a second time, must pain him.

Zeyd stuck a pair of screwdrivers under his belt and clutched a wrench. Nansen experimented with a meter-long rod, repair stock; it was blunt, but wielded by a saber man, it could strike or thrust as lethally as a sword. "Are you prepared to hunt Brent down?" he asked rhetorically. "Very well. Mam, I hate to expose a woman to danger—"

She grinned and jerked her weapon. "Up yours."

For a flick of time he smiled back. "You and Selim search the lower deck. Don't take chances. If you spy him, don't attempt a capture; trail at a safe distance, curvature between you and him. Or if you find him denned, keep watch. Lajos and I will join you as fast as we're able. Similarly for the upper deck, which we will take."

"What about me?" Dayan demanded. A knife gleamed in her hand.

"You have to hold this point and make it our information center. You are best qualified. Set the intercom system to deliver a message at every speaker, every . . . five minutes. A short one, asking him to surrender, promising to spare his life if he does. He can go unarmed—nude, to make certain—to the common room and wait for us."

"Do you really believe that will change his mind for him?" Ruszek scoffed.

"No, but we are obliged to try."

"Well, it may make him still madder," Ruszek said indifferently.

Nansen continued instructing Dayan: "Sweep the ship continuously with the monitors. We four will check with you whenever we're at an intercom, and you will keep us informed."

"I'm a soldier's daughter," she protested. "Let me hunt."

"Soldiers stay where they are most needed. Brent will know how dependent we are on this post. He may attack, perhaps shooting through the door. If that happens, take cover. If he gets in somehow, use the torch on him. But I hope we'll already have come to your call."

The mutinous look fell from her. "God be with you," she said, not altogether steadily.

Against emergencies, the captain had a master key that could override any lock program aboard. He slipped aside as a door retracted. Cautiously, he peered around the edge. Sundaram's cabin lay vacant. Dayan's latest futile plea lost itself in silence.

"This is no good," Ruszek complained. "He wouldn't trap himself in any such box. He's on the lower deck, in that maze of storerooms and park and everything, dodging around like a rat. Hanny will only spot him by accident. We should be there, too."

"I'm not so sure," Nansen answered. "What could he hope to accomplish on that level? Not that he's likely to be very rational anymore."

"If he ever was, the murdering bastard."

"Intercom check." Nansen entered the cabin and touched the plate. "Hanny?"

"I have him!" Dayan's voice shrilled. "Number Two spacegear locker. He's just coming out of it, suited."

"What? ¿Es el totalmente loco?"

"Come on!" roared Ruszek, and dashed off.

"Send Mam and Selim there when next they call in. We two are on our way."

The locker stood open. Again Nansen activated an intercom.

"He went into Spoke Two," Dayan told him. "Bound for that exit, I'd guess."

"What the devil? No shuttle at it. He'd remember that, whether or not he's realized that we'll have stalled them both. Is he wearing a jetpack?"

"No."

"It takes time to fasten one on," Ruszek said. "He hasn't got time. Nor have we. Help me on with a suit. I'll go after him."

"Are you crazy, too?" Nansen snapped.

"Listen," the mate retorted, "a good spaceman can make the jump across. He's good. I'm better. Even if you free the shuttle, it'll take too long. I think he's counting on that. We did fight the robots together. I know him a little." He stepped into the locker and unracked an outfit.

"The weapons. He must be making for them. I will go."

Ruszek came out dragging the suit. He put his free hand behind his back. "No time to fight about that. Match me, odd or even."

Nansen choked down a command and imitated the gesture. "Now," he said. Both hands leaped around. Three fingers were outspread on his, two on the other man's.

Ruszek laughed. "Ha, first fun I've had in daycycles."

Nansen scowled but went after the additional hardware. Ruszek shed his pajamas and slipped on a skinsuit. He spread the opened outfit and put feet in the legs, right after left. He drew the fabric up and put his arms in. It slithered, molecules aligning as embedded sensors directed. When he brought the front edges together, they fused. He stood as if in a second skin, white and tough, moisture-absorbent, powered for sensitivity and flexibility.

Nansen inserted earplugs and lowered a fishbowl helmet. Its collar made the same kind of seamless juncture. Harness secured a biostat case on Ruszek's back—air tank, composition regulator, temperature control, radio. Kneeling, Nansen guided feet into gripboots. Circuitry completed itself everywhere, unseen, like nerves healing; suit and man became an integrated system.

It was not meant for hard or prolonged service. It would keep the wearer alive and functional for several hours under ordinary conditions of vacuum and radiation, no more. But in its simplicity it could be donned by a man alone—faster if he had help.

Nansen rose. "Mam and Selim should join me soon," he said. The helmet included an audio amplifier. "He and I will come after you. Don't risk yourself needlessly. Keep track of Brent if you can. The three of us will take him."

Ruszek shook his head. Light gleamed on the bald pate and on drops of sweat caught in the big mustache. "No good. The worst chance is that he'll reach the arsenal, wherever it's hidden, before we catch him. He could mow us down, or cripple the engines, the whole ship. Hanny— He could make Hanny die in the cold and dark."

He set off down the passage, Nansen alongside. The maul swung to and fro in his grasp.

At the exit room Nansen offered his hand. When Ruszek took it the fabric felt cool and rubbery, like a snake. Ruszek nodded, swung around, and swarmed up the ladder into the spoke, out of sight.

*   *   *

Ordinarily he enjoyed the 180-meter climb, dizzying perspectives, aliveness in muscles, a sense of heightened strength as weight lessened. But it was too slow. He left the rungs at the bottom landing and hastened over the catwalk to the platform opposite. The railcar waited. He boarded and set it whizzing through the tube.

Deceleration at the end tugged harder than the pseudogravity there. He jumped out and approached the airlock. A red light warned that no shuttle was docked here. "I know, you idiot," he said. His fingers stabbed at the manual board. The inner valve drew aside. He entered the chamber. The valve closed.

"Do you wish to cycle through?" he heard in his earplugs.

"Yes, and fast!" he told the machine, pointlessly except for the fury fuming in him.

Air pumps brawled diminuendo. He felt their throb in his feet and shins until they had evacuated the chamber. The two or three minutes it took stretched themselves. The outer valve opened and he saw, across ten meters, the cliff that was the flat end of the cylindrical hull.

This near the hub, it was only dimly starlit. Wan flickers pulsed across it as the wheel rotated. He had no other immediate sensation of spin. However, when he reached the exit, he discerned vague shapes: ports, bays, the second shuttle. Seemingly it was they that whirled past. He did not look beyond them to the stars. That way lay vertigo.

Instead he poised on the rim, gauged with a precision that was mostly subconscious, and sprang. The impetus tore his soles loose from the weak centrifugal acceleration and he soared. Here he could not escape seeing the heavens stream around him. He set his teeth and ignored them.

Tangential velocity bore him outward. As strongly as he had jumped, it should not carry him past the edge in the less than two seconds of his crossing—not quite. But it would land him at a speed that could break bones and whatever hold his boots laid on the hull. He twisted about, readying.

Impact slammed. His upper body, relaxed in cat fashion, swung freely. Tissue absorbed shock. As he skidded and lost contact, he brought a foot down. It also flew off, but it had dissipated energy. His other foot touched and dragged. On the fourth stamp, he rocked to a halt. All the while he had gripped his hammer.

For a moment he hung slack, weightless. Pain seared through his injured shoulder. At the end of the sleeve that housed its magnetic bearings, the wheel turned, enormous, a mill athwart stars that now gleamed as if they were eternally fixed upon the sky.

"Hoo-oo," Ruszek muttered. "Did you get flung clear, Al, boy? That would simplify things."

He was nearly at the verge of the cylinder. Recovered, one sole always touching metal but the stride long and quick, he stepped across the right angle onto the vast curve.

His sight swept down the length of it—turrets, bays, webs, masts, murky against the constellations. He swore and started around the circumference. Of course he wouldn't see Brent from here. If Brent made the passage, he'd seek the midships entry lock, which happened to be some eighty degrees off.

Ruszek rounded the horizon.

He jarred to a stop, swayed forward, peered. A radio detector cobwebbed the querning after wheel, but a lesser motion caught his eyes. Distance-dwindled, a shape went slowly, black, across the Milky Way.

Brent, almost at the entry lock. Lacking a safety line, he walked very carefully. Ruszek had more skill. He half ran. Having turned off his transmitter before he left, he could call in his mother tongue, into the infinite silence, "All right, I'm coming to kill you." And, after a moment, a whisper: "For Hanny."

Vision was a blur of dusk and shadow. He could hope to draw close unnoticed. But he had said Brent was a good spaceman, too. Wary, constantly glancing about, the fugitive saw the pursuer. Ruszek saw the pistol rise.

He swung the hammer thrice and hurled it.

The bullets ripped into him, through him. Air gushed from holes too big for self-seal, a ghost-white fog spattered with black. In starlight humans cannot see red.

The maul hit Brent in the belly. It knocked him off the hull. He drifted away. His limbs flailed. He screamed. Nobody answered. He reached the after wheel. A spoke smote. The fragments of him exploded into the emptiness around.

Ruszek's boots clung. His body straightened and waited for his shipmates. They found a grin still on his face.

Nansen and Zeyd approached the Tahirians. Dayan stood in the background, a sidearm at her hip, but nobody supposed it would be wanted.

Ivan advanced, parleur in hand, to meet the humans.

"(You will release these two you hold,)" the captain ordered.

"(Is the conflict over?)" Ivan asked.

"(Yes. Brent is dead. So are Ruszek and your friend Cleland.)"

Anticipating a visit, the captors had given parleurs to their captives. Simon signaled from ens tether, "(We believed all of you were our friends.)"

"(We three did not do this willingly,)" Ivan said. "(There seemed to be no alternative.)"

"(There is,)" Nansen replied. "(You must accept it.)"

"(We shall.)"

"(You will give no further trouble?)"

Ivan met the human gaze. The scent from en was like autumn winds over rain-wet dead leaves. "(None. The cost of resistance is too high. We will do as we are told.)"

"Can we trust them?" Zeyd wondered.

Leo heard. Either en had that much English, or en guessed the meaning. Screen and attitude spelled: "(You can trust us. We do not fear for ourselves. We never did. Achieve your desire, mad ones, terrible ones, then bring us home and go away and leave Tahir in peace. Is that a correct price for our help?)"

"(I mourn for what might have been,)" Emil said.

Nansen blinked and squinted. Crow's-feet spread from the corners of his eyes. Fingers on touchboard wavered slightly. "(It may be yet. In spite of everything, someday it may be.)"

"**Unto Almighty** *God we commend the souls of our brothers departed.* . . ."

Nansen read the service through to the end. His crew responded according to their faiths, or kept silence.

At a signal, robots obeyed their programming. From the common room, the humans saw, on the screen, a probe leave the ship. Starlight touched two sheeted forms lashed to its sides.

It took on velocity and swiftly vanished, bound for the black hole. There was no other grave.

Nansen led the way to the wardroom, through the gap where the door had been. The room itself was cleaned and restored, bright and comforting. The servitors had prepared a buffet. A feast, however modest, is also part of a funeral.

He found himself raising a goblet of white wine to ring on Dayan's. His reserve cracked. *"Adiós, hermanos,"* broke from his throat.

She gave him the strength he groped for: "Yes. And tomorrow we'll get on with our work."

41.

Daycycle by daycycle, leap by leap, language grew into being.

Early on, the visual code became four-dimensional, figures depicted from various angles in space and shown changing with time. These representations would quickly have gone from solid geometry through non-Euclidean geometry to bewilderment, had not a computer simultaneously developed the appropriate equations. "Phase spaces, Riemannian spaces— I think they perceive them, live in them, with direct experience," Dayan said. "When we send a set of tensors, does that come across to them as a . . . an object?"

"Yes, the conditions we live under must be as strange to them as theirs are to us," Sundaram mused. "Stranger still, then, is that our transmissions do not leave them utterly baffled."

Hypertext evolved, symbols in multiply connected arrays. Ever oftener, context revealed meanings, which led to the adoption of new symbols and more sophisticated grammar. For this, Simon was invaluable. Adapted to chaotically changeable environments, sensorium extending to single photons and electron transitions, ens instincts bred intuitions of what a message might refer to. On the other hand, it was usually humans who worked out the form of a reply or of a question; they were better at abstract thought, and their species had developed mathematics further.

When Simon proposed expanding the code, Yu designed and built circuits to employ sonics. Though the beings at the other end of the communications scarcely employed sound themselves, they promptly got the idea and returned equivalent signals. It never led to direct speech, but it did give expression to a wider range of concepts. "Like music, rhythm, tone—saying things that words can't," Mokoena suggested. "M-m, no, I don't suppose that's a real comparison." However, she and Zeyd found it useful in describing their own kind of life, its chemistry, variousness, histories, folkways, perhaps a hint at its feelings and dreams.

Dazzlingly fast, the language expanded. The aliens seemed to make no mistakes, go up no blind alleys. When those aboard the ship did, the exchange quickly revealed where they were wrong. The code that resulted was a sort of human-Tahirian hybrid, heavily mathematical and graphical, individuality and emotion only implied—both parties burningly wanted to know! It did not translate well into English, still less into Tahirian. Yet there was discourse.

Einstein said once that the most incomprehensible thing about the universe is that it is comprehensible.

To Nansen came Emil and asked, "(Would it be possible to take the remaining boat on excursions? We could make many worthwhile observations, for example, of the black hole and its beams from a more canted orbit.)"

"(No.)" A parleur could not utter the man's sympathy for this spacefarer, idled and isolated. "(We cannot risk our only landable craft. Have you three nothing at all to do?)"

"(Leo and Peter will mate—without begetting, of course. The joining of life is a high art.)"

Is it enough, by itself, to fill months or years for them? Nansen thought. *Not among humans. Even Jean and I—* He dodged away from the memories suddenly crowding in on him, as they so often did. "(We have a few probes left. Let us by all means lay out a research program for them.)"

"(I anticipated you would hold the boat in reserve)," Emil said. "(It has occurred to me that we can get more information from the probes—they will survive more missions before the unforeseeable overtakes them—if they are directed by us, not entirely by robots, from closer than the ship. Could we not put together a protective capsule with such controls and a motor? Low acceleration would suffice, and the excursions need not be hazardously lengthy.)"

"*¡Por Dios!*" Nansen cried. "(That is an interesting concept indeed.)" His mind leapfrogged. Shift cargo around to clear a large volume in the hull. Bring what tools and other equipment were necessary across to that workspace; spare materials were already abundantly stored over there. Keep busy, keep engaged— "(Let us talk further.)" *Thank you for this, you who have not surrendered to apathy or to sorrow.*

Hard labor would be a blessing. He had been following the revelations from Sundaram's group, fascinated; but he was a layman, with nothing to contribute. Robots kept house. *Envoy* had no present need for a commander. He seldom even presided over dinner. His fellows generally snatched what food and sleep they must, at whatever hours were least inconvenient, and went back to their science. After that which they had undergone together, tacit consent had put them on first-name terms with him. He had recognized other overtures, tentative moves to lessen his aloneness, and had not responded. He appreciated their kindness, but appreciated more that it did not press itself upon him. The notion stayed with him that it was unwise, undutiful, for the captain to bare any wounds.

Once only, Mokoena got him aside and suggested a euthymic. He declined. "Well, grief must run its full course one way or another," she said. "If this is your way, you'll either break or you'll recover faster than otherwise, and I don't think you'll break. If ever you want to, see me again." He thanked her and left.

He had exercised. He had read, watched a number of dramas, listened to much music, attempted to brush up his rudimentary Chinese and learn Hebrew. His sketches and his clay sculptures went better, but he was no genius in this field, either.

He slept poorly. Often when awake he abruptly realized that he had been staring for half an hour into vacancy. Or he paced the corridors, up and down, back and forth, like a caged animal.

He could order an ending, a return. At this stage, it would feel like a betrayal of Jean. Emil's wish, born out of Emil's need, beckoned him onward.

Discovery unfolding—

Think of the black hole, monstrous mass monstrously awhirl, a throat down into an annulment that is also a transfiguration to the unmeasurable and unimaginable. Think of the matter vortex, captured, indrawn, torn asunder, gyrating in a magnetic field so intense as to be well-nigh material itself, shaken by resonance, racked by chaos, flung back out in great bursts of flame and seething back down again, naked nuclei colliding and fusing and erupting in wild new particles, photons turned into pairs and pairs annihilating to photons, a lightning storm of energies, and pervasive beneath it the subtle, all-powerful tides of the vacuum, of ultimate reality. Think of this as it comes to the event horizon, where space and time themselves are an onrushing, intertwining undertow around that strangest of shores.

What can happen there is impossible in mere abysses of light-years or at stars that merely burn.

It does not occur at every black hole, just as organic life does not occur on every planet. Conditions must be right. Maybe these are even more rare. Here, though, about this body, it lived.

Life is not a thing or a substance. It is information, a flux of patterns; it is the business of being alive. Organic biota are organic only because no other element has the versatility of carbon, to make the molecules that encode the data and carry out the processes. In a newly dead man the molecules are mostly the same as before, but that particular flow of events has ceased. There is no reason in principle why corresponding events cannot occur in a different matrix. In fact, many computer programs and robots are so complex and changeable that it is a largely semantic question whether or not to call them alive.

If the mightiest artificial intelligences, far surpassing our capabilities of logic, lack true consciousness, this is because it is not a separate thing, either. It is something that an entire organism *does*. We would have to supply the deep old animal parts of the brain, a nervous system integral with the whole, muscles, viscera, glands, drives, instincts: and thus the end product would be a creature much like ourselves. In the nature of the case, we cannot design a body for a superior mind. Evolution might conceivably carry on where we left off; but then, it might conceivably work further on us.

It might work on nonchemical life. It did.

Already people aboard *Envoy* had speculated. Now surmises took definite shape.

What they learned was partial, perhaps roughly equivalent to nineteenth-century knowledge of biochemistry, genetics, and phylogeny. It could no more be put in words than can the essence of theoretical physics. The researchers must needs try, for each other's benefit if nobody else's, but they realized how crude their approximations were.

In the intricate and mutable space-time geometry at the black hole, infalling matter and energy interacted with the virtualities of the vacuum in ways unknown to the flatter cosmos beyond it. Quasi-stable quantum states appeared, linked according to Schrödinger's wave functions and their own entanglement, more and more of them, intricacy compounding until it amounted to a set of codes. The uncertainty principle wrought mutations; variants perished or flourished; forms competed, cooperated, merged, divided, interacted; the patterns multiplied and diversified; at last, along one fork on a branch of the life tree, thought budded.

That life was not organic, animal and vegetable and lesser kingdoms, growing, breathing, drinking, eating, breeding, hunting, hiding; it kindled no fires and wielded no tools; from the beginning, it was a kind of oneness. An original unity differentiated itself into countless avatars, like waves on a sea. They arose and lived individually, coalesced when they chose by twos or threes or multitudes, re-emerged as other than they had been, gave themselves and their experiences back to the underlying whole. Evolution, history, lives eerily resembled memes in organic minds.

Yet quantum life was not a series of shifting abstractions. Like the organic, it was in and of its environment. It acted to alter its quantum states and those around it: action that manifested itself as electronic, photonic, and nuclear events. Its domain was no more shadowy to it than ours is to us. It strove, it failed, it achieved. They were never sure aboard *Envoy* whether they could suppose it loved, hated, yearned, mourned, rejoiced. The gap between was too wide for any language to bridge. Nevertheless they were convinced that it knew something they might as well call emotion, and that that included wondering.

Certain it was that the former, abortive efforts of the Tahirians to make contact had awakened some kind of passion, and the beings were doing whatever they could to establish communication with these better-qualified newcomers. That was astoundingly much.

Hitherto Nansen had not used the virtual-reality terminal in his cabin as anything but a tool, an aid to understanding. He would evoke something—a change in procedures, a modification of a piece of equipment, an unfamiliar astronomical configuration—and study it, try it out, in different aspects under various conditions, until he learned what he wanted to learn. Like most people, he had played with pseudoexperiences, fantasies, but that was long ago, in adolescence on Earth, and seldom. He did not fear addiction, he simply preferred truth.

Now he sought back. His project with Emil offered him hard labor and the deep sleep that follows it, but first the work required careful planning, and too often he drifted from a conference or a computer to raw memory. Since he refused drugs—before prescribing, Mokoena would want to explore his inmost needs—he thought a little spell in childland might help.

It did not take him long to set up the program, complex though it was. Elements of landscape, artifacts, personal features and traits, historical or fictional situations, everything anyone had cared to have entered, were in the ship's database. The computer would combine them according to basic instructions, partly randomly, partly fractally, governed by principles of logic and aesthetics unless he specified otherwise, sketching a world. Likewise would neurostimulation suggest sensory input. Imagination would do the rest, the vividness of dream within the coherence of structure, the unexpectedness of life within the boundaries of desire.

Nansen shaped a small, crooked smile. "Surprise me," he said, a phrase he had acquired from Dayan. But of course any surprises would spring from himself.

Loosely clad, he attached the bracelets and anklets, donned the cap, snugged every contact against his skin, and stretched out on his bed. For a moment he hung back, half reluctant. Then he grimaced, pressed the switch, and lowered head to pillow.

At first he only saw his illusion. Hearing soon commenced. Tactile sensation followed, temperature, equilibrium. As brain and nerves adjusted and endocrines responded, the primitive centers—gustatory, splanchnic, olfactory—grew active, too. Meanwhile the knowledge that this was entirely within him receded, to wait until he called for it, like the value of e or the date of Paraguay's independence.

He rode from the *estancia*. Clouds loomed immense on his left, blue-shadowed white walls and cupolas. Elsewhere sunlight spilled unhindered, glowing off countless wings, down over an endlessness of grass. The wind sent long waves across the plain and around the red anthills, sighed through scattered groves, streamed over his face with odors of sun-warmed earth and horseflesh. Hoofs thudded, muscles rippled beneath his thighs. He rode Trueno, the stallion who was his in his boyhood, whose death first taught him sorrow. The black mane fluttered, the black coat sheened, wholly alive, one with him. Gaucho-clad, pistol at right hip, cavalry saber at left, Ricardo bore west for the mountains.

House and herds slipped under the horizon. At an easy, space-devouring trot, he entered treeless solitude. Sky, sun, wind, grass, were all the world, a vast and healing presence. Day declined infinitely slowly. Yet when at last light ran level, washing the land with gold, it seemed he had barely left the house of his fathers.

Birdflight led him to a water hole. He drew rein, dismounted, cared for the horse, switched on his glowcoil, toasted some meat and made tea, readied for night, and in his bedroll looked at the stars of home.

Awake at dawn, mounted shortly after sunrise, he went on over country that rose faster than any map ever showed—no Gran Chaco to cross, no gradual upsurge of foothills, but sudden steeps, brush low and harsh among boulders, canyons through which rivers rang down from the snows that reared afar against heaven. Two condors wheeled on high. The air grew ever more cold. Trueno climbed, hour by hour, tireless, being now immortal.

Toward evening the castle hove in view, silhouetted gaunt on a ridge but with banners bright over the turrets, afloat in the whittering wind. Ricardo's heart sprang. Yonder waited the mage who would tell him the goal of his adventure and the comrade who would fare at his side. He knew no more than that. He shouted and struck heels to flanks. The stallion broke into a thunderous trot.

They saw him. Trumpets sounded. A drawbridge lowered, its chains agleam with sunset. One rode across and galloped recklessly to meet him, cloak and plume flying scarlet behind, one slender and lithe, his friend of the road ahead. They lifted their swords in salute. Horses met, reared, halted. *"¡Hola, camarada caro!"* Ricardo greeted.

And "Welcome, skipper, a thousand welcomes," said the husky voice; and below the helmet was the face of Jean Kilbirnie.

Nansen roused.

He lay for a while in darkness, weeping, before he could sit up and remove the apparatus. Afterward he swallowed a stiff whiskey, which was not his wont, and hurried to the gym. Nobody else was on hand to watch him work himself to exhaustion.

He would stay with reality.

42.

"Incredible, inexplicable," Sundaram said. "Communication, a common language, established this swiftly and surely—when we and the Holont have nothing in common."

He had invented that name for the quantum intelligence. Zeyd, who felt uncomfortable with the idea of mutable avatars—yes, God could do all things, but this raised difficult questions about the soul—suggested, "The great flowerings of civilization on Earth came about when different cultures met, didn't they? Maybe it is like that with us and the holonts."

"Do not forget Simon," Yu said.

Mokoena's eyes shone. "A galactic flowering—"

"Thousands of years hence, millions, if ever," Dayan said. "What we need to know here is *how* the process goes so fast. Let's concentrate again on asking about physics."

The answer emerged in the course of daycycles, not through dialogue but through demonstration. When Dayan fully grasped its nature and explained to her teammates, the fine hairs stood up on her arms.

"Telepathy would have been spooky enough. This goes far beyond. The Holont knew we were coming and what we would try. It told itself—they told themselves—by a message that went back through time."

"No, that cannot be!" Yu disputed, shocked. "It would violate every principle of logic and, yes, science. The conservation laws—"

Dayan shook her head. "When I began to suspect, I consulted our database." As if defensively, her tone went into lecture mode. "The history's lain forgotten because the whole thing was, in fact, deemed impossible. As prestigious a thinker as Hawking insisted nature must rule time travel out somehow, or the paradoxes would run wild. However, there are actually no paradoxes, provided self-consistency obtains. You cannot go back into the past and change what has happened, no matter what you do. But your actions can be a part of what did happen.

"Several of Hawking's contemporaries, Kerr, Thorne, Tipler, described several kinds of time machine, each perfectly in accord with general relativity. But they all required structures that looked physically impossible— for instance, a torus with the mass of a giant star, rotating near the speed of light, with more electric charge than the interstellar medium would allow and a magnetic field stronger than anything in nature could generate. Or a cylinder of material denser than any nuclear particle, also spinning close to light speed and infinitely long. Or— Well, the theoretical possibility seemed to be a cosmic joke on us, a bauble forever dangling just out of reach."

"And now . . . conditions at the black hole," Sundaram breathed.

Dayan nodded. "Yes. Not that even that allows any of what I mentioned. As nearly as I can tell, the holonts can't personally travel backward through time." Low, not quite evenly: "As nearly as I can tell."

She drew breath. "What they can do is something suggested back in Hawking's era by Forward. They can operate on that sea of particles and energy they exist in. They can form gigantic nuclei, atomic weights vastly greater than anything we've ever achieved, and keep them stable. Electromagnetic forces deform such a nucleus and set it spinning— speed, density, field strengths as required. I'm not sure yet whether what they get corresponds to the Kerr smoke ring or a short, wasp-waisted Tipler cylinder, or maybe something else. Anyhow, it causes a warp in space-time, a tiny 'hole' through which particles of sufficiently small wavelength can pass. That means highly energetic gamma-ray photons. Well, photons can be modulated, and modulation can convey information, and if you can send a message, in principle you can do anything.

"The holonts know how to communicate with us because the holonts in the future have already done it. They sent the knowledge back."

Yu looked at a bulkhead as if to see through it, out to star-strewn immensity. "That brings home to us how little we know, how little we are, does it not?" she whispered.

Dayan's voice clanged. "I would say we need to keep a sense of proportion and not get above ourselves, but we'd do wrong to feel humble. The holonts *want* discourse with us. I don't think that's purely from curiosity. I think that, somehow, we're important to more than ourselves."

At Nansen's call, his cabin door opened and Yu came in. He rose from his desk. Her glance flitted briefly about. She had not been here for weeks; hardly anyone had but him. The room was again neat, almost compulsively so. Kilbirnie had tended to get things into mild disarray. Her image filled a screen, not animated, a single instant of her smile. A few pet objects of hers stood on table and shelf. Air still bore the coolness and heathery tang she liked. But the background music was Baroque, and his attention had been on a sculpture. He stood as erect, immaculately clad, and reserved as always.

"Sit down, Wenji," he invited. "What can I do for you?"

They took chairs. She went straight to the painful point. "I thought you would rather I gave you this news in private."

He raised his brows. "Yes?"

"I have reviewed the plans you and Emil have worked out for that crewed, probe-controlling capsule."

He attempted humor. "We didn't ask you to review anything else." Tautly: "Have you found a mistake? We thought we were ready to start the robots on construction."

She sighed. "You can if you wish. You have run a perfectly good design program. But it didn't take account of some factors, such as cramped work space. I find that to build this thing to those specifications will take weeks."

"Oh." He sat motionless.

"My impression is that you two want it as soon as can be."

"Yes. Not that the astrophysics itself can't wait. Emil, though, Emil is so happy again, now that en will have something real to do. And it seems to have helped the morale of the other Tahirians also."

"And you yourself—" She chopped the sentence off. "The basic problem here is that a vessel suitable for beings of the two races—safe, adequately life-supported, controls and communicators easy to use—it becomes elaborate. That includes being rather large. If it were meant for just a human *or* a Tahirian, it would be much, much simpler."

He stared at her out of a face become a mask. "Are you certain?" And then: "My apologies. Of course you are."

"I have run a modification of your program," Yu said. "A vessel for one person of a single species could be ready in ten daycycles or less."

Nansen was silent about half a minute.

"Very well," he replied. "Let it be for Emil."

Her careful impersonality dissolved. "Do you truly mean that, Rico? This must be a bitter disappointment."

"Delay would be worse for en . . . and, as I told you, even ens fellows. The situation has been approaching horror for those poor Tahirians. If Emil can go piloting, and share ens pleasure in the special Tahirian ways, it should change their feelings for the better. And they are also crew."

"You, though. What of you?"

He shrugged. "I'll find other ways to keep busy. . . . No!" he snapped. "No whining. This is a ship meant for humans. Any who can't make a reasonable life aboard her is a sorry *canijo*."

Yu refrained from mention of those who were gone. Seeking a diversion, she turned her gaze on the half-completed clay figurine. It was a bust, not in his former representational manner. The head was misshapen in some purposeful fashion, the visage and its expression still more.

"Your hobby," she murmured. "But this is unlike anything else I have seen from you."

"Tahirian influence," he said. "I thought, I suppose like everybody, that every school and style was exhausted long ago and there's nothing to do but make variations on them. Tahirian art gave me new ideas. Perhaps the black hole and the fact of the holonts has, too. At any rate, a pastime."

"You are not doing this just for amusement," she said. "It is too grim. Terrifying, in a way. I don't know why, and that is part of the terror."

"Well," he said roughly, "I don't doubt your analysis of the engineering matter is correct, but I would like to go over it with Emil, as well as your new design. Will you download them for us?"

"Of course." Her undertone continued: "Yes, what we bring back may revitalize art on Earth, together with science, technology, philosophy, everything."

He yielded enough to what was in him that he muttered, "Assuming we get back."

"I expect we will, given your leadership," Yu replied, "but what we will find, I think not even the Holont knows."

Trouble crept likewise over Zeyd. Once he had prepared an explication of his science, transmission of its details was work for a computer. Unlike Mokoena, he could contribute little to the ongoing examination of fundamental questions—the nature of life and its evolution, whatever the form it took. Bit by bit, daycycle by daycycle, it was borne in on him that now he did best to keep out from underfoot. The efforts of his friends to tell him otherwise only made it worse.

He pursued such outside interests as he found. Among them, he took up fencing after he and Nansen improvised outfits. He grew more observant in his faith, reread the Qur'an, pondered new interpretations of it for the universe unfolding before him. Mostly he maintained a cheerful demeanor and was quick with a quip.

But Mokoena knew.

"I shouldn't say this yet," she told him. "I will, however, if you will keep it confidential for a while."

They were in her cabin, late one evenwatch. She had dimmed illumination to the level of candlelight and made it rosy. A screen showed poplars shivering and shimmering in a double row, at the end of which a dome and a minaret stood above white walls. Ventilation blew with the same soughing warmth. He looked up from the chair in which he slumped. "Why the secrecy?" he asked.

She stood above him, dark, full-figured, lightly clad, her eagerness more heartening than any spoken sympathy could have been.

"Announcement would be premature," she said. "Unscientific. Leaping to a conclusion we may never actually be sure we have reached. And still, I can't hold it in any longer. I have to share it. Who better than with you, darling?"

He sat straighter. "Yes?"

"We—we're learning more about the holonts. What they are, how they can possibly *be*. Not just patterns, mathematical abstractions. What embodies them? How can it be stable?"

She rejoiced to see and hear the awakening in him. "After all our puzzlings about that, is Hanny getting a definite answer?"

"We are, together." She stroked his cheek. "That includes you. Your data showed the holonts how our life works. Then they could draw conclusions about it." She paused, like an athlete readying for a sprint. "It is too soon. This interpretation may be wrong. But it does seem— Selim, it does seem the configurations are not transitory. They have a certain permanence. And life like ours, it's pattern and process, too. Does it impose its own trace on the vacuum? Some direction on the randomness, some change in the metric? Do these last? Selim, maybe the holonts—maybe the Holont thinks they do!"

He could not stay seated beneath that mood; he rose to meet it. "What does this imply?"

"Don't you see? That death isn't the end. That . . . something lives on afterward."

"I have always believed that." Wryness: "I am supposed to."

"Here, scientific proof—what that could mean to . . . to everybody!"

He kept himself judicious. "Fascinating. I certainly want to know more. But your inference strikes me as a non sequitur. I think the soul, God, the purpose and meaning of existence, will always be matters of faith."

"We'll see," said defiant enthusiasm.

The crew sat in their common room, in the half-ring of council. Nansen was at the center. Dayan stood before them. At her side, Mokoena with a parleur translated for the Tahirians who waited at the edge. Stars gleamed through night in the viewscreens, Milky Way, nebulae, sister galaxies.

"What we are learning—and learning to wonder about—is marvelous and magnificent and overwhelming," Dayan said into the hush. "A hundred years would not teach us everything. A thousand years might not. But, with all respect for the biology and astrophysics and whatever else, this newest finding is too important to wait for a regular report.

"I want to emphasize that it is a finding, neither a possibility nor a speculation but a fact. The Holont appears to have made a special effort to explain it to us. I have gone through the mathematics repeatedly, with computer aid, and verified the theorem. I have a feeling that this is what the Holont has really been working toward—because it has had word from the future about what this can mean to the future."

She heard the susurrus of human and nonhuman breath.

"The Tahirian physicists were wrong," she told them. "I don't say they lied. Doubtless they were quick to believe what they wanted to believe, a reason to end starfaring. It doesn't matter. The truth is, a zero-zero transition is no threat.

"It has zero probability of upsetting the cosmic equilibrium. Or less than zero. You see, the energy transfer actually makes a bond, like the transfers of virtual particles that create the forces holding atoms together. Yes, the effect is quantum-small. But it is finite, it is real. Every voyage brings the universe that much further from the metastable state, toward true stability that can last forever."

Mokoena's fingers flickered. Tahirian manes trembled. From Emil wafted a scent like wind off the sea.

Nansen stood up. His look passed over each of them before he said, quite calmly, "Now we must go home."

43.

No trace remained of Terralina. After Tahirians demolished the buildings, fourteen hundred Tahirian years of weather and growth erased whatever was left. They worked likewise on the site itself. Where a stream had run through a meadow surrounded by forest, a river flowed brown and sluggish across turfland. Trees had become sparse. Their kinds were different, too, low, gnarly, their foliage in darker browns and reds; nor was wildlife the same. Weather hung warm and damp, with frequent wild rainshowers. The planet's axis was shifting, the polar zones shrinking. Someday they would again march forward.

The humans had scant reason to care. They would only be here a terrestrial month, the span grudgingly granted them—a month of spaciousness, sunlight, wind, romp, rest, not virtual but real, before they embarked for unknown Earth. They erected their temporary shelters and settled in.

It was doubtless as well, though, that the place was altered in all except its isolation. Too many memories could have awakened.

The sky was cloudless when Sundaram and Dayan went for a walk. They moved rather carefully, not entirely reaccustomed to the weight. Heat drew vapor from wet soil, a fog that eddied upward a few centimeters, white above umber, and baked pungencies out of it. Tiny wings glittered by; larger ones cruised overhead. From the river, half a kilometer off, hidden behind reedlike thickets, boomed the call of some animal, over and over.

"Yes," Sundaram said, "it was enlightening to speak with those linguists." Segregated though the crew was, occasional scholars visited.

Conversation almost had to be in person if it was to deal with anything but trivia. He smiled rather wistfully. "And good to see dear old Simon again, one last time. Our talk clarified certain points for me. I will have much to think about on the way home."

"Might you come nearer to an idea of the Holont's semantics?" Dayan asked.

"That is beyond me. But our contacts with it and the Tahirians have been richly suggestive as to the basics of our own minds. In the end, this may prove to be the true revolution we bring, insight into ourselves." He quelled the note of enthusiasm. "Daydreaming. First we must give form to our thoughts so that we can test them."

"Well, we all have a lot to think about."

He glanced at her. The clear profile was somber against heaven. "You don't complain," he said gently, "but I imagine you feel a dreadful frustration. A glimpse of fundamental new knowledge, and then we left."

"Why, no," she replied. "I've been sincere. None of us were really sorry to go. What we did learn will keep us busy for the rest of our lives, won't it? In fact, Wenji and I expect to be working the whole way back."

"How, if I may ask?"

"We hardly know where to begin, there's so much. For instance, preliminary designs of field-drive spacecraft suitable for humans. And besides the acceleration compensator, what other applications of the principle are there that the Tahirians never thought of? And newer to us, maybe even more important—I think I'm starting to see how that electron manipulation from a distance that the Holont can do works. Quantum entanglement. . . . The uses in communication and nucleonics, energy sources. . . . Transmissions across time. . . . And more and more, including what you've found out about the mind and Mam's found out about life, possibly life after death. Oh, people will be engaged for centuries to come with what we bring them."

"To the extent they can be," Sundaram felt obliged to say. "That may be limited. They will have no black hole to study, no Holont to converse with."

He was not a physical scientist or technician. Preoccupied with his special explorations, he had not chanced to be present when this subject came up on shipboard, or else had paid no attention. She corrected him. "They will know the phenomena exist, that such things can be made. That should be enough for them to go on."

"If they care to."

"Yes. If. We don't know what their civilization will be like."

They walked on awhile. The noise of the water beast receded.

"All right," she said abruptly. "Time I told you why I asked if we could have a private talk."

"I did not wish to press you."

"No, you wouldn't. Kind, tactful—and, mainly, you understand the human soul."

"Oh, please."

"I mean in different ways from how Mam does as a physician and psychologist, or any of us do from everyday experience. Your, well, probably yoga is the wrong word, but your spiritual guidance. I remember how you helped Lajos, calmed him down, eased his pain, that nightwatch when we were sealed into the wardroom. I suspect you've quietly helped others along the way."

Sundaram shook his head. "I have no secret Eastern spiritual technology. In fact, it's a myth."

"Self-command, perception—there are right ways and wrong ways to try for them, aren't there? The same as with anything else. You know at least some of the right ways. Now everybody needs your counsel."

"Why do you say that?"

She fell silent once more. Mists thinned as temperature climbed. The turf squelped less and felt springier.

"We're a crew, we surviving half dozen," Dayan answered at length. "Our relations were never easy. They finally got murderous. And that was when we only had to cope with strangeness, loss, exile in space and time. We're better knit together now. But what when we meet our far-future kin, when they come at us in ways no nonhuman ever could? How can we keep this hard-won . . . crewdom of ours? I think we have to, because it'll be all we really have. But can we?"

Sundaram's smile was more compassionate than amused. "I cannot very well offer a seminar in brotherhood, can I?"

"No, but you can . . . lend strength to . . . individuals as they need it. Just be willing to. They'll soon know."

"You have Ricardo Nansen especially in mind, don't you?" Sundaram prompted softly.

Dayan swallowed. "I don't believe we can stay together without him."

"He will not desert us. That isn't in him."

"No, but— He's been so remote," she quavered. "Polite, dutiful, firm but considerate—and nothing else. Nothing behind his eyes."

"Oh, there is. He simply does not show it."

They stopped, as if they had read an agreement in one another's bodies, and stood face-to-face. "Why not?" she pleaded. "I thought . . . here, resting, wounds healing, he'd come back to us—his spirit would—but as soon as we were established, he went away. *Why?*"

"He told us he wanted a change of scene."

"It doesn't make sense. Unless he's broken inside."

"You care very much, do you not?"

Dayan stood mute.

Sundaram smiled now as a man would smile at his troubled young daughter. "Put your fears aside, Hanny. He has taken the deepest hurt of any of us. He—" After a few seconds: "He did speak several times with me. I may not reveal what he said, of course. But I can point out the obvious, which you in your own pain seem to have let pass by. Ricardo

Nansen is an aristocrat. He does not readily bare his feelings. To come to terms with his grief, he wants a surcease, a time alone. The captain is never alone, always on call. I helped him arrange it with the Tahirians. I may have given him a thought or two to consider. He will return to us, also in spirit."

Dayan laid fist in hand and looked past her companion, hopeward. Finally she turned her gaze to him and said, "Thank you. I wish I knew better words, but thank you."

Sundaram bowed. "*Shalom,* Hanny."

The island lay solitary, the top of a midoceanic volcano. From its crater the slopes fell rough and bestrewn, hundreds of meters down to surf. Woods blanketed the lower reaches in bronze and amber. Flocks crowded the skies, swimming creatures lanced the waves. Winds blew mild, full of salt and fragrances. Nevertheless the island was uninhabited. A population kept well under the carrying capacity of the planet had no land hunger. Besides, the benign climate would not last, and meanwhile geologists foresaw eruptions. An aircar was a rare sight on these shores.

One rested, a bright bubble, above the black sands of a beach, near a shelter. Nansen and a Tahirian stood outside.

"(I am glad it was you who came to take me off,)" said the man on his parleur.

"(Would you not rather it were Simon or, better, Emil?)" inquired Ivan.

"(We bade our good-byes when we landed from the ship. They were—)" Nansen paused. The breeze ruffled his hair. Beyond the little quadruped who confronted him, sea tumbled blue, indigo, and white. Surf whooshed low, crumbling rather than breaking, with none of the violence he had seen along coasts of Earth.

"(They are friends,)" he said. "(I always wished you, too, could be my friend.)"

Stance, gesture, and sharp, gingery odor did not altogether reject him. "(That is difficult, after what you have done to my people.)"

"(Those others do not see it as harm.)"

"(No, many have not. But the lifetimes since you first arrived here, during which we were away at the black hole, have been less than serene.)"

"(Everything seems peaceful.)"

"(Yes, seemingly. Yet our society is trembling, old customs abandoned, restlessness rife. The very purpose of maintaining stability is in question. This latest flood of new information, new concepts that your return has brought, it will have consequences still less foreseeable, perhaps uncontrollable.)"

"(Is it bad that possibilities open up?)" Nansen argued. "(I envy your race its nearness to the black hole. You can discover more than we today can imagine, thousands of years before we will be able to.)"

"(What cost does progress bear?)" Ivan retorted. "(I have studied what you related of your human history. I witnessed the slaughter aboard ship.)"

"(Need it happen to you? Cannot you make choices as free as ours?)"

"(I hope so. I realize you did not intend to disturb us. You could not know. It chanced, as the collision of a stray planet with Tahir might chance. The cosmos goes deeper than our minds ever will.)"

Ivan was still for a span. "(I do not hate you,)" en admitted. "(I would even like to be your friend.)"

Hand clasped hand.

They let go. "(But you must not disturb us more,)" Ivan begged. "(Leave us to cope with what you have left us. Depart before you raise more discontent, more questions.)"

"(I suppose we always will, wherever we are,)" Nansen wrote on his parleur as stoically as he would have uttered it.

"(Yes, because your race is mad.)"

"(Maybe. And maybe that is why we voyage.)"

The wind blew, the waves ran.

44.

The Thyrian nation was loyal to Jensu and indeed provided the Governance with many of its best constables, but clan ties still counted. Thus it came about that soon after he received his commission, Panthos was posted halfway around Earth to North Meric, where he reported directly to the Executive of that continent, his great-uncle. Given the growing unrest there, opportunities for conspicuously useful service and consequent rapid advancement in rank should be frequent.

"If you survive them," cautioned the old man. "Rats' nests of tribes, peoples, classes, religions, godknowswhats, scourings of wars, migrations, revolutions, conversions, history—much too much history, much too little of it ours."

Straight and trim in his new gray uniform, optionary's bars newly gleaming on his shoulders, Panthos replied, "They won't dare rebel, any of them, will they, sir?"

"Not yet. Not in my lifetime, maybe not in yours. They hate each other worse than they hate the Coordinator. But they do riot. If we can't keep that within bounds, it will stir up notions, and *that* will not be unwelcome to certain Jensui magnates— Never mind."

"I see what you mean, sir."

"I doubt you do, except very vaguely. Well, you'll learn. Don't expect any favoritism."

"I don't want any!" Panthos exclaimed.

Firix overlooked the breach of military manners, this time, and finished: "I'm far too busy for it. I will try to get you assignments suited to your degree of experience and to developing you as an officer." His features unbent.

"For your part, you'll come to dinner this evening. I've no end of questions, family, the estates, friends, everything, even the animals and adapts."

In the course of the next year or so Panthos learned about homesickness. Telepresence was thin rations when you never had the bodily reality. Besides, a man was generally too tired at day's end to make a call, which would have been at an inconvenient antipodal hour anyway. Or he had to attend some social function or he and his fellow juniors were taking their much-needed relaxation or he was playing with a joygirl or—whatever it was.

He also learned that maintaining the Coordinator's peace involved more than policing the Solar System.

At first he was stationed safely in Sanusco, meeting few natives other than servants, purveyors, and gentry, Jensuized in greater or lesser degree. Going on patrol through the streets, warrens, and sublevels, he discovered that the inhabitants were not a picturesque, undifferentiated rabble but individuals, who belonged to ancient cultures and held by ancient faiths. This education was interesting, occasionally delightful, now and then dangerous. He acquitted himself well, acquired the basics of two important languages, and was put in command of a platoon. They went widely over the continent as need arose, to assist a garrison in difficulties or to apply their special skills directly.

They went at last to Tenoya.

Firix first gave Panthos an intensive private briefing. "It's as nasty a hole as you'll find anywhere," the Executive said. "Aswarm with fanatics. Arods, you know. Nowadays their priests don't preach insurgency, but they do tell and retell how their valiant ancestors resisted the Pacification, and it wouldn't take a very hot spark to detonate the whole region. If this Seladorian business gets out of hand, that could just possibly be it."

Panthos frowned, searching a memory lately overburdened. "Seladorians? A cult, aren't they, split off from Arodism, but peaceful?"

The Executive scowled. "Peaceful in theory. In practice, unshakeably determined. And only partly Arodish. They've taken notions and practices from a wide range. Their prophet's father was a Kithman who left his ship to marry an Arodish woman. That made them outcasts in her people's eyes, and they had to move to Kith Town. She never felt at home there, and after he died young she returned to Arodia with her son. I can imagine the influences on him and in him. It doesn't help matters a bit that in the end Selador was martyred.

"Now the Seladorians in Tenoya have begun actively expanding their area of cultivation. That's brought on conflict with their neighbors, which has brought on killings. Retaliating for several deaths, a band of believers has wrecked a number of robots belonging to Arods, and even some municipal machinery. Their creed has technophobic implications, and the extremists among them are mechanoclasts.

"The city's aboil. The garrison's barely able to keep a semblance of order. A control team has to go in and attack the trouble at its heart. I'd frankly prefer a more seasoned man, but every one of them is engaged elsewhere. And this could be the making of your career, Panthos."

Ardency blazed. "Thank you, sir!"

The session went on for a pair of hours. At the end, when they parted, Firix said low, "I wish it didn't have to be you. Not that I don't have confidence in you, but—your mother's been my favorite niece."

"I'll be fine, sir," Panthos assured him. He snapped to attention and lifted his arm in salute. "Service to the Coordinator."

Firix's response was correct but without fire. Perhaps he was thinking of that painted giggler who sat in the Uldan Palace.

Panthos chose a slow transport for the flight to his destination. It gave him the time and the equipment-carrying capacity for direct mnemonic input. He arrived with some knowledge of the political situation and well-informed about the geographics. Nonetheless, what he saw from aloft struck him hard.

Perhaps it was the westward desolation, a rain-gullied plain stretching farther than his sight, dust scudding between scattered shrubs and clumps of harsh grass. Eastward the land sank down to a former lake bottom. That vast expanse of moister soil was green, cropland and groves streaked with irrigation pipes and studded with units processing the materials the plants yielded. Attendant robots moved about; brief sparks flashed where metal reflected sunlight. After the throngs in Sanusco and other cities—and the castles, preserves, villages, and archaic human-worked plantations in their hinterlands—desert and sown felt alike forsaken. Thyria seemed light-years distant, a dream half remembered.

Perhaps it was Tenoya, sprawling over square kilometers. Toward the center, folk and vehicles beswarmed the streets. Tenants filled cyclopean buildings once devoted to other purposes but not yet fallen. Small houses made from wreckage huddled beneath. Here and there lifted the bulbous spire that marked a temple. Three antique towers, refurbished, soared in graceful lines and pastel hues close to the fortified garrison compound.

A haze blued the city core, dust and smoke, man sign. At night, Panthos knew, lights would flare hectic. But, more than the surrounding hectares of ruin and abandonment, this life shocked him. He thought of maggots in the corpse of a beautiful woman.

Enough. He had work to do.

The carrier set down in the compound. He led his men out, told them to wait, and reported to the summarian. "I suggest an immediate reconnaissance, sir," he said. "We're fully prepared, and in fact want some movement after all that sitting. It'll familiarize us, and a show of force ought to make for a healthier attitude."

"I'm not sure," the senior officer replied slowly. "Yesterday we got word that Houer Kernaldi is in town. We don't know when he arrived. Maybe days ago."

The note of hopelessness, the acceptance of being pretty well bottled up within these walls, chilled Panthos. He kept his tone respectful. "Who, sir?"

"You haven't heard of him? Houer Kernaldi. Double name, you notice. A Kithman by birth, but a Seladorian convert. He's been evangelizing and organizing for a good ten years, while maintaining connections with his kinfolk."

He must be a lonely one, Panthos thought. If he'd abandoned the star ways, what had he left but tiny Kith Town and the rare ship from outside? Well, there were his fellow believers here on Earth, few though they were. And his god—or Atman, Entelechy, Ultimate Motive, Meaning, whatever the word was in various languages. The Executive and the educator program hadn't told Panthos much about that. They didn't know much. "A troublemaker, then, sir?"

"Not really, at least not by intent. He's never preached sedition, and may well be trying to calm his followers down. It could have the opposite effect, as crazy as everybody in Lowtown is."

"I definitely need to meet him. Permission to go out, sir?"

"I have orders to allow you broad discretion," the summarian answered resignedly. "But remember, if you get into a broil, it may touch off general rioting, and if that happens, we may not be able to rescue you."

Panthos doubted the most besotted fanatic would care to attack a band like his. Still, he should avoid provocation. He took them through the main gate in close order and at a slow pace, not thrusting through the crowds but passing through, causing people to move smoothly aside, as a boat parts the sea.

That was a wistful image. The summer sun burned in a bleached and empty sky. Shadows lay hard-edged. Heat seethed in air so dry that breath stung nostrils. It struck from walls, hammerblows. Stenches worsened with each step onward, unwashed humanity, rankly seasoned cookery, dung, offal, sometimes a dog or giant rat ripening in death. The natives clamored from shopstalls, shrilled at each other; the shuffle of their sandals mingled with wheel-creak from carts and blare from the occasional motor vehicle. They were mostly Arods, lean, of medium stature and light brown skin, black hair hanging braided, faces high in cheekbones and flat in nose and slant in eyes, men generally in dingy white gowns, women in layers of gaudily striped cloth. A lively lot, Panthos admitted; hands waved, feet hopped, mouths moved incessantly. Sometimes a gaunt yellow desert dweller or a tall ranger from the northern bottomlands came by.

Briefly, Panthos felt lost—he, his troop, his civilization—among these and a hundred different foreignnesses around the globe, grains in a dust storm that blew on and on forever. Nonsense! He led the Coordinator's men, constables of the Governance. Their two dozen embodied mastery.

Always awesome were the Warriors, two and a quarter meters tall, identical in thick body and stony countenance: adapts, their genes shaped not for civilian service but for battle. The riflemen were generally more useful, being more flexible in their ways. The flittermen, little fellows who looked as if the apparatus on their backs would soon crush them, were the least impressive. However, if things turned jeapordous, suddenly jets would lift them off the ground, whirlyblades deploy, and the opposition find itself covered from above.

Panthos marched in front, unarmored, bearing only a sidearm, the golden rings of Jensu on his cap like a target. That also belonged to the show.

Eastward the streets zigzagged down, narrowing into lanes, pavement cracked and pitted, until the platoon was in shadowed canyons under a ragged strip of sky. Walls gaped with holes, revealing the detritus behind. Panthos reviewed his data. Here was Lowtown, where war and quarrying had uncovered the remnants of earlier cities—before Tenoya, Arakoum; before Arakoum, Cago. . . . If collapse had not choked a building or if people had grubbed it clear, they occupied it afresh, roofed the top and shuttered the windows with whatever materials they could salvage, peered out at the newcomers, came forth and trailed him in a flock that grew steadily bigger, noisier, more hostile.

To them the constables were invaders. This quarter that they had made from ruins was itself centuries old.

Paceman Bokta advanced to the optionary's side. "They're in an ugly mood, sir," he said.

Panthos nodded. "I can see that," he replied. "And hear it and smell it."

"Reminds me of once in Zembu, before your time, sir, when we were putting down Migoro's Rebellion. On patrol through a district kind of like this. I never found out what set 'em off, but in an eyeblink a howling mob was at our throats. We had to shoot our way clear back to cantonment. Left four good men behind, torn to shreds."

"Do you think we should withdraw?"

"Well, no, sir, can't do that exactly. We could turn at the next intersection and take the first upbound street after that. They'll suppose we're only making a quick survey." Bokta's leathery countenance had stiffened. Plainly, he didn't like the taste of what he advised.

"Do you know they will? These aren't Zembui."

"No, sir. Maybe they wouldn't get bumptious. I just thought I should take leave to mention it."

The veteran was no coward. Nor was a crack unit, forewarned, likely to suffer serious casualties. On the other hand, if they had to kill, the consequences could go far beyond serious. As never before, the loneliness of decision caught at Panthos.

He mustn't hesitate. "This may be our last chance to find somebody who'll negotiate," he said. "We will proceed."

"Yes, sir." The paceman fell back into formation.

As if to bear him out, a noise awakened ahead. Raw yelps echoed between walls, above a growl that took chilly hold of spine and scalp. The throng dissolved. Men, the fewer women, and the yammering urchins shouted, jostled, ran toward the racket, disappeared down the crooked passages. Emptiness loomed and yawned.

Nobody was left to keep the platoon from returning to base, and return had become impossible. "Alert!" Panthos snapped. "Forward!" He broke into quicksteps. Boots thudded at his back.

The canyon opened. He had reached the Seladorian purlieu.

Another world. Another universe? Right, left, and behind, walls rose in their ravaged tiers like hills enclosing a valley. In front, afar, Panthos spied the lake bed, hazy green to the horizon. Green, too, were the terraces that descended intricately before him, but paler, the green of hardihood and frugality. These grasses, grains, bushes, and trees were not biosynthesizers, they were life in its own right, food for their cultivators. The single extravagance was flower beds, flaunting to the sun. Houses and utility buildings stood along paths, a layout planned for optimum use of space. They, too, were made from salvage, but sturdily and neatly, colored rose or yellow or blue.

Recalling what he had learned, Panthos guessed how the Seladorians had toiled, generation by generation, to create this oasis. More to the point today was their effort to expand farther. Yes, they had acquired lawful title to what they set about razing. That mattered nothing to the inhabitants they displaced, or to kindred and friends of the newly homeless. Besides, in Arodish eyes Seladorians were blasphemers. They wanted to abolish the machines on whose productivity depended the subsidies that kept poor folk alive. Drive them into the desert! Exterminate them! If it weren't for the damned interfering Governance—

At first Panthos saw no rioters. They had spilled off onto lower terraces. Screams and cries tore through the heat. Smoke began to rise. The structures wouldn't burn, but what was in them could, and it was ill to think about dwellers who hadn't escaped.

He studied the map in his brain. "We'll make for the bottom ledge," he said. "Refugees will have. Hold your fire till I give the order."

The platoon jogged across the uppermost terrace and scrambled down a stone stairway. Some of the mob raged below. They kept their distance from the constables, shrieking their hatred. Most were on the third level. Men surged from the homes they were plundering. Shouts; rocks and debris thrown; the troopers glared and kept going. A bruise, an impact that drew blood, corpsmen could take it. For a while.

Before patience and discipline broke, they reached the fifth and final terrace. On foundations that must have belonged to a dock, it jutted sheerly out, its edge a cliff. The expanse was all garden and orchard except for a building larger than any above, decked in flowerful vines. The Seladorian temple—no, they called it a communion house. This was hallowed ground.

Several hundred people were there. As abruptly and insanely as the violence started, the attackers had not pursued, not quite yet. Instead they went for the residences and whomever didn't get away. Those victims couldn't be many, for believers hadn't tried to bar doors, nor bolted panicky in every which direction. Somebody had taken quick, effective leadership and brought them here. Mothers bore babies, youngsters trotted at their skirts, men helped the old and the lame along. Children wailed, a few adults wept, but in stumbling wise they moved toward the refuge.

They were garbed like their persecutors, except for one who trotted back and forth beside them. He wore a blue cloak over his gown and carried a staff. With calls and gestures, he herded them on their way.

A few cheered raggedly when they saw the Jensui. The cloaked man waved them to keep moving and hurried over to the platoon. He was short, hard-bitten, less dark than the others, nose craggy, eyes without obliqueness—Kith, by the look of him.

Panthos drew to a halt. "Form your line," he commanded. "If any rioters show, shoot above them, warn them off." To the leader: "Are you Houer Kernaldi?"

"Yes," replied the man, his Jensui accented but fluent and steady. "You arrived in bare time, Optionary. Thank you. The Ultimate is with you."

Panthos grinned. "Happenstance is. Are you in charge here? Don't they have a, uh, priest or councillor?"

"I don't know where Honrata is. May she be safe."

"Meanwhile they look up to you, eh? Well, you did a good, forceful job. But this is a blind end. You're boxed in."

"There was no other way to go. The sanctuary doors are stout. I hoped they'd withstand battering till a rescue squad came."

That could have been too long, Panthos thought. He suspected the summarian wouldn't mind having the Seladorian problem taken off his hands. Afterward he'd shoot several arbitrarily arrested offenders. The Arodish high priest would protest the executions while privately feeling relieved himself, and that would be that.

However, here Panthos was, bearing the authority of his mission. "I'll call for an airlift to bring you to safety," he said, and raised his transceiver bracelet.

The response he got hit him in the belly. "We can't," a subcommander groaned. "The whole damn city's erupting. Mobs are collecting around every Jensui property. We've got to keep force at the sites, all sites, or else they'll turn into lynch-and-loot packs."

"Hoy, you can spare a flyer or two to ferry us."

"Sorry. The summarian told me to tell you." He must have monitored the call, Panthos thought, but not wanted to give this matter any more time than that at this moment. "It'd be too provocative, he said. Better to let this thing burn itself out where it is than risk it spreading through the whole province. We've spotted you by satellite. You're secure where you are, aren't you? Stand guard till we have calm again. Service to the Coordinator."

The voice cut off. Panthos lowered his arm. "Did you hear?" he asked Kernaldi.

"I did," the other said without anxiety. "You will protect us?"

"Of course. You're subjects of the Governance."

Men appeared at the top of the stairs. They bounded down. "Fire high," directed the paceman. Fulgurators flared and boomed. It was a more effective demonstration than bullets or sonics. The men scuttled back up out of sight. Their curses and obscenities trailed them.

"We're safe," Panthos said. "We just have to wait. No fun in this weather, but if you can keep your followers quiet, we'll manage." He felt confident of that. Here was a natural-born commander.

Kernaldi shook his head. "I'm afraid not, Optionary. No water."

"What?"

"I checked that immediately when we got here. As I feared, nothing flows. The pipes are fed from above. Somebody has turned the valves. They aren't all witless hysterics. This hasn't happened randomly. There has been a certain amount of advance planning."

"Um." Panthos considered. Each man of his carried a canteen, and would need each drop in it. "The soil must still be moist. We'll find vessels, dig down, squeeze out what we can for your weakest"—infants, the aged, the infirm. "That ought to keep them alive till morning."

"I doubt it." The tone was dispassionate, setting forth fact and logic. "Besides, will we be free then? This siege could go on for days, if the constabulary takes no action to stop it. And, Optionary, think of the spiritual side. The psychological side, if you prefer. Everything else of these people's is being destroyed. This garden is their center and symbol. If we— they themselves—uproot it, will they ever have the heart to rebuild?"

"Maybe they can't," Panthos said. "Maybe they should go back to the old faith and the old ways, rejoin their folk."

He promptly regretted his words. The small man stood erect and replied—if a knife could speak, so would it have spoken— "That is impossible. We are what we are. We will die here, or flee to Seladorian communities elsewhere, but we will not surrender."

Panthos kept silence for a span, watching the fugitives. Most were braving the sun, leaving the shelter of the sanctuary to the vulnerable among them. Mothers comforted children, fathers led them to what meager shade lay at the building or under trees. Exhausted, stunned, they nonetheless bore themselves well and talked softly. Always their glances went back to the evangelist.

"What is this lifeway of yours?" Panthos asked.

Kernaldi smiled. His voice eased, the tone of one reasonable man to another. "That's nothing to explain in a single quick lecture, my friend. How much of the history do you know?"

"Very little. Tell me what you can."

Still Kernaldi spoke calmly. "Selador was not the first to see that all existence is unity and life its culmination—its purpose, for how can a lifeless universe have meaning? Intelligent life, awareness, is the goal. Rather, I should say, it's the forefront, for it's to evolve onward, till at the end it is identical with the Ultimate that realizes itself through life. We humans, though, have taken a wrong turning. If we persist as we are, we'll become more and more irrelevant to the Meaning, or even, on Earth, a threat to it. In the course of time, our race will go through misery to extinction." He shrugged. "In everyday language, a mistake of nature's. Selador didn't want that to happen."

"He, uh, preached against machines, didn't he?"

"No. He was not technophobic. It's unfortunate that some of us today are. Having a technology is part of being intelligent. But humans have taken it too far, and in bad directions. They've adapted themselves to it, rather than it to the Meaning. They've cut themselves off from the living world. Too often, they're its enemy." Kernaldi gestured. "The desert here was once woodland and prairie. Our souls have shriveled like this country. Our duty to it, to the future, and to ourselves is to restore it and begin to live wholly with life."

He smiled again, ruefully. "But now I am preaching. Sorry. I'll only add that a great many local people, both high and humble, hate the idea. It would make *them*, or at any rate their descendants, the enclave."

"I'm surprised they don't regard it as just a daydream," Panthos said, wishing he could be kindlier.

Kernaldi took the remark in good part. "Oh, it is possible. I won't live to see it carried through, but we can make a start, and will if we're given the chance. Including the right sort of technology." He lowered his voice. "Bioengineering doesn't have to produce monsters. Apologies to those brave men of yours, but they are an example of what I'm talking about. Our scientific knowledge is valuable, but we should use it to restore a natural world that is in accordance with our own natures. Spacefaring is another example. It gave us many wonderful things and insights, but it is not an end in itself—that attitude has also produced monsters, of the spirit if not the body—and the time is overpast for us to take what we have gained from it for the enrichment and enlargement of life and mind, here and now."

Had Kithhood brought him to his faith? wondered Panthos. Generation after generation within metal, cruising the hollowness between the stars; alien planets, alien beings; on his own brief visits to Earth, an ever dwindling Kith Town from which Earth grew ever more estranged. . . .

Kernaldi put aside the emotion that had begun to show and went back to practicalities. "Well, obviously, in the course of time we Seladorians have developed our peculiar rites, observances, practices; and we stick together, if only because we have to. That alone gets us disliked. And we have our conflicts with the Governance. As a Kithman, I understand all this very well."

Sharply: "Have I said enough? Your turn. What about these people you see before you?"

The sun was a fire, the air a furnace. In the darkness of the sanctuary, a baby cried.

Panthos was young. Decision came fast. Yet he felt quite coolheaded as he answered, "You're right. Holding you guarded is no real protection. We'll escort you to the garrison."

Kernaldi regarded him for half a minute before asking, in the same level tone: "Isn't that against your orders?"

"I've received no direct orders." Panthos felt he had better speak openly; and he wanted to. "When we've left this spot, we can't turn back. That'd certainly mean a fight. When we get to the compound, they can't refuse you water, food, and shelter." As for himself, he should suffer no worse than a reprimand, and maybe nothing more than a tongue-lashing from the summarian. After all, he commanded a special force, dispatched by the Executive, whose grandnephew he was.

Kernaldi raised hand to brow. Though he had had nothing to do with Kithfolk, Panthos recognized the starfarer salute. "Thank you, sir. You are a man."

Wheeling about, Kernaldi went among his followers, to and fro, in and out, talking, touching, being what he was. Panthos caught fragmentary phrases. He saw what assurance and order they wrought.

"I think we can overawe the mob and pass through," he told Bokta. "Regardless of what happens, shoot to wound or kill only if there's absolutely no other choice, and only at those directly up against us. When in any doubt whatsoever, hold your fire. Is that clear, Paceman?"

"Yes, sir," Bokta replied. "I wish it wasn't," he muttered. A veteran could get away with such remarks.

Kernaldi herded the Seladorians into line. Bokta deployed the platoon forward, behind, and on either side. The flitters lifted. "Let's go," Panthos said, and led the way.

Up the stairs, where formation got tricky. Over the terrace above. As he expected, the rioters shrank back, right and left. They snarled, some of them screamed, a few threw objects, but they made way for the constables. Smoke reeked. Pale under the sun, flames danced over piles of household treasures. Whirlyblades whickered.

People and platoon surmounted the last level, crossed its defiled greenery, and went up a deserted street. Walls brimmed it with shadow, though heat still sucked on skin. Boots slammed stone. Doorways and windows stood shut. Nobody called from lean-to shops or hovels built out of shards.

The top of Panthos's mind crouched watchful. Underneath, he thought how he longed for a cold beer. And when he got back to Sanusco, there was a girl . . . and then furlough, home. . . .

A rifle barked. He never heard it, nor felt the slug crash through his skull.

Weapons swiveled about. "Hold fire!" the paceman bawled. No telling exactly where behind this crumbling concrete the sniper lurked, or what women and children might be shivering nearby. The optionary had issued his orders.

"O Ultimate—" Kernaldi knelt down by the sprawled body. He closed the eyes.

No further shot came. Probably the killer had laughed and run. "Take him up," Bokta bade after a short while. A Warrior gathered what was left of Panthos and cradled it against his chest. Kernaldi had been calming his flock. The march proceeded.

"Now," Kernaldi said, "the Governance will have to keep us protected."

45.

On the voyage back to Sol, Nansen often sought the command center. There was seldom any need for it. As ever, *Envoy* mostly conned herself, making leap after zero-zero leap so smoothly that her crew never noticed the transitions. Only when she was about to pause and orbit free, in the normal state, for the taking of observations, did captain and engineer stand by their posts, and that was more from a sense of duty than because they anticipated any problems.

But in between such times, when he wanted to be alone and felt as if his cabin were closing in on him, he would come sit among instruments and quietness, dim the interior lights, activate the great viewscreens, and lose himself in the splendor around.

Late one daywatch, about at midpassage, he heard a light footfall behind him. Turning his head, he saw Dayan enter through the dusk he had made. She wore a gray coverall and he could not make out the red of her hair, but stars and Milky Way touched it with frost. As he rose from his seat, she caught her breath. He wondered why. It did not occur to him that he stood limned against the cosmos.

"Well, welcome," he said. His pleasure was as genuine as his surprise.

"I'm . . . not sure I will be," she answered.

"You always are, Hanny."

Her gaze dropped, lifted anew toward his, and held steady. The change in her mood, from the optimism and exuberance of her projects with Yu, was like a sudden cold wind upon him. She plunged ahead: "I'm sorry to interrupt your thinking."

"I wasn't. And I wouldn't be sorry if you did."

"But— I suppose you can guess why I'm here."

He smiled. "Because I happen to be?"

His fragile cheerfulness broke under her words. "I thought you should hear first, privately, and I didn't want to wait till you were in your cabin. I'd have had to fend off everybody else's questions." She glanced away, at a cloudlet glimmering in the crystal blackness, a nebula where suns were coming to birth. "Besides, this place is more right, somehow."

"It's about your latest observations, isn't it?" he asked slowly. They had not been quick or easy, she alone out on the hull. Sundaram, Zeyd, and Mokoena lacked skill to help her; she had declined Nansen's and Yu's offers, declaring that, slight though the risk might be, the ship could spare neither of them.

She nodded. "Yes. I've finished reducing the data."

He folded his arms and waited. Ventilation rustled, no louder than bloodbeat in ears. At this point of its cycle the air verged on chilly, with an autumnal smell.

"No further room for doubt," Dayan said. "Starflight in the region of Sol is—has been—decreasing. Steeply. Toward extinction."

Twilight shielded faces. "It had begun to seem that way," Nansen murmured.

"We weren't sure. Statistical fluctuations— Now, though, the tracks I measured this time—" She swallowed. After a second she had forced dryness on her tone. "A total of nineteen. The maximum distance from Sol was fifty-five light-years, plus or minus three. The mean distance was about twenty."

"Down from sixty-two flights averaging fifty light-years each," he recalled. "Ten weeks ago."

"A thousand years ago, star time," she reminded him, needlessly, desperately.

"And now—no, 'now' is meaningless—these wave fronts new to us are twenty-five hundred years old," he mused. "Human starfaring peaked maybe four thousand years after we left home. Then the ebb set in."

"Figurative figures," she said, regaining prosaicism. "I'll have more exact values in my report."

Nansen stood mute for a little. The stars gleamed multitudinous in constellations that still were strange to Earth. "Do the numbers make much difference?" he replied. "What matters is what we find when we come . . . home. Or don't find."

Defiance stirred. "Or as the Yankees used to say, 'We ain't licked yet.' For all we know, enterprise has been recovering."

He looked at her. Eyes caught starlight and gave it back out of shadow. "Do you really believe that?"

The liveliness died. "I'd like to. But probably I don't."

"It does seem as if every other race that tried came at last to the end of its strength, or its desire, and gave up. Or will someday. Why should ours be different? What growth curve of any kind rises forever?"

She trod one step closer. "Don't take it so to heart, Rico," she said from low in her throat.

"I shouldn't, true. The irony of it—" His armor cracked enough for her to hear. "We can't speak of the cruel irony, can we? The universe isn't cruel or kind or anything. It simply is. It doesn't even care about its own survival."

"Your God ought to."

"Well," he sighed, "the Church taught that someday time also will have a stop."

She touched his hand. "Rico   "

"*¿Sí?*" He sounded startled.

"If it is so—if *Envoy* is the last human starship—don't let it break you." Dayan's voice lifted. "A bitter disappointment, yes. To all of us. But we didn't fare for nothing. We had our voyage, we made our discoveries, we *lived*. And this won't be the end of life, either."

"No," he must agree.

"If humans aren't adventuring anymore, could they be at peace, as the Tahirians wanted to be?"

"I doubt it."

"We never really had a hardwired drive, a need or instinct, to explore. You and I heard a lot of rhetoric about that, back in those days, but the fact is, most people in most of history were content to stay put and cultivate their own gardens. Exploration, discovery, was a cultural thing."

"And an individual thing," he insisted.

She beheld him crowned with stars. "Individuals like you."

"And you, Hanny."

"But would peace be so terrible?" she pursued. "Suppose Earth is tranquil and beautiful. Suppose we can find something for ourselves like your *estancia*. Then I could gladly settle down."

"Do you remember the *estancia*?" he asked wonderingly.

"How could I forget? That short while I spent there with you was as happy a time as I've ever known."

"Hanny."

She mustered resolution. "All right, Rico. I've been meaning to say this when the chance came. Couldn't earlier, of course. But it has been more than a year for us since we lost Jean."

His machismo crumbled. "I—naturally, I've had thoughts—but—"

She smiled in the starlit gloaming. "But you're the captain and a gentleman and wouldn't let yourself notice how I've lately been waving my eyelashes at you." In a rush: "Rico, we've six months of travel left. After that— We can't guess what, after that. But we have this half year."

"To explore what we've found, yes."

"And more than that."

"To be happy in," he said, amazed.

46.

Where the gorge was narrowest the river at the bottom ran at its most furious. Gray-green and white-foamed, it roared between cliffs, spouted off boulders in the shallows, breathed chill and damp into the sunshine above. Debris from farther upland whirled and bounded through the current, sticks, brushwood, sometimes a dead animal, a capsized dugout, or a fallen tree. Here the gap was small enough that the Susuich could throw a bridge over.

Emerging from the shadows and blue foliage of woods, Vodra Shaun stopped at the brink to see what it was she must cross. Iron-ruddy rock fell ten meters to the water, with twice that distance between the sides. A suspension bridge would have been appropriate, but no natural fibers had the strength necessary—at least, none in this region did—and as yet the Susuich trade with the Hrroch did not include steel cable. Instead, the builders had trimmed spindly local trees. Planted in holes and crevices halfway down the cliffs, poles slanted upward to meet other members and form trusses that supported two stringers on which short sections lay transversely. The whole was lashed together with rawhide. Construction had obviously demanded skill and daring, and possibly several lives.

Dau Ernen halted at her side. "It looks fragile, doesn't it?" he said.

"Well, I could wish we weren't quite so heavily loaded," Vodra confessed. She grinned. "But then, I've wished that ever since we set out."

Their burdens were indeed considerable, even in a gravity field 10 percent less than terrestrial. Besides sleeping bags, tent, medikits, and assorted gear, they carried dried food for two months. Nothing that lived on Brent could nourish them. Kithfolk hardly ever had occasion to go backpacking. Vodra herself had done it exactly once before, on her last visit to this planet. Dau had never, and struggled manfully at first. Young, in good condition, he toughened as the days passed on the trail.

Ri had already stepped onto the span. "Follow, follow," he called. "We have far to go to the next worthwhile campsite."

Standing there against the sky, he made a handsome spectacle. Long, slender save for a barrel chest, the proportions were not human, but suggested a refined, abstract sculpture of a man. The head was different, plumed, round-eared, eyes big and golden above a curved beak. A kilt decked the red skin. Little more encumbered him than a rifle and knife, of Hrroch manufacture; traveling through this wilderness, his homeland, he lived off it.

Vodra lifted the transponder hung about her neck to her lips. "We wonder if we can get safely across," she told him. The instrument converted her utterances to the trills and whistles that she herself could not have produced in any intelligible fashion. Human spellings of Brentan words, including names, scarcely counted as crude approximations.

Nor was the language she used an equivalent of his; it emerged as Hrrochan. Hitherto Kithfolk had only had serious dealings with the civilization beyond the eastern sea, technologically ahead of any others. Ri was among the Susuich who had acquired its tongue. The knowledge came from traders who, pushing west from their coastal colonies, established outposts in the mountains. Over the years it had qualified Ri to act first as an intermediary between them and his overlords, now to guide a pair of strange beings farther west to the heart of his country.

He waved a four-fingered hand. "Be careful to keep your balance," he advised. "Come!"

"Well, I suppose we can," Dau said in Kithish after Vodra translated for him.

"We'd better," she replied. "Plain to see, this culture has no use for the timid. If we're to get any profit from our expedition, we have to act bold."

Ri waited for them. His original attitude toward the humans, half wary, half marveling, had turned into comradeship. When Vodra reached him, Dau at her back, he made the clucking sound that perhaps corresponded to a smile and turned about to lead the way.

The bridge was barely a meter wide, without rails. Its thin structure trembled underfoot. Swollen with snowmelt, the river raged beneath.

Ri saw the danger first. He shrilled and burst into a run. Heavier and less gracile by heritage, tens of kilos on their shoulders, the humans dared not.

Ri was also too slow.

That the thing should have happened just then was wildly unlikely. Or was it? Maybe the bridge needed rebuilding every few years. Vodra hadn't thought to ask.

A tree came downstream, not one of the gaunt local sort but a mountain giant, oak-massive, uprooted by a spate or a mudslide or the crumbling of a bank. Wide-spreading, spinning as it tumbled, its branches snagged in the truss. The battering-ram momentum of the trunk drove them forward. Wood snapped and rattled. The truss broke. The bridge collapsed.

Spacefarers had quick reflexes drilled in. As she felt the footing go, Vodra undid her bellyband and pulled her arms free of the pack. She glimpsed Dau doing the same. The bridge toppled slowly, down through the members that had upheld it. She grabbed hold of the nearest piece and clung. It eased her fall.

But then she was at the bottom and the river had her.

She felt neither fear nor the cold. She was too busy staying alive. A part of her seemed to stand aside, watchful, and quietly issue orders. Fill your lungs before you strike. The water is thick with glacial flour, you're nearly blind underneath it, but watch as best you can. Maybe you'll see a boulder in time to evade it. Swim upward. Break the surface. *Breathe.* The torrent drags you down again. Don't thrash, move minimally, save your strength; you'll need every erg of it. Up. *Breathe.* Look around while you're able. The right bank is closer. Work toward it, but beware of rocks. In this stream, you could hit hard enough to break bones. Under again. No way to kick boots off. Well, they won't sink you. Not till you've grown too weak. Up. *Breathe.* Where's the sun gone? Shadow; a strip of sky far overhead, insolently blue and calm; brawling water— Look out! Boulder ahead! A big one, to stick into air. Swim sideways. Now, bend legs, kick, use your feet to push yourself off. Onward. Don't gasp so. You're not completely winded yet. And the current is slowing a little.

And more. The stream was past the steepest part of its fall toward the lowlands. It had widened, too, and was therefore shoaling, through what was almost a canyon rather than a defile. The palisades were much higher, though. On the right they blocked off the sun. It touched the leftward heights, a wash of gold over their rustiness, but that deepened the gloom down here.

Still, she could see a ways. Not far off lay a small beach. The water was less noisy. "Halloo-oo!" she heard, and cast a glance back. Yonder came Dau. He'd been lucky, caught a balk of wood and gained flotation. Not just for himself, she saw. One arm held Ri across it, face up. The Brentan flopped, ominously passive, as the timber wallowed.

When Vodra's feet touched bottom, her observer-pilot went away. Suddenly she was herself, aware of painful bruises, sobbing and shuddering with cold. She waded ashore and dropped onto a gravelly crescent nestled against the cliff. Stranded brushwood covered most of it.

Dau grounded. Less exhausted, he carried Ri out. The sight shocked Vodra alert. She scrambled back up.

"Are . . . are you all right?" Dau stammered. She saw the anxiety on his face and knew it for genuine. It wasn't merely because she was the sole fellow human in a thousand kilometers or worse. She was the closest to a real friend he had gotten thus far. Everybody else in *Fleetwing* was courteous, even helpful, but a newcomer didn't soon settle into full crewdom. Too many traditions, customs, mores, turns of speech, all the nuances of belongingness, were too dissimilar. Vodra had taken the shy boy from *Argosy* under her wing. It was one reason she'd chosen him for her partner on this trip. Give him a chance to prove himself.

That might turn out not to have been a favor.

The thought flitted off. "Hold!" she exclaimed. "Careful there! He's hurt. Badly." Ri lay lax in Dau's clasp. The long limbs hung down, the head lolled, eyes closed, beak agape.

"He must have hit something when we fell," Dau said. "I saw him and snatched. Unconscious. I don't know—"

"You can't," Vodra interrupted. "I've learned some Brentan anatomy. Here, kneel, let me ease him to the ground."

Her fingers searched across the red skin. It felt hot. Well, the normal body temperature was higher than hers. She'd like to snuggle close beside him. No, never mind the chill, not till this was done. No serious contusions visible. But— Yes. That jaggedy lump, halfway between neck and waist.

She rose. "Not good," she said. "I think he has a broken back."

Dau took his gaze from the water, stone, and murk around them. "We'll bring him to sick bay—"

"He's not our species," Vodra said. "We don't have regrowth techniques for his biome. Luckily, an injury like this isn't as bad for them as for us. If we handle him properly, he should recover."

Dau fumbled in his coverall and drew his radio transceiver from a pocket. Awkwardly, shaking, his numbed hands groped at the keys. A green light came aglow, tiny in the shadow. "It still works," he said with lips gone blue. And *Fleetwing* had, as always, placed relay satellites in orbit. "I'll call for help."

"Wait," Vodra commanded. "Rescue isn't that simple."

He blinked. "Huh?" His teeth clattered. He suppressed it. "Oh, yes, a spaceboat can't land down here. B-b-but she surely can s-s-somewhere above, nearby." He looked at the steep. Scored, craggy, bushes and dwarf trees growing wherever seed had found soil, it would be hard but not impossible to ascend. "We'll c-climb up."

"Not dragging Ri along. Especially if we want to keep him alive."

"Oh— But we can't stay here," Dau protested. "We'd starve. No, we-we'll freeze to death. That boat had better land soon."

"It had best not land at all, anywhere in this country," Vodra told him. "Have you forgotten?"

Long ago, when Kith ships explored as well as traded, their crews naturally bestowed names on planets of interest that they found. *Fleetwing*, ranging farther than others, made the most such discoveries, and thereby won the exclusive right to deal with them. Every catalogue of myth was drained early on. *Fleetwing*'s people felt it proper to call worlds where sentient beings dwelt after the crew of *Envoy*. They were half mythic anyway.

Brent was unusually terrestroid and promising. The Hrroch, in particular, had attained ironworking. More to the point, they were extraordinary agronomists. While nothing was humanly edible, they had a wide range of biologicals to offer, from luxurious textiles to microbial chemistry. If shrewdly marketed, these should fetch high prices on human-inhabited planets. Of course, once the idea was there, presently someone would find it cheaper to synthesize than to import. But meanwhile the Hrroch ought to hit on new ideas; Kith trade goods often stimulated inventiveness. And art—pictures, patterns, statuary, architecture, music, literature, dance—evolved with a civilization. Likewise did events, language, culture, psychology, an ongoing stream of information. The Brentans were humanlike enough for their minds and works to be comprehensible. They were alien enough for these to be unpredictable, wellsprings of excitement and inspiration.

Hence their world became a port of call for *Fleetwing*. About once a terrestrial century she arrived from the stars to take orbit and send her boats down. The welcome was always eager. The Hrroch were fascinated, the wares they acquired were fabulous, discourse with crewfolk who had learned the tongue was as enlightening as it was astounding, and you didn't need speech—signs would do—to show the rest around and have fun with them. These advents lived on in memory, lifetime after lifetime. They conditioned the history.

Perhaps they gentled it. Brentans had their dark side, conflict, violence, oppression; but they never seemed to wreak the absolute horror humankind knew of, while concepts of peace and justice seemed to come easier. Scientific method was harder for them to grasp, whether for cultural or genetic reasons, but by now the Hrroch were in an industrial era, with steam power and mass production.

Had that somehow engaged too much of the spirit? Or did every civilization everywhere in the universe eventually expend its creativity? Already on her previous visit, *Fleetwing* had found the art disappointing. This time originality was well-nigh dead.

Not quite. A few brilliant new motifs shone like starbursts in a dark nebula. Kithfolk inquired. The work was from overseas, where colonists traded with the Susuich, the dwellers beyond the Cloudpeak Mountains.

Would the Susuich admit guests? Well, maybe. They were a clannish, reclusive folk. Some unfortunate incidents in the past had reinforced the attitude. No Hrroch any longer ventured west of the uplands. Humans, though, *starfarers,* were different. A party of them could fly to a trading post. Interpreters would be available.

Negotiations took a while. The rest of the crew didn't mind. A spell of leisure, on living turf beneath sun and leaves, on lakes and in breezes— they were shipfolk, spacefolk, but Earth was their grandmother and this half-Earth lifted from them some of a weariness so deep in the bones that they did not really know they bore it.

Word came at length. A flying vessel could touch down at the border village Chura. It could let two strangers off but must then immediately depart, returning only to fetch them at the same spot. A guide would take them as far as the town Ai. They must not expect admission to the Abode of Songs or other holy places. However, the chieftains were willing to discuss possible barter relations.

"Arrogant, aren't they?" Captain Graim said.

"I'd call it forlorn," Vodra replied. "They're bewildered, maybe terrified, but putting up a brave front. We need to respect it."

The need was not physical. The Kithfolk had guns, missiles, robots, every means of conquest. But that would destroy the very thing they sought, and also something within themselves.

"Agreements? Science? Trade? Corpses can't do anything!" Dau explained. "Besides, if w-w-we don't report in this evening—"

"I know," Vodra said. "Let me make the call."

Her own communicator was intact. Radio waves leaped aloft and back down to that settlement on the eastern seaboard where Arvil Kishna had brought the spaceboat he piloted. The signal activated the transceiver he carried on his person.

Dau stood by. He caught bare snatches of talk. The river boomed too loud, noise ringing off canyon walls. He shivered too hard. And he was not yet accustomed to the *Fleetwing* dialect.

Vodra put the unit back in her pocket. "He'll call Chura," she said. The Susuich had agreed to leaving a communicator there. "He'll ask its chief what can be done, if anything."

"But how . . ." The words faltered and died, for Vodra ignored them. She squatted down beside Ri and examined him more closely.

When she had finished he said, in his wretchedness, "You care more about him than us, don't you?"

"He's a thinking being, too," she answered sharply. "They all are, the Brentans. I've known them, off and on, for hundreds of their years"— while she herself had been through less than sixty. "Every time, it's hurt to say good-bye, knowing I'd never meet those friends again. I don't want to lose one more unnecessarily."

"I'm sorry," he said, contrite. "I shouldn't complain."

"Well, let's take care of ourselves . . . and him. First, out of these wet clothes. They make the windchill worse. We'll need them dry by nightfall."

He gulped but obeyed. For a moment, seeing her trim form, he reddened. She ended that by paying it no heed. Following her example, he spread his garments over bushes under the cliff. The gravel hurt his feet.

"How can a chief . . . yonder in the mountains . . . notify local people . . . to help us?" he asked.

"I don't know," she admitted, "but the bargaining about our visit went quicker than runners can account for. Drums, maybe." She gave him a close look. "You're shaking yourself to pieces."

"I'll t-try to keep warmer." He started jogging in place.

A laugh escaped her. "Bobblety, bobblety, bobblety! No, that won't work for long. Not at all for Ri. The trick will be to stay alive till help arrives. Or till the natives have tried and failed, and Arvil comes after us regardless."

"How?"

"I've had groundside experience, you know." Stooping, she drew the guide's big knife. While she whacked at the dead brush, she gave instructions. He was a novice, but like most Kithfolk he had passed considerable time in virtualities, which included forests, lifeways of the past, and the like. Cold lashed him. He quickly understood what she meant.

A shelter grew beneath their hands. Lop off a forked branch about a meter long. Prop it erect between rocks. Lay a three-meter length—that took some searching—with one end in the crotch, the other on the ground. Lean pieces against this, slanting, for ribs. Cut branches off live shrubs and trees. Weave them into the framework; their leaves make the beginning of walls. Stick lesser pluckings and cuttings in anywhere, anyhow, until the sides are closed. Throw boughs and leaves beneath, a carpet against the wet gravel. The work itself will force blood to move.

It was nearly done when their communicators buzzed. Vodra spoke with the pilot. "Yes, the chief wants to make a rescue attempt," she told Dau. "Arvil's not sure whether that's for the sake of pride or precedent or what. Nor can he make out how they propose to do it."

"Or if they can. . . . No. I said I wouldn't complain."

Vodra smiled and clapped the young man's shoulder. "Good. You *are* going to do well aboard *Fleetwing*. All right, let's complete our job."

She eased Ri into the shelter before laying a semicircle of stones before its entrance. "Reflector," she explained. Meanwhile Dau gathered firewood. A flamelighter from her coverall started a small blaze within the arc. They both crawled past, inside, and huddled together, hands spread toward their hearth.

Some warmth crept back into them. He glanced at her. Through the dusk he saw matted dark hair, sharp profile, firm breasts, flat belly. The crow's-feet and gray flecks didn't show; she could have been his age. Her flank glowed against his. She smelled of fire smoke and woman.

"You—you shouldn't be starfaring," he blurted. "You're meant for a pioneer."

She gave him back his look. "But I am a starfarer," she answered. "So are you. Or you'd have stayed groundside," when the *Argosy* crew voted to end their voyaging and disband, for the trade had grown too sparse to support every ship remaining in the regions that she plied, and too many among them had lost heart.

"Yes, starfaring was my life," he sighed, "and I'm lucky you happened to be there and would take me on." The flames cast slight, uneasy glimmers into the murk where they hunched. Outside, the river rumbled and hissed. "Though I can understand why most of us were glad to settle down on Harbor. It's . . . homelike. Compatible." He had said that often before. Today he went on: "Not like Aurora."

"*Fleetwing* hasn't touched at Aurora for about—a thousand years, I think," Vodra said slowly. "It isn't on any of our regular routes, you know. Nor do I recall much talk about it at any rendezvous we've made. Has it changed greatly?"

"Yes. I've watched it happening. Oh, they stayed friendly enough, in their outlandish way. And . . . last time we were there . . . they seemed more interested in what we had to offer, what we had to tell, than their, uh, their great-grandparents were the time before. But it was just novelty to them. Nothing important."

"I know. I've seen the same on Olivares. Different from Aurora, no doubt. In either case, no longer our civilization."

Serrated towers dispersed over lands apportioned according to intricate rules of kinship. Robes and masks worn in public. Ceremoniousness governing deadly feuds. Multisexual group marriages. Rank achieved by passing examinations, within a hierarchy serving a God who was a demiurge. . . . That was in the western hemisphere. People on the eastern continent were more enigmatic.

Not that any of them were hostile, or their societies worse than most. But they cared little about the stars or what starfarers brought.

"*Argosy* never got to Olivares," Dau said. "*Fleetwing*'s traveled farthest of any, hasn't she?"

"Maybe." How could you tell, when it was oftenest a matter of chance which ships you met at which world, after centuries? "And maybe that's why she keeps on traveling."

Was anything left of the original structure? A worn-out part here, a broken part there, replaced, as the millennia swept by. . . . Yes, that was also getting harder to do, repair facilities far-scattered and expensive. To be expected, when demand for their services dwindled. . . .

"I haven't asked this before." Was Dau seeking comfort in conversation? "Too much else to learn. You've kept exploring, going beyond known space, when others gave it up. Have you found any more planets where humans could live?"

"And there are no natives they'd have to dispossess? Yes, two possibilities. It didn't make a big stir when we mentioned it at rendezvous. Why should it? Who'd want them?"

None from Earth, probably, Earth from which the first seeds blew outward on a wind now stilled. Vodra was a child when *Fleetwing* last called there. She remembered talk of Seladorians everywhere, buyers nowhere, and Kith Town, well, tolerated. Afterward she seldom heard any suggestion of going back.

"From Harbor, at least," Dau said. "Dreamers. Malcontents. It's no paradise."

"No human place ever was." Vodra fed more sticks to the fire. It crackled and jumped, red, yellow, and blue. A bed of coals was forming. That was what would really see her and him and Ri through the night. "None ever will be, I suppose. But how many would go? How'd they pay for a migration? Those planets are not New Earths, any more than the rest were. Less than Harbor or two or three others, in fact. It'd take a huge investment, and then toil, sacrifice, death, for generations, before they were hospitable to our race."

"With nanotechnics and robotics to produce, Kith ships to ferry—"

"Where's the capital coming from? And we Kithfolk, we can't travel for nothing. We have to live, too, and meet our running expenses. If enough people wanted it enough—" Vodra shook her head. "But they don't."

"And so we limp along on whatever trade we can scrape up," Dau said bitterly. "More and more desperate. Like this excursion of ours here."

"Not desperation," she maintained. "Scientific interest, if nothing else. And the hope of something tradeworthy. Wait, I should check how Ri is doing."

She wriggled past him to hunker above the Brentan. Dau leaned over her shoulder. In the vague, shifty light he saw the chest rise and fall, the eyes partly open but blind. He heard how breath labored.

Vodra returned to the entrance. He joined her. "If he were human," he offered, "I'd say he's sinking."

She nodded. "Yes. I don't know how long he'll last without better help than we can give."

She stared beyond the low flames to the river, the opposite cliff, and the shadows. He barely caught what she murmured.

"Take down the sky.
We shall no longer hide from nothingness,
Now she is gone.

Or he," she added to herself.

"What?" he said, astonished. "Why, I know that poem. I love it."

She turned her face to him. "You do?"

"Yes. *'All daybreak broken—'* "

"Then it reached your ship, too? It's Brentan, you know."

"It is?"

"Oh, a translation, adapted for humans, of course. But we heard it in Hrrochan. Later we sold reproduction rights on Feng Huang, Harbor, and Maia for good sums." Defensively, because he was young, his ideals vulnerable: "Why not? Bringing it to them was a service."

"Of course. We dealt in information, too, in *Argosy*. It wasn't that kind, though, at least not often."

"They're wonderfully musical and poetical everywhere on Brent, as far as we've seen. Maybe that's due to the nature of their speech. If we can get the Susuich to trust us— That cultural treasure their religion keeps hoarded—"

"Yes, I heard."

"I'm sorry, Dau. I don't mean to be patronizing. I'm tired, my skull's empty, I babble about whatever sounds hopeful."

"I'm glad you do," he said. "It keeps me going."

They drew closer.

Nothing untoward happened. He was bashful and she was wise. After a while their clothes were dry enough to don. Yet those hours lived always within them. Long afterward, when he was the newly chosen captain of *Fleetwing*, he would order an energy gun to engrave her name on a loose asteroid, a memorial among the stars.

Night fell. Chill deepened. The fire wavered, but heat radiated from its bed and the stones beyond. The humans dozed.

A cry roused them—not a shout, a triumphant skirling, like the pipes of ancient warriors bound into battle. They jerked awake and stumbled forth. A full moon had risen over the eastern steeps. Its light flickered and flared on the river. A creature like a gigantic snake, head high, surged downstream, coil upon coil swinging to and fro to drive it onward. Half a dozen Brentans rode on its back. When they saw the pair on the shore they and their mount swept into the shallows. They sprang off.

Vodra beckoned at the shelter. One who must be some kind of physician went inside. His night vision was superior to hers. When he came out, another interpreted for him: "We shall care for Ri here until he is ready for carrying elsewhere. He will live and regain health. You have done well."

A third, with a bronze armlet that seemed to betoken authority, touched a fourth and spoke. The interpreter said: "As for you two, K'hraich will now guide you. When you reach Ai, you may enter the Abode of Songs."

47.

Earth shone in the viewscreen as the brightest among the stars, lapis lazuli, with Luna a nearby point of tarnished gold. To Nansen in his command center, it was as if nothing had changed, as if he had never been away. Observation of them and their sister planets gave the exact time span. A few millennia were not enough for chaos to change their orbits beyond calculation.

Lives—of humans, civilizations, dreams—went faster. The length of recorded history had—what? tripled?—through how many births and agings and deaths, end to end, since last he beheld his world?

Envoy would not get there for another day. How slowly it passed. Already, though, her crew spent most of their waking hours at duty stations, straining to discern and understand and keep guard against whatever the unknown might cast at them. Only Nansen was idled. The captain must hold himself ready to decide and command. But nothing happened except reports, and thus far the data were sparse. It was a lonely feeling. Silence pressed in on him.

Dayan's voice broke it, urgent over the intercom. "Hold. Another signal just registered. It goes on."

"I have it, too," said Yu. "Here's a visual." The display appeared for Nansen also. To him it was like previous ones, shifting waveforms, a graphical equivalent rendered by a computer as an aid to study.

Dayan sighed. "The same kind as the rest."

Sundaram repeated his earlier judgment: "No language. A stereotyped code."

"Signals between robots," Yu agreed. Radio and laser beams that *Envoy* chanced to intercept along her path.

Strange. Shouldn't the technology be far advanced, undetectable by mere antennae? Or maybe this ought not to be surprising.

"Is everything in Solar space robotic?" wondered Mokoena. She spoke from Sundaram's workroom. On the return voyage she had learned sufficient linguistics to become his assistant.

Nansen harked back to telescopic glimpses of a few asteroids and Mars as the ship moved inward. "Off Earth, evidently yes," he said. "And minimal." *Industries, settlements, human presence growing when we left, the germs of whole new nations—empty now, abandoned, one with Nineveh and Tyre.*

Mokoena's tone shuddered. "What of Earth itself?" Their transmissions ahead had drawn no response.

Zeyd avoided the worst inference. "A limited economy. Not necessarily impoverished. It could recycle with high efficiency to support a small, stable population." Machinery purred around his words. For his part, he had qualified himself for second engineer, not expert but able to take routine off Yu's hands.

"Like Tahir," she said. "People who have turned their backs on space."

Nansen looked past Earth to the stars. They shone cold and remote. None of the rare traces of travel had seemed to touch Sol, coming or going.

Dayan's dispassion cracked. "Why the devil don't we make directly for where the last starships are?"

"Earth is the mother world," Sundaram said gently.

"Yes," Mokoena added. "Don't you care to know what she's become?"

"And we promised we would come back," Nansen finished.

To eyes watching from polar orbit, the planet danced from day to night and back to dawn, agelessly beautiful. Still were the oceans a thousand shades of blue, burnished under the sun, starlit and moonlit after dark. Still did land masses sprawl, green, tawny, dun, in their familiar shapes. Cloud dappled the whole with fleeces and great swirls. The ice caps reached farther than formerly; snowfields ruled over most mountains. But this had merely enriched the temperate zones and mildened the tropics. In the cold valley of the glacial cycle, technics held global winter at bay.

Subtle arts, Nansen thought when he studied the instrument readouts. More carbon dioxide and methane than he once breathed—not that he'd notice the difference—and doubtless the concentration was well controlled. However, that couldn't be the whole story; the factors and interactions that make climates are millionfold. If a cybernetic system maintained this balance, it could not simply measure physical quantities and compute how much of what should be increased or decreased. It must be integrated with the ecology, the entire living world; for life is itself a geological force.

Installations seen on Luna and in Earth orbit strengthened his impression of a system complex, powerful, and self-sufficient. Though none aboard *Envoy* could tell what those domes, dishes, towers, lattices, and less nameable structures were for, she picked up indications of solar energy collected and beamed to chosen Earthside locations that varied minute by minute; and there appeared to be a widespread, buried electrical network, coupled to nodal points where buildings clustered aboveground.

Otherwise they saw something like an Eden. It was no single garden. Down from tundra and taiga swept wind-billowing steppes; boreal forest yielded to broadleaf woods and these to jungle; wings stormed above marshes and along seashores; plantations and croplands mingled in, not as conquerors but as parts of a planetary whole. Habitation was in scattered villages and a few small, compact cities. Traffic between was thin and largely aerial. No galaxies of illumination clustered on the dark side, though Nansen speculated that lighting was designed to minimize sky glow.

Alone in the command center, he heard Yu report yet another fruitless attempt at making contact. "Again, nothing."

"I wish we had the Holont trick in our hardware," snapped Dayan. "Give their damned electronics a good shaking."

"Patience," Mokoena advised. "We can't expect their equipment to be compatible with ours, can we?"

"We can expect some technical wit," Dayan retorted. "And even some provision for our return."

"After eleven thousand years?" gibed Zeyd.

"Keep trying," Nansen said.

Abruptly the formlessness in his outercom screen coalesced into a face.

Dayan whooped. "Transmission from the ground! They've figured our system out!"

"What breed of human is that?" breathed Mokoena.

Nansen stared. The head was both long and wide, the features male but beardless, skin amber, shoulder-length hair reddish black, nose thin, lips full, eyes big and violet. The mouth opened. Musical syllables resounded.

"More to the point," Sundaram asked, awe in his tone, "what language is that?"

"Over to you, Ajit," Nansen said for them all.

It went quickly. A few computer-generated pictures and diagrams established the fact of *Envoy*'s journey and the approximate date of her departure from Sol. Then it was a matter of trying out ancient languages lying in scholarly databases. When this brought forth Chinese, Sundaram explained that English was the mutual tongue aboard. Presently he could call his shipmates to join him in the common room. They sat, in their various degrees and ways of tension, before the big screen they had used for entertainments. Dayan had reprogrammed the system for two-way transmission.

The groundside scene was of graceful columns and ogive windows open on a garden. A line of men in close-fitting green uniforms were perhaps an honor guard, though they bore no visible weapons. Their features were varied; races had not completely melted together. In the foreground a tall woman in a flowing, iridescent robe occupied an elevated seat. She was of the type the crew had first seen. Her coifed head bore a golden circlet from which arched two stylized wings. Beside her stood a stubby, balding man, dark white. His long tunic and flared trousers were gray, nondescript, carelessly worn. "A professor, I'll bet," Dayan whispered into Nansen's ear. He tried not to smile, as solemn as they seemed on Earth.

The woman crossed hands on breast. Nansen rose, gave her a salute, and sat down again. She spoke. When she stopped, the little man piped up. "The Unifier Areli bids peace, pax, calm, harmony," he said. His accent made the English hard to follow.

"Thank you," Nansen replied. "We are peaceful, too, of course. I gather that you know what our mission was."

"I finded mention in databases. Rare. Many records lost. Most that concern *Envoy* be from *Ronai-li*—they say Kith—stories, songs of they."

"Doesn't even the Kith, whoever they are, remember us better?" Mokoena muttered.

The man had been translating for the woman, who sat impassive. However, perhaps he heard, for he turned back and explained, "Few, few Kith visits. Prior—lastest one, more than three hundred years in past. Near-lastest, a century more soon. Some Kith—" He searched, found the word, and finished: "Kith folklore was collected. *Envoy* be in it."

"But they've essentially forgotten us here on Earth," Yu said.

"Eleven thousand years," Sundaram told her. "Periods of turmoil, apparently. A great deal was inevitably lost, including from computer files."

"If they were interested, they would have gotten it back."

"But there are humans at other stars, are there not?" Nansen asked intently. "Some ships travel yet, don't they? You must be in contact."

"*Irb,* yes, news by laser." The man shrugged, a gesture that included bridging the fingers. "From far places." Mostly irrelevant, his tone implied. He smiled. "You have big news, no? Interested, we."

"A novelty," Zeyd growled aside to Mokoena. "The ship back from Punt, with pygmies to amuse Queen Hatshepsut. Are we much more significant?"

Again the man was bringing his leader(?) au courant. When his attention returned, Nansen said, "You evidently do not know our names.

Allow me to introduce us. I am Ricardo Nansen, the captain." He didn't give it in full. Hispanic nomenclature had frequently confused foreigners—when there was a Spanish language, a Paraguay, an *estancia*. He went around his group.

"I be Lonnor, student, expert, professional of beginning robotic period," the man replied. Areli spoke to him. "We be—we are uncertain of biosafety," he conveyed. "You have data, text, virtuals?"

Mokoena took the word. "Of course. Don't worry about any diseases we might carry. We left with none and haven't been exposed to anything we could catch, or that could infect Earth life generally."

"Biology changed be possible."

"M-m, yes." She rubbed her chin. "We could be a hazard," she said to the others. "Our *E. coli*, for example, may be exotic and dangerous now. Or there could be something that we have no immunity to. Yes, a quarantine period is needed." To Lonnor: "I will see about sending you our complete biological and medical file, right down to the DNA." Her teeth flashed. "And I'll be fascinated by what you give us." Zeyd nodded vigorously.

"Meanwhile," Sundaram proposed, "we can exchange every kind of information."

"We should be able to rig compatible virtual-reality sets," Dayan added eagerly.

"Yes, yes, we hope," Lonnor agreed. "Many future-want—will want—to meet you."

"In person?" demanded Yu.

"No easy bring you down." Lonnor considered. "You have vehicles for make-land?"

"I think it would be best if we don't use our boat," Nansen said slowly. *Our single remaining boat.* "Nor should we all go at once."

It wasn't that anybody was likely hostile. Still, theirs was a totally foreign world; and the knowledge *Envoy* carried was beyond price. Come worst to worst, crewfolk who had stayed aboard must steer her elsewhere and reveal what she had.

Nonetheless— His gaze went to the viewscreen which Earth filled with her glory. How could he go without at least once more feeling her caress in his feet and bones, while her winds kissed him farewell?

48.

They had never heard of a field drive here, or apparently anywhere in the space known to man. Was that historical accident, or did the invention require a Tahirian kind of quantum mechanical insight, guided perhaps by hints the Holont gave those visitors before they fled from it and withdrew from the stars?

"Don't be too specific with your colleagues, darling, about this or anything else," Nansen warned Dayan. "Not till we understand the situation better."

"It won't be hard to stay vague." She chuckled. "Right now, it's impossible not to, what with the communication barrier." Her mood sank. "Besides, I have a feeling they're not particularly anxious to learn."

"Really? Have you any idea why?"

"I get a powerful impression that to them, for God knows how long, science has not been a search but a body of knowledge. Almost like a theology, though without the religious kind of passion." She forced a grin. "They've elaborated their interpretations of natural law and how it works—I'm tempted to compare them to rabbis and the Torah, century after century—but anything really new, calling for reconstruction work on the foundations, that'll be very hard to accept. My guess is that this generation, and probably the next, never will."

Mokoena and Zeyd reported a similar attitude toward their scientific fields. Nobody disputed that there could always be surprises. Certainly, what the travelers had to relate excited an interest that in some individuals became enthusiasm. However, this was detail, another example of what well-established principles could lead to. Tahirian psychology—

history, culture, entire perception of reality—drew still less heed. Dayan interpreted the placid reaction as, "So it's alien, so what?"

Yu said that while technology was obviously high, little appeared to have changed for millennia, except that some parts of it had been dropped because they no longer served any useful purpose. That did not necessarily imply decadence, she remarked. After all, in her birth era people hadn't built Roman-style aqueducts or gigantic hydroelectric dams. The sort of competitiveness that drove material innovation, whether or not there was any current need for it, was simply not in this society.

Once translator programs were available, conversations went more easily, with a wide variety of persons. Likewise, guides conducted virtual-reality tours of the world, walks through its important or beautiful sights, into worksteads and museums(?) and homes, nearly anywhere requested. Notwithstanding, comprehension continued to be elusive. Capitalism, socialism, despotism, democracy, every arrangement the crew remembered, seemed now as inconsequential as mercantile guilds or divine right of kings had been to them.

It was clear that robotics and nanotechnology had made all necessities, services as well as goods, and perhaps all comforts, too, free, like air and sunshine. There was presumably some way to control their distribution and maintain a stable population, but whatever coercion this required was not obvious. "Probably social pressure does most of the work," Nansen speculated. "The great majority likes things as they are."

Yet, talking among each other, the *Envoy* company came to wonder if "stagnation" meant anything, either, on this world in this age. "The equilibrium may be more stable than any of the long-lived human civilizations of the past achieved," Sundaram mused, "and that may in large part be due to the fact that, no matter how much internal variegation it enjoys, it is now the only civilization on Earth. The thread of communication with the local stars and the very rare visit of a starship apparently have even less effect than its slight contact with the Roman Empire had on Han Dynasty China. Nevertheless, people have spoken to me of progress. I do not yet grasp quite what they mean by that." He spread his hands. "Spiritual? Humanistic? I think we shall need a long intimacy before we can begin to understand."

And then we may not like what we learn, Nansen refrained from saying.

Bringing him and Zeyd down was an awkward business, which required much advance planning. Flesh and blood no longer made passages across interplanetary space. Those who wished to experience sister globes contented themselves with virtuals. That art was well beyond anything of eleven millennia ago. The fact that no one seemed addicted to it said something profound about their society, but the newcomers weren't sure what.

In the end, the two men crossed from the ship to the robotic boat in their spacesuits.

"I *am* sorry," Nansen told Dayan, holding her close to him in their cabin just before he went. "It does feel like a dirty, selfish trick on you. But—"

"But you've explained the reasons, and they're valid, and mainly, I'm going to miss you like hell. So shut up already and give me a last big, wet kiss." She grabbed his ears and pulled his head down to her lips.

Areli the Unifier herself had suggested that the first visit, perhaps all, be by a small party and discreetly handled. *Envoy*'s arrival had roused "strong general interest." (Sundaram had an idea that no word for "sensation" existed, that the culture valued tranquility, self-control, and good manners too much. "Confucian?" asked Yu, and answered herself: "No, doubtless no analogy really fits.") It had been necessary to screen applicants for direct contact with the crew, and millions had tuned in on each conversation. ("Well, we are extraordinary," Mokoena observed, "although I won't be surprised if most of them stop caring in a few more months.") A conspicuous, publicized group would be everywhere encumbered by well-meaning crowds, besieged with invitations, swept off to festivities. ("Which seems to contradict your view of the zeitgeist, Ajit," Dayan remarked, "except that, no matter how persuasive their social conditioning methods are, I don't believe they can make everybody identical. It could even be that a few cranks would try to attack us.") If the honored guests from the remote past wished to walk again on their mother world, best they go essentially incognito.

That suited Nansen well—so well that he came to suppose his original dim suspicions had been unjust. *Which perhaps helps show how foreign Earth has really become,* he thought with a slight shiver.

The question was who should go first. His overriding priority was the safeguarding of the knowledge his expedition had brought back, and getting it to those humans to whom it would make a difference.

He considered: Yu, engineer, interpreter of technical data from Tahir and the star cluster. Dayan, physicist, who came closer than anyone else to comprehending what the Holont had had to tell; furthermore, along the way Nansen had given her simulations and a little practice in flying *Courier*, so that she was his auxiliary pilot. Mokoena, who could delegate her biology to the computers but not her hands or her presence as a healer. Sundaram, linguist, the nearest thing the ship had to an anthropologist, who could do his work over the laser channels while reserving himself for the folk of other stars. All, Nansen judged, indispensable. That left him and Zeyd.

His decision had raised only minor protest, which soon died. The years and the light-years had knit them that closely together.

Zeyd's appointed (anointed?) guide was a young man called Mundival, of Areli's mixed-race type. Mnemonic induction techniques had given him a good command of English as reconstructed from the databases. He was ardent, well-nigh worshipful; he could not hear enough about starfaring and its pioneer days, or do enough for the starfarer. Just the same, Zeyd couldn't help envying, a bit, Nansen, who'd gotten a most attractive young woman. Not that either of them would— However— Oh, well.

Mundival proposed a walk through a city. Clothes varied broadly, sometimes fantastically, according to individual choice within parameters Zeyd had not learned. Dressed in inconspicuous tunics and trousers, they two wandered along the paths that wound over a high hill and around its foot. It was late spring in the northern hemisphere, a season of jubilance after the stark winter of these parts. Sunlight spilled across blossoms and leaves. Trees vibrated with wings and carols. A breeze drifted sweet. Dwellers went loosely clad, children skipping, youth and maiden hand in hand, elders dignified but generally cheerful. Sometimes a car purred by, robotic, more often carrying loads than passengers.

Elya occupied a height between two landscapes. Westward swept plains of grass, dotted with stands of trees, where wild herds roamed— big animals, brown and shaggy, developed from lesser creatures to replace the extinct grazers that belonged in such an ecosystem. East and north the terrain dropped to an enormous bottomland, intensively cultivated. There it was robots that moved, tending the biosynthetic plantations, processing the products.

The population here numbered some one hundred thousand. Most of them lived in houses set well apart among gardens and groves. Their places of business were similarly modest, schools, shops, ateliers, inns, decorous recreational establishments. Many served pilgrims to the Sanctuary and the shrines nearby. That quasi-temple rose majestic above surrounding trees, natural stone carved with an exuberance of foliage, flowers, fruits, and vines, towers branching like boughs against the sky. When the Sanctuary sang, the music went as waterfall, thunder, and joy from horizon to horizon.

No two the same, other buildings were mainly underground, with only an upper level in the air. Passing an especially curious structure, drapelike curves in blue-and-white stripes surmounted by a roof that was a living organism, Zeyd confessed, "In spite of my virtual tours, I am afraid everything is rather bewildering to me."

"I ammed—I was not certain how it would be for you, sir," Mundival replied. "We lost so much information during the evil millennia. And what we keep is too much for one human brain."

Yes, Zeyd reflected, the total might be fragmentary but must be overwhelming. How closely could he number the rulers of medieval Egypt or say what their individual fortunes had been? "This is marvelous, of course. Is it typical?"

"Not truly. No place is. This one is more historic than most."

Mundival gestured at some nearby remnants of massive walls, recalling ages when men thought and wrought larger than now. City lay buried upon city beneath Elya, the whole way down to Chicago. Micromachines had done the archeological work on them centuries ago. Ruins like these were merely curiosa.

Like a ship from that same past?

"Elsewhere is different," Mundival said. "I believe you have seen. You shall betread if you wish. Territories, biomes, inhabitants, lives, all be— are different, all around Earth. Life varies." He searched for a word. "Spontaneity is life, Selador taught."

Zeyd frowned, picking his own words with care. "Forgive me, but I still don't quite understand. I gather that religions, customs, even laws vary from group to group, and each develops as it chooses, or splits off to start something new. Doesn't that lead to conflict?"

"All are Seladorian," Mundival said earnestly. "Different deity or none, different usage, yes, but all accept the oneness of life. That means, too, the oneness of humans." He hesitated. "It shalled—it should."

Zeyd knew of no faith that had ever brought universal harmony. He wondered how meaningful these cultural uniquenesses were, and what measures were now and then necessary to maintain the global peace. Regardless of what it called itself, he didn't think Seladorianism was just a philosophy.

"But not many believe this out among the stars?" he asked cautiously.

"No. It is far to there, and they are strange—"

The young voice did not condemn; suddenly it throbbed. The young face glowed. *Perhaps,* Zeyd thought, with a tingle through his nerves, *we are not quite living fossils after all.*

A vast lake, almost an inland sea, filled the heart of what was once Paraguay. Its creation had been part of the general transformation of Earth through several centuries. Machines, most of them millionfold and invisibly small, kept watch over it, monitoring, correcting, guiding the further evolution of lake, land, and life. Yet as he stood on the shore, to Nansen it seemed as if newly come from the hand of God.

Water sheened argent to the edge of sight. The sun was a great gold-orange globe wheeling down to the horizon. It cast a molten bridge toward him, which broke up in little fires where wavelets lapped in the shallows and lost themselves among reeds. Sometimes a fish leaped, like a meteor that rose before it fell. Wings swarmed through deepening, nearly cloudless blue overhead; cries drifted faintly across distance. Ashore, enormous blossoms and delicate tall trees were new to him, engineered for subtle purposes, but they perfumed the evening coolness and drew an arabesque over heaven.

"Yes," he said after silence had grown long, "my forebears rest in a good place."

"I am glad you are pleased," answered Varday. She touched his arm. "We had better turn back. The guests will be arriving."

He took a moment to enjoy the sight of her in the sunset glow. Like Zeyd's companion, she was of the Unifier's type. Early on, he had suppressed an impulse to ask exactly how equal everybody was. Let it suffice him that the breed was a handsome one—in her case, lovely, for she was gracefully formed, with hair a dark ruddy cascade over bare, amber-hued shoulders.

"Yes, that's right," he agreed. "I look forward to meeting them." They fell into step over the soft turf.

"You are kind to permit that I invite my friends." Her voice flowed easily, melodiously. Accent added charm. "They were delighted."

"Well, you have been more than kind to me. Besides, I do want to meet people, not in masses or at some official function, but individually."

"I wish conversation could be more free. If you were willing to undergo a mnemonic in a modern language—"

"No, thanks." He had more than once declined the neurological process. "First I should get a general impression of your world. There'll be time later, if we so decide." He knew his—and Zeyd's—excuse was lame, but neither cared to say outright that he didn't entirely trust whatever else the program might instill.

Varday lapsed into the solemnity of youth. "You cannot know the spirit of a people unless you speak with them unrestricted."

Nansen shrugged. "Not always then, either." *Or ever? Are they any more candid today than in the ancient past?*

Varday nodded. "That is true. We may have changed too much from what the star folk are. Often since you came I have wondered if that may not be the deep reason why the Kith scarcely ever call on us."

"Oh, surely not. You aren't hostile to them in any way, as I've heard people once were."

Varday shivered in the breeze. "People were not sane."

He tried to drive off the specter with dryness. "From what I've gathered—tell me if I'm mistaken—there simply isn't a trade to ply. Planets, or at least planetary systems, have long since become self-sufficient. They don't need to import. Newness, fresh ideas, or stories—but this culture of yours, here on Earth, isn't much interested even in that."

It comforted neither of them. *Is any culture anywhere?* he thought, with recollections of recorded communications from other stars. *No voyages now seem to go past the sphere of the known, if only because the radius has grown too great and nobody wants the fate of* Envoy. *As ships die or their crews disband, they are not replaced. . . .*

And she exclaimed: "It shouldn't be so! *We* shouldn't be!" She gulped. "I used to think about this sometimes. And then you came back to us."

They walked on. The sun was down, the sky still bright in the west, but dusk seeped from the ground and spread from the east with the swiftness of these latitudes. Lights began to twinkle in the village ahead. A tune chimed.

Varday tossed her head. The hair rippled along her back. "This is to be a happy occasion," she declared. "Forgive my loss of laughter."

It was not the first time he had seen sudden melancholy fall on her as they traveled about. She bounced back equally fast, with cheer to lighten his own inner darknesses. "You'll make it be, my friend," he said.

They entered the village. It was in and of this clime, houses square, earth-toned, each surrounding a garden court. Only the local Sanctuary, foam white tower with a helical spire in which rainbow colors played by day, stood out. Residents wandered the streets, relaxing in the cool. Mostly they wore white robes and headcloths, trimmed with bright colors. Pet animals were popular, cockatoos on wrists, long-legged hounds, vividly marked cats, creatures more exotic. Where illumination fell strongest, several artists and musicians followed their callings. Nansen did not recognize the implements and instruments. Everybody greeted him and Varday as they passed. He had merely been named to them as a visitor from elsewhere. That was no novelty.

The mansion stood on the far edge of town, not very big though ornamented with pilasters, changing iridescences, and a winged cupola. Varday had explained that it belonged to an association of which she was a member, and currently she had the use of it. Bubblelike aircars had already delivered some guests and returned to wait for the next demand for their services. More set down while the door parted for Nansen and his guide.

Inside was a chamber where abstract murals slowly refashioned themselves, aromas wafted, and music played in the background—music resurrected from his era, mainly by transmission from *Envoy*'s database, in his honor. A buffet stood generously spread. Food and drink were excellent nowadays, though moderation in both appeared to be universal. Most of the gathering were young. They merged zestfully around the starfarer, without pressure or presumption, informal because etiquette and restraint were ingrained.

Of course they wanted to hear about his voyage. The basic account had gone worldwide, but incidents, anecdotes, sidelights must be numberless. Nansen spent the next two or three hours largely seated, talking. Beside him, Varday held a small device programmed to translate back and forth. She was right, it didn't make for intimate conversation, but it served well enough here.

"... and we left the star cluster and continued on our way," he said.

"Does it abide in its unhappy state?" asked one girl.

He shrugged. "We can only answer that by going back."

She hugged herself. "I will never be able to see it again without a shudder."

"It's like something out of Earth's blackest past," said another.

"Oh, now," countered a young man, "that was a rousing story."

"A dreadful story," maintained a second youth. "Forgive me, Captain Nansen, but if mistakes lead to madness among the far stars, too, we are well free of them all."

Some assented, some frowned. Nansen went quickly on to milder tales.

Later there was dancing. Varday had learned some steps from his time and was his sole partner. The rest made a game of devising their own to fit the archaic melodies. She was warm and lithe in his arms.

After a span he didn't measure she suggested some fresh air. A couple already out in the court murmured a salutation and returned inside. Tact?

The door contracted behind them and shut off sound from within. Early dew on roses glimmered beneath stars and Milky Way.

"You have a beautiful world here," he said. "I didn't hope to find anything like this."

I hoped to find humans in the freedom of the galaxy, and something of its grandeur in their spirits.

She nodded. How slender her neck was, beneath the heavy hair. "Three thousand years of peace."

"Thanks to . . . Selador." *Who seems to have done better than the Christ they seem to have forgotten.*

"And those who came after, martyrs, preachers, workers." Her basic seriousness was again upon her. "To this very day. Each one of us, in every generation, must do the work over again."

"How?" he wondered.

"Against the beast that is born in us. We must never let down our defense or believe the past is safely dead."

He knew that education included virtual experiences of former events. It struck him now that some of those must be cruel. Psychotherapy afterward could take away the pain, but the scars would remain, reminding. *Could this whole civilization be a retreat from the horror that was history?* "Peace." He was unable not to ask: "Do you never grow restless?"

"Of course we do." She sounded defensive. "We make our adventures." *Yes, I've seen some recordings of breakneck sports.*

"And we create," Varday said.

When did anyone last create anything really new? He had inquired, during his long-range dialogues while he lingered in quarantine orbit. Artists of every sort—yes, and scientists—were evidently satisfied to play variations on themes long canonical. Most effort and ardor went into exploring and re-enacting the accumulated works of the ages. No one lifetime sufficed to exhaust that heritage.

"Not everybody can be . . . original, can they?" he demurred, then feared she might take offense.

She did not. Looking up at him, her eyes were big and abrim with starlight. "No, not in public ways," she answered softly. "But everyone can make life itself the highest art."

Her invitation was unmistakable. They had been well behaved throughout, by his standards. Hers—? A wish stirred—would Hanny really mind?

As if summoned, a spark rose over the westside roof and hastened across the stars. "Why, look," he said, and realized how relieved he felt, "I do think that's *Envoy*."

Probably she recognized his tone. Probably she wasn't too disappointed. She spoke gravely. "Your ship. Your life's meaning."

He glanced his startled question at her.

"We of Earth today seek what we may find in ourselves," she told him. "You seek elsewhere, outward."

Did her voice tremble the least bit?

*   *   *

From the southeastern shore of the Mediterranean Sea, down over the Arabian peninsula to its end—though neither of these bore the names Zeyd remembered—was rain forest. Nor did he know most of its plants and animals. Many had not existed when he left home.

He stood with Mundival at the edge of a clearing. Ferns brushed his calves, wet, a touch of cold here where sultriness hung on after dark. Below a black wall of trees, a fire blazed and roared. Flamelight wavered on smoke; sparks leaped. Before it bulked an altar hewn from a stone. A hundred or more people were gathered in front, naked to the night. This was their form of Sanctuary, their unifying and affirming ritual.

Robed at the altar, their leader lifted her arms on high. "In the name of Selador," she chanted, "oneness." Mundival whispered a translation in Zeyd's ear.

"Helui ann! Helui ann!" boomed the response. Mundival did not render it. Perhaps he couldn't.

"For everything that is life, oneness."

"Helui ann! Helui ann!"

And yet at home they lived and worked, in their scattered communities, as members of global civilization, made trips everywhere around the planet, partook of its all-embracing communications web. Two or three of them had shown Zeyd around, and through Mundival had described rationally—with a certain passion, but rationally—something of the balance between humankind and nature in this land, a balance not only ecological but sacred.

The liturgy went on. Drums and whistles joined in. The people began to sway and stamp their feet.

The voice grew shrill. ". . . bring down the falsehoods of the Biosophists . . ."

A carnivore screamed, somewhere off in the dark. Zeyd wondered how serene Earth really was and how long its peace could endure.

Kith Town lay empty save for robotic caretakers, a museum of antiquity. The styles, furnishings, possessions in its buildings had changed over the millennia, but gradually and never entirely. Even the newest homes, forsaken just centuries ago, haunted Nansen with hints of his childhood.

Visitors were rare. Anyone who felt curious could employ a virtual. However, a service center included sleeping quarters.

Nansen got up before dawn. Varday waited outside her adjacent room, as they had agreed. He didn't want to say more than a good morning, and her culture put her under no compulsion to talk. They went silently out together, into silence.

It was cold; breath smoked, barely visible by starshine. Murk overspread the hemmed-in street. Footfalls rang hollow.

The houses ended at a sharp and ancient boundary. With the sky clear above them, the pair saw better. A few lights glimmered on the ground afar, lost beneath the stars. Closer by, snags of walls and pits that had been foundations broke the gray of hoarfrosted grass and brush. From time to time, a city had engulfed the starfarers' dwelling place.

"They come no more," Varday said, barely loud enough for him to hear, and needlessly, except for whatever need was in her. "It is so seldom a ship arrives, and so brief a while. The crew stay in a hostel, or they stay aboard."

Do they sense they are no longer wanted? Nansen thought. *Their wares are of no more use. The stories and questions they brought from beyond were often troublesome.*

He stopped and looked aloft. She did, too. Constellations had changed shape, not greatly but noticeably. He pointed toward what he knew as Ursa Minor. "See," he told her, "there was our North Star." It was Delta Cygni now, not very near the celestial pole.

"Does it still call to you?" she asked, as low as before.

Impulsively, he threw his cloak around them both and his arm around her waist. Nothing more happened between them. They stood side by side waiting for the sun.

A lodge lay in the Himalayan foothills, surrounded by beauty. Isolated, robotically tended, it had no other guests at the moment than the travelers and their guides. They met in a room too big for four, where colors flickered in the walls, a symphony of birdsongs played, and drifting odors stirred obscure feelings.

"Yes, we've decided between us," Nansen said. "The others would like to set foot on Earth, too, but only in a few special lands." *Only for piety's sake, or to seek a final forgetting of what is no more.* "After that, we go away."

"Why?" protested Mundival.

"We have nothing to do on Earth," Nansen replied. "Yonder, we may."

"You are welcome here! You would be heroes all your lives!"

Zeyd looked into the troubled countenance and answered as gently as might be, "Yes, we could do well as storytellers, no doubt. But what of our children?"

"They will be welcome, too—"

"Welcome to become Earthfolk. I'm sorry. I don't say that would be bad." Zeyd tried to smile. "They might find more happiness in your ways than in ours. But we are starfolk."

Jean's folk, thought Nansen.

Varday stood up from her seat and held her arms out to him. For the first time, he saw tears start forth upon her. They gleamed down the amber cheeks. "Then will you take me with you?" she cried.

49.

The young Venture League had acquired an old building in Argosy for its headquarters. Its academy occupied one suite on the seventh floor. But then, that school for starfarers was still unborn, little more than a dream and some experimental programs. It would not want a campus until the starships that were themselves, as yet, little more than plans in computers began to be built.

If ever they did.

The room where Ricardo Nansen and Chandor Barak sat was light and spacious. Opalescence swirled like slow smoke in walls and ceilings, except for the fourth wall, which stood open on a balcony. There flowers glowed in planters—geraniums, marigolds, forget-me-nots, because Harbor had never evolved much in the way of blossoms. Air flowed warm, bearing murmurs of the city. Though it was summer in this hemisphere, to Earthside eyes the sunshine spilling from the blue would have had a mellow, autumnal quality. By now Nansen was used to it, and Chandor's people had been on the planet almost since *Envoy* first departed from Sol.

Like many of them, the director and prospective commander of the academy was medium tall, with tan complexion and features that bore memories of northern Asia. However, his eyes were green and the mustache and bobbed hair dark blond. Somewhat of a dandy, today he wore a purple blouse with upward-flaring red collar, rainbow-striped kilt, and gold trim on his floppy half-boots. Otherwise there was nothing foppish about him, and the fact that his mother, Chandor Lia, was president of the Duncanian continent had not been decisive in choosing him for this post. It hadn't hurt, but what counted was that he had proved himself an able administrator who shared the dream.

"Yes, we have to ride the comet," he was saying. Nansen, who had gained fluency in the language but hadn't encountered all its idioms, was momentarily puzzled, then translated from context, "catch the tide" or "strike while the iron is hot."

How much else don't I know yet? The question pierced him daily. And he hadn't even been very active in public affairs. Steering from Sol to Tau Ceti . . . tumultuous welcome . . . appearances, interviews, celebrations . . . lectures, conferences, helping interpret the torrent of data downloaded from his ship . . . getting Hanny and himself established, the whole crew, and that handful of Earthlings who threw everything away that they might go with him to an unknown destiny. . . . The years stormed through memory.

He hauled his attention back to Chandor. If his influence—and, yes, the substantial sum he became able to contribute—had made the founding of the League possible, then it behooved him to answer this appeal for his help.

The director leaned forward, intent and intense. "Our beginning may have been too successful," he said. "We're in danger of being over-whelmed. Hundreds of youngsters are applying, clamoring, to us. If we can organize them into a nucleus, something active, actually taking the first steps forward, we'll recruit thousands, around the globe and throughout the system. But if we don't show any real accomplishment soon, I'm afraid the excitement, the support, will die."

"That fast?"

"There'll be forces working to quench it. Are you aware, sir, what powerful interests are against us? They look on our goal as insane. They don't believe a serious revival of starfaring is possible. They want the capabilities you've brought developed and used at home for undertakings they know will be profitable."

Nansen scowled. "This is a free society, isn't it? How can they forbid us applying our knowledge to make money and spending the money as we see fit?"

"They have funds, resources, and influence of their own, more than we'll have for years. They can undercut our fledgling businesses, put pressure on those who'd help us with financing, and flood the world with disparaging, discouraging propaganda. I've reason to think they're already subsidizing the Seladorian missionaries."

"Can a few evangelists make any difference in the time span that concerns us?"

"If the eloquent preaching the laser beams carry from Earth gets featured regularly in major news media, perhaps yes. What you have revealed is so new. How many people have understood the implications? For millennia we've been resigned to—the stars only lights in the sky, a few threads of communication, a rare ship with an alien, clannish crew."

"Do you seriously think we're threatened?"

"No, not really, thus far," Chandor admitted. "I fear we soon can be, but it need not happen if we keep our momentum—and if we don't suffer some major setback; but that's beyond our control.

"And so, Captain Nansen, I believe we must take the wave of hopefulness you've raised and give it the impetus to mount higher. We should begin accepting recruits now, start their education, prepare them to receive the next Kith vessel and befriend her people. She may arrive at any year, you know."

"Hm. Are you ready for such an effort?"

Chandor nodded. "Yes. We have our database organized, adequate staff, ample computer capacity. Of course, at first we can only offer home-study courses, but they ought to lay a firm foundation. By next year we should have facilities for simulator training, and in two years for the elements of practical spacemanship. A small cadet corps, true, but a *corps*, a living body."

"That's quick work," Nansen said, impressed.

"Work worth doing! I asked you to come see me—this sort of thing goes far better in person—to counsel us on what to teach and how. We have the theory, you have the actual experience. And you are the hero. I could well say you're the prophet. We need your imagination."

Nansen felt uncomfortable about that. But no matter. The zeal before him lighted his own fire afresh. This was not about gain or glory, it was about the nature of humankind and humankind's place in the universe.

A musical note sounded. "Pardon me," Chandor said, and to the visiphone: "Accept. Proceed."

"Search for Captain Ricardo Nansen," stated the voice.

Chandor gave his visitor a surprised look. Nansen nodded, equally unsure what it meant. *Hanny, are you all right?* "I am here," he said.

The scanner found him. The wall opposite generated an image panel. He saw a short, dark man in a tunic with an emblem on the left breast. A transparency behind showed dusk falling where he was. Nonetheless Nansen recognized the high-peaked roofs, archaic, unlike any hereabouts; and he knew the man also. It was Kenri Fanion, calling from the Kith village on the Isle of Weyan.

"Apologies for disturbing you, Captain Nansen." He spoke in the dominant language of Harbor. Once in conversation he had confessed that his Kithish was rusty; they didn't use it much anymore in the settlement, apart from rites and ceremonies. Besides, it had drifted from the versions spoken in the ships into a dialect of its own.

Yet, though he had never gone to the stars, he was a Kithman in blood and heritage, his community the last abiding rendezvous, he an information broker for a living but by dedication a member of the Kith's Tau Ceti service establishment. He addressed the commander of *Envoy* straightforwardly but with awe in his eyes.

"It could wait," he said. With grimness: "It will have to. However, I thought you should know immediately, before the news comes out."

Nansen grappled calm to himself. "Thank you. What is it?"

"I have just heard from Shipwatch," the system of orbiting instruments

that kept track of starship trails. "Bad word. A vessel bound for us . . .
won't arrive."

Chandor gasped. "Say on," Nansen ordered.

"Shipwatch has recorded a trace." *From far off. Else the craft, running
close to the speed of light, would be in telescope range.* "Suddenly it
blanked out."

"They may have gone normal for a while to take observations or for
some other reason," said Nansen, knowing how empty his words were.

"It's been five hours, Captain. And why would they lay to at all? They
know this vicinity." A tic pulsed in Fanion's cheek. "We'll keep alert for a
sign, of course. But I think something has gone radically wrong."

"Do you have a location?"

"About seven and a half light-years distant, inbound from the Cassiopeia sector. We'll have a better figure when the readings from the far-
orbit stations come in." *Longer baselines, for triangulation. Not that a
few billion kilometers either way are important, across a gap like that.*

Chandor's knuckles stood white above the arms of his chair. Somehow he achieved the same quietness. "Cassiopeia. That suggests *Fleetwing*. She hasn't been here often. Generally she's plied remote parts, the
Brent and Olivares regions, or even farther."

Fanion's head jerked, a nod. "Yes. The oldest left, wasn't she?" He
blinked hard. "Well, I suppose death finally caught up with her, too."

"Too?" asked Nansen.

"Word reaches us eventually, by laser beam if not by ship. Whether or
not a particular vessel has called on us in centuries, she'll have done so
elsewhere. When nobody's seen or heard of her for a very long time—
then nobody ever does again."

*The things that can fatally happen. . . . But what did? There shouldn't
be any hazard in a familiar region like Tau Ceti's, nothing she hasn't
dealt with over and over in her thousands of star-years.*

"That's my message, Captain Nansen," the Kithman finished. "I wish it
weren't. I'll inform you as soon as we learn more."

"If you do," Chandor said.

"Yes, if. God keep them yonder." Fanion ended transmission, maybe
afraid he couldn't have gotten through the usual formalities.

Ghosts of nacre drifted in a wall gone bare. The sky outside shone as it
had no right to shine. The city mumbled.

"God keep us all," Chandor said, "and the hopes we had."

"What do you mean?" Nansen demanded.

"You should know, Captain. How few and far between the Kith ships
are. Now we probably won't see any for more than a hundred years.
When you and I are dead."

"Unless another one happens to be bound here, too."

"Hardly." Chandor's tone flattened. "It could chance to, I suppose,
as thin as the trade is and as loosely organized as it always was. But in
general, the ships settled long ago on a cycle of routes. It's complicated

and variable, no doubt—I don't know the details—but roughly speaking, if this was *Fleetwing*'s turn to call on us, nobody else will for at least a century."

"Oh, yes. Pardon me. I've heard that, but forgotten."

Chandor smiled sadly. "Understandable, sir, as much as you've had to learn in four short years, and as much as you've been doing."

Staving off grief as best he could, Nansen forced some resonance back into his voice. "This doesn't have to be a disaster for the League."

"I'm afraid it is, sir. Our opponents will be quick to take advantage. The psychological effects—"

"Well, you know your society better than I do." *A free society with an ideal of enterprise, where the story of the great pioneering era has the power of myth. Would its young really surrender their newborn dreams so soon?*

Maybe. Those dreams are so very new.

"And, you know," Chandor trudged on, "we were counting on a shipful of starfarers, their experience and example, their help."

"Yes. We were." *He's right, this could be the blow from which we can't recover.* "They may not be lost." *Don't let it sound forlorn.* "They may start up again—have started up again—and arrive in another seven or eight years."

Chandor shook his head. His shoulders sagged. "I can't believe it, sir." He drew breath. "Once, before *Envoy* returned, I got to wondering about the mysterious disappearances. I've been interested in the Kith my whole life, you recall. I retrieved everything about them that's in their database on Weyan. It goes back millennia, and includes many observations made elsewhere. Three times in the past, Shipwatch systems have detected trails—not bound their way, as it happened, but detectable—that suddenly ended. No one knows why."

"Did no vessel make a search?"

"None were on hand. Except—let me remember—yes. A ship that stopped at Aerie, decades after an observation there, did go look, since the distance was fairly short, a few light-years. But she found nothing. Cumulative effects of uncertainties in the data, during the time that had passed. The search volume was too huge."

"Wouldn't survivors have broadcast a signal?"

"None was detected. The searchers gave up. Nobody else ever made such an attempt. They couldn't afford to."

A chill coursed through Nansen. He tautened. After a minute he said, gazing past the other man, out at the sky, "Perhaps we can."

Chandor gaped. "Sir?"

"Let me use your visiphone, please."

First Nansen called Dayan at their home and spoke briefly with her. Thereafter he told the communications net to find the rest of *Envoy*'s crew, widely scattered over the planet. It was to bid them get in touch and come to him as soon as possible.

"Now, pardon me," he said, rising. "We'll talk again later. Meanwhile, carry on."

"Yes, Captain," Chandor whispered. In his face bewilderment struggled with something that dared not yet be rapture.

Nansen had ported his aircar two or three kilometers from the Venture building. He liked to walk. He did not like the stares he drew on a street. Not that they meant trouble. Most were friendly, many close to adoration, especially in this city. A few were wary or even resentful—*Envoy* had brought great strangeness to Harbor, and already the changes were felt—but not blatantly. Nor did anyone hail the famous man, though some nodded or gave him the hand-to-temple salute of deference. He simply didn't enjoy being a spectacle.

The boulevard was wide, lined with the sweetly curved double trunks and feathery orange foliage of lyre trees. Vehicles glided along it, pedestrians through the resilient side lanes. The buildings behind were seldom more than ten stories high, set well apart on lawns of golden-hued native sward or green terrestrial grass. They ran to fluted or color-paneled façades with turrets elaborately columned and spired. Argosy was founded about six hundred years ago, by Kithfolk who despaired of wandering. Assimilation was not entirely complete. Ancestral genes revealed themselves here and there in small, trim bodies and craggy visages. More pervasive and meaningful was ancestral tradition, an ethos half forgotten, now stirring awake. It made Argosy a favored site for an organization that aimed to launch fresh emprises among the stars.

And Harbor itself is a favored world. Jean's world. We were lucky, arriving when we did, when a new civilization is reindustrializing the planetary system and dynamic individualists are seeking their fortunes. It can't last.

Though who knows what real interstellar traffic, whole fleets of ships, might bring about that never was before in human history?

Having claimed his car, he set it to wheel out past city limits and take off. Field drive, miniaturized for bubbles like this, would make it safe to land and lift anywhere. That alone meant enormous wealth for the innovators. But let somebody better qualified find the right managers to reap it. Nansen was no businessman; his skills and goals lay elsewhere.

From above he spied a cluster of buildings lately erected, laboratories for research and development in the nascent technologies. The League's financial backers did not lack vision—if their vision was largely financial, what of it?—while today's computers, robotics, and nanotech made for rapid progress.

The sight fell behind him and he flew over a tawny plain. Shagtrees lined riverbanks with vivid yellow, fireplumes with scarlet. This part of Duncan had reverted to nature during the death agonies of the Mandatary; several circular marshes were warhead craters. Reclamation was under way, hampered by disputes over ownership. Twice, however, he crossed a broad swathe of green, cropland and pastureland, where a village nestled as a center for single farmsteads.

Not too favored a world. Population rising steeply again, more and more lands overcrowded. Yes, technics feeds, clothes, houses, medicates everybody, but it can't create living space; and poverty is relative. The economy today is ruthless; for each person who succeeds, a hundred or a thousand go under. And there are other malcontents, misfits in religion, politics, lifeways—and some who look at the stars with a pure kind of longing.

At least open land could still be had, square kilometers of it, if you could pay. Nansen's aircar slanted down toward his *estancia*, where Dayan awaited him.

He had not copied the house of his childhood. That would have been a mockery, here where grass was only slowly spreading outward and only terrestrial saplings rose from it. Flower beds decorated a lawn, but a big arachnea dominated, like a spiderweb against the sky, swaying and rustling in a wind that smelled faintly of spices no human ever tasted. Two dogs lolled near the porch, panting in the warmth, but the glittery mites dancing in the air around them were not insects, and a sunhawk overhead, watchful for prey, had four wings. Yet the house was high-ceilinged and rambling, stone-floored, red-tiled, and a fountain played on the patio.

The *Envoy* crew sat near it, under a vine-draped trellis. Household staff had brought drinks and withdrawn. There was no need for servants as such; in most respects, robots would have done better. These youngsters, though, were like apprentices, here to be with Don Ricardo and Doña Hanny, to learn from them and someday win berths on their ships. They were like family.

But they were not those who had fared with Nansen. His glance ranged over his crew. As erstwhile, they were in a semicircle facing him. His beloved sat on the right, her hair a flame above a cool white gown in the fashion of Duncan. Sundaram sat beside her, the usual mildness on his brown visage, the usual contemplativeness behind it. Yu showed a measure of weariness. Zeyd's lean frame was tensed. Mokoena's arms cradled an infant.

Nansen stood up. "The meeting will please come to order," he said.

It was not pomposity. They needed a touch of ritual to focus their attention. Until the last of them arrived, they had talked mainly about their roles on the planet—Yu and Zeyd planting the seeds of an industrial revolution, Dayan and Mokoena of a scientific revolution, Sundaram trying to guide the religious and philosophical transformations that were afoot after the revelations from the Holont. Now they must turn their minds back to the deeps.

Nansen sat down. For a span only the clear song of the water sounded forth.

"You know what the situation is," he said. "The question is, what shall we do about it?"

Mokoena responded promptly. "First, I think, we had better ask if we should."

They were not surprised.

"We have too much to lose." She held her baby closer. "Everything we've gained, homes, new lives; everything we're accomplishing."

"Yes," Sundaram concurred. They could hear his reluctance. "Why squander the years we have left, and *Envoy*, to seek a derelict?"—*Envoy*, the sole working starship in tens or scores of light-years.

"Are we certain she is a derelict?" Nansen answered.

Yu's eyes brightened. "Do you mean this might be just a quantum gate malfunction?" The light faded. "If so, the energy shift probably destroyed the vessel, or at least the crew."

"Or maybe not. Hanny, will you explain?"

Looks went to the physicist. She spoke fast, impersonally, as if to keep emotion out from underfoot. "You remember what we learned at Tahir and the black hole, about the Bose-Einstein condensate having a small probability of going unstable. Not all the borrowed energy goes smoothly back to the substrate. It's reclaimed instead from the surrounding matter, violently. This is in the data we downloaded here, of course, but in that cataract of information, it seems to have gone almost unnoticed.

"Well, since we mastered the modern computer systems, I've used their power to work on the equations, off and on. I've only mentioned this to Rico. Damn it, there hasn't been time to prepare a paper! But I've found a solution that suggests how to eliminate the danger. A matter of devising quantum-wave guides." She could no longer wholly restrain herself. "Oh, when humans go back to the stars, they'll go with that, and field drive, and so much else!"

"If they go," Sundaram said.

"Yes," Nansen conceded. "Chandor Barak, whose judgment we'd better listen to, thinks that most likely we have a threshold to get across—here, now, on Harbor—and if we don't, star traffic will continue dying till it's as extinct for humans as for . . . all others?"

"We expected a Kith ship would become our ally," Zeyd said. "But this disaster—"

"They may be alive aboard her," Dayan stated.

"What? In God's name—"

"That's something else that's come out of my solution. The manner of energy reclamation when a gate fails. It takes the form of deceleration of matter in the immediate vicinity. That would definitely ruin the engine part of any ship. But, depending on what the energy differential is, the front section might not be too badly damaged, and the deceleration might not be lethally high."

"I've studied plans of Kith ships," Yu breathed. "They show an emergency nuclear power plant forward in the hull. Given self-sealing, self-repair—an essentially intact life-support system, recycling everything—the crew could survive."

Mokoena spoke raggedly. The baby sensed her unease and wailed. She rocked it. "Recycling is never perfect, you know. A ship is not a planet. She can't hold a full ecology. She doesn't have plate tectonics, or any broad margin of tolerance. Wastes accumulate, toxins, unusables. Adrift in mid-space, with no proper means of flushout and replenishment—if a crew did live through the shock, I wouldn't give them more than twenty years."

"What a ghastly, slow death." Zeyd turned to Nansen. It blazed from him: "But Rico, you think you can save them!"

"If they are in fact alive, which we don't know, I think perhaps we can," the captain replied carefully. "And I think it's worth trying."

"Allah akbar!" Zeyd cried. "The old crew faring again—"

Mokoena laid a hand on his arm. "No," she said, gentle and immovable. "I'm sorry, Selim, darling, but no."

"She's right," Nansen agreed. "It's more than your child, and other children we mean to have. It's everything we're building here. The whole future we've dreamed of, lived for. Your advice, example, and inspiration are absolutely essential. Your duty, all of you, is to stay."

"But not yours?" Yu challenged.

"I'm the most dispensable. The League can carry on without me—if people see that it is carrying on, that the industrial and social foundations for a starfleet are being laid—if they can keep a hope alive that the work will be rewarded in their lifetimes."

"What will you do for crew?" Zeyd growled.

Nansen smiled. "Oh, we have no dearth of adventurous young souls. They'll fight to go. Fifteen years' absence won't seem terribly consequential to them, and anyhow, they'll experience just a few days. But they'd better have a seasoned commander."

Sundaram shook his head. "Fifteen years for us without you, dear friend. Or perhaps forever."

"We've time to be together," Nansen said. *"Envoy* can't leave tomorrow. Her gamma makes her safe enough from a quantum accident. But there are other kinds. And the Kith did make technological advances while we were gone. She needs a dozen sorts of retrofits. And the crew will need training, and— I don't suppose we can start for at least a year."

Mokoena's gaze rested dark upon him. "An added year for them in that ship. You're cutting it close, Rico."

"I have no choice. Nor, really, about going. But I want to consult and work with my former crew."

"You realize, don't you," Dayan broke in, "I'm going also."

"We'll argue about that later," Nansen said roughly.

"We will not." Dayan rose to her feet. "There is no argument." She came over to stand above him. "I'm experienced, too. How can you imagine I'd accept fifteen years without you, and being too old for children when you got back? Meshuggah!"

50.

For thousands of years among the stars, for hundreds of her own years, the ship had been great and proud. She was akin to *Envoy* in her general plan—seen across fifty kilometers, the unlikenesses were few, the most obvious a proportionately larger hull—but of more than twice the linear dimensions, ten times the burden. Even the wreckage of her had kept majesty; Nansen remembered Machu Picchu, Kerak des Chevaliers, the Lion Gate at Mycenae. It still belonged in the reaches she had sailed; he remembered the Gokstad ship, the *Mary Rose*, the *Constitution*, and thought that *Fleetwing* had found a better ending.

But maybe the ancient crews had found better deaths.

He reduced viewscreen magnification, retaining light enhancement, to survey the entirety again. Lesser wounds dwindled out of sight and he saw the forward wheel turning as before, slower than his because it was bigger but creating interior weight as of old. That meant the frictionless magnetic bearings around its hollow axle were there, which meant that the superconductors generating the fields were operative, which meant that a fusion power plant was, which meant that life within the rim might yet be possible.

The force boom, though, projecting from the hub to make and shape the radiation screen fields, was warped, a fourth of its two-kilometer length snapped off. The outer hull was rotating, oppositely to the wheel, something that should never have happened. That it had not long since grated ruinously against the inner hull was a tribute to the remnants of the bearing system—to the engineers who designed it and the honest workers who built it, dust these many centuries. The eight boats that had docked on the exterior, two sets of four spaced equally around the circumference, were gone. The magnetics that held them fast had failed, doubtless in the moment of catastrophe, and they drifted off with the debris.

The huge cylinder terminated in ripped and ragged metal. A few interior members stuck out, torn across, like bones in a compound fracture. The inner hull was hidden from view, a stump. No after wheel spun athwart the Milky Way. Its fragments were also forever lost. They might not have receded fast, but in sixteen years they would have traveled into tracklessness.

Nansen consulted a display of data his instruments had obtained and interpretations his computers had calculated. The dry figures joined with the stark sight to tell him *Fleetwing*'s story.

Her normal-state velocity in the galactic frame of reference had been about seventy-five kilometers per second. When the substrate reclaimed the unpaid part of her debt, as much matter decelerated to zero as would carry that much energy at that speed. It occurred in a fractional second, thus with appalling force. In ship terms, the zero-zero engine immediately crashed aft, rending off its section of the inner hull. The pieces rammed into the solid hub at the end. They bore it and the plasma accelerator it supported away. Unsecured, seized by incidental forces— electrostatic, if nothing else—the after wheel withdrew as well. Whirling and wobbling, its axle sleeve struck the outer hull, smashed through decks, entangled structure. Its linear momentum left a hole agape in the stern of the cylinder, its angular momentum left a spin. *Fleetwing* pitched and yawed. That put more torque on the long, thin mast than it was meant to bear, and it gave way.

Not that it or its screen fields were needed by then, Nansen thought. *This ship will never again race with light.*

Incredible, that the systems up forward could save anything of her, yes, actually restore a kind of stability.

No, perhaps not really unbelievable. She was made so well that she had already endured everything else the cosmos threw at her. And likewise her Kithfolk.

He stood in *Envoy*'s command center with Hanny Dayan and Alanndoch Egis. His second officer was youthful; all aboard from Harbor had seen less life span than he and his wife. She was fair-haired and gray-eyed, tall in her one-piece blue uniform; but starfaring ancestors had bequeathed her her face.

Consoles, meters, displays, encompassed them. The air at present bore a tinge of pine smell. Retrofits had not changed old *Envoy* much.

Alanndoch stared at a radio monitor. The instrument searched from end to end of that spectrum and back again, lest a message come in that the audios were not tuned for. "No answer yet," she said, uselessly and desperately. "Are they dead, then? Their broadcast goes on." She *was* young.

"It would," Dayan reminded her. "Automatic. Evidently the best transmitter they could rig was crude, but they built it rugged. The call will continue for decades more, till the power plant gives out."

Nansen ran a hand through his hair. It was going white at the temples. "They should have seen us," he muttered, just as pointlessly. "If nothing else, they could modulate or modify that signal. Interrupting it every few minutes would show that they're alive."

Dayan's voice bleakened. "Maybe nobody looks out any longer. Maybe they've turned off their viewscreens. Sixteen years of watching naked space—"

"That doesn't sound like what I've heard of Kithfolk," Alanndoch said.

"After all this time, under those conditions, what may they have become?"

"Dead." Alanndoch's head drooped. "We're too late."

Seven and a half years—half an Earth-day for them—to the approximate location. Zigzagging to and fro, zero-zero jumps that closed in on the goal. Laying to, straining outward with opticals, neutrino detectors, every capability on hand. The radio signal, barely obtainable, a broadcast gone tenuous over these distances, and no more than a wave band not found in the interstellar medium; yet unmistakably a beacon, proof that somebody had survived the disaster. (Well, *Fleetwing* was massive, and no doubt bore a considerable tonnage of cargo. Evidently the shock had not jarred her fatally hard.) Homing in on the source. A final approach under normal-state boost. Matching velocities at a safe remove. Quest completed.

Found: a wreck and a mindlessly radiating monotone, alone amidst the stars.

Nansen's fist banged on a console panel. "No, it's not for nothing," he said. "At the very least, we'll learn the details of what happened. The future needs to know."

Dayan flung off her despair. "Good for you, Rico!" She clapped his shoulder. "Let's start."

Alanndoch likewise brightened a little. "Oh, yes, we must board." She regarded the others. "But, Captain, Scientist," she well-nigh pleaded, "you shouldn't. Please reconsider. Don't risk yourselves. You've crew who're willing, anxious to go. Beginning with me."

"Thanks," Dayan said. "But Rico and I have earned the right."

For her, he thought, *the right to be not yet used up. To defy time once more, time that has devoured everything on Earth which was hers.*

For me— He spoke in his wonted sober fashion: "We have argued this already. I well know the doctrine. The commander should stay with the ship. However, Dr. Dayan and I have more than training"—brief, though intense. "We have experience"—since before *Envoy* departed Sol, and at worlds unknown until she fetched up at them, and at the black hole; for a moment it felt to him like the full eleven thousand years. "We have by far the best chance of coping with anything unexpected. Stand by."

Dayan's demand rang heartening. "We'll certainly want you and the whole crew later. If we find survivors, you'll have tricky work to do."

"At worst," Nansen finished, "you shall take our ship home."

51.

The wreck swelled in the forward screen until it blocked sight of the stars. Spin brought an emblem into view, scarred and scoured, then took the blue-and-silver wing away, then swung it back. Nansen turned his space-boat and proceeded parallel to the hull at a distance of meters, seeking a place to make contact. Field drive gave marvelous responsiveness; this was almost like steering an aircraft.

Almost. Never quite. Robotics handled most of it, with more speed and precision than flesh could, but the basic judgments and decisions were his, and a mistake could kill.

He worked his way aft, turned again, matched velocities, and rested weightless in his harness. Before him yawned the hideous hole where the after wheel and plasma accelerator had been. He called a report to *Envoy*. Dayan, at his side, probed the interior with radar, detectors, and instruments more subtle, still experimental, that employed her new knowledge of quantum physics.

"As we thought," she said after a few minutes. "The midships emergency bulkheads must have closed immediately and sealed the front end off. The fusion reactor there is in regular operation, supplying ample current to all systems that are functional." She frowned. "The readings at the wheel aren't so good, but from here I can't make out just what the trouble is."

"That's what we want to discover," he said. "Ready? Hang on."

As slowly as might be, he maneuvered around the hull and forward. A hundred meters from the bow end of the cylinder, he went into a circular path around it—not an orbit; the gravity of even this enormous vessel was negligible. To stay on course required a constant, exact interplay of vectors. He fought down a brief dizziness and concentrated on matching the rotation "below" him.

And now: approach. He had picked a smooth area, free alike of installations and of damage. However, it spun at nearly two hundred kilometers per hour. A slight miscalculation could mean that a housing slammed into him. The boat stooped. Contact shivered and tolled in the metal. At once he made fast. It would not have been possible to do so speedily enough with magnetics, but an electron manipulator inspired by the Holont gave him talons. Silence washed over him.

Weight tugged, as if he were hanging upside down. Stars streamed in the viewscreens. *Envoy* hove in sight, merely a glint among them unless he magnified. "We're docked," he told them aboard.

"*Elohim Adirim!*" Dayan gasped. A lock of hair had come loose from her headband and wavered like a small flame. "That was *piloting!*"

Nansen realized he had been necessary. He also realized he had not by himself been sufficient. "Thank the boat," he said.

Her name was *Herald II*.

Donning spacesuits and securing equipment to take along was a slow business. Weight amounted to about one-tenth terrestrial, in the wrong direction. They helped one another. Nansen saw Dayan's distress when he strapped a pistol to his waist. "The last thing I want is to fire this," he said, "but we simply don't know."

"That's the horror," she answered, "that you might have to." Her neck straightened. "Well, I won't believe you will until *I* have to."

They kissed quickly before they attached helmets. After that their appearance was unhuman, heads horned with sensors and antennae, blank visages, insectlike eyes that were optical amplifiers. They cycled through the personnel lock, planted gripsoled boots on *Fleetwing*, and moved off cautiously, a boot always emplaced. Drive units rested on their backs, but a return to this whirling surface would be an acrobatic feat. "Yes," Nansen murmured, "we two definitely had to be the first. Already I'm finding things to warn everybody about."

Dayan's breath was harsh in his audio receivers.

Step by step, they advanced. A coaming lay in their way. "That's a lock," Dayan said.

"I know," Nansen answered. They had studied the plans of the ship, taken from the Kith database, with equal intensity.

"Are you sure we shouldn't try to go inside here and proceed through the hull?"

"Yes, I am sure. Too many unknowns."

They crept around the portal. "I . . . I'm sorry," Dayan said. "That was a stupid question. I'm feeling a bit spinny."

Medication staved off nausea but couldn't do everything. They clung to a sharply curving world that wanted to hurl them from it, blood coursed too heavily in their heads, and a night sky whirled beneath them. "Don't look at the stars," Nansen advised.

Dayan swallowed. "Ironic," she said. "The stars are what this is all about, aren't they?"

They reached the end of the cylinder and crawled over the edge. She lost her footing. He grabbed an ankle barely in time and hauled her back. *"¡Nombre de Dios!"* he groaned. "Don't *do* that!" Twenty meters from them, the spokes of the wheel scythed across heaven.

"I'm sorry—"

"No, no, I am. I should have been more careful of . . . of my partner."

He heard a chuckle. "Enough with this modesty contest. But thank you, *b'ahavah.*"

Progress became easier, here where the centrifuge effect pulled sideways. It was somewhat like walking in a stiff wind, which lessened as they approached the center. Nevertheless they kept their caution. "I feel well again," Dayan said after a while.

"Good." *Oh, more than good, beloved.*

They came at length to an occupied shuttle bay. Although the little vehicle had been designed centuries after those that *Envoy* bore to Tahir, it seemed crude compared even to the early field-drive models she now carried. Nansen helped Dayan unlimber the tripod that was part of her burden and snug its feet to the hull. It gave her a framework to which she could fasten her instruments. When he had finished, the single sound he heard was breathing. Somehow the stillness made the wheel that rotated on his right all the more monstrous.

Dayan busied herself for several minutes.

"I was afraid of this," she sighed. "It confirms the readings I took aft. The launch control is dead. Probably the power supply to the computer was knocked out in the disaster."

"What about the others?" Besides the lost boats, *Fleetwing* had carried eight shuttles; her people had more occasion to go to and fro than his ever did, and numbered many more. He glimpsed those that were docked in the wheel, whirling past.

"I can tell from here, the entire lot is stranded, at least on this side."

"Well, frankly, I'm not very regretful. I didn't like the idea of trusting an unfamiliar system that might have been damaged in unobvious ways."

"How will we evacuate survivors?" *If any.*

"That depends on what the situation is. At the moment, I think the best procedure will be for our engineers to make what modifications are necessary for us to use a shuttle of *Envoy*'s. We'll convey it over, steer it to a wheelside bay, and ferry the people across to the hull. First we'll doubtless have to do some repair work there, too. They can pass through it to an exit port, and our boats will bring them to our ship. That may involve a large number of trips, but it looks to me like the most conservative, fail-safe plan. Meanwhile, let's repack your gear and execute the maneuver I rather expected we would."

Did a sob answer his deliberately impersonal words? He decided not to ask. Dayan went about her tasks as competently as always.

The truth came out as he slipped a cable off his shoulder and began uncoiling it. Under low weight and Coriolis force, it writhed from him like a snake. He heard her voice gone high and thin. "Rico, I'm afraid."

Astounded, he could merely say, "We don't dare be afraid."

"Not for me." She caught his arm. "For you, darling." Her free hand jerked toward the wheel. "I'm remembering how Al Brent must have died."

"That was long ago and far away." Six thousand years and light-years. Not enough to grant forgetfulness.

Her tone firmed. "Let me go first. We can better spare me."

"No." He shook his head, unseen by her within the helmet. "I've had much more open-space practice. We stay by the plan we've rehearsed."

"But if you are—caught—"

"I won't be. If somehow I am, you return at once to the boat and take her back. Do you understand?"

"Yes," she said after a moment. "Forgive my foolishness. It's just that I love you."

"And I you. Which is another reason I cannot let you lead." Maybe she visualized his grin. "Besides, allow me my machismo."

She laughed shakily and embraced him. Their helmets clinked together.

The cable, a thin and flexible strand stronger than any steel, floated in an arc. He used the molecular bond attachments to stick an end to the front of her suit. She fixed the other end to the back of his. When he leaped free, she waved, then stood waiting, a soldier's daughter.

He activated his drive unit and curbed his outward flight. The next few minutes would be touchier than rendezvous and docking had been. Though turning speeds this near the hub weren't great, they were opposed; the space between units was narrow; the angular momenta were gigantic. He lost himself in the crossing, as a man may lose himself in battle or a storm at sea or the height of love. Not reckless by nature, he still found in unavoidable danger the fullness of life. The blood sang in him.

His mind stood aside, wholly aware, coolly gauging and governing.

He drew near a spoke, fifteen meters from the axle, and adjusted vectors until the eight-hundred-meter length was steady in his eyes. He edged inward. He swung his body around. His boots made contact. The impact was slight. He must have matched velocities within a few centimeters per second. Excellent! He took half a minute to stand triumphant among the marching stars.

Peering back, he verified that the cable was not fouled. He reached around, undid it from his suit, and attached it to the spoke. "All clear, Hanny," he called. "Are you ready?"

"Yes, oh, yes."

"Jump."

The line began to straighten as her mass moved offside. He caught hold and pulled, hand over hand. Draw her in. He felt how she used nudges of drive to counteract drift. Good girl, grand girl. Probably she could have made it safely on her own, as he did. But why take a needless risk? Whoever met the wheel while flying would spatter through space in chunks. He *was* better trained.

That was why he had elected to walk from the boat, rather than flitting directly. The first engineers to come, led by Alanndoch, must duplicate his transit. But they were young and—well— Maybe they could rig a net for those who followed. And eventually they'd have a shuttle from *Envoy*, for easy passage between wheel and hull.

That's if we find any reason to do the work. His exultation congealed.

Dayan arrived. He hugged her, one-armed, and gathered in the cable. They'd want it again later. Lateral weight here was about one-twentieth *g*, though Coriolis force complicated movement.

Dayan went to the entry port. "Uh-oh," he heard.

"What?" He got the strand back on his spacesuit and joined her. She pointed. "This is not an airlock according to plan," she said.

"No." He examined the hinged metal box that had been added in front, the traces of welding and hand tools. Cautiously opening the door, which faced spinward, he saw through murk that the box was a chamber barely adequate to accommodate a man. The door was airtight. When dogged shut, it could be opened with a single turn. A tube fastened at the rear seemed to have been a battery-powered lamp. An inscription was painted on the inside of the door. He had acquired enough Kithish to read it:

BLESSINGS
FAREWELL

He reclosed the box and stood for a dark moment before he spoke. "Why did they make this?"

"More important," Dayan replied, "how?"

"Hm?"

"We don't know what else they did. If we can get in at all, we may cause terrible things. Like if we can't shut the lock valves, the air inside will escape."

A wind bearing corpses, as winter winds blow withered leaves?

"You are right," Nansen said. "Perhaps the next port is accessible."

They started off, to the hub and across to the spoke they wanted. The wheel gyred in silence and cold.

*   *   *

They arrived. "This lock looks intact," Dayan said. "We can deal with it."

Can we deal with what's behind it? wondered Nansen.

He pressed the plate for entry. Nothing stirred. "Circuits dead," he declared. "Don't stop to probe, Hanny." He leaned his muscles against the emergency manual truck. Gears worked; the valve swung ponderously aside. "Hold," he said. He couldn't make *Envoy* out among the stars, but his suit had sufficient broadcast power. "We're about to go in," he announced. "We'll be cut off from contact for a while."

"How . . . how long shall we wait before dispatching . . . reinforcements?" Alanndoch asked.

"Wrong word," Nansen replied. "Whatever we find inside, it won't be hostile." *Or so I pray.* "The enemy is around us." *The universe, our enemy and our glory.* "Give us twenty-four hours. After that, proceed at discretion, but remember always, your first duty is to bring our ship home."

"Luck be with you, Captain, Scientist."

"Thank you." Nansen switched off and beckoned to Dayan. They entered the chamber.

As Nansen spun the valve shut and lost sight of the sky, blackness closed in. Dayan turned her flashbeam on. In vacuum it threw a puddle of light on the side opposite. Reflections diffused dimly into gloom. Nansen saw her as a bulk of shadow and a few vague glimmers.

He closed the valve. No air gushed in. The pump wasn't working, either. Groping, he found the command plate for the inner valve and pushed it. As he expected, the servo did nothing. If there was an atmosphere beyond, it pressed on this exit with tonnes of force.

Despair tasted like iron. "Living people would have made repairs," he rasped.

"Not necessarily," Dayan said. "Tinkering with embedded circuits, using inadequate tools, could well make matters worse. If ever they had reason to go outside, they could, more slowly, by the backups. Maybe the hydraulics here aren't jammed. People could maintain those."

Nansen tried. The truck resisted his hands. He marshaled his strength and heaved. It was as if he were trying to pull his bones apart. Then the truck turned. A faint thread of light appeared before him. Through his helmet he heard the first whistle of inrushing air. The truck turned more and more easily.

Vision hazed. "Frost!" Dayan cried. "Ice on our lenses!" Water vapor. The breath of life.

They trod into hollowness. Standing on the platform, as their suit exteriors warmed and the rime smoked off, they saw a great shaft stretching emptily upward and upward. Its fluorescence was more chilling than the tomb darkness of the lock chamber. On one side a railcar track converged away into the distance, on the other side a ladder with occasional rest stops. That was a long climb.

"Air." Dayan's voice shook. "I'll crack my helmet and smell it."

"No, don't," Nansen ordered. "Not till we know what it's like"—pressure, composition, corruption.

"Right. My testing kit—"

"We won't stop for that yet. We'll have a look first." *What we find may make everything else, our whole journey, irrelevant.* "Come."

The railcar rested inert. He sighed and sought the ladder. As they descended the hundreds of meters, their weight rose toward Earth normal and their burdens grew heavy.

Mute, side by side, they debarked at the top and went through a bare room into a passageway.

Greenness! Plants in handmade boxes stood as far as they could see, leafing, blooming, fruiting, blanketing trellises, vaulting the overhead, rose, lily, violet, bamboo, pumpkin, dwarf juniper, trumpet vine, grapevine, things that Earth never knew, a riot of life.

"*Life*—" Dayan reached, trembling, humbly, to touch a flower.

They had not gone much farther when three persons met them.

The strangers loped down the corridor with tools in hand that Nansen didn't recognize. He hadn't had time to learn everything about this era. The detached part of him supposed they were implements to cope with crisis. The noise he and Dayan made could have signified trouble. His mind sprang to the people themselves.

An older man, a younger man, a young woman, short, dark, lithe, strong-featured: Kithfolk. They were skimpily clad and skinny but looked healthy. Joy roared in him. He unsecured his helmet and clapped it back off his head, to breathe mild air and green scents.

The three had skidded to a halt. They stared, stunned, at the miracle. Time whirred past before the older man whispered, "You—you are from outside?" It was in an old-sounding but comprehensible version of the principal language on Harbor, whither they had been bound.

Dayan had bared her own face. "Yes," she answered, not steadily. "We're here to bring you home."

"After, after . . . these years," the woman stammered. "You came."

The young man whirled about and ran off. His shouts echoed. The woman fell to her knees, raised her eyes, and poured her thanks and her love out to her God.

She wasn't loud. The other man stood fast. He was gray-haired, his countenance furrowed, clearly a leader. Maybe later the knowledge of deliverance would overwhelm him, but at the moment he had recovered and his tone was almost level. "Welcome aboard. A million welcomes. I am Evar Shaun. My companion here is Tari Ernen. We are crew of *Fleetwing*."

Nansen did not, at once, respond in kind. That it was *Envoy* which lay nearby might have been too much, just now. "We detected the failure of your zero-zero at Harbor," he said. "We came as soon as we were able. Why didn't you reply to our calls?"

"We didn't know," Shaun said. "Most electronics failed when the thing happened." Of course, he'd have no idea what the thing was. "We have had no viewscreens since then." Luckily—no, not luck; good engineering—such systems as light, temperature, and ventilation were separate, simpler and more robust. "Only by going outside at the end of a cable have we seen."

Tari Ernen got back to her feet. "Every year," she said. "We marked every year with a sight of the stars. On our birthdays."

"How are you?" Dayan whispered.

"We live," Shaun replied. "We have made ways of life that kept us sane." After a little: "It will be . . . not easy . . . becoming planet dwellers."

"No children anymore," Ernen said. "We children grew up. We would not have our own. Not when we knew it would be at least fifteen years before rescue."

"And likeliest forever," Shaun added stoically, stating a fact to which he had been resigned, which his emotions did not yet quite recognize was no longer a fact.

"You have lost this ship," Nansen said, "but we are building more. They will need crews."

The pair gaped at him. It must be too great a wonder to grasp at once. Then Ernen sobbed, "We *shall* be starfarers again?"

"Thank you, thank you," Shaun mumbled.

Before everything dissolved in bewildered passion, Nansen threw a question that had been dogging him. "How many are you?"

"A-about two hundred," Shaun said.

"What, no more? Did you, uh, did you lose many in the disaster?"

His heritage—culture, chromosomes, spirit—arose in Shaun and he could answer quite evenly: "The shock injured most of us, but few fatally. It did worse and irreparable damage to the life-support systems. What was left could not serve all of us for the length of time we must wait. We would die in poison and filth from our own bodies. You see how we have planted gardens everywhere, to keep the air fresh and provide food, but that was not enough, either.

"The aged and infirm, and others chosen by lot, went into space, one by one. We rebuilt a lock to make it gentle for them. They drift among the stars. Their names live in honor."

Nansen stiffened. "How did you make them go?" he demanded.

Shaun met his gaze. "There was no need of force. They went freely. They were Kith."

"They are Kith," Ernen said. "Forever."

Dayan bowed her head and wept.

52.

Tended with devotion, Earth life had spread widely across the *estancia* in the years of their absence. Again, after millennia, Nansen and Dayan rode out over a plain where grass rippled and groves rustled beneath the summer wind, light streamed long from a westering sun to lay gold over the green, and wild creatures ran and wild wings soared.

For a span they galloped, rejoicing in the surge of muscles between their thighs, flying manes, drumming hoofs, sweet horse odor mingled with smells of soil and growth. When they reined in, buildings were lost to sight. Alone within the horizon, under the enormous arch of sky, the riders continued at a walk. Saddle leather creaked.

"Freedom!" Nansen said.

Dayan glanced at him. "Freedom?" she asked.

A trifle abashed, because he didn't like dramatics and this had been an outburst, he explained, "To live our lives as we want."

Her brows lifted slightly. "Why, we've always had that, you and I." With a look aloft: "Maybe more than anybody else ever did."

"Not lately. I didn't think you enjoyed it much, either."

"M-m, true, I hadn't known how many *duties* being famous and celebrated involves. But the crowds meant terribly well." She grinned. "And we—you especially—put it to use."

"Not very efficient use on my part, I fear. Ceremonies and speeches and having hundreds introduced to me—not my kind of work."

His mood had lowered. He was dissatisfied with his address to the parliament and people of Harbor. Pieces of it came back to nag at him.

"*. . . Our first starships are ready, ships better than any known before,* *thanks to the union of human technology with the new knowledge brought from afar. The* Fleetwing *folk are here, ready to counsel, instruct, be officers aboard. More Kith will join with us as we meet with them, on this planet and others. But it will no longer be only they who go starfaring. Henceforward, all can who have the strength, the skill, and the wish. . . .*

"From Fleetwing *we have learned of two worlds where humans can make homes. Many more certainly exist, but these are a beginning for whoever has cherished the dream. . . . The planetary engineering systems that we are building will make settlement easy where once it was hard, and possible where once it was impossible. . . . Given capabilities like these, and the capital investment that the Venture League is prepared to make, starfaring will become profitable—not marginally, not for a few, but for everyone. Therefore it will go on, growing of itself. . . .*

". . . the revelations, the inspirations we will gain from other races than ours. . . . We will awaken those who wish to be awakened, to join us among the stars. . . .

". . . millions of years, so many starships flying that they weave universe and substrate together, making existence eternally sure. . . . What we have learned about communication across time suggests that the cosmos may have evolved us in order that we shall at last save it. Can this be true? It is imaginable. . . .

"For us today, enough: that we are going back to the stars and will never forsake them."

"I didn't like the things I said," he confessed, "nor the way I did."

"What was wrong?" Dayan inquired. "I thought your talk went fine."

"Too florid."

She nodded. "Not your style. Well, it was written for you."

"I don't care to be a mouthpiece. And I spoke like a poorly programmed machine."

Dayan laughed low. "Rico, Rico. You had a job to do, you found it distasteful, and now you worry whether you did it right. Tell me, did that speech express your beliefs?"

"Of course. Otherwise I would not have given it."

"No, you wouldn't have. Very well, then, you were being honest. And as for your delivery, I assure you, darling, it didn't matter. You were *you*, the captain of captains. That was what they wanted and needed."

"But it's wrong," he protested. "I don't deserve that sort of prestige. Nor do you, *querida*. We didn't lay the foundation or build the house"— the enduring house of the starfarers. "Wenji, Ajit, Mam, Selim," four comrades grown gray, "and those who worked with them, here on Harbor," diligently, patiently, sometimes fiercely, year by year by year, "while we were gone—they are the ones."

"In a way, yes," Dayan replied. "In another way, no, not entirely. Our mission, humans bound off to save humans, it . . . embodied everything.

It made people *care*, through all that time. Ajit's told me he thinks it made the crucial difference."

"But that doesn't make sense!"

Dayan shook her head, smiling. "Oh, Rico, when did anything human make real sense? Our race is crazy. Maybe that's why it's the race that's going to the stars. No, my dear, you'll never get away from being a symbol, a hero."

"Well," he grumbled, "at least you and I will have private lives again."

"Mostly, I trust," she agreed. "And raise lots of little Nansens."

He brightened. "They'll be Dayans, too."

The sun went low and the riders turned back. They had come farther than they noticed, and dusk found them still out on the plain. The sky was violet westward, dark eastward, where the lights of home glimmered remote. Above them the earliest stars were blinking forth.

Dayan murmured something.

Nansen glanced at her shadowy form, close beside him. "What?" he asked.

"Oh, I—I was just looking at those stars," she answered, her voice almost too muted for him to hear. "Some lines came to me. In English— um— *'Have you curbed the Pleiades?'*"

He nodded. "Yes. I remember. *Job*. In Spanish— But a traditional English version has stayed with me. . . . *'Canst thou bind the sweet influences of Pleiades, or loose the bands of Orion? . . . or canst thou guide Arcturus with his sons?'* What put you in mind of that?"

"I got to thinking. If our children—surely some will—if they travel yonder, we'll lose them forever."

"Perhaps not," he said. "Once we've discovered how to build a holontic time communicator—it'll mean more than the future talking to the past, you know. It'll mean calling across the universe."

"And in that way also making the universe one." She sighed. "A grand vision. You and I won't live to see it, though." Mastering forces so mighty would take many human lifetimes. "Unless we do live on afterward. . . . No, I can't say what the limits are for us. That would be as arrogant as to say there are no limits ever. But—"

She was silent awhile. They rode toward the hearthlights. More stars appeared. The wind had gone cold.

"I only know," she said, "that whatever we may someday become, we will never be God." Suddenly her laugh rang forth. "But we can have fun trying!"